KATABASIS
A NOVEL OF FORE WORLD

KATABASIS

A NOVEL OF FOREWORLD

— BY —

JOSEPH BRASSEY, COOPER MOO,
ANGUS TRIM & MARK TEPPO

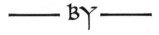

Text copyright © 2013 by FOREWORLD LLC

Published by 47North, Seattle
www.apub.com

ISBN-13: 9781477848210
ISBN-10: 1477848215
Library of Congress Control Number: 2013941687

Cover Illustrated and Designed by Alejandro Colucci

To James Rhys Brassey.
This is what your father was working on,
young James, in the months prior to your birth.

CAST OF CHARACTERS

In the East

Cnán – Binder, Shield-Brethren guide
Feronantus – Shield-Brethren Knight Master, the Old Man of the Rock
Haakon – Shield-Brethren initiate
Istvan – Hungarian horse-rider, Shield-Brethren companion
Lian – Chinese noblewoman, once a part of the *Khagan's* court
Percival – Shield-Brethren Knight Initiate
Raphael – Shield-Brethren Knight Initiate
Vera – leader of the Shield-Maidens
Yasper – Dutch alchemist, Shield-Brethren companion

Ahmet – Seljuk mercenary
Bruno – Lombard mercenary
Evren – Seljuk mercenary
Gawain – Welsh mercenary
Haidar – Persian mercenary

Gansukh – Mongolian hunter, emissary of Chagatai Khan
Alchiq – *jaghun* commander, known as Graymane to the Shield-Brethren

In Rus

Alexander "Nevsky" Iaroslavich – the *Kynaz* of Novogorod, a prince of the House of Rurik
Andrei – a prince of the House of Rurik
Hermann of Dorpat – the Prince-Bishop of Riga
Illarion Illarionovich – Ruthenian noble, a survivor of the Mongolian invasion
Kristaps – the First Sword of Fellin, Livonian knight
Nika – Shield-Maiden, a survivor of the fall of Kiev
Gorya – Ruthenian mercenary
Iakov – Ruthenian mercenary
Illugi – Danish mercenary
Makar – Ruthenian mercenary
Onikii – Ruthenian mercenary
Ozur – Danish mercenary
Svend – Danish mercenary
Taras – Ruthenian mercenary
Thorvald – Danish mercenary
Vasya – Ruthenian mercenary

1241

VETURNÆTUR

CHAPTER 1:

GHOSTS IN KIEV

Illarion stood upon the edge of a broken battlement beneath the star-speckled night sky. There was no moon, which meant the desolate ruins of Kiev were lost in the darkness beyond the citadel's walls. Here and there, tiny sparks winked at him from the sea of darkness—fires dutifully tended by the scattered remnants of the population that had once filled the city. The only sound he heard was the voice of the cold wind, moaning as it slithered through gaps in the ruined walls. On nights like this one, it was very easy for him to think that he was the only one left, the only survivor of the rapacious Mongol hordes that had swept out of the East.

Once, Kiev had been the most beautiful city in all of Rus, but the horde—hundreds of thousands of men and horses—had thundered across Rus, trampling and destroying everything in its path. Some cities, like his own Volodymyr-Volynskyi, had thought they could withstand a Mongolian siege, and the price of their hubris had been the horrific death of every man, woman, and child of noble birth. The rest were allowed to flee so that they would spread the word of what happened to those who dared to fight back. These pitiful survivors fled to Kiev, bringing their fear with them, and by the time the horde arrived, the city was hideously swollen with refugees.

Illarion had not seen the destruction of Kiev; he had only witnessed the aftermath a year later when, in the company of a band of Shield-Brethren, members of the *Ordo Militum Vindicis Intactae*, he had passed through the ruined South Gate in search of a mystic artifact.

In the labyrinthine caverns beneath the cathedral, they had found nothing—no artifact, no guidance from ghosts of fallen Ruthenians, no cryptic message to be deciphered. They had found only flesh and blood enemies, members of the *Fratres Militiae Christi Livoniae*—the Livonian Brothers of the Sword. With the aid of a company of *Skjalddis*—Shield-Maidens—who still held the citadel in the center of Kiev, Illarion and the Shield-Brethren had driven the Livonians out of the caves.

When the Shield-Brethren continued east, chasing their mad quest to save Christendom by striking at the heart of the Mongol empire, Illarion had realized his place was not with them, but with Kiev. Some nights, when he prowled the battlements alone, Illarion wondered if he stayed behind simply because he was afraid—afraid that Saint Ilya would never respond to his entreaties. That the saint was gone. That all of the old ghosts were gone. That Rus was dead, and that this winter would never end. The stories told about Saint Ilya's grave were that it was the hiding place of the egg that held the soul of Koschei the Deathless. Had the mysterious egg been destroyed as well, thereby ending the life of Rus's last immortal hero?

The night offered no answers to Illarion's endless questions, and when the sky was void of the moon, it was even easier to let go of the endless questions. He could walk along the crumbling walls with no purpose, no destination, and—looking behind him—no past. What use was to it be afraid of what might come if he didn't exist?

The wind stirred, toying with his white-streaked hair as if it were trying to remind him of what he was missing. His right ear was gone, cut from his head by the Mongol gleaners who prowled the fields of dead after the horde was done with an enemy city. He, unlike his wife and children and so many others, had not been entirely dead.

Some nights when he was lost in the depths of a sweat-stained sleep, he would remember rising from the piled corpses, animated with the urge to fight back, but when he woke in the morning, the dream seemed to be only a mere figment of a tale he had overheard around a camping fire.

Power had rested upon his shoulders once, and luxury. He had commanded a household of servants, had possessed retainers, and paid men who fought in his service. But it had never fit him well. As a boy, he'd been drawn to the training yard, had benefitted from a position where men were expected to fight, and his father had hired the finest swords in the land to teach him. When he had grown to manhood, he had spent several years in the service of another boyar as a retainer, and a brief time as a sword for hire when his family believed him to be on a pilgrimage. It was on those journeys, in the years before he returned home to marry the bride picked for him, that he had first met the Shield-Brethren— and eventually Feronantus, the cold master of the northern citadel. His life had changed, then, and but for the rift between the church of the east and the church of the west, he might not have come home. How different might life have been, had *that* been his fate?

He heard gravel crunch behind him, and he stirred slightly, shaking off the layer of morbid thoughts that were accreting to him like layers of ice. He knew his visitor had stepped poorly solely to warn him of his approach, and he turned his head to indicate that he had heard the signal. He had been outside long enough that his eyes had grown accustomed to the tiny gleam of the distant lights, and he could make out enough of the silhouette of the person approaching to realize it was one of the *Skjalddis.*

"Moping in the dark?" she asked, and by her voice, he knew it was Nika. Green-eyed Nika, who appeared oblivious to both the weather and the endless despair of life in Kiev.

"Aye," he said with a short laugh. "'Tis better to do it up here where the wind carries my sobs away from the citadel."

She stood next to him, less than a head shorter than he, and she seemed to be both listening and looking intently. "It is both the best and worst night for a raid," she said after a moment or two of introspection.

"There are no Mongols left," Illarion said. "They've taken everything of value."

"Not everything," she countered.

"There are easier cities to plunder," he said. "I wouldn't wait around either."

"Still…" She cocked her head, listening intently again.

Illarion caught himself before he spoke, and did the same. He was at a deficit, having only one ear, and after listening for a few seconds, he had to admit he heard nothing but the wind as it sighed across the crumbling crenellations of the wall.

"Do you hear it?" Nika asked.

Illarion shook his head.

She glanced at him; he gestured at the hair obscuring his missing ear, and she nodded. "It's only on nights like this, when the moon is hiding and the wind is from the north. It is…"

"What?" Illarion asked, his curiosity aroused. He briefly wondered if Nika was playing with him, spinning a nursemaid's tale as if he were a wide-eyed boy.

"After our sisters failed to return…" She paused, and Illarion bowed his head in respectful memory of the party of *Skjalddis* who had left Kiev with the Shield-Brethren months ago. "I kept vigil on many nights," she continued. "I was waiting for some sign that they would be coming back, and it was during the near darkness of a new moon that I started to hear the sounds of…of their ghosts."

"Their ghosts?"

Nika made a noise with her mouth that was not unlike the low moan of the wind through the stones of the wall. Illarion shivered briefly at the sound; it made the skin along his back crawl, but he covered his apprehension with a snort of laughter. The sound was harsher than he intended, but it felt surprisingly good nonetheless to have something to laugh about. "Ooooo," he said, aping the same noise that Nika had made.

She nudged him with her shoulder. "Ah, you have heard them," she said.

"Aye, I guess I have," Illarion admitted. He struggled to think of what to say next, but his tongue was still and his mind was empty; the tiny spark of humor that had fluttered to life between them guttered and went out, swallowed by the night. Carried away by the wind.

"When I was a young girl, I was in love with the wind," Nika said. "As a child, when it howled and shook the timbers of our tiny house, I was never afraid. I would lie awake, listening to its cries. My father worried, of course, but my mother pointed out that I was silent during the storms. What better nursemaid could new parents hope for? When I was older, I would let my hair down when the winds came and run in the meadows. It was my mother's turn to worry. 'What man would want such a wild woman?' she would lament to my father. 'The wind cannot give us grandchildren. It will abandon her; the storm will steal her heart one day, and leave nothing behind but a hollow shell.'"

"Did it?" Illarion asked, wondering how often this story was repeated across all of Rus.

"My heart?" Nika shook her head. "The wind blew my father's fishing boat into the rocks one day. He got caught beneath the sail, was battered against the rocks. By the time we managed to pull the canvas from the water, there was nothing left of him but a bloody stain. It was my mother's heart that the wind stole."

Illarion thought of the planks that had been laid down across the families of Volodymyr-Volynskyi. Hearing the screams of those underneath as the horses stamped across the field of wood. "Who suffers more," he wondered, "those who are slain or those who are left behind?"

"There is no answer to that question, Plank," Nika said. Illarion had not told the story of his survival of the destruction at Volodymyr-Volynskyi, but it had circulated among the Shield-Maidens nonetheless, almost as if it had been whispered to a few of them by the wind itself. At first, Illarion had bristled at the nickname, but he had gradually realized that the time in his life when he might have objected to it was long gone.

"Aye," he sighed, knowing she was right. He exhaled, letting out a breath he had not realized he was holding in, and stared out across the empty expanse of Kiev.

To the east, the darkness was becoming less absolute. Tiny dots were swirling around, starlight snared in a mist rising from the Dnieper River. As he watched, the mist thickened and started to creep into the broken ruins like a river breaching its bank and slowly engulfing the surrounding fields. The wind shifted, dancing around the citadel so that it blew into their faces now. Blowing the mist toward them.

Nika put her hand on his arm. "Do you hear it?" she whispered, her grip tighter than necessary.

He did. The sound was distant at first, far enough away that it might have been trees falling in the forest, or the thump of rocks rolling in the river, but it was too persistent—too rhythmic—to be natural.

"Mongol riders?" he whispered to Nika.

She shook her head. "That is not the sound of hooves," she said enigmatically.

Illarion stared at her, trying to ascertain what she wasn't telling him. He half-turned, unsure whether he should merely stand idly on the battlement when an unknown host approached the city—a host, judging by the sound, of a size that would find their meager defense of the citadel to be little more than the sting of a gnat.

"Wait," she said, grabbing his arm.

"We have to warn the others," he said, pulling free of her grip. Nika did not move, and Illarion could not fathom why she wasn't concerned. With an exasperated exhalation, he stayed as well.

The fog slithered across the ground, devouring the distance between the river and the citadel walls at an unnatural rate, and the wind blowing against his face was warm. It carried strange scents—the musk of blossoming flowers, a bittersweet crispness that reminded him of orchards in the spring, and the smoky aroma of smoldering cedar and cypress—as well as a distant thrum of sound. At first, Illarion thought the noises were nothing more than the echo of night birds, calling to each other, but as the sound became clearer, it fell into sync with the rhythmic beat of the march. The words were oddly familiar and yet utterly foreign, and he instinctively realized he knew what sort of song it was.

"They're singing," he said. "It is like one of the battle songs sung by the Shield-Brethren."

"Aye," she answered, somewhat breathlessly. "We sing one like it ourselves, but..."

The voices echoed as if from some deep chasm, far away and out of sight. The fog reached the base of the hill, the mists wreathing around stones and broken houses, through trees and over the bones of the dead, and Illarion thought he saw shapes in the mist, always at the very edge of his vision, melting back into the fog when he tried to focus upon them. The sound of leather-shod feet grew louder and louder as did the singing voices, and Illarion found himself wondering how the noise had not alerted the rest of the citadel.

Nika touched his arm again and pointed, and the hairs on the back of his neck rose as he looked down and saw figures stepping out of the mist. They had broad faces with strong noses and close-cropped hair; they carried heavy shields emblazoned with shadowy sigils. Illarion recalled the shields that hung in the great hall at Petraathen, the mountain citadel of the Shield-Brethren.

I never took the final test...

Each rank remained solid for a brief instant, their stony faces staring up at Nika and Illarion, and then, as the next rank formed and crashed into them, the forward rank fell apart, splashing back into the wave of fog lurching against the wall. The ghosts swirled around the wall, forming and dissolving with a mindless relentlessness that made Illarion want to scream. The shout stuck in his throat and he could feel it swelling in his chest, struggling to get out.

The mist parted suddenly, as if it had been cut by the sword of an invisible giant, and in that instant, all of the faces disappeared. The mist trickled away, running back down the hill like rain water sluicing off the hard rock. All that remained was a solitary figure—more solid than any ghost and yet even more improbable than the phantom host that had just thrown itself against the walls of the citadel.

The figure looked to be an impossibly old woman, stooped and bent, her hair wild and matted and covered in dirt, as were the wretched rags that hung about her gnarled form like sodden cobwebs. When the mist was gone, she lifted her ancient face and fixed Illarion with the most terrible pair of eyes he'd ever beheld, their baleful gaze lancing like a bolt through his heart. As he stood, transfixed by the vision, the crone's withered right hand slowly rose and, with a deliberate, unerring gesture, pointed towards the frigid north.

The world seemed to fade, and Illarion's vision narrowed until his eyes could see nothing but the old woman's dire stare.

The scream that had been caught in his throat withered and died, slipping back into his gut with a whimper. His eyes burned as if he had been staring too long into a fire, and he struggled to find the strength to blink.

When he did, the crone was gone.

Beside him, Nika stirred, as if she, too, had been released from the grip of some unspeakable glamour. He shivered, as the wind had shifted again and its breath was fiercely cold once more.

"Did you see...?" he asked, reluctant to put into words the vision he had witnessed.

"Aye," Nika said, her voice as unsteady as his. "I saw the ghosts of my fallen sisters."

"No," Illarion said. "There were men, carrying heavy shields, like the Greek infantry once did. And...and there was an old woman."

Nika stood close enough to him that he could make out her features in the starlit night. There was still a trace of fear in her face, but mostly Illarion saw a fierce determination in the Shield-Maiden's eyes. "I only saw the faces of dead *Skjalddis,*" Nika said. Her throat worked and her eyes widened slightly.

"You have been keeping a vigil," he whispered, realizing she had been lying to him earlier. "You've seen them before."

"Every month," she admitted. "When there is no moon." Her eyes were bright now, tears reflecting starlight. "But I never saw the old woman," she said. "Not until tonight."

"Who is she?" Illarion asked.

Nika let loose a short bray of laughter, a cruel sound that was quickly swallowed by the night. "She showed herself because you were here," Nika said. "You're the one who summoned her."

"Me?"

"Aye," Nika said. "You stayed when the others left. You had family here. You are part of Rus. You have been down into the crypts and seen the grave of Saint Ilya. You know the stories."

"They're just stories," Illarion protested.

Nika stepped closer to Illarion and peered into his eyes as if she were trying to see some flicker of light hidden deep within. "You know who she was," she said softly. "From the stories. The witch with the leg of stone. The witch who knows what must be done."

Illarion's heart was pounding. He looked at Nika, and though he already knew the answer, he could not stop himself from asking, desperate that she should tell him otherwise.

"Nika," he whispered, "what is it that must be done?"

"You must go north," she replied. "That is where Baba Yaga has instructed you to go, and wherever you go, my sisters and I will follow."

CHAPTER 2:

CROSSING THE GAP

He had not seen the sun for a week; the sky had been blotted out by a white fury of a storm that clung to the peaks of the mountains with the tenacity of a wild dog. The slopes were covered in snowpack that would not melt for many months, and his horse labored slowly, picking its way carefully across the ice-bound ground. More often than not, he walked beside it, gently pulling the reins to keep the beast moving. It was a sturdy beast; it had carried him all the way from the heart of the Mongol empire, but he doubted it would be with him for the entirety of his journey.

This was not unexpected. He had made certain choices over the years that had isolated him; if asked, he would not have spoken of consciously creating his self-imposed exile from those he cared about, but he knew. It was the way of the *Vor*. He saw its patterns well enough to know the path that would be his and his alone.

The Heavenly Mountains were a long chain of tall peaks that separated the Mongol homelands from the steppes roamed by the Turkic tribes, and the Zuungar Gap was one of the few passes that were not heavily patrolled by the *Khagan*'s men. It was too high—too exposed to the frigid wind—to be a trade route. Not since Hannibal had there been a commander of such fortitude to attempt such a risky crossing. And Hannibal had brought elephants with him.

Feronantus had just the one horse, and the Spirit Banner of the Mongol empire.

It was a gnarled stick of hard wood, covered with generations of scars. When it had come into Feronantus's possession, it had sported a crosspiece of cedar and a silk banner as well as several dozen strands of knotted horsehair. He had knocked the crosspiece off and discarded the banner, but had left the horsehair strands. They did not freeze. He did not like touching them.

The banner was strapped to his saddle, pointing in the direction he wanted his horse to go, and the horsehair streamers floated and danced in the wind with utter distain for the ambient temperature. Whenever he stopped for a few hours of sleep, he would find his beard crusted with ice when he woke. The horsehair remained untouched.

He suspected the only reason his horse had not died already was because the banner was keeping the animal warm. Soon, there would come a night when the clouds would dip too low and the wind would be too cold, and he would have to take the banner for himself, and that would be the night when his horse died.

He had made much harder choices in the past, and he suspected there were one or two more that would be put to him yet. He didn't spend too much time fretting about the animal's death. It was inevitable. He had seen it in the swirling pattern of the *Vor*.

◆ ◆ ◆

He had first felt the touch of the *Vor* during the summer of his eighth year. Like all orphans claimed by Athena and given a home at Petraathen, he had learned how to hold a sword as readily as a hoe or a switch or a trowel. They were allowed only wooden weapons—nearly straight pieces of oak capped with ugly and ill-fitting hilts—and they were not allowed to learn any of the true art of fighting. The sticks were not long enough and the balance was all wrong, because their *oplo*—the fighting master of the *Ordo Militum Vindicis Intactae*—was not interested in having to break them of too many bad habits when they were old enough to hold real steel. What they had learned those first few years was how to *not* let go of their swords. How to use them, instinctively, to defend themselves. How to attack—even as clumsy as they were—when given the slightest opportunity.

His *oplo*, a veteran named Peregrinus who had gone west while other crusades had gone east, was a giant of a man who moved with the incredible agility of a feral cat. Every day, he would stalk the boys for an hour or so, making sure they carried their swords. At the evening meal, the other knights could tell which boys had been caught by the *oplo* by the red welts across the backs of their hands.

Feronantus had been careful to keep his wooden sword with him, eager to foil Peregrinus's attempts, but after several days, he had sought out the *oplo* and demanded to know why he had been neglected. "You have caught all the other boys," he complained. "Some more than once. But I have not seen you." He dropped his sword in the dirt and held out his hand, palm down. "I am ready."

Peregrinus crouched and picked up Feronantus's sword, cradling it lightly in his hands. "Why are you eager to be punished?" he asked.

"I am worthy of punishment," Feronantus said. "I am just like the others."

Peregrinus took Feronantus's hand and carefully wrapped the small boy's fingers around the misshapen hilt. "No," he said quietly, staring intently at the boy. "You are not. I *have* been looking for you, but you are never where I expect you to be." He turned Feronantus's hand over and lightly stroked the unblemished back of the boy's hand. "It is not enough to be worthy of punishment," he said. "The one who metes out the punishment must earn that right as well. Do you understand?"

Feronantus nodded, though he was not entirely certain he did.

The following morning, as he was squatting to take a shit, Peregrinus had appeared next to him and placed his foot firmly on Feronantus's blade which was resting on the ground. He flicked it away, and Feronantus had felt his muscles tighten uncontrollably. "This isn't fair," he complained.

Peregrinus snapped the switch, and Feronantus felt the tip lay open the edge of his ear. "Fair?" the *oplo* hissed. "If we were on a battlefield, would you ask your enemy to wait until you had wiped your ass?"

Feronantus felt tears threaten to start, but he held them back. Blood dripped down his ear, and his naked rear was cold and exposed, but he did not move.

Peregrinus watched him for a moment longer, and then nodded curtly. "You may live long enough to thank me for this lesson," he said with a hard smile.

Feronantus stared up at his *oplo* and, with a shiver, *knew* that he would. Peregrinus saw something in Feronantus's gaze and took a step back. The switch twitched in his hands, but he thought better of it after a second. "Get that cleaned up," he said, thrusting his jaw toward Feronantus's bloody ear.

◆ ◆ ◆

He nearly lost the fire when he added the heavy branch. The kindling and materials he had used to start the fire had turned to ash, and he had no choice but to add damp wood; otherwise he would lose the fire entirely. The branch was a thick piece of fir that he had pulled from deep within the tree's canopy, hoping that it would be less soaked than the outer branches. The log threw off a heavy plume of white smoke—his own contribution to the winter cloak laid about the mountains—and the ashes beneath the log whitened as if all heat had been drawn from them. After a few moments, during which Feronantus held his breath in anticipation, a tiny tongue of flame licked the end of the log. It was followed by a second, and Feronantus relaxed his vigil on his meager fire. Confident that it wouldn't go out in the next few minutes, he left the tiny camp and walked the short distance to where his dead horse sprawled in the snow.

They had reached the peak of the pass a day or so ago—it was hard to tell night from day when the clouds were so impermeable about the mountain tops—and Feronantus had thought that he might have been mistaken about his horse, but when his animal started to lag, he started to watch for a possible camp site. On this side of the gap, there were shrines for Khan Tengri, the god of the Mongols. He found a few that were marked by faded scraps of linen wedged between the top two rocks in crooked cairns, but they offered no protection from the wind. As he and his wobbly horse limped along the edge of a ridge, a steep drop down to a craggy mouth of broken stones on his left, he spotted an irregular cluster of rocks like a moss-covered crown atop the skull of a dead giant. His horse balked at the nearly flat incline up to the ring of stones, and as he tried to coax it onward, it shivered uncontrollably and then collapsed.

He collected the Spirit Banner and his kit from the dead horse, carrying them back up to the smoking fire, and then returned for his saddle and bags.

The log was burning slowly, popping as it dried, and it was still putting off a lot of smoke, but not nearly as much as when he had first put it on the fire. Several of the tall stones near the fire were glistening, their icy shells starting to melt from the fire's heat. As best he could—his back and hands were stiff—he cleared the snow from the ground at the base of these stones. He chipped as much of the ice from the stones as he could, and only after he put another branch on the fire and was assured that it wouldn't smother the flames, did he spread out one of his heavy blankets and sit down.

Feronantus thought he had closed his eyes for merely a moment, but when he looked at the flames again, the first log was nothing more than a charred rib of wood and the second was half devoured by fire. He stirred, a flash of anger lending a brief flush of color to his pale cheeks.

This isn't fair...

Peregrinus had died in the Holy Land, when Richard Lionheart had taken Arsuf from Saladin. The Shield-Brethren had come to the crusade with the English king, and they had been fighting nonstop since they had arrived. Of the three dozen new initiates who had gotten off the boat in Acre's harbor, less than half survived the siege of Arsuf. Their *oplo* and several other veterans had fallen in the service of Richard as well, and by the time the English king had decided to return home, there was no longer any distinction between initiate and veteran. They were all survivors.

Feronantus glanced at the Spirit Banner, which he had propped up with several rocks so that it leaned upright against a nearby shrine stone. The horsehair strands were bedraggled and kinked with knots, and the staff was so old that the wood appeared to be gray in the dim snow-light of the winter evening.

Am I wrong? he wondered. *Have I abandoned everything for a warped stick?*

The staff of the banner was nearly five feet in length, and the wood had been ash once, but time had hardened it to nearly the strength of iron. It had belonged to Temujin, Ögedei Khan's father, and according to the stories Feronantus had learned during his recent travels across the Mongol empire, Temujin had been given the staff by mystics who dwelled in a sacred grove near Burqan-qaldun. With the banner, Temujin had become Genghis Khan—the Khan of Khans—and all of the wild clans had bowed to him. Genghis's dream of a unified empire had been realized by his sons, and when the armies of the Khan of Khans had come to the West, threatening Christendom, Feronantus and a company of his fellow Shield-Brethren had journeyed east, to the heart of the empire. It had been their intention to kill Ögedei Khan—Genghis's son and the current Khan of Khans.

Even though the death of the *Khagan* would trigger the *kuraltai*, the feverish election of a new Khan of Khans, it would only postpone the devastation of Christendom. The Mongol hordes would come back, and unless the kings of the West put aside their petty differences to band together against the common enemy, they would be overrun again.

Would the banner be enough? Would the West rally around it like the Mongol clans had for Genghis? Would he be able to use it to command a host the size of which would rival that commanded by Alexander the Great?

Feronantus climbed to his feet and reached for the banner. The wood was warm in his hand, and he prodded the dying fire with the worn end, breaking up the coals. Hanging on to the banner for support, he leaned over and put a few more branches on the fire. The new wood smoked and sizzled, enveloping him in a cloud of white smoke. He stepped back, coughing and waving his hands to clear the smoke from his face. His left hand, still holding the banner, felt as if it were being pierced by a thousand knives, and he shifted his grip.

His thumb rubbed across a ragged spur, an aberration on the otherwise smooth surface of the banner.

Feronantus backed away from the fire until he was pressed against the weeping stones. His eyes watering from the smoke, he peered at the spur on the banner. It looked like the stump of a tree branch, the scarred remnants of a tiny growth that had been sheared off. He had stripped enough saplings of their leaves and branches to recognize the swelling of the wood around the base of such a protrusion and the way the bark peels away when the leaf is yanked off.

How is this possible? he wondered. The piece of wood had been severed from its parent for many years. How could it still sprout new growth?

Out beyond the circle of stones, someone let loose a long series of chest-rattling coughs, and Feronantus forgot about the mystery of the banner. His right hand fell to the hilt of his sword and he peered into the gloom beyond the weak light of his fire. A shape stirred, becoming more than a gray shadow against the white sky and ground, and then it became several shapes—man-sized and horse-sized. Feronantus heard the familiar jingle of a western harness as a man staggered against the outer rocks, a pair of horses nearly pushing him forward in their effort to get close to the single source of warmth on the mountainside.

The man, covered in a layer of hoar frost, fell to his knees and crawled closer to the fire. His face was a mass of ice, his beard a bundle of broken icicles. He collapsed, nearly landing in the fire. His arms were outstretched as if he were trying to embrace the flame.

"Istvan," Feronantus croaked, recognizing the near-frozen figure.

Istvan groaned upon hearing his name, and his moans became more pronounced as the fire began to thaw the ice on his face and chest. Feronantus looked at the pair of horses, recognizing the tack on each. *He's alone,* Feronantus thought. *They haven't found me.*

Istvan had brought an extra horse, almost as if he had known that Feronantus would need one.

Such was the mystery of the *Vor.*

Istvan rolled onto his back, and the white mist of his exhalation rose and twined with the guttering smoke from the fire.

"All-Father," the mad Hungarian croaked.

The thousand knives pierced Feronantus's left hand again as the horsehair strands fluttered around the staff of the Spirit Banner.

CHAPTER 3:

THE WINTER PASSAGE

The horse had been foundering all day, and as evening approached, Raphael announced he was going to slaughter it. Cnán felt a momentary spasm of horror, but her reaction was overwhelmed by a flood of relief that the company would be building a fire. It had been many days since the last time she had been warm, and she didn't dare try to count the days, fearful that such an accounting would only make her burst into tears. She was no stranger to long journeys and uncomfortable terrain, but the last few weeks had strained even her fortitude.

They found a stretch of ground that was sheltered from the wind in two directions, and as the Shield-Brethren went about the making of camp, Cnán and Vera wandered over to the nearby tree line to gather fuel for the fire. The other member of their company—Lian, the Chinese woman who had accompanied Haakon from the *Khagan*'s camp—did not join them, and Cnán wasted no breath wondering aloud to Vera why the Chinese woman did so little in the preparations.

She had made such a mistake once before and the *Skjalddis's* response had been stinging and brusque. *Are you jealous?* Vera had asked.

There was no mistaking the Chinese woman's beauty. She was several inches taller than Cnán, with lustrous black hair and a delicately shaped face. She spoke none of the languages known by the Shield-Brethren, but via the light touch of her hand and a series of exaggerated expressions that annoyed Cnán endlessly—she acted like a tawdry village mummer—Lian found ways to communicate with the men. Cnán, whose unkempt hair and slender build had allowed her to be mistaken for a boy on more than one occasion, was all but invisible next to Lian. Vera's northern heritage had been blunted by several generations of Ruthenian blood, but she was still pale and hard—shale to Haakon's granite, if they were to be thought of as being carved from stone—the sort of woman who would appeal to these men purely out of admiration of who and what she was. Vera, however, had already chosen one of them as her companion, and so she was invisible to them for other reasons.

Why am I even worrying about this? Cnán snapped a low branch from a scraggly fir, adding it to the pile in her arms. It wasn't jealousy that she felt. She wasn't trying to vie for the attention of the Shield-Brethren. The youngster, Haakon, had propositioned her once, and she had turned him down. Not because she hadn't found him desirable, but merely because both knew such a liaison would have been a fleeting distraction. At the time, she had thought she would never see him again, more so when she had agreed to accompany the Shield-Brethren on their mad crusade to the heart of the Mongol empire. How strange it had been to journey all the way from Legnica in the West to the mountains north of Karakorum and find the pale-haired youth waiting for them.

She liked Yasper, the nimble-fingered Dutchman who knew more about powders and reagents than the art of killing a man with a sword, but he was prone to talking of matters that made her head swim. The most innocent comment could launch him into an hour-long monologue about the alchemical mystery of snow-fall. Raphael had become their leader, and the weight of such responsibility kept him removed from the rest of the company, but for those times when he sought Vera's counsel.

Which left Percival, the regal Frank who was the most beautiful and the most terrifying of the company. She had seen him crush the spine of a Mongol *bankhar* with a mace one moment and then calmly and attentively inquire as to her safety the next. Her childish infatuation with him had faded away during their long ride across the steppes, but once Lian had joined their company, she had found her feelings were not as dead as she had thought.

Juggling her collection of branches into the crook of her left arm, she grabbed one of the broken branches jutting out from the round trunk at the top of a fir that had broken off during a wind storm. The trunk caught on every rock and root as she dragged it back toward the camp, and she cursed and yanked and pulled, pouring her frustration and annoyance into the task.

Yasper spotted her first and trotted over to help. He tried to take the bundle of branches from her, and nearly tripped over the heavy branch when she shoved it at him. "Oh, of course," he said cheerfully, dancing around the thick branch.

Percival, she noticed, was showing Lian how to arrange kindling and moss in order to start a fire—a task Cnán was fairly certain he had shown her at least once before.

Yasper yelped as she dropped the heavy branch onto his foot.

She noisily dumped her armload of branches beside Percival and Lian. Lian jumped at the sound, reminding Cnán of a rabbit being spooked out of hiding by an owl, and Percival put out a hand to calm her as he glanced up at Cnán. "Ah," he said, noticing the branches. "Just in time. Thank you, Cnán. Would you be so kind as to tell Lian—"

"Tell her yourself," Cnán snapped, and she stomped off before she said anything more.

Yasper was huffing as he dragged the heavy branch up. He dropped it as unceremoniously as Cnán had her branches, but he had the grace to do so several yards away from the fire pit. "I'll get a hatchet," he said, out of breath. "We can cut this up into several pieces."

"I'll get it," Cnán said. As she turned toward the few remaining horses, she nearly bumped into Vera who had an armload of wood of her own.

"We could use some more wood, little one," the Shield-Maiden said. "Leave the blade work to others." Behind her, Cnán saw Haakon and Raphael crouched around the body of the dead horse. The skin on one of the haunches had been pulled back already, and Haakon's arm was moving vigorously as he cut the meat away from the bone. His forearms were stained red with blood.

Flushing, both from the rioting emotions in her heart and from her stomach growling at the thought of real food, Cnán stormed off toward the tree line again. She could blame the weather for the way she was feeling—being cold and hungry always sapped one's strength and lowered one's defenses against mental confusion—but some of it ran deeper than that. She had been traveling with the Shield-Brethren for almost a year now, and in that time had come to be quite attached to many of the members of the company. Not necessarily in a romantic fashion—her lingering feelings for Percival, notwithstanding—but like family, for lack of a better word.

Family.

She was a Binder, and she had her family already, but they were scattered, and she felt their presence and read their thoughtful concern via marks carved in the boles of trees, in complicated sequences of knots shoved into narrow hiding places at trade markers, and in subtle arrangements of stones and twigs and leaves that weren't accidental patterns left by the wind. Such love and community was affection at arm's length, at best, and such satisfaction that she received from finding signs of her sisters in the wild paled in comparison to laughing at one of Yasper's quirky jokes or finding an excuse to discuss the perpetually dismal weather with Percival.

What gnawed at her with increasing savagery was a sense that her new family was falling apart. She was the only one who saw the end coming, and she didn't know how to stop it.

They'd crossed the empty steppe once already, surviving the mind-numbingly dull ride across the endless landscape. She knew the Shield-Brethren were liable to summarize their journey east as merely an *interesting* journey. They were not prone to hyperbolic talk of their deeds, and *interesting* barely started to cover what they had accomplished. Of the group, Yasper was the only one who was still prone to marvel that not only were they still alive, but they appeared to have managed to escape any sort of pursuit. Cnán, however, wasn't as convinced; nor were Raphael and Vera, who found regular excuses to circle back on their trail to make sure no one was following them. As they had reached the mountains and traveled through the Zuungar Gap, the weather had grown more vicious and they had given little thought to anything more than maintaining westward motion. Cnán had hoped that the harsh weather would lessen after the Gap, but the storms had only gotten worse. Even after they came down from the mountains—Khan Tengri was nothing more than a thin finger of stone in the distance—the ground remained coated with a heavy layer of snow.

It was difficult to find landmarks, and even more difficult to find food for the horses and shelter from the winds when they tried to rest. Her confidence at being able to find her way back to the rock—an isolated trading post that was their goal—lessened every day. She couldn't even seek guidance from the stars—the persistent cloud cover hid them from her—and the sun was never much more than a diffuse glow behind the heavy layer of dark clouds. It should have taken only a few days to ride out the belly of the storm that hung over them, but the gray clouds seemed to move with them.

It was winter on the steppe; she and the others were the fools who thought it would be anything less savage and miserable than it was. But they had had little choice, hadn't they? The *Khagan* was dead. His sons and brothers and cousins and other relatives who thought they might have a chance at the throne were coming back to Karakorum. The Empire was no place for a handful of armed Westerners and a pair of refugees like herself and Lian.

More than once, shivering under her thin blanket, she had considered the idea that they would disappear. The wind would steal all the heat from their bodies, and then the snows would cover them. They might be found once the seasons turned, but more likely, they would die and thaw and be gnawed into pieces by the hungry beasts that roamed the empty steppe. *How silly*, she would chide herself, *to save the West and then to die so ignobly.*

She had to find the rock. She had to get them home again.

✦ ✦ ✦

It was not the first time Raphael had eaten horse, and the meat was a heavy weight in his tight stomach. Like the company itself, the animal had been gaunt and under-nourished, and he was glad he had cautioned Haakon and Yasper to prepare less than they normally would have. No one ate much; they were all suffering from a lack of consistent meals. Raphael had hoped that a full belly and a warm fire would quiet his restless mind and allow him some much-needed sleep, but after an hour of fussing and twisting under his narrow blanket, he gave up. Even though the wound had healed well, the muscles in his lower back tended to twist themselves into knots.

He pushed his blanket aside and sat up. The fire had dwindled to a warm orange glow, and he could make out Haakon's slumped shape on the far side of the pit they had dug in the frozen ground. The boy was supposed to be on watch, and Raphael felt a momentary twinge of jealousy that Haakon was able to enjoy the rest that eluded him. *Let him sleep*, he thought as he reached for his saddlebags. Why berate the boy when he could readily take the watch? His stiff fingers found the leather shape of his journal, and he plucked it free of the bag and carried it with him as he got to his feet.

He made a quick circuit of their camp, falling into the old habit of walking widdershins. There were those who considered walking in opposition to the sun's route to be bad luck, but Raphael had learned long ago that *luck*—good or bad—had little to do with keeping a company safe. The night circle was one of many quirks that made the Shield-Brethren different from the other martial orders, though no one gave much thought to whether such differences made their order more or less successful than the others. The *Ordo Militum Vindicis Intactae* had a lineage that went back more than fifteen hundred years. If a practice worked, you didn't wonder overmuch as to its source or rationale.

And yet, was this blind obedience to the old ways responsible for the situation he and the company found themselves in? How had he, whose tongue had gotten him into so much trouble over the years, kept his thoughts to himself during their journey east? Had it been the enormity of their task, the daunting impossibility of their mission, that had kept him silent?

Raphael paused at the corpse of the dead horse. The body was already stiff and cold; he should have had Haakon cut more meat. The task was going to be more difficult in the morning. He hadn't thought ahead. *That's the issue, isn't it?* he thought. Their mission to Karakorum had been a success. They had accomplished an impossible task, but their leader—the man who had convinced them that killing the *Khagan* was the only way to save Christendom—had abandoned them at the very moment of their success. Feronantus had taken the Spirit Banner of the Mongol empire and left them behind. Why? Raphael had pondered this question a great deal in the weeks since, and he had found no suitable answer. He had even found himself praying for divine guidance on several occasions, though he was terrified of receiving any response from his queries. *I'm just going to have to ask him myself,* he thought as he shook off the cloak of morbid thoughts that was settling about his shoulders.

He recalled the dead horse they had found near the Zuungar Gap—the first sign that they were still following Feronantus. If it hadn't been for the pair of skeletal wolves who had been trying to gnaw off a chunk of frozen meat, they wouldn't have found the snow-covered corpse. After scouring the surrounding area for an hour or two, looking for incongruous humps covered in snow, they had found the shrine and signs that someone had built a fire there.

Yasper had been fascinated by the ridged patterns of ice on one of the standing stones, and the inquisitive alchemist had had to be dragged away when they had gleaned the meager clues left by their erstwhile leader.

During one of Raphael's numerous visits to the court of the Holy Roman Empire, the Holy Roman Emperor, the brilliant and highly educated Holy Frederick II, had inquired as to what Raphael knew of the legendary Feronantus. Did Raphael know why Feronantus had been exiled to Týrshammar? How many of the stories coming out of England were true, and how many were bellicose fables? Had Feronantus been the companion of Richard Lionheart when the English king had been captured on his return from the crusade? Was it true that Feronantus was one of the few men who had beaten William Marshal? Over the years, Raphael had had the opportunity to answer many of Frederick's constant questions, but on the subject of Feronantus, he had been able to offer little knowledge. It wasn't that he sought to abstain from enlightening the Holy Roman Emperor; it was that the answers to his questions were maddeningly obscure. His own curiosity piqued by Frederick's questions, Raphael had sought out those who could tell him of Feronantus's history, and he had been stymied time and again. There were numerous stories about the Old Man of the Rock, and he had been surprised to learn that the more audacious stories were more likely to be true than not, which only compounded the confusion of Feronantus's past. How could such an illustrious hero end up the master of the most remote stronghold in Christendom?

Raphael suspected the answer to that question would reveal a great deal about the sort of man who would abandon his faithful companions. At first, Feronantus's decision had felt like bold-faced betrayal; in time, however, Raphael had come to realize it was an act of cold calculation. If there were to be reprisals for what the Shield-Brethren had done in the forest near Burqan-qaldun, the company—minus Feronantus—would be an easier target to track than a single man, riding alone.

Raphael shivered as a breath of cold air slithered into his cloak and down the collar of his tunic. He pulled the worn cloak tighter and hunched his shoulders to try to block the wind from trying again. His hair was shaggy and unkempt, and he had given up trying to keep his beard trimmed months ago. It wasn't as untamed as Yasper's, who looked as if he was trying to cover the lower half of his face with a bird's nest, but it was almost long enough that he could start braiding the ends in the northern style. He was grateful for the warmth all the hair afforded, though, and the beard no longer itched as fiercely as it had a month ago.

He began walking again, mainly to keep warm more than from any concern about the security of their camp. Once they had passed through the mountains and reached the central steppes, he had stopped looking over his shoulder multiple times during the day. The Mongols wouldn't stop hunting them, if they knew where the company had gone, but the farther they got from the heart of the empire, the more certain he was that they had escaped. As soon as they reached the rock, they could resupply from the cache that had been left for them by a friendly trader. With a little luck, they could even manage to pass as mercenaries along the trade routes with no one the wiser.

He ran his thumb along the edge of his journal, playing with the leather cover. Part of him wanted to hunt down the old man; part of him reminded him that the company was his responsibility. They looked to him for guidance and leadership. Was abandoning them to pursue Feronantus any different than what had been done to them? He had put off making this decision, figuring that Feronantus would, at least, be making for the rock as well.

His fingers let the wind tug the journal open, the pages fluttering as the wind explored his rough sketches and scattered entries. Could the wind read the variety of languages he wrote in? At first, making notes had been an opportunity for him to practice whatever the local tongue had been during his travels—it allowed him to fix the words more firmly in his mind. It was a trick he had learned from Frederick. After they had left Kiev, he had stuck with Latin, figuring that there were only a handful of people in the east who could possibly read it—and most of those were men in his own company.

The last entry he had written before his world had been turned upside down had been the record of a statement made by Feronantus. He put his thumb down, holding the pages still, as the wind reached that page. He had been angry when he wrote the words; the letters were thick slashes of charcoal on the parchment. *Our lives have no meaning,* Feronantus had said, e*xcept that which is given to them by our deeds, and by how our comrades remember us.*

The wind shifted, blowing against his face and nearly tearing the journal out of his grip. He raised his hands and shielded his eyes; he could see little and hear nothing but the noisy cry of the wind, but he sensed a storm was coming.

◆ ◆ ◆

The wind slapped the felt tent, and Lian couldn't tell if it was going to collapse the whole structure or tear the stakes out of the ground and whisk the tiny shelter away. She felt like a tiny animal, and she tried to quell the shivering in her legs. Beside her, Cnán lay stiffly, trying to be as far away as possible from Lian while simultaneously cuddling close to share body heat. Cnán didn't like her, a reaction Lian had seen time and again at Karakorum and to which she gave little thought. Jealously between women, especially the concubines and other unattached servants, was an undeniable facet of court life. Everyone wanted what someone else had, and the luxuries and comforts afforded the prettier ones were always a source of ire.

She doubted any of the concubines at the *Khagan*'s palace would recognize her; months ago, she might have been shocked at such a possibility, but such concerns—along with many others—were behind her now. She wasn't a captive in the company of these knights from the West; while they were too noble to slit her throat and leave her for the wolves, they weren't entirely trusting of her either. Cnán was the only one who spoke any Chinese—though the woman's accent was odd, even to Lian's ear—and she spent as much time as she could with the pale lad, Haakon, who had a rudimentary understanding of the Mongol tongue. From him she had learned enough of the western trade tongue to start with the others, even though the brutal weather made idle talk infrequent. Still, she knew something about talking to strange men; she had been useful to Master Chucai in that she knew how to appear attentive, flatter when necessary, and coax all manner of information out of a man without him being aware that he was telling her anything.

And then there had been the young pony, Gansukh. The emissary from Ögedei's brother, who had come to Karakorum to put an end to the *Khagan*'s drinking. She never would have guessed that this unrefined hunter would become her lover and sometime protector.

Beneath her furs, she slipped a hand inside her robe and felt for the tiny lacquer box tucked in an inside pocket. It soaked up heat from her body; on nights like this one, it felt warmer even, as if it was generating heat for her. Gansukh had pressed it into her hands shortly before he had left with the *Khagan* on Ögedei's fateful hunt, and she had kept it with her when she had made her daring escape.

The theft had been an odd moment of sentimentality, and she still wondered why she had taken it. Did he mean that much to her? It was a preposterous idea, really. She was a Chinese woman, an escaped slave, and she was fleeing Mongolia, China—all of the east. She was heading into the west, like one of the characters from the folk tales she had heard as a child. A lost soul, wandering into the unknown. She had no idea what lay ahead of her, though she knew what was behind her—beyond the snow-capped mountains.

Death.

She had turned her back on death. She clutched the box and her robe in her hand, and tried not to pay much attention to the howling wind. Another storm was coming. The company wasn't very sheltered, and the tent was, truly, rather flimsy. She should have been more worried about freezing; her life, so recently renewed and reinvigorated, might be stripped away by the wind.

Lian felt so sleepy—her hand was warm, her breasts were warm. The wind howled outside the tent, but it couldn't come any closer. *It'll pass*, she thought fleetingly, falling into a dream of lush greenery.

1242

VESNA

CHAPTER 4:

VOLQUIN'S DRAGON

The frigid waters of the Velikaya River lapped against the hull as the rowers brought the boat closer to the shore. It was early morning, and the first touch of the sun had raised a layer of fog that extended past the banks of the river. Fortunately, there were men standing on the shore, suggesting the limit of how far the boat could travel. They wore white tunics stained with mud and stitched with black crosses that seemed to float in the morning light. *Black, not red,* thought Kristaps, frowning. Black was the color worn by the members of the Order of Teutonic Knights of Saint Mary's Hospital in Jerusalem, while he, along with the men in the boat, was a member of the Livonian Brothers of the Sword—wearers of the red cross.

It was a reminder of how far his order had fallen. First, Schaulen, and then the disaster at Hünern where they had lost their second grandmaster, Dietrich von Grüningen. The remnants of the Livonian order had been forced to seek sanctuary in the ranks of the Teutonic knights, and had it not been for the intercession of Cardinal Sinibaldo Fieschi, Kristaps would have abandoned the Livonian order entirely.

What use, he had asked the cardinal, *is an order that cannot serve God by the strength of its might? What fools were they to offer their faith and devotion to an ideal so aged and weak that it could not defend itself?*

Such an order has no use to us, the cardinal had replied. *An order's usefulness lies not in the words spoken by its master, but in the actions of the man and those who follow him.*

The cardinal's words were uppermost in Kristaps's mind as the keel of the boat ground against the shore—*those who follow*—and Kristaps dropped out of the prow and into the sand, one hand adjusting his sword to keep the scabbard from brushing the water. He saw the eyes of the men on the shore take in his attire, and he noted the ones who gave little starts of surprise. *Would they follow?* he wondered.

"Who commands here?" he demanded, fixing the nearest man with a hard stare. The man flinched, and Kristaps fought the urge to strike the man across the mouth with his hand.

"Her...Hermann of Dorpat..." the man said. His tone grew stronger as he spoke, as if his spine was stiffening with each word. "Who are you, sir, to be asking?"

"I come from Rome with a message for your master," Kristaps said, ignoring the man's question. He was a head taller than the other man, and as he stepped closer, he stared over his head as if the Teutonic knight were nothing more than a mere peasant—as if all of the men wearing the black cross were nothing. Not far from the beach, the walls of Pskov rose out of the fog as if the Novgorodian city were floating on a cloud. Atop the wall, the pennant of the Teutonic order snapped in the crisp wind.

"You, sir—" the man began.

Kristaps cut him off. "I am Kristaps, First Sword of Fellin," he snapped, pitching his voice so that all of the men on the beach could hear him, "and, by the grace of God and His representative in Rome, the Grandmaster of the Livonian Order of Sword Brothers."

He was delighted to see the effect of his words—not just his name, but his new title as well. After the defeat at Schaulen, most of the Sword Brothers had given up the red for the black and he knew some of those cowards had ended up here, in Rus, fighting to expand the holdings of the Teutonic order. Other former members of the *Fratres Militiae Christi Livoniae,* however, would relish the chance to reclaim the red. As word spread of his presence, they would rally around him.

Hermann of Dorpat, the Prince-Bishop of Riga, was a longtime friend of the Livonian order, and despite the order's recent spate of ill fortune, Kristaps knew he had at least one ally in these lands. A competent ally. The sooner these Teutonics were willing to follow him, the sooner he could accomplish the will of Rome.

And reclaim the honor of his order.

A second man stepped forward, his tone much more contrite and apologetic. "Forgive us, *Heermeister,*" he said, dipping his head. "Word had not yet reached us of your elevation. What of..." He paused, whether unwilling to speak the name of the previous grandmaster or unaware of it, Kristaps wasn't sure.

"*Heermeister* Dietrich fell victim to a foul betrayal," he said curtly. "One I mean to avenge."

Neither man said anything, and Kristaps marched past the rank of Teutonic knights who had come to greet him and his men. He fixed his gaze on the walls, setting his mind to the task ahead of him. The campaign of the north was his responsibility now, and only after he was successful would he have the resources to accomplish his true mission: the utter destruction of the Shield-Brethren.

✦ ✦ ✦

It was remarkable how intact Pskov was, given what it had endured. Rus had been weakened terribly by the invasion of the Mongol horde, and as the armies of the *Khagan* moved west, the destruction of each city was like another cut on a body already mortally wounded. When the *Khagan* died, the horde had returned east, trampling what tiny seedlings of hope had managed to break the hard ground of the steppes. Rus was, in Rome's opinion, malleable—ready to be brought more firmly under the yoke of the Church.

The cardinal had not told Kristaps all of Rome's plans, but he had an inkling of the machinations taking place in the wake of the battle at Hünern. At first, the retreat of the Mongol horde had been linked to the death of Onghwe Khan and the dissolution of his Circus of Swords, and the wild tales that had accompanied him on his journey to Rome had sung the praises of the Shield-Brethren, which was impressive, given the fervent pace he had set. Stories of Andreas, Rutger, and the rest of the Rose Knights haunted his every waking moment. Never mind that Andreas had been dead before the final battle had begun, and that the Shield-Brethren would have been crushed if it had not been for Kristaps' men and the other martial orders at Hünern.

Later, when he was in Rome, word arrived that the true reason for the withdrawal of the Mongol forces was the death of the Khan of Khans. *A hunting accident*, the report said.

And Kristaps had found himself wondering again what Feronantus and the other Shield-Brethren had been doing when he had seen them in Kiev.

The cardinal had been intrigued by Kristaps's story of what had happened in Kiev the previous summer. Like Kristaps, he wondered if the Shield-Brethren had had something to do with the *Khagan*'s accident. If such a supposition were true, then the fame of the Shield-Brethren would only increase much more dramatically if rumors were given leave to spread.

We need a victory of our own, the cardinal had said. *We need the appearance of strength—if not the actuality of it.*

"This does not look like a city that was taken by force," he noted as he strode along the main road of Pskov. He saw no burned houses, no sign that barricades had been set up or taken down.

The second man who had spoken to him at the beach trotted along beside him, trying to keep up with Kristaps's long stride. "When we came, they met us in the field," the man explained. "Six hundred men. The bulk of their militia. Few of them had maille, and most had never really fought a pitched battle before. The battle was…" The man gasped for air. "It was over quickly."

Kristaps made a noise of approval. At least the taking of Pskov had been handled well. A permanent settlement that could serve as their compound made the rest of the campaign easier. They would not have to waste time and resources providing for the basic essentials for the men. He could focus on finding and defeating his enemy.

The Novgorodian Prince, Alexander Iaroslavich, whom the locals called *Nevsky*, was somewhere in the wilderness. The curious rumors he had heard during his river journey to Pskov said that the people's savior wandered the wilds with his sworn swords, preparing to return in force to drive out the invaders.

It was the sort of fanciful nonsense that made Kristaps want to burst into fits of derisive laughter when he overheard the whispered talk among the local citizens, but the stories were not to be disregarded entirely. Common folk were wont to sing merrily of their heroes—such songs gave them hope after all—but every story had some truth to it, and he had to pick out these little details so as to gain a better understanding of the man whom he had to defeat.

At the end of the street was a sprawling structure that was too small to be a castle and too grand to be a wealthy landowner's estate. More men wearing the white and black of the Teutonic Knight loitered out in front, looking more bored than alert. Eventually they noticed Kristaps approaching and snapped to a modicum of readiness.

Kristaps stopped before these men, eyeing each one in turn. His escort, panting slightly from the brisk walk, caught up with him, and he waited for the man to catch his breath. "He's here to see the Prince-Bishop," the escort wheezed.

No one moved, and so Kristaps stepped forward, intent on opening the door to the house himself, but one of the Teutonic knights took a step to his left, blocking Kristaps's progress. Kristaps stared at the man, calmly watching his face for any sign of what he might do next. "You're in my way," he said quietly.

"You're wearing the wrong colors," the Teutonic sneered. "The Sword Brothers are no more. Not since Sch—"

That was as far as he got before Kristaps's hand smashed into his mouth. The man staggered back, blood flowing from his lips, eyes wide with shock. Other guards started to draw their swords, and Kristaps had already put his hand on the hilt of his blade when his escort—having regained his breath—started shouting. "Stop! Stop!"

When he had everyone's attention, the escort explained. "He's the *Heermeister* of the Livonian Order," he said. "Here on orders from Rome. Let him pass."

The guards relented, but didn't sheathe their swords entirely until the escort repeated his last sentence again. The blood-ied man glared at Kristaps, but lowered his gaze when Kristaps took a step in his direction. He got out of the way, and Kristaps approached the door without further mishap.

They'll learn, he thought as the door opened. *My way will be the only way.*

He would not make the same mistakes as his predecessors. He could lead these men to glory, but only if they feared him. Otherwise, like the men he had met this morning, they wouldn't follow orders without questioning them. He needed soldiers, not self-styled tacticians.

◆ ◆ ◆

The Prince-Bishop of Riga sat in a study at the back of the estate. A fire burned in the hearth, and its light made the sparsely furnished room appear empty and cavernous. A crude tapestry depicting a trio of horsemen chasing a pair of stiff-legged deer hung on the wall to the left of the door. Hermann of Dorpat bent over a narrow desk, reading scraps of parchment and linen by the firelight. Kristaps stood quietly by the door, giving the Prince-Bishop an opportunity to notice him. His patience was not very generous, and after he tired of looking at the tapestry, he cleared his throat and crossed the room to stand in front of the desk.

Hermann of Dorpat looked up from his reading. His eyes possessed an energy one did not often see in quiet church men, and a keen look to his sharp features that bespoke reservation and competence. He had the broad shoulders of a man who had once wielded weapons or done difficult work, and the thick middle of a man grown used to eating well after many years. He examined Kristaps's face intently, as if striving to mark the First Sword of Fellin firmly in his mind, and then his gaze fell to the red sword and cross on Kristaps's tabard.

"Ah," he started with a tiny shake of his head. "So you have arrived." His fingers dug through the messages on his desk. "I have it here somewhere. Yes, this one." He held up a piece of parchment that carried the broken seal of Rome. "Well then, let me offer you congratulations on your elevation, *Heermeister* Kristaps." He glanced down at the piece of parchment in his hands and his eyes quickly scanned the message written therein. "Welcome to Pskov. I pray you can serve God and the church with all the fervent skill of your predecessors, may they be blessed."

"I thank you," Kristaps replied. He put his hands under his tabard and brought out the sealed message that had been given to him by the cardinal. He offered it to Hermann and stood back as the man took it and broke the red wax seal. As Hermann read the orders from Cardinal Fieschi, Kristaps listened to the popping and crackling noises coming from the fireplace.

"I'm afraid I don't entirely understand," Hermann said with a sigh as he lowered the note. "Fellin is a long way from Pskov, as is much of Rome's influence. What purpose is being served by putting you in charge of the northern campaign?" His fingers tapped against the edge of the letter. "I have matters well in hand here."

"With all due respect, our mutual benefactor disagrees," Kristaps replied in a voice that restrained its irritation with curt politeness.

Hermann glanced at the letter, turning it over to see if he had missed a critical paragraph. "I fail to see how that conclusion is reached by the scant sentences that this cardinal has written."

Kristaps leaned forward and gently pushed the message down. "Sometimes the messenger is as important as the message."

Hermann stared at Kristaps for a moment, a flush rising in his cheeks. His eyes darkened and Kristaps fought the urge to smile.

"During your journey to Pskov, you may have noticed that winter has not quite released its hold on this land," Hermann said coldly. "Spring comes late in Rus. Rome knows little about the difficulty of fielding an army during the cold season."

"That is why they sent me," Kristaps reminded him. "It is the opinion of our mutual benefactor that the republic of Novgorod needs to be properly rescued in the wake of the Mongol invasion. There are many children of God who must be embraced before they succumb to heathen temptations. Before they are overwhelmed again by the devils from the steppes."

Hermann snorted. "Such flowery language to justify such military action," he said. "Rome cares not for Rus or its people. It simply wants more wealth, and citizens under its protection will tithe to remain in the fold, won't they?"

Kristaps let the offhand remark slide over him, keeping his focus upon the man rather than the banter. "Our masters have their reasons, Your Grace," he said, "but our place is to remember who is master and who is servant, who speaks for Holy God and who is obliged to obey. Our place is to follow orders."

"I note that this message lacks the explicit orders that you seem to be implying, *Heermeister*," Hermann said. "But for the sake of argument, I will at least indulge you. What would you do, were the command of this holy crusade in your hands?"

"As I came to your estate, I saw how readily your men had taken Pskov, and I wondered why you hadn't marched on Novgorod already if their militia were as poorly numbered as Pskov's," Kristaps said. "But then I heard stories of this man, Nevsky, and it all became clear to me."

"Nevsky has an army," Hermann said.

"And where is this army?" Kristaps asked. "In Novgorod?" He didn't wait for Hermann to answer him because he really didn't care to hear the Prince-Bishop's excuses. "You shouldn't be concerned about his army. It doesn't matter if it is in Novgorod or if it is with him. It is the stories that should concern you. Tales of Nevsky's exploits against foreign aggressors make him a beloved figure. He is the only hero the Ruthenians have left, and as long as he lives, they will not give up hope. If you strike at Novgorod without first slaying him, they will hold tight the dream of being liberated by their lost prince. Therefore, the most important task to be accomplished is the death of their savior."

Hermann considered this, his fingers lightly drumming on the desk. Kristaps took stock of the Prince-Bishop's contemplative expression, and found the man's thoughtfulness to be to his liking. Many were too proud—too aloof with their airs of being God's servants—to truly contemplate the more unsavory requirements of performing God's work, and they would shirk from doing what must be done.

"I suppose you imagine that I have a man in the enemy's camp who might be able to do such a thing," Hermann said as he pushed back from the desk. He shook his head as he walked over to the hearth and picked up the metal poker leaning against the wall. He turned toward Kristaps, holding the poker as if it were a sword. "This man should merely walk up to the prince"— he jabbed the poker lightly at Kristaps—"and, like this, put several inches of steel into him. Is that what I should do? What I should have done already?" His lips curled slightly as he turned away from Kristaps and used the poker on the logs in the hearth. A fountain of sparks leapt up from the Prince-Bishop's assault. "It is one thing to demand 'Why have you not killed this man?' when he is standing in the same room, or even living within a short distance of where you stand, but Alexander Iaroslavich is not here." He waved the poker around. "He is no fool. I have men out looking for him, but they either cannot find him or they don't come back at all. Does it make sense, *Heermeister*, to waste men and resources chasing this ghost when I could be strengthening the base of my power here instead?"

Kristaps stared into the fire, his thoughts straying to the arena in Hünern and his fight with the Shield-Brethren knight, Andreas. "You don't chase your enemies," he said, "unless you know you've the better horse, or better yet, you've a horse and he has none." Andreas the horse thief, fighting desperately with his spear against Kristaps's sword and maille. He had thought Andreas a prideful fool for entering the arena without a sword until the knight turned his back and ran toward the Khan's box at the other end of the arena. Only then had he realized that he had never been the knight's true target. "You make your enemy come to you. You offer them something they think they want, something they cannot refuse. A feint, exposing an opening your opponent thinks is his *one* chance to destroy you."

Hermann poked at the logs in the hearth with a casual indifference, mulling over Kristaps's statement. Kristaps knew that Hermann of Dorpat was one of those men who had reached his station in life by virtue of shrewd negotiation and decisive action.

He was not above taking a risk when the reward was significant; it was merely a matter of carefully articulating the risk, and giving Hermann the opportunity to frame the risk in his own mind. Once a decision was made, Kristaps would have the freedom he needed to accomplish his task. It was better to let the Prince-Bishop think the decision was his to make; he would give his blessing more readily.

"Walk with me," Hermann said suddenly, dropping the poker onto the floor. "I wish to show you something."

✦ ✦ ✦

He followed Hermann of Dorpat out of the estate, where they picked up an escort of four bodyguards. The Prince-Bishop walked briskly toward the wall surrounding the city, his cloak wrapped around his body to ward off the brisk wind. The fog had been blown away while Kristaps had been inside the estate, and the pale blue sky was clear.

"The wind blows from the north almost constantly," Hermann said. "The locals are fearful of it, as they believe it means a short spring and a shorter summer."

Kristaps said nothing, though his thoughts were tumbling over one another. He watched the bodyguard carefully, noting how these men were not as indolent as the men at the gate had been.

Hermann led him through a narrow alley between houses to a wooden stair that went up to the battlement. The Prince-Bishop went first, and Kristaps followed, his back twitching at letting the four men crowd behind him. Pskov's defenses were not the most fabled in Rus, and they did not even begin to approach the grandeur of Kiev, but they were nonetheless high enough to afford a view of the surrounding lands. As they reached the top, Kristaps could see thick clouds marshalling north of the city. They would arrive in a few hours, most likely dumping their load of snow on the city.

"What you do you see, *Heermeister* Kristaps?" Hermann asked, his arm sweeping to encompass the land outside Pskov.

"I see clouds and empty fields and a forest of ugly trees. I see a hard land that is not ours. Even if we conquer it, it will never welcome us."

"I know what happened at Schaulen," Hermann said, folding his arms across his chest. "I know the name your first *Heermeister* had for you, Kristaps of Fellin. You are not a stupid man, that much is clear, but are you a man with the necessary subtlety to bring these people to heel?"

Kristaps looked at the Prince-Bishop, waiting for him to say something of import. There was more coming, he knew, and it was best to let the Prince-Bishop say what he felt was necessary. If patience was subtlety, then he could demonstrate that he was capable of it.

"The heretics of the east have managed to lay the blanket of their false doctrine across this land," Hermann continued, "but it was not so long ago that this place, and all the people in it, were pagan to the core. This land is brutal and hard, and the people in it doubly so. They do not yield easily, and they do not change their allegiances readily. They know the forests and the fields better than we do. They know their old and secret paths and they know their forbidden lore. Even the most ardent Eastern Christians still leave a bowl of milk to appease the *domovoi* they know reside in their homes. You can conquer a land, bring it to its knees with sword and fire, but even a defeated people will always hold to the ways of their ancestors over yours. In time, the old ways would bring them together, and they would challenge you. Just like they did at Schaulen."

"The mistakes at Schaulen were our own," Kristaps replied, keeping his voice calm. "And what you speak of has been the crisis of any conqueror for the last thousand years." He shrugged, dismissing the Prince-Bishop's concerns. "Burn enough houses down, and the people will forget their own names in favor of the ones you give them. It is a matter of will. Doing God's work is never easy, and one must understand and be ready to do what is necessary in order to achieve God's wishes."

"And would you burn all of this if God called for it to be so?" Hermann asked, staring at Kristaps as if he was seeing the knight in a new light.

"I believe," Kristaps answered, "that when God's representatives on earth give you a holy order, you must accomplish it, and not make excuses about how hard the people and the weather are."

Hermann gave a derisive snort as he looked out over the bleak wilderness beyond the edge of the walls. "Even if I had been able to find Alexander Iaroslavich earlier this winter, I don't have enough men to fight him in the field. We have allies coming, which will bolster our numbers, but the Danes will not bring me any closer to the prince than I am now. The Novgorodians distrust the Danes twice as much as they do men from Dorpat and Riga," Hermann said.

"Why is he out in the wilderness?" Kristaps asked. "Why is he not guarding Novgorod directly, or marching against you now, if these Ruthenians are such masters of this frigid land?"

"There was a matter concerning tributes and taxes," Hermann replied. "After beating the Swedes back at the Neva—where he earned that silly designation—he sought compensation for his men from the boyars of Novgorod."

"A not unexpected request," Kristaps said.

"Aye," Hermann agreed, "but pride intervened, and Nevsky was sent into exile without any compensation at all."

"But the boyars will change their minds, won't they?" Kristaps said. "That's why you are wintering here, to give them time to panic and call him back."

"Aye," Hermann said. "And then we'll know where he is."

"He'll gather more men," Kristaps said. "You're allowing him the opportunity to increase his numbers." He shook his head. "It's a matter of pride, isn't it? He'll want to be seen; he'll need to be seen. He will want assurances from the boyars and people of Novgorod that they won't treat him badly again. To make sure that doesn't happen, he'll made a concerted effort to get the people on his side."

Kristaps turned his head shake into a nod. "He'll want recognition before he acts," he said, thinking out loud. "That is when he will be vulnerable, when he is among the people, reminding them of how badly they need him."

Hermann glanced at him, and Kristaps saw the gleam in the Prince-Bishop's eye. "It is a risky proposition," he said.

"If there were any other way, you would have tried it already," Kristaps pointed out.

Hermann laughed and indicated that they should walk along the parapet. "You surprise me, Kristaps," he said. "I would not have thought you capable of such a soft touch."

Kristaps glanced at the four bodyguards before following Hermann. The wind continued to bluster about them as they walked. In the streets below, Kristaps could sense the tension that always seethed beneath the surface of day-to-day affairs in an occupied city. A change in sovereignty split the people as readily as it could unite them, as loyalists clung desperately to their former convictions whilst collaborators sought to enrich themselves, and readily flocked to protect the new power that was responsible for their good fortune. That tension could be used by any side of the conflict that understood how to move men, how to manipulate them and make them do as suited their designs.

A soft touch? Kristaps kept his opinion to himself. A carefully worded compliment was sometimes more useful than an outright threat. Whatever kept your enemy off guard.

"You think the prince will come to the rescue of Pskov?" Hermann asked.

"He has to," Kristaps said. "A prince in exile is not a prince. Even when Novgorod deigns to bring him home, he will still seek the love of the people. Until he is sure of their devotion, he will be constantly reminded of what he has lost." Kristaps smiled, baring his teeth against the wind. "Once he returns to Novgorod, he will no longer be able to do as he pleases. He will act in a way to ensure the people's love. He will come to Pskov, and we will kill him."

CHAPTER 5:

ONE OF US

The messenger knelt in the tent, his long cloak of furs doing an ill job of masking how he shook from the cold he had endured to reach this encampment. Outside, the night wind made the hide walls ripple with its angry, icy lash; inside, braziers burned sweet-smelling coniferous wood, filling the air with a warmth that could not quite drive off the chill from without.

Melting snow dusted the messenger's shoulders, and his short cropped hair framed a youthful face. He bore no weapons, having left sword and bow in the hands of the heavily scarred retainer who stood watch outside the door. His eyes were a light blue of the sort common in the north. Despite the dirt on his clothes, he had the look of a boyar's son, nervous but eager to succeed, and as afraid of failure as he was hopeful for success in his mission.

Illarion felt a small knot twist in his gut—equal parts pity and grief. *Had it not been for Onghwe Khan, this boy could be my son,* he thought. He looked away from the boy, directing his gaze at the other person in the tent—the man whom the messenger had come to see.

Sitting in a dark chair, wrapped in surprisingly utilitarian garments for one of his station, was Prince Alexander Iaroslavich. He had a long, young face and his dark eyes had a weight to them that made his gaze hard to meet straight on. In years, he was little older than twenty, but the beard lining his jaw made him look older, and there was an energy about him that lay beneath the austere expression with which he watched the kneeling man. The Novgorodians had taken to calling him *Nevsky* after the battle of Neva he'd won in his nineteenth year. They had named him and then exiled him, and now they were asking him to come back.

The messenger fidgeted, looking sidelong at Illarion. Nevsky had heard his words, but was taking a long time to respond. Illarion had no advice to offer the young man.

Finally, Alexander sighed and the messenger stiffened, his gaze snapping back to Nevsky.

"Was there any dissention in the Veche?" Alexander asked. "Were they unified in this…*request?*" The prince's tone was quiet and congenial, but Illarion heard the stress laid on the last word. In the brief time he'd been with Alexander, he had learned to hear the undercurrents in the prince's diction. For all his youth, there was a hardened veteran—in both war and politics—that lived within that body. *I am who I am because I have earned it,* this voice said. *Do not take me for a fool.*

"They speak with one voice," the messenger gulped, "and I am that voice. Lord, Novgorod the Great is in peril and, as one, the people call their *Kynaz* to his duty."

As a prince of Novgorod, Alexander had been responsible for coming to its defense and negotiating its relations with foreign powers, all under the watchful, but distant, authority of his father, Iaroslav, in Vladimir. When the Mongols had come, Alexander had struck bargains with Batu and the other Khans: in return for taxes and obedience, Novgorod and Pskov were to be spared. The people had looked upon Alexander as their savior, and in retrospect, Illarion wished he and the other nobles of Volodymyr-Volynskyi had been less proud in their defiance when the horde had come to their walls. Shortly after the battle of Neva, where the young

Alexander earned the name of Nevsky, the prince had laid claim to rights that the ruling boyars of Novgorod—the Veche—had been unhappy to grant. Their solution had been to exile the prince.

"Do you think I have abandoned my duty?" Alexander asked.

The messenger looked down at the floor of the tent, trying to hide the glimmer of fear in his eyes. Illarion stirred slightly, feeling the knot in his gut again, but he remained silent. While it had been clever of the boy to keep Alexander's focus on him and not the Veche, the ploy had brought the entire weight of the Veche's actions down upon his shoulders.

"I...I would not be here, my Prince," the messenger said, "if I thought such a thing were possible."

Alexander glanced at Illarion, a thin smile touching his lips, and Illarion inclined his head in return.

"I find such faith reassuring," Alexander said quietly. "And I would hope that the Veche is of the same mind as you, as well as the same voice. I, too, am filled with faith—faith that the Veche has come to realize that their security must be paid for. Or do they still believe that men will die for them out of *duty*?"

The messenger touched his lips briefly with one hand, considering the prince's question. "Will you heed the Veche?" he asked, opting to interpret the prince's question as a decision.

"I might," Alexander said. He clapped his hands, summoning the retainer from outside the tent. "See that he is fed and given a warm place to sleep. His ride has been long, and I can see that he is exhausted. God alone knows how difficult it was to find my camp in the dark."

The retainer, a bearded man with a northern look who was one of Alexander's sworn *Druzhina*, nodded in response and gestured for the messenger to follow him. The young man rose, seeming at once nervous and relieved, and made to follow the retainer. But he paused before he left the tent. "Is that the message you wish for me to take back?" he asked.

"Yes," Alexander said. "Remind them that if they wish to lay claim to me in the guise of *duty,* I will expect the same from them."

After the retainer and the messenger had left, the prince leaped out of the chair and began to pace around the tent. His face lost some of the severity it had held during the messenger's visit, and his posture relaxed. "I had been planning on returning anyway," he said to Illarion. "It will be easier now that they are expecting me."

"Pride can slow a man's actions," Illarion said.

Alexander peered at his face for a moment and then laughed. "You are like an old grandmother," he said. "I never know if you are talking about me"—he gestured at the wall of the tent—"or those old fools in the Veche."

Or myself, Illarion thought fleetingly, an image of the old crone he had seen outside the citadel walls in Kiev flashing through his mind.

"Though it does not matter whether it was my zealousness or the Veche's wounded honor," Alexander continued, a frown pulling at his mouth. "The Veche may not trust me, but they will not stand in my way, and the militia of Novgorod will be at my back."

"Dare you lay your trust there?" Illarion asked.

Alexander walked over to a small table shoved against the wall of the tent where a number of hide maps were scattered. From previous examination, Illarion knew they were out of date, but the inked details were of little import to Alexander. He hadn't lived a cloistered life—much of his boyhood had been spent traveling between his family's extensive holdings; as a result he knew the intimate details of his country better than any city-bound mapmaker.

"Perhaps it is a dangerous assumption," the prince admitted as he shuffled through the maps to find one to his liking. "But this Hermann of Dorpat still has an army in Pskov. When the spring thaw arrives, he will march on Novgorod; otherwise, why would he be wintering in Rus when he could be in the comfort of his own home? Time is running out for the Veche, and I suspect they've called up what reserves they have and have realized they do not have enough men to make the Teutonics reconsider their plans."

He found the map he was looking for and spread it across the top of the others. "They lack battle-tested commanders, and foolishly hoped that the Prince-Bishop would abandon Pskov when winter came." He shook his head. "Naive fools. Winter did not stop Batu Khan from marching up our rivers and defeating my grandfather, my father, and my uncles in their turns. These knights know it is possible to conquer Rus; they might not have a strategist as brilliant as the Mongols, but they can follow a course laid by others."

Hermann of Dorpat was the Prince-Bishop of Riga, a trading city that lay along the river route that the Vikings used to reach Byzantium. Livonia had been brought under Christian rule by the Livonian Brothers of the Sword and when the order was broken by a pagan army of Semigallians and Samogitians at Schaulen, Hermann had turned to the Teutonic Knights, who had only been too happy to crusade in the north. Bolstered by former members of the Livonian Order, Hermann's army of Teutonic Knights had set their sights on Mongol-battered Novgorod.

"It isn't just the weather, though," Alexander mused. "They outnumber us and their knights are better armored. Why have they held back?"

"Uncertainty," Illarion said as he walked over to the table and looked at the map Alexander was considering. "The Mongols have a tendency to feign a retreat. This *kuraltai* could be another ruse. Had Hermann marched earlier, he might have done so only to discover the horde waiting for him."

"This...what did you call it?"

"*Kuraltai.* It is the ceremony where the Mongols chose a new *Khagan*—their Khan of Khans."

"And they all have to be present for this *kuraltai* to happen?"

"If they want to be considered for *Khagan*, yes."

Alexander shook his head. "And if the previous *Khagan*, Ögedei, had not died, how different would our lives have been? Batu would still be in Christendom and Hermann of Dorpat would not be nipping at my heels. He is like the scrawny scavenger who only shows his face after the bear has gone."

"Aye," Illarion agreed, his thoughts drifting to the company of Shield-Brethren whom he had last seen at Kiev more than half a year ago. Had Feronantus's wild mission been successful? Had any of them survived their journey into the heart of the Mongol empire?

"We will show ourselves at Novgorod, which will make the Veche happy," Alexander said. "Then we will gather what militia they have and march. Word will reach our enemies and force them to decide whether or not they will move."

"Hermann is a careful man, from what I have heard," Illarion mused. "He will have to see this as a chance to crush you in the field before he commits his men."

"That is my hope."

"And if you make yourself an irresistible target..." Illarion trailed off.

Alexander smiled at him. "What good am I to the people of Pskov if I die here, in the woods, a victim to the weather and my own boredom?"

✦ ✦ ✦

For some of Nika's sisters, the tales of the stooped, toothless crone were as real as the ground upon which they stood. That hadn't been the case for Nika—brave strong Nika who could move through the wilderness with none the wiser to her passing, who could kill a man and be gone before his friends even knew she was there. For her, the stories of Baba Yaga had been nothing more than fairy tales, until the night in Kiev when the mist parted and showed her both the future and the past.

Since then, the bleak Ruthenian nights had held no comfort for her. The wind was a sinister beast, slithering and moaning in the darkness. During her nocturnal vigils, she would wrap herself in multiple layers of furs as protection against the wind, but when it blew out of the north—as it did this evening—she could still feel its chill touch.

She heard the approach of two sentries and she turned her head slightly so they would know she was aware of them. They gave her a wide berth, keeping her outside the quivering circle of lantern light. They stared as they passed, and she did not rise to the bait and stare back. The weak glow from the lantern was disturbing her night vision as it was.

Not all of the *Kynaz*'s men were happy sharing a camp with the Shield-Maidens.

The *Kynaz* had accepted Illarion and the Shield-Maidens into his camp readily enough, but Nika and her sisters still had to establish themselves in the same way they always had to do when faced with those who did not understand or respect them. It had only taken a day or so before a loud-mouthed braggart made the first rebuke, proclaiming loudly to several other like-minded men that a skinny wench like Nika would be much warmer in his tent, on her back on a pile of furs. She had suggested that if he believed her to be so helpless, he should carry her back to his tent, and when he had tried to pick her up, she had knocked him to the ground and broken his arm. Illarion had been appalled at the violence, but the *Kynaz* had understood why she had done what she had done. Alexander needed experienced fighters, and who had more value: the man in the dirt, weeping and moaning about his arm, or a warrior like her? *There will be no more pissing contests,* he had said. *The Shield-Maidens are our guests and our equals.* And that should have been enough, but she knew it wouldn't be. There would always be those who did not understand them, and hatred would always be coupled with such ignorance.

As long as such stupidity did not endanger those she loved— or all of Rus, for that matter—Nika did not waste much thought on men like these. People would talk and would stare and would think themselves entitled. That was the way of the world, and weeping and moaning over it did not make it go away. Warriors had to concern themselves with their strength and their ability to protect those who they had sworn to guard.

The sentries passed, and the light from their lantern illuminated the snow-flecked walls of a row of tents. Shadows squirmed on the tents as the light passed, making patterns in the wind-blown snow that reminded her of the striations in the walls of the caves of Kiev. Cryptic messages left by the dead.

As the sentries reached the end of the tents, they suddenly changed direction, and Nika saw the reason for their course correction. If there was anyone less liked by the *Kynaz*'s men than she and her sisters, it was Illarion Illarionovich. They called him *ghost* and thought him cursed. He was bad luck, a phantom who had returned from the dead. He walked with his head held high, seemingly untouched by the wind, and he did not look at the men as they scuttled out of his way. It was as if they did not exist to him. His eyes were focused on a different world, a realm beyond this one.

He wasn't a ghost, Nika knew, but something worse. Death had rejected him, filling his bones with a hellish sorrow that would never go away.

And Baba Yaga had chosen him.

She knew the old stories well. Faery tales of princes named Ivan, of Koschei the Deathless and other, older things great and terrible. She knew that there was more truth to the legends than most thinking men imagined, but had thought the older terrors gone from the world since long before the days of Saint Ilya.

Koschei had been the last menace to dabble in the black matters best left to the old stories, and he had been dead for centuries. But the enemies of Rus had awakened something when they had ravaged the land. *Some things should stay buried,* she thought.

"May your heart keep you warm, little sister," Illarion said as he reached Nika's side.

"And yours you," she replied a little stiffly. She always felt self-conscious echoing this greeting with Illarion as she knew what he had suffered at the hands of the Mongols. "I saw the messenger," she said, eager to talk of something else. "Has Novgorod finally relinquished its death-grip on their pride?" Leaders who would not do so in the face of conquest were, in Nika's opinion, unworthy of their high seats.

"They have," Illarion replied. "The Veche have recalled the prince. In the morning, we're to make preparations to march."

"Lord Novgorod the Great," Nika mused, "I've not been there since I was a little girl."

That seemed to surprise him, which was not all that shocking. He'd once been a boyar, and those from high places were always surprised to learn how far someone without wealth or status could go, given the chance.

"We won't be there long," Illarion said, staring off into the darkness beyond the camp. "Once the prince has reconciled with the Veche, he hopes to march again."

"Against the Teutonic army in Pskov?" Nika asked.

Illarion nodded. "Aye. There is more, though. I understand that Hermann of Dorpat has Livonians in his ranks."

Nika's hand fell to the hilt of her sword. "Livonians?"

"Aye," Illarion said. He nodded toward the smaller cluster of tents behind Nika. "Let us walk," he said.

Nika fell in beside Illarion, and they began a circuit of the Shield-Maiden camp. Unlike the sprawling mass of the *Kynaz's* camp, the Shield-Maiden tents were arranged in neat arcs. There was no direct path through the tents, and from several key positions, a few guards could watch every approach. The organization of the tents would split any force into discrete lines that would be easier to defend against with a smaller force. As she and Illarion walked the night circle around the verge of the camp, she spotted the steadfast shapes of several other sisters who were also on the nocturnal watch.

"I have been troubled by the presence of the Livonian Order in Kiev last year. What were they hoping to find there?"

"Relics," Nika said.

"But we didn't bring any with us, which would suggest that there were no relics to guard."

"Is that the only reason you think we stayed in Kiev?" she asked.

Illarion shook his head. "No, but when the Shield-Brethren came, you let them down to see the grave of Saint Ilya. And while they were down in the tunnels, they encountered that group of Livonians led by Kristaps. What were they looking for?"

"The grave is empty," she said. "It's always been empty."

He stopped and his gaze swung across the Shield-Maiden tents and the sprawl of the *Kynaz*'s camp. "I do not like uncertainty," he said, his gaze settling on the darkness beyond the camp. "I do not like the mischief that is spawned by old legends."

"It is her way," Nika said.

A thin smile creased Illarion's face and he idly reached up and tugged at the end of his beard. "Alexander accused me of sounding like an old grandmother when I spoke like that to him. You neither agree with nor dismiss my fears. All you say is *It is her way*. As if that is explanation enough for a weary soldier like me." He stopped pulling on his beard, and in that moment when he stood still, Nika got a glimpse of the fear that lay beneath the cold mask he presented.

Around them, large flakes of snow began to fall. The wind had fled, and in the emptiness that followed, the skies were filling with slow-falling snow. A flake landed on Nika's cheek, a cold kiss that melted into a tear. "I have heard many stories," she said, "and until very recently, I thought little of them beyond what I learned as a small girl. But I saw her as clearly as you. Do we share a madness, then? Or was she really there? I don't know, Plank. *It is her way* may be the plainest explanation I can offer you."

"You are asking me to believe something that may run counter to all that I have been taught," he noted.

She hesitated as the teardrop slid down to her chin. "Yes," she said finally.

Illarion raised his face to the sky and closed his eyes against the falling snow. "Then I choose to believe she was there, little sister. Otherwise, as you say, it is a madness that we share. This world is mad enough that we need not add to it. Let us be clear-minded." The thin smile returned to his lips. His shoulders straightened, the weight being raised again. *Weight makes you stronger.* Nika recalled one of the lessons drilled into her by the older Shield-Maidens. *If you refuse to be crushed, you will grow to hold it up.*

"Aye," Nika said, wiping the wetness from her face. "Let us believe."

"I do not intend to tell the prince of…what *we* saw that night," Illarion continued. "But *I* need to know. I need to know what you think is out there, watching us. Waiting for something to happen."

"There are stories of Baba Yaga that have been passed down by my elder sisters," Nika said. "She used to come more often— before we began to worship in accord with the priests in Kiev. She would come both in times of plenty and of sorrow." Nika whispered, stepping closer to keep any others who might hear from listening. "Men talk of *domovoi*, or think they see *gamayun* flitting through the trees, but they do not *remember*. She is wisdom, yes, but she is also terror. She is the wrath of the land, and that fury has never been very discerning. Do you understand?"

"Aye, I do."

"I do not know if you mean to follow Saint Ilya's steps, or whether it is a hero or monster that lies in your heart," Nika said.

"Are they all that different?" Illarion wondered.

"What has singled you out is as fickle as the wind and as terrible as the winter," Nika continued, undeterred by Illarion's query. "She is the harbinger of all the things that should stay in the dark forests at night. I do not know if the Mongols awakened her when they came from the east with their strange sorcery and foreign gods, or if the Livonians disturbed her with their meddling, but she is here now." She swallowed heavily. "This is what I believe, and it makes me afraid."

"Why," Illarion asked, "does she hold such power over you and your sisters? You said she was to be obeyed, but why do you follow what terrifies you so?"

Nika took a deep breath. "If the stories are true, then once, long, long ago, she was one of us. Baba Yaga was a Shield-Maiden."

CHAPTER 6:

WOLVES

Alchiq brought his horse to a stop, raised his right arm, and curled his fingers several times. His wispy beard was as pale as his hair, and his skin was dark and weathered from many years spent in the saddle. He was old enough to remember Genghis Khan's rise to power and was a much better hunter than Gansukh, who was no slouch himself when it came to tracking prey, even though he had spent the last six months ensconced at the *Khagan*'s court in Karakorum.

Gansukh gently pulled on the reins of his own horse, drifting behind the older man. Alchiq wasn't stretching his arm; he was sending Gansukh a signal. The curling motion of the fingers mimicked the way Alchiq laid his fingers around the end of his arrow when he laid it across his bow. However, the signal didn't distinguish between whether they were being hunted or there was an opportunity for game. Either way, the response was the same.

Gansukh pulled the mitten off his right hand and pushed it into the front of his fur-lined coat. With his left hand he slid his bow out of the leather sheath that hung from his saddle. Alchiq leaned forward in his saddle, his head cocked to the side. Whatever he was hearing was getting closer.

More than a dozen paces separated the two of them—an old habit of Mongol riding parties—and Gansukh was far enough back that he couldn't hear what was commanding Alchiq's attention. Which also meant that whatever was out there in the mist most likely wouldn't hear him either as he slipped his bow out of his quiver and leaned forward, stroking the neck of his horse to calm it.

The weather had improved since they had crossed the gap in the Heavenly Mountains: the afternoons were normally clear and dry, but the nights and morning were still bone-numbingly cold and shrouded with fog. They rarely spoke to each other, a silence that was neither uneasy nor uncomfortable, and when they did, it was usually in short sentences.

Three nights ago, Alchiq had pointed out a line of tracks in the snow and had said a single word. *Wolves.*

The fingers of his right hand now warm from having stroked his horse's neck, Gansukh drew an arrow from his quiver and nocked it. He tapped his horse's barrel lightly with his heels, nudging the animal forward, as he strained to hear. The fog muffled all but the sound of his horse's exhalations.

Two mornings ago, the wolves had come into their camp. They had known the beasts were out there; they had seen the glint of their eyes beyond the light of their fire each night. The wolves were wary of the light and heat of the blaze, and the first night the men had fed the fire throughout the night, which meant neither of them slept well. The second night, Gansukh had fallen asleep almost instantly after brushing down his horse, and when Alchiq woke him hours later, he had been dreaming of Lian.

An hour later, when the fire was nothing more than a bed of fading coals, the wolves came. He killed two with his bow, and chased off the rest with a pair of freshly lit torches, but not before the gaunt beasts had killed one of their three horses.

Gansukh had hoped it would be enough. With two dead and a fresh kill, the pack could gorge themselves.

But hunger was a cruel spirit that always returned.

Gansukh glanced at Alchiq's raised right hand. The index finger didn't bend like the others. There had been an altercation several weeks ago with a party of Oirat riders. Alchiq had wanted their extra horses and they hadn't been terribly eager to sell them. In the subsequent fracas, one of the Oirats had pulled Alchiq out of his saddle, and while the pair had been fighting on the ground, the Oirat had latched onto Alchiq's fingers. Alchiq had killed the man before losing any digits and, no stranger to battlefield injuries, he had kept his fingers clean and wrapped. The skin was healing on both fingers, but there was something wrong with the knuckle on his index finger.

Alchiq could still pull his bow, but the motion was slow and Gansukh could tell the crooked finger pained him.

Gansukh's horse exhaled noisily, setting to the left and then reversing course to the right. Gansukh heard the wolves too, a whisper of paws against the hardened crust of the snow. Alchiq dropped his arm and drew his short sword. *They're coming from the sides,* Gansukh thought, and he caught a flash of motion at the edge of his vision.

He loosed an arrow and reached for another before he was consciously aware of what was coming at them. He heard a yelp of pain as he tracked another target. His horse pranced sideways, whinnying in fear, and his second arrow went wide. As he reached for his third, Alchiq's horse reared, hooves flailing.

Alchiq was out of his saddle before his horse could fall and pin him, and as the older man got his feet under him, a gray and white shape darted out of the fog and slammed into him. Gansukh heard Alchiq grunt as man and wolf went down on the snow-slick ground. He didn't bother trying to put an arrow into the wolf. It would be a difficult shot as the two wrestled on the ground; besides, Alchiq had a sword.

Gansukh loosed another arrow at a wolf that was snarling and snapping at Alchiq's horse, and the beast spun away, the shaft of the arrow protruding from its neck.

Alchiq was shouting now, the wolf answering with short yelps and growls. Gansukh could smell fresh blood, and when he glanced down at the ground, there was crimson spatter staining the snow. Alchiq's horse snorted and stamped, its eyes wide with fear, and Gansukh's horse was no less afraid. They wanted to run, but they didn't know which way to go, which meant there were still more wolves surrounding them.

Gansukh slid off the left side of his horse, hoping to reduce the directions from which he could be attacked. After checking to his left, he peered under his horse's belly. He saw nothing but brush and snow. And fog. It was too thick. The wolves' ambush had been exposed; now they were keeping their distance.

Alchiq swore loudly, and Gansukh glanced over, peering around the withers of his horse. The older man stood, a bloody wolf corpse at his feet. There was blood on his chest and arm, but it didn't look like his.

Something grabbed at his left foot, and Gansukh lost his balance, leaning against his horse for support. Instinctively, he pulled his foot in, and whatever held it let go. He swept his bow around in a wide arc as he turned, and he caught sight of an all-white wolf darting out of reach. The beast lunged at him, and he jammed his bow between his body and the animal. The wolf snapped its jaw shut, its teeth closing a mere finger's width from his arm, and he smacked it across the snout with his bow.

The white wolf retreated but not very far. It crouched low to the ground, its teeth bared, a low growl rising from its throat. Alchiq yelled behind him, issuing a challenge to the wolves, who answered with angry calls of their own. Gansukh's horse stamped its hooves and he kept his back pressed against its flank to prevent another wolf from flanking him.

Gansukh watched the white wolf carefully, and when its front shoulders bunched, he raised his bow and drew the string back in a fluid motion. The wolf jumped as his bowstring sang, and he dropped his bow, reaching for the knife in his belt. The wolf slammed into him. Gansukh pulled his head back to avoid the sharp teeth as he fumbled for the hilt of his knife. He shoved his left forearm under the beast's chin, and he could feel the wolf's hot breath on his cheek as the beast tried to bite his face. His knife came free from his belt and he stabbed upward. The blade went deep, and the wolf barked in pain and wiggled away. He lost his grip on his knife.

His horse, spotting the blood on the snow, tried to bludgeon the injured wolf with its hooves, but the wolf darted beneath the horse, threading its way through the stomping hooves. Gansukh tried to dodge his angry horse while keeping an eye on the fleeing wolf. A bloody smear indicated in which direction the animal had fled, and Gansukh lumbered after it. He caught sight of it, struggling to get through a line of brush. The hilt of his knife, protruding from its chest, caught on the bare branches. The wolf twisted and flexed, snapping at the knife hilt, and Gansukh fell upon it heavily, reaching easily for the slippery hilt. He shoved the blade further into the beast and twisted the blade, getting a good grip on the hilt. He yanked the knife free and blood flew in wild arcs, painting the snow with thin crimson lines. The wolf collapsed.

It was only then that he realized his arrow had not struck the wolf. Slightly puzzled by how he had missed—the wolf had been less than three paces from him—he pushed up from the dead animal and staggered back toward the pair of horses and Alchiq.

The horses stood nearly shoulder to shoulder, still unsure which way to run, and Gansukh gave them a wide berth. He was sticky with wolf blood, and he didn't want to spook them any more than they already were. He found Alchiq standing near two wolf corpses, his short sword in his left hand, his right covered with blood that trickled steadily onto the snow.

Alchiq sensed his presence and spun around, his sword raised, but he lowered it when he recognized Gansukh. He was breathing heavily, and there were several deep scratches on his left cheek. "Wolves," he said, gesturing with his sword to the two dead on the ground.

Gansukh nodded as he cast about for signs of any remaining wolves, but he saw and heard none. The horses were still spooked, but their eyes were no longer wide.

"It's over," he said.

Alchiq was looking at his right hand, seemingly entranced by the flow of blood from it. "Finger," he said, waving the bloody hand at Gansukh.

"What?" Gansukh said, trying to focus on what Alchiq was showing him.

"Wolf got it," Alchiq said as he rotated his wrist so that Gansukh could more easily see what was missing. The index finger was gone. There was nothing left but a ragged flap of skin hanging over a shard of bone. "Was only getting in the way," Alchiq said, his eyes glittering.

Gansukh crouched and cleaned his blade in the snow. By the time he finished, the excitement of the fight had started to drain away and his hands shook slightly as he slipped his knife back into his belt. Deep in his throat, something like a cough started, but by the time it rose into his mouth, it had become a hiccupping laugh.

Alchiq's face split with a wide grin. "They're going to have to try harder," he said, holding up his other hand and wiggling all of his remaining fingers. "I still have nine more."

Gansukh started to bellow with laughter and Alchiq joined him. The horses stared at the two men, their ears twitching. *They don't understand*, Gansukh thought, wiping at his eyes. *It's not the sound of fear.*

Gansukh had a glimmer of insight into what drove Alchiq, and while the other man's bravado was worthy of recognition in the best Mongol fashion, the rest troubled him. They were chasing a band of Western knights who had crept into the heart of the Mongol empire. *As long as he can ride a horse and wield a sword, he won't stop*, Gansukh thought.

Was he willing to go that far as well?

CHAPTER 7:

THE VIRGIN

They eschewed anything that suggested civilization. They tarried at streams long enough to refill their water skins and allow their horses to drink, and then they moved as purposefully away from moving water as possible. Gullies, depressions, divots, and other variations in the terrain that would provide a modicum of respite from the constant wind of the steppe were passed over as suitable camps. When they spotted herds of the wild deer, Istvan would ride, wide-eyed and screaming, until the herd spooked. They rode several hours past sunset every day, and did not start again until the sun had burned off the meager fog that tried to cling to the scrub. The Turkic lands from the Heavenly Mountains to the wide rivers that carried traders north and south across the steppe were vast and wide, and if the Virgin blessed them, they would be able to pass across these lands without notice.

When they did stop at night, they lit no fire. Feronantus would jam the Spirit Banner into the ground, flinching slightly every time he did so, and they would huddle around the stave, trying to sleep. Istvan shivered constantly at night; his body still hadn't recovered from its exposure to the winter snows. It was as if the chill had gotten into his bones; it would take a month or more in a desert climate, Feronantus suspected, before the Hungarian would be warm again. While the steppe nights were chilly, he could recall nights at Týrshammar that had been much colder.

His bones ached for other reasons.

He couldn't have said with any conviction whether the Spirit Banner kept them warm at night or not. Certainly, it didn't exude heat as it had that night on the gap, when Istvan had staggered into his camp, half frozen, but Feronantus always noticed that the ground around the banner was softer in the morning. The horses always cropped at the scrub closest to the banner.

He checked their course against the stars when he could see them, and by his reckoning, they were farther west than the rock where the company had met Benjamin on their journey east. In another few weeks, they would reach the river that ran past Saray-Jük, though they were far north of the Mongol-controlled town. Once they crossed the river, he would have to make a decision about where he was going to go. If the *Vor* hadn't already told him by then...

Feronantus had spent his entire adult life devoted to the Virgin, and his reward—nay, to speak of the gift given to him thus was to suggest that he deserved it, that the motivations of his actions were nothing more than an obsequious need to be commended for his sacrifices—his *insights* were furtive glimpses beyond the veil of mortal existence. He had never been granted a rapturous experience like the one that had come over Percival in the woods after the death of his warhorse; the Virgin had never spoken to him as *plainly* as she had others. Nor was he a self-deluded charlatan who fancied himself a crude divinatory. When the fate-sight came over him, he simply *knew*.

At the *Kinyen* when Istvan, firmly in the grip of his mushroom-fueled madness, had spoken of the All-Father's staff, Feronantus had believed the Hungarian was speaking to him. The Virgin was preparing him for the choices he would have to make, and when the company had closed their trap around the *Khagan* at the cave of the great bear, he had seen the staff. He had found the *Khagan* in the open and was about to kill Ögedei Khan himself when the *Khagan's* champion had intervened, waving the Spirit Banner between them.

That had been the first choice, and when he had hesitated, the *Khagan* had fled. When he and the others had caught up with Ögedei, Feronantus had not been surprised to find the *Khagan* facing off against Haakon, their lost acolyte who had made his way east as a captive of the empire.

And lying there on the field had been the Spirit Banner. Ignored. Forgotten. Waiting for someone to take it up.

That had been the second choice, and he had not hesitated that time.

He knew there was one choice still to make. He had had months to examine the signs: the sigils made by the stars in the night sky, the garbled words tugged out of Istvan's mouth at night by prescient night breezes, and the directions suggested by the leaning trunks of the wormwood that grew across the steppe. The *Vor* had one more secret to share.

✦ ✦ ✦

The oaks sheltered them, the massive canopy of branches over their heads a verdant sky. Maria often dressed in the local style, but she had forgone the wimple that afternoon, letting her dark hair cascade loose down her back. It had been a long time since he had seen her hair unbound and he marveled at how long it had gotten.

They walked through the forest without any clear destination in mind, pleased to get time away from the others. The band of merry ruffians was growing and soon it would become inordinately awkward to sneak away. They would have to either confess their relationship or forgo it entirely. Feronantus suspected it would be the latter.

"Do you believe in signs and portents?" Maria asked. She had plucked a long-stemmed yellow flower, and with the flower tucked behind her left ear, she was tying the remaining stem into an intricate knot. "That the divine can send us messages?"

"Visions?" he asked.

"Sometimes," she replied.

"How do you distinguish between the presence of the divine and a mere hallucination?" he asked.

She smiled at him, her fingers still working. "Careful, Feronantus," she cautioned. "That is the sort of philosophical question that will get you noticed by the local parish priest." She inclined her head. "Even if it is a good question."

"A man can learn the rudiments of swordplay fairly quickly, and when all of your opponents know the same techniques and counters that you do, it becomes increasingly difficult to lure them into a crossing that is to your advantage. Our *oplo*—our instructors—sought to teach us something they called *Vor*. Fate-sight. If you knew all the remedies and counter-remedies, the only way you could win a fight was to be smarter and quicker. Eventually you would begin to see parts of the fight before they happened; you would just know what was going to happen next before your opponent did."

"Has that ever happened to you?" she asked.

"Once, I think," Feronantus admitted.

"You *think*? You're not sure?"

He offered her a rueful smile. "The *Vor* doesn't announce itself. It doesn't shake you by the shoulders and whisper tactics. You simply..." He struggled to find the right word. "...*know*."

"Can you feel this *Vor* when you are not in combat?"

"No," he replied.

"Are you sure?" she asked.

He laughed at her question. "What could the *Vor* possibly show me?" he asked.

"Do you know the stories of Hildegard of Bingen?" she asked, and when Feronantus shook his head, she continued. "Hildegard was a devoted daughter of God who was visited time and again by angelic visions. Her family had her committed to a convent so that she could be cared for, but few—especially Hildegard—believed her visions to be caused by some malevolent affliction. She painted what she saw, marvelous drawings of angelic creatures with wings filled with eyes and shining spheres of light. Over time, many a bishop and king consulted her, hoping she could divine their futures, but all she had for them were her beautiful—but cryptic—drawings. Since her death, some have claimed that it was the fact that she had foreseen these things that caused them to become true. As if God had made the world through her, and what she drew was merely a pale representation of God's intent."

"You think she felt the *Vor*?" Feronantus asked.

"It would seem that she did, don't you think?" Maria asked in return, glancing down at the knot she was tying. Satisfied with her work, she raised the intricate shape to her eye and looked at him through it. "What would you do if you saw what might come to be? Would you embrace it or avoid it?"

"I would avoid it," Feronantus said.

And she had smiled sadly at him as if she had already known that was going to be his response.

✦ ✦ ✦

He and Istvan would ride for days without speaking, and occasionally they would drift so far apart that he would lose track of the Hungarian on the open steppe. Then, when the sun was about to leave the sky, the horizon aglow with orange and yellow bands, Istvan would ride up, his horse blowing heavily. *Lidérc*, the Hungarian would claim. At night, malignant ghosts would start to swarm; in the encroaching gloom, he would spot the shining beacon of the Spirit Banner and ride as quickly as he could to evade the phantoms.

Feronantus did not put much credence in ghosts, though he was well aware of the power that faith could have on a man. Just as it could buttress his soul, faith could terrorize. If vengeful spirits came to drag a man down to Hell because he had strayed from the righteous path, then fleeing such foul visitors was merely a way to return to the proper path. Did it matter how a man let his faith guide him as long as he had faith in something?

It was the sort of question that Maria liked to put to him; in time, he had come to understand why she pressed him so. Her hand was undeniably present in the concessions King John had given to the lords of England and to the freepeople of the island. And when the *Electi* of Petraathen had exiled him to Týrshammar, he had brought that selfsame spirit with him.

She was with him now, her hair tangled in the black braids of the Spirit Banner.

Lately Istvan had taken to muttering a long Magyar word when he approached the Spirit Banner, and Feronantus had tried to piece it together but had given up after awhile, intuiting what it meant without having to know the word. *Athena Promachos. Vindex Intacta.* The name changed but she remained constant.

When the Virgin's grace came over his brothers, they were not given insight into mastery of the martial arts; they were afforded other visions. Was Maria right in stressing that these were merely another aspect of the *Vor*?

CHAPTER 8:

NEWS OF THE WORLD

The rock was an aberration on the steppe, a slab of stone that stood resolute against the wind—a giant's finger, forever pointing to the east. The surrounding terrain was as flat as anywhere else on the steppe, and if the clouds were low or the wind was blowing snow, it was possible to miss the rock for there was no indication of its presence other than its black shape. The eastern edge of the rock was higher than the western edge, and in the winter months the northern side was perpetually in shadow.

There was snow on the ground in the shadow of the rock, and Cnán shivered as she and Vera and Raphael lost track of the sun behind the bulk of the spire. There was less snow than the last time she had explored the north side of the rock. The weather had been warm enough to start melting the ice, but the respite had been short lived, and the snow had a hard icy crust on it now.

They had been at the rock for several weeks, recovering from their desperate flight through the winter storms. The company had become separated, and during the frantic efforts to find one another, Cnán and Lian (and their nearly dead horse) had been found by a pair of Western mercenaries. Gawain, a Welshman who spoke the trade tongue with a lilting accent, and Bruno, a dark-haired man from Lombardy, had brought Cnán and Lian to the rock. The pair, along with two dark-eyed Seljuk brothers who were traveling with them, continued to range about the rock, searching for the rest of the company. Over the next few days, everyone had been located. Suffering from malnutrition and exposure, the presence of an established camp at the rock was a haven they eagerly welcomed. Some, like Cnán and Raphael, cycled through fever spells—drifting in and out of bouts of wearying illness. The wound in Raphael's back had slowed his recovery.

She searched for the notch in the rock, trying to remember the sequence of bumps and textures that would lead her to the secret hiding place. It was a Binder message shrine, and she had visited it when she had first been well enough to wander about camp. She and Vera had been waiting for Raphael's fever to subside before they showed him what they had found. The narrow slot in the rock that led to the shrine was difficult to see unless you were looking right at it, and she was almost ready to retrace her steps when she spotted a crack in the rock. When she stood in front of it, the crack revealed itself to be a narrow slot that went back into the rock.

She could wiggle through readily enough, while Vera had to keep her back absolutely straight; they both waited on the other side of the cleft in the rock for Raphael. He moved slowly, easing himself toward the tight gap, and if he hadn't been as emaciated as he was from their journey, he wouldn't have been able to slip through.

Cnán led them along the tight passage, which made a sharp turn and then spilled out into a tiny grotto that was open to the sky. Sunlight made the opening appear to be dappled with blue and orange, and the ground was free of snow. Banks of green moss ringed the base of the narrow sanctuary, making it appear as if they stood inside the trunk of an ancient tree.

The walls of the grotto were a palimpsest of writing, marks made with charcoal and chalk that had been erased, overwritten, and amended. Shoved into cracks in the rocks were strands of hair—both human and horse—braided and knotted in the secret code known to the Binders. *Rankalba.* Finger talk. To the casual viewer, the scene would appear like a shrine to animal spirits, an altar of offerings to forgotten pagan gods; indeed, some of the drawings on the walls were representations of animals and hunters, lending credence to the illusion of the grotto's primitive function. But there were messages in the hunting scenes too. The beasts were marked with cryptic patterns of dots and squiggles that could easily be mistaken for decorative markings, but the sequences were an abbreviated version of the finger talk, much like how the Roman armies communicated back and forth about troop movements in a manner that their enemies could not decipher.

Raphael examined each of the leavings with great interest. "Are they all messages?" he asked, his voice still raw and rough from his illness.

"Aye," Cnán said. "Some of them are quite old and meaningless now, but they haven't been taken down."

"Why not?" Raphael asked.

"A Binder would never remove a message left by another. When the one who left the message returns, she may remove it if she so decides. In some ways, it allows us to keep track of one another." She touched a strand of black hair that was knotted in several clumps. "This one, for example, says that there is snow in the Zuungar Gap," she said. Her fingers moved expertly, tying an intricate knot just below the last set. "I've just added a note that the passage is very difficult."

She moved on, pointing out a row of horse-shaped drawings. "These are notations about caravans on the Silk Road. Do you see the tiny marks held within each horse?" She tapped each horse in turn as she deciphered the marks. "Silk, silver, cedar, rice, salt, furs, and horses."

"Someone is moving horses along the Silk Road?" Raphael said.

"Aye," Cnán said. "But…" She looked at Vera.

"What?" Raphael asked, glancing back and forth between the two of them.

"Our rescuers, Gawain and Bruno," Cnán said. "They're mercenaries. You should examine the horses in the paddock when you get a chance. There are more than a group of sellswords should have, which is good for us if we can convince them to sell us some."

"But the bigger question is where did they get them?" Vera said.

"Do you think someone might be looking for them?" Raphael asked.

"The Seljuks patrol constantly," Cnán said. "We've managed to convince them to let Haakon patrol too. Ostensibly, they're all keeping an eye out for Mongols, but the boy suspects they're watching for someone else. They're in no rush to leave the rock, and it makes sense to wait until winter truly breaks, but a true merchant would be more interested in getting them to a market, like Samarkand."

Raphael nodded absently, the various Binder messages still distracting him. "What about this one?" he asked, pointing to a scrawl of tiny marks like the tracks of small birds.

Cnán cleared her throat. "That one says the *Khagan* is dead."

"Aye," Raphael said. "That is true. We were there. Why did you write this message?"

"I didn't," Cnán said. "Someone else left it. It also says that a *kuraltai* has been called. The other Khans are returning to Karakorum. The Silk Road will be crowded. Every merchant between Samarkand and Constantinople will be traveling to Karakorum. As will every provincial tribe. The steppes will be crawling with riders."

"Does the message say how the *Khagan* died?" Raphael asked, a frown creasing his forehead.

Cnán deciphered the third line of the message. "A *hunting accident*," she translated.

"But no mention of us?"

Cnán shook her head. "Just that he died while hunting in the sacred lands of the Mongols, near where his father brought the clans together."

"A not undignified end," Vera said.

Raphael glanced at her with a raised eyebrow.

"And then there is this one," Cnán said, pointing out the last of the markers that she wanted Raphael to see. "It says there is strife in the north," she said. "The Teutonic Knights are crusading against Novgorod and Rus."

"Anything from Kiev?" Raphael asked.

Cnán shook her head. "There is no mention of Kiev, but I would not worry too much about a lack of news. It usually means nothing has changed."

Raphael leaned against the rock wall and looked at the two women. "Why have you brought me here to see all of this? You could have simply told me while we were sitting around the fire; you could tell everyone."

"Everyone will have an opinion," Cnán said.

"An opinion about what?"

"About what our course should be," Cnán said. "Getting out of the reach of the Mongol Empire and across the Heavenly Mountains was a goal that we all agreed upon. Now, though, we are free to choose our own roads, are we not? Or are you still beholden to the one who left us?"

"Feronantus?" Raphael shook his head. "I was never beholden to him."

"Percival thinks otherwise," Cnán said.

"What? When did he tell you this?"

"During one of your feverish bouts. He grows tired of waiting. There is something burning in his mind."

Raphael pushed himself away from the wall and stalked about the tiny space. It was a little like being trapped in a cage with a wild animal.

"What about you?" he asked Vera as he paced.

"I would know of the fate of my sisters," Vera said. She nodded at the wall markings. "There is villainy afoot with the Western Church that it would send knights to conquer lands so recently devastated by the Mongol horde."

"There is no news of Kiev, which is far from the northern borders," Raphael said. "We don't even know the reason the Teutonic Knights are massing. It may not be for the reasons you mention. It might be Danish invaders."

"It might not be either," Vera said. "Knights, blessed by the Church, have crusaded in the north before. Rome tolerates the Eastern Church, but only slightly more so than it does repentant heathens."

"See?" Cnán said. "Different opinions. Can you imagine if we asked everyone what they wanted? Feronantus provided us with a reason to band together. We had a common goal under him, but where is he now? What are we to do?"

"I don't know," Raphael said simply.

"You should decide soon," Cnán said. "We can't stay here forever. Even though this land is not under direct Mongol rule, they do ride here. While the rock is out of the way for most caravans, it is still a landmark that traders use."

"Very well," Raphael said, holding up his hands. "I understand your concern." He clasped his hands together and sighed, raising his face toward the open sky.

"Do you want to ride after Feronantus?" Vera asked quietly as Raphael's silence stretched.

"Yes," Raphael said, and then shook his head. "No. I don't know."

"Where might he go?" Cnán asked.

"West, I presume," Raphael said. "Will he go back to Petraathen? Týrshammar? I don't know. I don't even know why he stole the Spirit Banner." He looked at Cnán. "You're the one who knows these peoples," he said. "What is the banner to them? What purpose could stealing it serve? Will it affect the outcome of the *kuraltai*?"

Cnán rubbed her arms. "It's just a banner. You've seen them. All of the clans carry them. That one belonged to Ögedei's father— Genghis Khan—and he supposedly received it from monks who lived on Burqan-qaldun. The mountain is a sacred place, remember? Borte Chino—she was the Doe—and Qo'ai Maral lay down together in the shadow of Burqan-qaldun, and Borte Chino grew heavy with child. Tengri watched over her until she could give birth to all the peoples that would become the Mongol clans."

"Like Adam and Even in the West," Raphael said. An idea seemed to occur to him. "Was there a tree? Was there a specific tree that Borte Chino lay beneath? Or ate the leaves from? Or something like that?"

Cnán shook her head. "I'm sorry. I don't know the stories all that well."

"Do you think there is a connection?" Vera asked. "If that story is like a story in the West, others might be similar too."

"Perhaps," Raphael said.

"Stories?" Cnán asked. "What stories?"

"Ragnarök," Raphael said heavily. "The battle between the giants and the gods at the end of time. It's one of the Northmen stories. I'm sure Haakon heard it growing up, and I'm sure Feronantus heard it too, during his time at Týrshammar. The King of the Northmen gods is named Odin, and one of his other names is All-Father. Odin tests himself by hanging from Yggdrasil, the World Tree, and he receives special wisdom from his sacrifice."

"Do you remember the *Kinyen* we had, out on the steppes?" Vera said. "Do you remember what Istvan said that night while under the influence of his devilish free-buttons?" When Cnán shook her head, Vera continued. "He spoke of a staff, and he called out to All-Father."

"Istvan often spoke of things that weren't real," Cnán said, feeling like she was pointing out something they already knew.

"Aye, that he did," Vera agreed. "But herein lies the particular madness which is so dangerous: what does it matter if he spoke of real things or not, if others found them real?"

"I don't follow you," Cnán said. "They're still not real. It doesn't matter what others think."

"Do you remember when Tonerre, Percival's war horse, was wounded in that fight with the Mongols?" Raphael asked.

"Aye," Cnán said cautiously. The Frank had taken his horse into the woods and given it a merciful death. She had watched him do it, and had seen what had happened to Percival afterward. She suspected the change that had come over Percival in the wake of killing Tonerre was what Raphael was talking about. "He had a vision," she said. "It's been haunting him ever since."

Raphael nodded. "The Shield-Brethren have a history of receiving visions from the Virgin. Some look upon these visitations as proof of love from the Divine; some see them as a curse, an unavoidable injury that we must sustain in return for the rewards offered by the path we take. I have seen great horror laid upon men who have been touched by the hand of the Virgin. I do not..." He shook his head and changed the subject. "Throughout our history, some of my brothers have received strange gifts. It has happened enough that some think such grace is the ultimate affirmation of our devotion." He hesitated before plunging on. "Some may even see the expression of such grace where it is not."

"You mean they imagine that they've had a vision when they actually haven't?"

Raphael nodded.

"But I thought you just said Percival had a vision?"

"I did. And he did."

"Then who are you talking about? Who didn't have a vision?"

"Istvan," Raphael said. "He was hallucinating due to the mushrooms. Whatever visions he saw were inspired by his own fevers. He was babbling, talking nonsense, and therefore his words could not—should not—be construed as divinely inspired."

Cnán rubbed the side of her nose. "I feel like I am being lectured by a scholar who has spent too many years studying scrolls written by Confucius. Everything you say is plain enough, but I think I must not be as well versed in your tongue as I imagined."

Raphael passed a hand over his eyes and sighed. "I am sorry, Cnán. Perhaps I have been pondering this for so long that I neglect to remember that others have not been party to my thoughts as long as I. It is not just a matter of speaking to your question, but also of your understanding my answer and not simply accepting it as a truism simply due to the fact that the answer came out of my mouth. Therein lies the crux of my current crisis, in fact. Everything I say may be true or false, but only I know whether each statement is such. You *interpret* my words as either true or false based on who you are and what you know. Do you see?"

"Do I see what? Are you asking me if that is a true or false statement?"

Raphael smiled. "There. Yes, you do understand."

"I'm not so sure that I do."

"Percival had a vision. You and I agree that that statement is true, yes? Because we both saw the transformation that came over him as the Virgin's grace touched him. Correct?"

"Yes," Cnán said. "I would agree with you."

"Istvan might have had a vision, but it was a figment of his own broken mind. Do you agree?"

"I would agree with that as well, but I confess I do not entirely see the same distinction you do."

"I fear that Feronantus *believes* Istvan's vision was divinely inspired. Now, if we had not witnessed Istvan's vision and

Feronantus came to us and said, 'Istvan has had a vision,' would that statement be true or false?"

Cnán hesitated. "It would be true," she said.

"Why?"

"Because I have no reason to believe Feronantus would lie."

"Exactly. When we first undertook this perilous journey, why did we do so? Because Feronantus said we needed to. It was our sacred duty to avert the destruction of Christendom and killing the *Khagan* was the only way possible. We took that statement as truth and acted on it. And yet, when the time came, Feronantus left us. He took a symbol of the Mongol Empire and rode off. What truth can we discern from his actions?"

"We could ask him if we ever see him again," Cnán said. "Beyond that, you're talking in circles. The *Khagan* had to die. That was the way to save Christendom. You did that. You and the Shield-Brethren. What Feronantus did after doesn't matter."

"It does matter," Raphael said. "You asked me if I was still beholden to him. Well, he is the master of the Rock, an elder of my order. I am bound to serve him, and in which case, I should chase after him and offer any aid I can give him. But if he has lost his way…" He trailed off with a shrug.

CHAPTER 9:

—

THE DREAMING GHOST

Illarion looked out over a strange and yet familiar city. He knew it wasn't real—that what he saw had been destroyed by the Mongols and that he was caught in the grip of a dream—but he stared nonetheless. It was Volodymyr: on his left, the gray stone spires of the church where his children had been christened strained for the sky, a sky that was the color of his wife's eyes; on his right, the staggered line of red and brown roofs that ran along the main boulevard between the city gates and the central keep. At night, the colors would vanish, and all that remained would be a trail of flickering lights along the boulevard, like flaming footprints left behind by the sun.

Illarion stood at the edge of the balcony, his hands gripping the wooden railing. Behind him was the main house of his estate, and even though he wanted nothing more than to turn around and go inside, he didn't dare. He was afraid even to draw a single breath or blink out of fear that it would all disappear. Then, one by one, the torches along the boulevard would go out too, and he'd be left in utter darkness. Utter suffocating darkness.

Under the planks, before the riders came. Before the screaming started.

He had died that night, hadn't he? What had risen up from beneath the sea of planks wasn't Illarion Illarionovich, but a ghost— a vengeful phantom that knew not why it had been given shape or what it must do to find release. It wandered Rus, as empty and void of love and life as every field and village. Rus was dead, trampled beneath the hooves of the Mongol horses, a sea of black and brown that had swept across the land from the east to the west. Like the flood of night, in the wake of the sun. Like death, in the wake of life.

Her eyes had been the same color as the sky. When the thunder came, the pounding hooves of the horses as they were driven back and forth across the planks, darkness flowed out of the center of her eyes, an ever-widening pit that devoured everything until there was nothing left of the blue.

He gasped as he heard the tiny cry behind him. He squeezed his eyes shut, and his hands gripped the railing even tighter. He tried to will himself to wake up, to flee this strange place that was both the Volodymyr he knew and the Volodymyr he would never know. It was his son's voice, happily giggling over something as inconsequential as sunlight glittering off a cloud of dust. He knew it wasn't real; the sound of his son's voice was only a mocking echo, a vestigial memory of something he had lost and would never have again.

Like his ear.

All that remained of his ear was a memory of the pain that had given birth to the phantom that he was. Floating in the bleak emptiness of his wife's dead eyes, he had left the world behind; then, on the verge of finding her again, the pain had snatched him back. Jerked him back where there was nothing but death and blood and pain. The black-bone had taken his ear, sawed it off his head with a dull knife, and the Mongol had stood there, dumbly staring at him, as he rose from the dead.

He heard his son's voice with his right ear. The phantom voice with the phantom ear. As he turned from the railing, he reached up and touched his ear, feeling its ridges and folds. It wasn't a dream; his son wasn't a dream.

But when he turned toward the house, the room was empty. When he wandered through the house, he found no one. The rooms were more sparsely furnished than he remembered, and instead of growing angry at what he had lost, he clung more fiercely to the insubstantiality of his past. *None of this is real,* he heard himself saying. *I will wake soon.*

His mind had other ideas, though, and he wandered for what seemed like hours through labyrinthine halls, larger in truth than his household had ever been. The rooms were windowless, lit with stinking tallow torches that created more shadows than light. He imagined familiar faces, both living and dead, and he saw images that he knew belonged to others. They weren't his memories, but they were too vivid—too real—to be mere dream ghosts. He saw a fat man with a long stringy mustache, his body wrapped in eastern silks, lying in a hole that had been dug in the floor of one room. He saw a fire burning fiercely in a stone hearth, and flapping over the flames like a black bird was a banner made from strands of black horsehair. He saw a room filled with long planks of wood; before he turned away, he saw the tiny arm of his son reach up from beneath the planks, and between two planks, he saw a blue eye staring up at him.

He kept walking and the walls grew dark, slick with moss, and he stumbled more than once as the ground tilted downward. Soon the walls of his house were gone, and he was running through dank caves, surrounded by walls of black rock, veined with brown mud. He heard—*with his right ear!*—his son call out his name. *Ilya*, his son cried out, *Ilya.* He ran on, chasing the sound and he passed rooms that were familiar: the dark burial chambers of the Lavra, in Kiev; the ceremonial rooms beneath the mountain fortress, where the river ran.

But I have never been there, he thought, staggering to a stop. His tunic was soaked with sweat, and his face was wet with tears.

He distinctly heard the roaring sound of an underground river, and wondered how he could have ever confused that sound with his son's voice. *It is only a dream.*

A light bloomed, though from where he could not fathom, and he found himself in a large cavern. On the wall beside him was a carving of a man in maille, a flowered helm upon his head and another blossoming flower clutched to his breast. The figure lay upon a bower of branches, suspended high in a tree, and as he looked more closely at the carving, he realized some of the branches were actually roots of an enormous tree that was trapped in the stone.

He realized the cavern went back, beyond the tree caught in the stone, and as he wandered around the twisted confusion of stone and root, he found a supine body on the floor, dressed not unlike the figure carved into the wall. But the flower was missing from its chest; in fact, as he knelt beside the body he realized the corpse had no hands, and when he raised the ornate frontispiece of the helmet, he discovered the corpse had no face either.

He swore a vow, father.

His son was standing behind him, though it was not his son. Much as the landscape of Volodymyr had been both what it was and what it might be, so too was his son an amalgamation of the child he had known and the young man he had dreamed his son would grow up to be. He stood up, tears filling his eyes, and ran toward his phantom son, trying to gather the ghost into his arms. His arms closed around nothing, and he tripped over a root of the stone-bound tree and fell. He landed in a puddle that, as he tried to get up, grew deeper. He splashed in the pool, trying to find the bottom, which had suddenly dropped away from him. He turned, struggling to keep his head above water, and he saw a torrent flooding out from beneath the tree. A flood that swept up the faceless knight and roared over him—*a sea of black and brown, all the way from the east to the west*—and he choked on the water. His feet found some purchase, and he pushed himself upward, struggling to stay afloat.

He spotted her, crouching in the branches of the tree. The old crone, her stone leg still part of the wall. She watched him, her face twisted into a perverse grin, her eyes dancing with an unholy glee.

"Help me," he managed, speaking the only words he ever said in any dream he had had since his family had been killed. *Help me.*

The flood continued, and he felt his feet slipping. He stretched out his arm, even though she was much too far away to reach him, and his arm was stained red by the water.

Help me.

Make this pact, not by words but by blood. Her voice echoed in his phantom ear. She leaned out of the tree, holding out a long stick, and as he reached for it, the stick twisted in her hands, becoming a sword with a glowing pommel. He grabbed at it anyway, and screamed as the red-hot metal seared into the flesh of his forearm.

You will die and live and die again, Ilya, the old crone said, *until your tasks are done.*

You will die and live and die again...

Illarion awoke violently, bathed in sweat, and he hunched over, hugging his arms to his belly—fighting the urge to vomit. A buzzing sound echoed in his head as if his skull was filled with angry bees, and he gasped and struggled for breath as the bees drifted out of his head, one by one, through the puckered scar of his right ear.

Once the bees had left, taking with them the remaining echoes of the old woman's voice, the feelings of nausea passed as well, and Illarion gradually found the strength to sit up. His forearms still stung, but when he pushed back the sleeves of his tunic, he saw no marks on his flesh. No rings of scar tissue like those on Percival or Raphael or any of the other Shield-Brethren he had known. *Because I never took the test,* he thought.

He lay back on his bedding and stared at the peak of his tent. Pale rose light seeped through tiny gaps between the pieces of hide and canvas that were stitched together to make his tent, and he surmised it was just after dawn. *Clear sky*, he thought. *Blue like—*

He shook his head, disturbing that thought before it could be finished, and refocused his attention on the Shield-Brethren initiation. He had been to Týrshammar, the cold fortress in the northern seas, and had studied the martial arts there. Like other sons of boyars and princes, he had heard stories of the Shield-Brethren citadel—Petraathen, the rock of Athena—where the most promising of students were taken and initiated into the inner secrets of the order. But he had not taken that journey; he had come back to Rus instead.

Illarion threw off the blanket and heavy fur that had been half-covering him and got to his knees. The tent wasn't tall enough to stand upright in, and the muscles in his lower back were already complaining—Nevsky's army had traveled hard yesterday. He slipped his sweat-stained tunic off and found a relatively dry patch with which to wipe his face and neck. He dug through his saddle-bags for a clean change of clothes and, once dressed, he crawled out of his tent.

Outside, the cold morning air was brisk but not as biting as it had been over the past week. They had come down from the mountains and were only a day's march from Novgorod, taking refuge in the thick forests that served the twofold task of obscuring their numbers and affording some shelter from the winter wind.

Even though his city and family were gone, he was still a boyar, and the title afforded him a place in the hierarchy of the *Kynaz*'s camp. His tent should have been with the other knights, but for all his Ruthenian heritage, he was an outsider to Nevsky's men. A ghost. An ill omen. And so he made his camp with the Shield-Maidens, which only added fuel to the stories being whispered about him. *A revenant who hides among the witches.*

Make this pact…

He pissed on the roots of a nearby fir tree. Afterward, he stared at the steam rising from the roots of the tree, rubbing at his right forearm. *Nothing more than a dream*, he thought.

He ducked back into his tent for his baldric and sword. Slinging the leather strap over his right shoulder and settling his sword against his hip, he strode toward the main camp, letting the smell of the cookfires guide him.

Warriors looked up from their trenchers as he passed, though most looked away if he glanced at them. He saw equal mixture of curiosity and fear, and the few who didn't shy away from his gaze would stare at his sword. It wasn't the finest blade Illarion had ever held, but most of the men-at-arms in Alexander's army were using weapons that had been passed down from grandfather to father to son. Many carried the shorter blades preferred by the Vikings, and small shields were in abundance. Most of Alexander's personal *Druzhina* were equally as well equipped as he—as were the Shield-Maidens. Some of the boyars had been trained in the west, and had the money and means to acquire their own kit. And there were others, grim-jawed men from the North—*Varangians*—like those who had fought in the service of Vladimir of Kiev long ago.

His hand was tight on the pommel of his sword as he walked, and when he heard the familiar clatter of wooden training weapons, he changed his course. His stomach was tight, and not from a lack of food. It was his head that needed aid—a different sort of sustenance.

He found them in a muddy space between tents, a patch of ground that had been trampled many times over. Two men were drilling with training weapons—wooden swords and simple shields—while another pair watched. A fifth man, circling the men at a safe distance, was barking advice at each fighter. The trainer—an *oplo* among the Shield-Brethren—was one of the tall Northmen, his blond hair and beard interspersed with braids.

Illarion paused, watching the two men batter each other with the wooden swords, not yet willing to make his presence known.

The younger of the two fighters checked a blow too slowly, and the stroke of his opponent's sword collapsed his guard entirely, the edge of his shield slamming into his nose while the sword smashed against his head. The fighter collapsed, blood squirting from his nose, and the watching pair howled with laughter. As the other fighter, a horrified expression on his face, stepped forward to apologize to the downed man, the Northman kicked the still-standing man in the backside. "That was your opponent's mistake," he snapped. "Not yours. Never apologize for making the other man bleed."

The second fighter, startled by the kick, started to stammer out a reply, thought better of it when he caught sight of the dark look on the Northman's face; unsure of what to do next, he stood there, awkwardly holding his training weapons, as the wounded man struggled to stand. The pair were no longer laughing, silenced by a stern glare from the trainer, but they were still smirking. The wounded man wiped at his nose and stared at the blood on his hand as if he couldn't quite believe its source.

"You find this entertaining?" the trainer asked. At first, Illarion thought he was referring to the pair of watchers, but then he realized the Northman was looking directly at him.

"Aye," Illarion said, realizing that strange sensation on his face was his mouth trying to form a smile.

The Northman grunted in reply, and then proceeded to wrest the wooden swords out of the hands of the students. He threw one at Illarion, who caught it deftly. "Care to show these oafs some real sword fighting?" he asked as he gestured for the pair to give up their shields as well.

Illarion grinned, the motion coming more naturally this time. The wooden grip felt solid in his hand. "I'd be happy to," he said, slipping off his baldric and sword and exchanging them for one of the wooden shields.

The Northman grinned, and waved Illarion forward. "Come, *ghost*, let us see what you know."

"And what shall I call you?" Illarion asked as he walked out onto the tiny field. He took a few practice swings with the sword, measuring its weight and handling. "*Dog? Rat?*" He glanced up at the Northman. "You have a name, don't you?"

The Northman spat on the muddy ground. "Ozur," he said, lowering his body into a defensive crouch.

"My name is Illarion," Illarion said. "Not *ghost*." He darted forward, swinging his sword in a short arc. The Northman jerked his head back, snapping his shield up and blocking Illarion's strike. "A ghost can't hurt you," Illarion said. "I can."

Ozur thrust his shield forward, trying to snare Illarion's, and his sword followed quickly, the point driving toward Illarion's face. Illarion caught both on his shield and pushed them wide as he stepped back. With a flick of his wrist, he disengaged entirely. Staying out of reach. "Me too," Ozur said with a wicked grin.

They circled each other, and Illarion felt the dream recede. His attention collapsed to the weaving point of Ozur's sword and to the circular shape of his opponent's shield. His body relaxed and all of the nightmarish tension in his shoulders and back sloughed away.

Ozur slammed his shield against Illarion's, twisting the edges together so that Illarion's arms were forced down, clearing the way for a sword to come over the top of the interlocked shields. A sharp jab at the face. Illarion ducked, slapping his sword along the left edge of his shield. Angling for a strike at Ozur's chest. The other man grunted and shoved, pushing both shields away, and he followed through with a wild swing at Illarion's head and shoulders. Illarion blocked, holding his sword firmly. The swords rattled together loudly, wood clacking against wood, and Illarion tried to slide his blade along Ozur's, but wood wasn't the same as metal and his blade didn't move as quickly as it should have. Ozur had time to pull back and avoid the strike at his hands.

Ozur stepped back, his guard still high, but he was out of measure. "What do you want here?" he asked Illarion. He was watching Illarion carefully. The Northman's eyes held a healthy amount of distrust, but there was curiosity as well.

"A good fight," Illarion said.

Ozur grunted in response. Illarion's answer was no answer at all. Wasn't that what they all wanted?

"They don't trust me," Illarion said, his gaze flicking toward the watching men.

"I don't trust you either," Ozur said.

"Are you afraid of me?" Illarion asked. He feigned a step to his left before darting forward, his shield clashing with Ozur's again. The wooden swords banged off the rims of the shields, and Illarion felt the breeze of Ozur's sword as it passed close to his face. He felt his sword strike something soft. Just a glancing blow.

Ozur backed away again, and this time his eyes were hard and his face was dark with emotion. "No," he said thickly. There was a line on his cheek, a mark left by the tip of Illarion's sword.

"I'm not a ghost, then?" Illarion asked. "Not a sorcerer or some dark thing from a midwife's story?" His words were not a question.

"Just a man," Ozur said. When he came at Illarion this time, he moved with a savage speed Illarion hadn't seen before. *He's really fighting me,* Illarion thought. *This is no longer a training exercise.* He gave ground instead of trying to match Ozur's attack. Ozur's shield struck his, and he felt the shock of the contact run up his arm. Ozur's sword flicked over the edge of the shields, nearly striking his shield arm, and he made the mistake of leaning back from the sword. Ozur drove forward, crouching behind his shield, and Illarion felt his defense crumble, his arm collapsing back against his chest. Ozur leered at Illarion, his braided beard much too close, and the pommel of Ozur's sword smacked Illarion in the forehead.

Illarion staggered back, his vision flashing white. He heard cheering from the watching men, and his single ear filled with a roaring sound. He blinked heavily, trying to clear his sight, and when he could see again, he saw Ozur had lowered his weapon.

"They don't know you," Ozur said. "They see how swiftly you've snared the prince's ear. Such influence makes them nervous, especially from one who should be dead."

"I'm not dead," Illarion gasped.

"Aye." Ozur grinned and pointed at Illarion's head. "And tomorrow you'll have the bruise to prove it."

Illarion raised his hand and felt the bump rising on his forehead. Ozur was right; he would have a very visible bruise for the next week or so. Perhaps it would be enough to convince the men that he was as real as they.

"Had enough?" Ozur asked.

Illarion touched the bump once more, wincing lightly. In the distance, he thought he heard a voice calling out to him. *Ilya, Ilya…*He shook his head, and readied himself again.

Ozur shrugged, and then abruptly launched himself forward with a scream. Illarion sidestepped, checked the blow with his shield, and snapped his weapon at the bigger man's shoulder with a flick of his wrist. It met with a crack as his opponent pivoted, catching the weapon high on his rim before cutting low. Illarion slammed his shield down onto the blade as he stepped to the side with his right foot and snapped off another stroke at Ozur's hip. They were both fighting in earnest now; Illarion was holding nothing back.

The big warrior grunted as the wooden blade struck home, and Illarion knew that Ozur would carry a mark from this bout as well. Ozur's grunt turned to a laugh as he struck high at Illarion's head. Illarion raised his shield to block the blade and the rim of Ozur's shield jabbed low at his midsection in a blow that would drive the air from his lungs. Illarion tightened all the muscles of his abdomen at once—his *oplo* at Týrshammar had taught them how to survive this blow—and the rim of the shield struck him hard, but he didn't lose his breath.

Illarion slammed his shield upwards and to his left, driving Ozur's sword arm wide, creating an opening that his opponent would have to cover. Illarion followed through with his sword and Ozur dropped his shield to block the thrust. The bait, taken.

Illarion let his weight carry him forward as he snapped the sword away from the feint, stepping inside the range of the Northman's sword. He slashed across Ozur's midsection, and if his sword had been sharp, he would have opened the Northman up from hip to shoulder. With a shout of surprise, Ozur stumbled back, tripping over his own feet and falling to the muddy ground.

There wasn't a sound from the watchers, and when Illarion stole quick glance in that direction, he saw the young men staring. Then the silence was broken by Ozur's roaring laughter. The Northman rolled onto his side, coughing as he hauled himself to his feet. He groaned as he laughed, his hands clutching at his chest and belly. "Who taught you to fight?" he chortled around a painful wheeze. "I haven't been hit like that in years."

"I spent some time at the Rock," Illarion said. "At Týrshammar, in the north."

"With the Shield-Brethren?" Ozur said, a look of admiration on his face.

"Aye."

Ozur laughed even more. "Why didn't you say so in the first place?" he groaned. He dropped his weapons and held out his arms as he stepped up to Illarion and gave him a brief hug. "That would have saved us both some bruises."

"Would you have believed me?" Illarion asked.

"I do now," Ozur said. He looked at the men standing nearby and waved a hand, dismissively. "Get out of here, you lazy fools," he said. "Don't make me set the ghost of Rus on you." The men scattered, pursued by Ozur's laughter.

The ghost of Rus...

Illarion didn't share the Northman's humor. When Ozur glanced back, he misinterpreted Illarion's expression. "It was a good hit," he said, clapping Illarion on the shoulder. "I look forward to the day when I see you perform it with steel on one of our enemies."

Illarion smiled weakly at the Northman. The dream was gone from his head, but his apprehension remained. Perhaps he should let Ozur hit him one more time.

CHAPTER 10:

THE SEVEN RIVERS

They went south once they escaped the Heavenly Mountains, putting the tall peak of the sky god behind their right shoulders. When he was lucid, Alchiq was angry about their course and he would harangue Gansukh until his voice gave out about the younger man's tracking skills, but his lucidity never lasted long. Gansukh lashed Alchiq into his saddle and ran a rope between their horses. Within a week, he had crossed the first of the seven rivers that lay between the mountains and the inland sea.

Further to the south was the trade route, the so-called Silk Road, and he knew their quarry would not risk traveling along that route. They were conspicuous as a small company, and too many would remember their passage. Alchiq thought they would stay north, out in the open steppe, and Gansukh saw no reason to disagree, but they needed supplies. They needed herbs and unguents for Alchiq's ruined hand.

One night, unable to sleep due to Alchiq's incessant nightmares, he considered smothering the old man with a blanket. It wouldn't take much. Their journey and his fever had reduced Alchiq to nothing more than skin and bones. Some days he was barely strong enough to stand. When Gansukh had finally drifted off to sleep, he had dreamed about the blanket in his hands. He had folded it up to a thick square, and once he got it over Alchiq's mouth, he had pressed down with his elbows to hold it in place. Alchiq had struggled fiercely, beating at Gansukh's arms with his bandaged hand, tearing open his wound again, but his strength had ebbed quickly. The dreaming had disturbed Gansukh, but not so much that he hadn't woken feeling more refreshed than he had in weeks.

That morning he had started to alter their course to the south. The dream was only going to get worse, he knew, and if he didn't do something to ease Alchiq's fever, he was going to end up acting out his dream one night. Would he even wake up as he smothered Alchiq, or would he kill the other man and lie back down without bothering to wake?

There were seven rivers that flowed in and out of the lake, the largest being the Ili. Gansukh knew there were a number of settlements along the rivers; the area had been subjugated by the armies of the *Khagan* several times since Genghis had brought the clans together. The Cumans, Kipchaks, Turks, and other nomadic peoples paid tribute readily to the *Khagan* and were all but ignored by Karakorum. They had learned how to exist under Mongol rule, and as a result, they had flourished as the trade routes opened up. There would be little trouble finding a village with a reasonably well-supplied market. With any luck, he could find a few more horses too.

✦ ✦ ✦

Along the eastern bank of the Aksu River, he found a flourishing fishing village. There were several taller buildings built back from the water's edge, and judging from the sun-baked brick half walls that surrounded these houses, they belonged to the local equivalent of the clan leaders. They were peaked roof houses with extended overhangs that curled up at their ends. The fanciful architecture was out of place with the nomadic lifestyle of many of the steppe clans and suggested the village was more diverse than he had expected it to be.

Alchiq was in one of his feverish dazes, where he slumped in the saddle, more dead than alive. Peasants and craftspeople noticed them as Gansukh led Alchiq's horse into the small village, but only because they were new faces, not because they were Mongols. Gansukh caught sight of several clan insignia before they reached the broad beach where the bustling mercantile center lay and he spotted the familiar sight of Mongol ponies, saddled and outfitted for steppe hunters.

He found space at a trough where he could leave the horses (along with the dazed Alchiq), so that he could venture into the stalls on foot. Alchiq couldn't untie himself from his saddle without raising some commotion and he wasn't concerned that someone would steal his horse.

If Alchiq hadn't sought to steal the horses from the Oirat, he wouldn't be here now, seeking aid.

The thought made him grit his teeth, and the look on his face must have been rather stark as the first few merchants took one look at him and turned their attention elsewhere. He got his anger under control and even managed to smile at a swarthy man with a turban and a white beard who eagerly wanted to sell him any number of dried gourds.

"No gourds," he said, waving the merchant off. The merchant jabbered at him in a Turkic dialect, and he shook his head and walked on. Somewhere on the other side of the row of stalls, musicians were playing. When he heard the jingle of small bells, a memory of another market sprang to his mind: outside of Karakorum, shortly before one of the *Khagan*'s grand festivals. He and Lian, the Chinese tutor assigned to him by the *Khagan*'s chief advisor, had spent the afternoon wandering around. He had been distracted by a dancer wearing bells, and she had been angry at him.

Lian.

He had tried very hard to suppress thoughts of her since the *Khagan*'s death. There were too many empty hours riding across the steppe, and a man could drive himself crazy trying to figure out what a woman was thinking.

That day in the market, she had been buying him a robe. A robe he no longer had, along with everything else that hadn't been on his horse when his tent had been burned. For a while he had thought Munokhoi, the ex-*Torguud* captain with whom he had had a deadly enmity, had set the fire. But Munokhoi had been in the woods, stalking *him*; he couldn't have been in two places at once. Alchiq had been the one to suggest an alternate culprit, but Gansukh had brushed off the old hunter's accusation initially. Eventually, however, he realized Alchiq was probably right.

Lian had set the fire.

First, she buys me a robe, and then she seduces me, and finally she runs away, but not before burning everything I own. He had learned a lot about the manners of court and he knew the traditional methods of courtship among the steppe clans; he was fairly certain setting fire to your prospective mate's belongings was not part of the typical rituals. Even in China.

He found a bald and bewhiskered Chinese man selling dried herbs, and via a combination of hand gestures and sniffing at the apothecary's pots, he found remedies that would ease Alchiq's fever and bring the swelling down in the old man's hand. The old Chinese man stared suspiciously at the battered coins that Gansukh offered, but he took the money regardless. Gansukh didn't bother being offended; coin was coin, he knew.

When he rifled through his tiny pouch after buying the herbs, though, he grew a little concerned about the scarcity of coin. Alchiq had some money too, but neither of them had much wealth. He had had little use for it previously, but now…

He passed a set of benches arranged around a dirt ring. Bare-chested men were wrestling, while onlookers wagered and shouted. Women with jugs of *arkhi* were wandering through the crowds, filling cups for a coin or two. Gansukh paused to watch the wrestlers. Neither man was very broad in the chest or tall, but they were both wiry and well-matched. The bout lasted several minutes, during which time each man seemed to be on the verge of subduing the other. After the third such reversal, Gansukh began to suspect the wrestlers were in collusion, allowing the other to escape in order to increase the wagers being laid against them. His interest waning, Gansukh made to wander on, but he paused as he overheard a piece of a conversation between two rotund merchants who were loitering behind the benches.

Kuraltai, one of them had said. The election of a new *Khagan.*

Gansukh kept his eyes on the wrestlers, but the rest of his attention was directed at the merchants.

"They're all heading for Karakorum," the one wearing red said. "It could take months—years, even—to pick a new *Khagan.* Every horse I could borrow or buy is hauling wagons east."

"All of them?" asked the other merchant. His plump fingers were constantly wiggling, the sun flashing off his rings. "Even Batu?"

"Especially Batu," the red merchant replied. "His armies are taking what they need as they come east, and no one is buying anything along the Silk Road. They're all looking toward Karakorum."

The empire, collapsing in on itself, Gansukh thought as he continued on. The death of Ögedei had left a void at the center of the Mongol empire, and all of his sons and uncles and cousins were rushing to fill that void. Behind them was every other *ordu* chieftain, hoping to curry favor with the new Khan of Khans. If, and when, another was elected.

As he walked back toward the trough and their horses, he wondered what it was that he and Alchiq hoped to achieve.

What empire were they trying to save? Or were they just seeking vengeance?

✦ ✦ ✦

He mashed up the herbs and made a foul-smelling tea that Alchiq refused to drink. He took one sip and spat it out onto the fire. Gansukh, having expected such behavior from the old man, smacked him on the shoulder with an arrow—the end with the fletching. Alchiq growled at him, his red-rimmed eyes glaring like the eyes of an angry boar. "Drink it," Gansukh said, indicating the cup with the arrow.

"No," Alchiq snarled.

Gansukh raised the arrow again, and when Alchiq put up his right hand to intercept the switch, Gansukh whipped him across the wounded finger stump. Alchiq howled, and started to struggle to his feet. He was looking for his sword, but Gansukh had taken it days ago.

"Drink it," Gansukh repeated. "And then I'm going to change that dressing."

Alchiq clutched his wounded hand in his good one. He had gotten to his feet and he glowered at Gansukh, his eyes still bright with fever. Gansukh kept the arrow between them, making Alchiq focus on the fletching. Slowly, the lines smoothed on Alchiq's face and the angry light in his eyes subsided. Gansukh flicked the arrow down at the cup that Alchiq had knocked over. "You're no good to me like this," he said. "You're slowing me down. If you don't drink this tea, I am going to leave you here."

Alchiq grimaced at Gansukh's threat, but he sat down and reached for the cup. He dusted off the wet dirt clinging to the rim and held it out. Gansukh slipped the arrow under his left arm as he picked up the pot and poured another measure for Alchiq.

"It's horse piss," Alchiq muttered after he took a sip.

"I don't even know why I am bothering to help you," Gansukh said. "You're not much better company when you are well."

Alchiq glared at him, and then showed his teeth in what Gansukh assumed was an attempt to smile. "You're a fool who is still thinking with his heart," he said.

"Aye," Gansukh agreed, recalling the thoughts that had kept him company while he had been in the market. "That I am." He tapped the pot which he had left close to Alchiq. "Drink the whole pot."

"I'm going to piss this out all over your boots," Alchiq said.

"It won't be the first time someone has stained my gear," Gansukh said with a shrug. "You remember what happened to the last man who had difficulties controlling where he pissed?"

"I do," Alchiq said. He put his head back and poured the rest of the cup into his mouth. "That was a fine killing," he said as he reached for the pot.

Gansukh figured that was as close as a compliment he was ever going to get from Alchiq on the matter of his duel with Munokhoi. "In the village, when I was buying supplies, I heard talk of the *kuraltai*," he said, changing the subject. "News of the *Khagan*'s death has spread. The horde is coming back."

Alchiq nodded, his lips still curling with each sip of tea. "Where are we?"

"Not far from the Aksu, in the Seven Rivers region."

"South of the lake," Alchiq grumbled. "They wouldn't have come this way." He waved his damaged hand at the pot. "All this way for tea. We've lost their trail."

"We lost their trail weeks ago," Gansukh said. "We knew the *Skjaldbræður* had to get through the gap, and so did we. But we knew we would have to find them on the steppe afterward. You assured me you knew where they would go, but after the wolves, you were taken by fever. If I hadn't gotten supplies, the fever would have boiled your brain. What would I have done then?"

"What would you have done?" Alchiq asked. "Would you have given up and gone home?"

"*Home?*" Gansukh said. "Where would that be, Alchiq? I failed in my mission for Chagatai Khan. His brother is dead. Am I supposed to crawl back to Ögedei's brother—who is, for all I know, riding for Karakorum to participate in the *kuraltai* himself? Am I supposed to beg forgiveness? 'O Great Chagatai, I didn't fail you; Ögedei was going to stop drinking as soon as he returned from his pilgrimage. It wasn't my fault these Western demons slew him.'"

"No," Alchiq said softly. "The fault is mine. I knew they were coming." He stared into the fire, his face sagging. "I first encountered them in the woodlands of the west, beyond the borders of the Ruthenian land that Batu Khan had recently conquered. I followed them to the ruin of Kiev, and when they left Kiev with a company of the *Skjalddis,* I found a *jaghun* of riders and pursued them further. We slew the *Skjalddis,* but the *Skjaldbrœður*—who numbered barely more than an *arban*—destroyed my *jaghun.* They slew almost a hundred men, and had I not lucked upon one of them as he gathered water, they would have sustained no casualties." He beat his fist against his leg. "One!" he exclaimed.

Gansukh found this hard to believe, and if this were any other man, he might have chided the story-teller for embellishing the tale, but he held his tongue. Alchiq was brusque, even by his standards, and he was not prone to fanciful stories.

"They were coming east, and I knew where they were going," Alchiq continued after he poured himself another cup of tea. "I knew what they sought to do, and so I rode ahead of them. I rode as fast as I could to reach Karakorum before they did. Master Chucai listened to my warnings, but he paid little heed to what I had to say. The *Khagan* never should have gone hunting with as few men as he did. Chucai knew that; he knew the threat."

Gansukh cleared his throat. "What are you saying?" he asked. "Chucai knew the *Skjaldbrœður* were waiting in the forest?"

Alchiq shook his head. "He was as surprised as the rest," he said. "And he'll limp for the rest of his life because he didn't listen."

Master Chucai had been with them when the *Skjaldbræður* had attacked the *Khagan* outside the cave of the great bear. One of the *Skjaldbræður*, a very tall man with a bow nearly as tall, had pinned Chucai to his horse with an arrow, and the *Khagan*'s advisor had spent hours attached to the dead animal before he had been found and cut free. He was, in Gansukh's estimation, lucky to have not lost the leg entirely.

"Why are you doing this?" Gansukh asked after a few moments of silence. He had asked the question before but previously Alchiq's only response had been to brush the question aside as if it were nothing more than the sort of pestering question asked over and over again by a small child.

"They killed the *Khagan* and took something that belongs to the empire," Alchiq said. "That's reason enough for any man."

And yet, we're the only ones who are chasing them, Gansukh thought. "And then what?" he asked.

Alchiq shrugged.

By the Blue Wolf, Gansukh realized, *he means to die on this journey. He'll keep chasing them until they turn and fight him. And he knows they will kill him, but he doesn't care. It's the only end he can see.*

There was another reason to chase the *Skjaldbræður*, but it wasn't one that he was willing to share with Alchiq. He wasn't entirely certain that he was willing to accept it himself.

They took something from the empire, he mentally echoed, and the thought felt foreign, as if he were trying to convince himself.

CHAPTER 11:

THE DIPLOMACY OF WAITING

After so long resting at the rock, Haakon started to go a little stir-crazy. Even though he was not confined to a cage, sitting around and doing nothing was too much like his time as a prisoner of the *Khagan*. He had, in fact, woken himself several times during the night from the dream he had had many times during his imprisonment—the one where he had escaped from his cage and stolen a horse. The next morning, he had told Percival and Gawain that he was going to go with the Seljuks on their patrol.

At first, Gawain had refused to let him join the scouts, but after Gawain and Percival had had a terse discussion by themselves, he had been granted leave to ride with the Seljuks. They shared only a few Mongolian words in common, which was fine with Haakon. There wouldn't be much to talk about anyway.

Even several months after his escape and reunion with the Shield-Brethren, he still struggled with understanding his place in the company. When he and the other trainers had come from Týrshammar to Legnica in response to Onghwe Khan's call for fighters, he never thought he would do much more than squire the knights of the order. Instead, he had been thrust into the thick of the gladiatorial bouts and after his first bout, he had been imprisoned and sent east with a caravan bound for the *Khagan*'s court—a prize warrior of the West secured by Onghwe Khan. Then, after months of languishing in the cage, he had been forced to fight again. Each time he had managed to beat his opponent, and then shortly after his escape, he had fought the *Khagan,* and killed him.

It was no small feat, and not a day went by that Haakon didn't dwell on that fight in the forest and on what the *Khagan* had said when he died.

The Seljuks followed a pattern where they rode in widening circles around the rock for the first hour, and then they split up, riding out until they could barely see each other. With the addition of Haakon to the scouting party, they could keep an eye on an even larger portion of the surrounding terrain. As a result, they tended to ride in circles for most of the morning and when the sun had passed its zenith, they would chose a different direction than that of the day before and ride away from the rock for another hour. Then they would turn to their right, ride awhile, and finally start back to the camp.

They had been doing this for about a week, and Haakon was starting to recognize some of the subtle landmarks around the rock. In the east, the ground was rougher, the endless plains of grass broken up with sporadic clumps of stone, like abandoned gauntlets of forgotten giants. Haakon knew when they were west of the rock because of the lack of rocky formations.

A long time ago, a river had run west and south of the rock, and the only landmark that remained was a meandering course of spruce and cedar. There were gaps in the trees, and whenever they rode through these breaks, they would flush out flocks of tiny birds.

Haakon was the westernmost outrider, and he had been riding parallel to the river's track for a half hour or so when he decided it was time to cut through the tree line. He nudged his horse to the right and the animal, knowing the routine, complied. The sky was mostly clear of clouds, and Haakon wasn't wearing a hat. It never got as cold as it did in Týrshammar, and the last few days had been warm enough that little snow remained on the ground.

His horse started as the birds spooked from the trees, a half-dozen tiny shapes winging into the sky. Haakon stared at the birds for a few seconds, wondering why they had spooked before he had even reached the trees and it struck him that they were flying toward him.

He fumbled for his crossbow even as he tried to arrest his horse's forward motion. The crossbow was cocked but not loaded, and he cursed as he tried to yank open the satchel containing the bolts.

A horse neighed on the other side of the trees, and his horse pricked up its ears and trotted a little faster. "No," he hissed, pulling at the reins and nearly spilling the satchel of bolts. He got a bolt in place and braced the crossbow against his shoulder.

A horse and rider emerged from the gap in the trees. Haakon took only a second to register tiny details of the pair—short pony, shaggy mane, rider wearing fur-lined jacket and peaked hat, Mongol bow held casually across the saddle—before he pulled the crossbow's trigger. The bolt rattled as it left the groove of the crossbow, and the rider reacted to the sound. The bolt struck him in the chest and he toppled backward, falling off his horse. The horse, a stolid Mongol pony, didn't panic when its rider disappeared.

There were two more riders behind the first horse, and Haakon grabbed at his reins and jerked his horse away from the gap. He heard shouts behind him as he snapped the reins hard, urging his horse to a gallop, and as his horse picked up speed, the first arrow sailed past his head. He crouched low in his saddle, knowing there were going to be more.

The Mongols rarely fired just one arrow.

◆ ◆ ◆

The prolonged stop at the makeshift camp gave Lian time to think—too much time, in fact—and she found herself second-guessing her decisions. Even though she had managed to convince a company of Westerners to bring her with them as they fled the empire, she didn't have any idea of what happened next. It was a frustrating place to be, especially given how pragmatic she had been in all her planning. At least, that was what she had been telling herself, but lately, she had started to wonder if she had merely made a long string of very bad decisions. And what had they all stemmed from? Gansukh's refusal to join her.

She had used her natural talents in an effort to convince the young steppe rider that he should leave the empire with her, and she had thought he could be swayed, but he had been steadfast in his duty to the *Khagan*. She couldn't decide what she felt about him, or if he really cared for her. Had she really loved him, or had it all been a ruse? They had used the threat of Munokhoi's ire to find shelter in each other's arms, but had that been the only reason? And when Gansukh had left the *Khagan*'s compound on that last day, why had he given her the tiny box that held the sprig? Why had he trusted her with it?

And why had she abandoned him?

The struggle through the winter storms over the past few weeks had been a convenient excuse to not think about what she had done. Food had been scarce, the weather had been bitterly cold and miserable, and all any of them had been thinking about was surviving each night. Putting one foot in front of the other again and again until the storms were behind them, until they were no longer wading through snowdrifts and sliding across icy ground.

But then what?

She learned their language as quickly as she could; in fact, Percival was the easiest to talk to. At first, she had thought he was entirely smitten with her, but she soon realized Percival was helping her learn the trade tongue out of *duty*. She was in need of assistance, and based on some personal code that he believed very intently, he was required to render as much aid as he could. He was very polite—and a very good conversationalist, as well— but she never learned anything about him. For all her efforts— and she caught herself using all of her wiles on more than one occasion—the Frank remained an enigma.

In fact, all she really learned for her efforts was how badly Cnán wanted to be noticed by Percival, and how much the Binder disliked her relationship with the knight. Not that there was much of one to be angry about.

The short one, Yasper, talked nonstop when he was nervous, which happened anytime she simply stood next to him and did nothing more complicated than breathing. She enjoyed listening to him prattle on, even though she understood less than half of what he was talking about. Of the new men, Gawain and Bruno were the only ones who paid her any attention. She understood them and they understood her; it had been easy to engage in light flirtation with them, and such talk only increased her opportunities to practice the trade tongue of the West.

While her family name afforded her a better life than that of a scullery maid or a concubine, she had still spent the better part of her adult life in servitude. Master Chucai had recognized her intelligence and once she had become part of his house, she had had access to books and scrolls. She had been expected to learn the subtleties of court life, and while mastery of these arts would have never gained her freedom, they did make a difference in the quality of her slavery. Lian was good at reading people, at deciphering the silences between words as well as the tiny gestures and tics that betrayed everyone.

This is how she knew Percival yearned—with a desire that almost pained him—to return to the West; that Vera's hatred for the Mongols ran very, very deep; and that Cnán was angry at her for merely being in the camp. Haakon had dreams about her that embarrassed him when he did remember them, and she had wondered once or twice herself what might have happened in those dreams. Raphael carried a mantle of sorrow that weighed heavy on him, a burden of betrayal whose source she could not discern.

She knew the four who had rescued them were running from someone, and all she was certain of was that it wasn't Mongols. Lately she had been wondering what Gawain and Bruno's past would mean to the Shield-Brethren when it caught up with both companies.

"Daydreaming again?"

Lian started from her reverie, discovering that Bruno had snuck up on her. She had been sitting on a rock not far from the fire pit. It afforded her a view of the surrounding plain, a view where nothing moved for hours but the occasional column of wind blowing through the scattered tufts of wormwood.

She ran her hand through her hair, pushing it back from her face. "This land makes it easy," she said, tilting her head to look at him. The rock jutted out of the ground enough that, when she sat on it, she could look him in the eye.

Bruno laughed. He was a broad-shouldered man with curly black hair and an equally curly beard. His teeth were large and straight and when he laughed, he showed them off. His nose was distinctive, easily the largest she had ever seen, but none of the others seemed to notice its size. His hands were large too; she could recall—without much difficulty—what it had felt like to be carried by him. How comforting that sensation had been.

"What were you thinking about?" he asked.

She shrugged, both from a lack of desire to tell him and from a lack of enough words in the trade tongue to say everything.

"Home?" he asked.

Lian snorted and shook her head. "Home is"—she pointed straight out in front of her—"so far away."

He gently took her arm in his beefy hands and rotated it so that it pointed off to her left. "That way," he said.

"It's still far," she said, letting her arm go limp in his hands. He wasn't in any hurry to let go.

He turned her arm again, crossing her body and leaning in close as he did. "My home is that way," he said, his chin close to her shoulder. "Lombardy."

She nodded, her arm still loose in his hands. "Lombardy," she tried, stretching out the word.

"Many forests and mountains," he said. "Not like this at all. And the sea. Oh, how I miss the sea. Do you know what that is?"

She turned her head toward him, and her eyes went to his lips. "Like a lake," she said. "But bigger."

He grinned. "Aye."

"I have seen it," she said.

"How is that possible?" Bruno asked. "I thought you said you were from a land beyond the Mongol empire. To the east. The sea lies to the west."

She laughed. "That may be, but I have stood on a beach and watched the sun rise out of the water."

Bruno stroked his beard thoughtfully. "It must be a very large lake," he said.

Lian shook her head. "Very well," she said. "I misspoke. It was a lake. But"—she cocked her head to the side and raised an eyebrow at Bruno—"how do you know that the body of water that you sailed on wasn't a very large lake as well?"

It was Bruno's turn to laugh. "You are clever, Lian. I grant you that." He inclined his head. "I confess that I cannot say, with complete conviction, that the *sea* I sailed upon did not have a far shore."

Lian turned her gaze toward the endless steppe. "I wonder how far away it is," she said, her heart tripping in her chest. Was she willing to go that far, or did each step take her farther away from all that mattered to her?

✦ ✦ ✦

Cnán had hoped a visit to the Binder shrine would nudge Raphael into some sort of decision, but his mind was still recovering from his latest bout with winter fever. He wasn't enfeebled like most who get lost in madness, but his thoughts were still caught around a central idea, like a goat tied to a stake. He could only range so far and, as he talked, he twisted in ever-tightening circles.

It was only after the three of them had returned from their meeting at the Binder shrine and she had made polite excuses and removed herself from the conversation that she realized what was truly bothering her. She admired Raphael. Whatever her feelings were for Percival—and while they were less confusing now then they had been last fall, they were still extant enough to cause the occasional bout of confusion and embarrassment—she did not regard the Frank in the same way that she regarded Raphael. Percival was erudite in speech, educated and well-traveled, and he was pleasing to look upon. He was, in many regards, a natural leader. More so than Feronantus, certainly, who could be best described as brusque, taciturn, and exasperatingly enigmatic. And with Feronantus gone, the company needed a leader. They needed someone with…*vision.*

The thought made her shiver.

Raphael, it seemed, was suffering from a *lack* of vision. *Which is worse?* she wondered. *Feronantus telling me only a fraction of what he thought I should know, or Raphael being unable to frame his thoughts well enough for anyone else to follow?*

Her wandering feet led her over to the fire pit where Yasper was tending to his endless alchemical experiment. Of all of the company, the alchemist was the least concerned about their lengthy stay. He was a constant presence at the fire, and while he would infrequently poke at the oblong cakes buried in the ashes, for the most part he simply sat on a large rock and stared at the pit of ashes and smoldering wood.

He glanced up as she approached, offering her a smile. His grin faltered as he saw the look on her face, and she quickly hid her frustration and offered him a smile of her own. "Still waiting?" she asked.

"'Tis the only constant in the subtle art of alchemy," he said. "Still no decision on where we're going?"

"I had hoped he was well enough." She shook her head. "But he is caught in a confusion about visions."

Yasper nodded as if he understood, all too well, that sort of confusion.

Cnán sighed loudly. "I do not understand how the Shield-Brethren can be so caught up in this question of whether or not one of their members has had a vision."

"As I understand it, their tradition is very old and they cling to certain beliefs very strongly. It is the basis for their faith, if you will."

"What about you, Yasper?" Cnán asked.

"What do I believe in?" He raised his eyebrows and looked at her as if to assess whether she was being entirely serious. "I'm an alchemist," he said. "I'm ardent practitioner in believing in the impossible."

"You're no help," she said with a sigh.

He laughed, and the sound loosened some of her annoyance. His laugh was a unique sound, almost like the call of a giant bird out of legend, and it came out of him in gusts. During their journey through the western forests, she would scout ahead of the company as well as spending time in the woods by herself, and she always could find her way back to the camp by following the echoing hoots of Yasper's laughter.

The tension left her shoulders, and she felt her fingers uncurl from the half-fists she had been holding them in. His laughter was like the rumbling course of an avalanche—snow and rocks breaking free from the icy mountainside and spilling down to the valley below. You couldn't stand before it; you could merely be carried along with it.

"Does that earnestness apply to your experiment?" she asked, nodding toward the cakes buried in the coals. "What are you making again?"

"Phoenix eggs," he said, and he laughed again when she rolled her eyes.

"Phoenixes don't exist," she countered, trying to hide the smile that was threatening to break across her face.

"Not yet," he said with a wink. "Give me a few more days."

The urge to smile won, and he beamed with pride at having changed the disposition of her face. With a final shake of her head, she let go of the conversation with Vera and Raphael. She had done what she could. Raphael would make a decision soon, she hoped.

She leaned forward, peering at the yellowed cakes nestled in the fire. They were rough, like dried mud, and when she examined them closely, she could see tiny crimson veins running along their surfaces. "But you made these," she said. "You can't *make* a phoenix. It's a living creature."

"Is it?" He tilted his head at her. "I thought you said they don't exist. If that is true, then why I can't make them?"

She groaned and put her hands over her face. "You're just as bad as Raphael," she said. "I ask a simple question and I get philosophy in return."

He touched her hands lightly, drawing them away from her face. His expression was tender and attentive, and his eyes were wide and imploring. "Cnán," he said gently, as if he were about to impart a grave secret, "maybe you should ask easier questions." And then he threw his head back and laughed again.

She laughed with him this time, slapping him lightly on the shoulder. When the laughter had run its course, they both stared at the ashes, and Cnán felt a strange awkwardness stealing over her.

"You don't like standing still, do you?" Yasper asked suddenly, just as she had been about to offer some pithy comment and take her leave.

"I…what?"

"All this sitting around," Yasper said, indicating the spread of the camp with a sweep of his arm. "No destination in mind, no plan for our departure. No horses, for that matter. It makes you uncomfortable."

"I…" The awkwardness was getting worse. "I travel a great deal," she finished, mentally kicking herself as soon as the words left her mouth.

"Aye," Yasper said. "We all have recently. I've spent more time on a horse in the last eight months than in the previous three years. And you? Where did you come from before you found us at Legnica?"

"I spent the winter in Samarkand," she said, waving her hand over his shoulder.

He turned and shaded his eyes, and after looking for a moment, he climbed up on the rock he had been sitting on and looked some more. "I don't see it," he said, looking down at her. "I don't know how you do that."

"Do what?"

"Know where places are without consulting a map or the stars."

"I'm guessing," she said. She indicated the rock behind her. "The point there? That's east. The sun, there—" she pointed at the blazing light in the sky.

"Is that what that is?" he said, mockingly.

"The sun, there," she continued, ignoring him, "means that we are on the southern side of the rock. Samarkand is south of us." And when she waved her hand this time, she made the gesture more broadly, covering the entire sweep of the southern horizon. "*Somewhere* out there."

"You're patronizing me," Yasper said as he hopped down from the rock. He picked up his fire stick and gently moved the ashes around his alchemical cakes. "It's okay," he said as she began to argue otherwise, "I probably deserved it with the joke about phoenix eggs."

"Probably," she said. She stood next to him, her shoulder lightly brushing his. "I don't like waiting," she admitted.

"I know," he said. He held out the stick and she took it without thought. Kneeling beside the ring of rocks, Yasper leaned over the fire pit and blew heavily on his alchemical cakes. White ash blew up, rising into the sky as it passed over the still-hot center of the fire. On the cakes, the crimson veins stood out in stark relief. "Something is going to happen soon," he said. "There's very little we can do to hasten its arrival."

"I know," she said.

◆ ◆ ◆

From the hemp rope that outlined the large paddock, Raphael watched Percival move among the horses. Most ignored him, but the pair of gray mares vied for his attention. He held his left hand out to one, who nosed his palm eagerly, as he ran his fingers through the mane of the other. The left-hand one snorted lightly as she discovered he had no treat for her and butted him lightly on the shoulder with her forehead. Percival smiled at her and scratched her neck affectionately.

"They're beautiful horses," Raphael said.

The mares lifted their heads, nostrils flaring as they checked his scent. Percival clucked his tongue lightly and patted them both reassuringly. "Indeed," the Frank said. "From Arabia. They're quite far from home."

"As are we," Raphael noted.

Percival noted something in Raphael's voice and realized the visit was not entirely a casual one. He left off his ministrations of the horses and approached the rope line. "What is on your mind, Raphael?" he asked.

A combination of sun and wind had darkened Percival's fair face to bronze and put red and yellow highlights into his beard. His eyes were a shade of blue that reminded Raphael of the Mediterranean, and he was struck by the similarity between Percival's face and some of the statues of Zeus he had seen on Cyprus during his travels.

"The last time we were at this rock, our company held council and re-affirmed our desire to end the *Khagan*'s life. We went east as one, and achieved our goal, but not without great cost. Now, we are but a handful of weary travelers, and our brotherhood is reduced to two."

"Two?" Percival frowned. "You don't count the boy? After what he's done?"

"Haakon?" Raphael shook his head. He pulled up the right sleeve of his tunic to reveal the edge of the pale scar that marked him as an initiate of the *Ordo Militum Vindicis Intactae*. It was an old brand, seared into his flesh during the ritual in the cave beneath Petraathen. "He hasn't been tested."

"Is that all that matters?"

"With regard to the final say of our course of action, yes. I am not considering Vera either, even though she is—by all counts— an equal sister to us." Raphael let his sleeve drop. "What keeps us together is fellowship and the necessity of companionship in order to survive the journey through the mountains, but that journey is complete. I would know your mind as to your ultimate destination."

"We should return to Petraathen," Percival said without hesitation.

"Should we?" Raphael asked. His gaze was mainly directed at the horses behind Percival, but he was watching the Frank's expression as best he could without being obvious. His own con-fusion about Feronantus was very clear in his mind—that was the one thing he *was* certain of—and he needed a clear perspective on his thoughts. Was Percival as conflicted about their course of action, or was it merely an odd affectation of their previous leader that was being dismissed as a character flaw? Percival held himself to a high standard, and while he had taken the same oath of fellowship and brotherhood, he maintained a more rarefied observance of the letters of their oaths than any other member of the order that Raphael knew.

Percival closed his eyes for a second, and when he opened them again, Raphael felt they weren't as focused. *He's guarded,* Raphael thought.

"We have lost brothers in battle," Percival said. "It is our duty to see that their stories are not lost and that their swords are returned to the Great Hall at Petraathen."

Duty, Raphael thought. *No other reason?*

"Of course," he said. "But we are not required to do immediately. Is there not some other task that remains unaccomplished?"

"I fought for him," Percival said. "I bled for him. He abandoned us. He fled the field of battle. Feronantus is no longer worthy of being called *brother.*"

"And you aren't curious as to why he fled?"

"No."

Percival's response was curt, but Raphael spotted a flutter in the Frank's left eye, a nervous tic that couldn't quite be suppressed. But before he could ask another question, a cry from behind him interrupted their conversation.

A figure atop the rock was waving madly. Raphael squinted, trying to figure out who it was as the figure shouted once more and then darted off, disappearing on the far side of the rock.

"Gawain," Percival said, his eyesight better than Raphael's. His hearing was better too. "He's spotted the scouts...but they're missing a horse."

CHAPTER 12:

TIGER, TIGER

At first, Feronantus overlooked the long pale orange and black shape as nothing more than a piece of rock, an exposed slab attached to a much larger formation that lay beneath the soil. The terrain over which he and Istvan had been traveling the past few days was no more or less flat than any ground they'd seen in weeks, but it seemed harder. As if the soil were nothing more than a thin skin over a plain of old stone. As such, he wasn't surprised to see the occasional bump in the landscape—places where the soil had been blown away to reveal the ragged skeleton of the world beneath the sandy skin. He had thought they might find the enormous rock where they had met Benjamin during their ride east, but they had missed it, apparently. Not that it mattered overmuch; the rock was a landmark that others would use, and he didn't want to risk encountering anyone. He and Istvan would not be able to deter a decent-sized band of marauders or Mongols.

The second time he saw the orange and black rock, he wondered if the striated stone was indicative of certain mineral deposits, and he briefly missed Yasper's presence. The Dutchman would have had an opinion, if not informed knowledge about the composition of the oddly colored stone. He considered pointing out the rock to Istvan, but the Hungarian was in one of his moods and was inclined to ignore everything Feronantus said.

The third time he saw the rock, he realized it wasn't a rock at all.

"Tiger," was all Istvan said when Feronantus finally pointed out the shape to the Hungarian. They moved upwind and left their horses near a pair of stones that were not going to wander. Istvan led him on a slow creep across the steppe—at one point, they wiggled for a good half hour on their bellies—until they reached the edge of one of the natural depressions that were scattered across the steppe.

A small stream trickled in from the north, and Feronantus realized he was looking over a shallow lakebed that was now nothing more than a dried basin with a tiny pool near the center. Out of the direct path of the wind, the wormwood was able to grow taller, and clumps of the bush clustered along the edge of the pond. Behind the wormwood were several stands of larch, still naked from their winter fright, and through the trees, they could see a herd of antlered deer, cropping the short grasses that had started to push through the permafrost of the steppe.

Istvan pointed, and Feronantus stared at the shadows creeping through the wormwood. The tiger was stalking the herd, moving with incredible patience through the brush. It was no wonder he had mistaken the tiger for a striped stone; if he hadn't been staring directly at it—well aware of what the shape truly was—he would not have noticed it.

Istvan rested his chin on his hands and squirmed slightly to make himself comfortable on the ground. "Watch," he whispered. "Usually you do not see a beast like this until it is too late."

Feronantus wondered where Istvan had seen a tiger before. He had heard stories of them while he had been in the Levant, during the crusade with Richard Lionheart. Some of his fellow Shield-Brethren had scoffed at the stories, thinking the tiger was much like the hippogriff or the phoenix—a creature out of legend. But he had seen men wearing cloaks lined with the orange and black fur.

A pair of stags with broad antlers patrolled the edge of the herd, alert for the sign of any danger. Each time either came near the copse of trees where the tiger was hidden, the predator became like a stone. Feronantus had never seen an animal display such patience and cunning.

They watched for more than an hour, during which time Feronantus felt cramps seize his legs more than once. He was no longer a young man to enjoy such protracted watchfulness, and he was about to tell Istvan that he was done watching when one of the two stags raised its head and gave a loud warning cough.

In an instant, the herd was in motion, the does driving the younger deer before them while the older males and the stags lagged behind. A blur raced out from beneath the trees, and one of the stags lowered its enormous spread of antlers, but the tiger was not interested in fighting an armed opponent. It streaked past the stag, intent on one of the older does who wasn't running as fast as the rest of the herd. The doe bleated in fear and dodged away from the rest of the herd, heading across the dry basin. In motion, the tiger appeared to be longer than a man was tall, and it ran with long loping strides. The deer scrambled and hopped and darted in a valiant effort to confuse the tiger, but the predator remained focused on its target. It got one paw on the deer's hindquarters, and the blow knocked the doe sideways. Before it could get its balance righted, the tiger was on it, its fanged mouth closing around the deer's slender neck.

The rest of the herd disappeared over the far rim of the basin, one of the stags lingering a moment. Feronantus stared at it, framed against the sky with its proud spread of knobbed antlers, and then it was gone.

In the basin, the tiger held its prey tightly in its jaws, the body of the deer slack. It was staring in their direction, and before

Feronantus could stop him, Istvan stood up and lifted his arm in salute.

"What are you doing?" he hissed at the Hungarian.

"We could have spooked the herd," Istvan said. "But we didn't, and now he has food." He looked down at Feronantus, a feral light in his eyes. "Perhaps he will not stalk us again because we have not interfered with his hunt."

"What do you mean?" Feronantus asked somewhat distractedly as he got to his feet. His knees complained, and his lower back was stiff.

"He's been tracking us for the last few days," Istvan said. "If it hadn't been for these deer, he might have attacked us tonight."

◆ ◆ ◆

It was a cold and clear night, and since they hadn't seen any sign of other riders for more than two weeks, Feronantus allowed a fire to be built. He wasn't entirely convinced the tiger would keep its distance, and that fear jabbed at his spirit like it had found a chink in his mental armor. He was not one to let fear rule his mind, and long ago he had learned the difference between terror and caution. Every man who goes into battle is aware of his mortality, but a great deal of the training within the order was meant to mitigate that fear.

In his mind's eye, he could see the muscles moving beneath the tight skin of the tiger as it ran and the strength in the animal's paws as it had slapped the deer to the ground. The tiger was more frightening than any berserker, and not merely because it ran on four legs and had sharp teeth. The berserker was merely a man, and Feronantus knew how to defeat men. He did not know how to defeat a tiger.

And through that tiny crack in his armor came other thoughts, like invaders through a breach in a castle wall. Did he know what was going to happen when he brought the Spirit Banner back to Petraathen? What were the *Electi* going to say when he showed up at the castle gates? Not only had he ordered and participated in the death of the *Khagan*, but he had taken a trophy as well, as if he were a mongrel mercenary. The elders of Petraathen had been disgusted with him for many years; the Spirit Banner would merely be the final straw. His fate would not be exile. Not this time.

But if he were right about what he saw in the *Vor*, then it had to be done. The order had to be set on the right path if it were going to be saved. The death of the *Khagan* had set in motion a sequence of events that had to be played out; it was his fate to see that future and know his part in it.

But as he had watched the tiger stalk the herd, his confidence had eroded, and when the tiger had swiped at the deer with his enormous paw, he had watched the deer be knocked from its path and wondered if he would survive such a blow. If God or the Devil or the Virgin—unhappy with his interpretation of her messages—reached down and swatted him, would he have enough strength to continue on? Was he marching doggedly onward, clinging to the hope that his instincts were right? Was that why he had left the others behind? They would quiz him endlessly about what he was thinking—Cnán, especially. The others might follow him without question, but Raphael was beginning to show signs of doubt.

Istvan snorted in his sleep and rolled onto his back. His mouth lolled open and a nasally snore drifted out. For not the first time, Feronantus marveled at the Hungarian's indifference to the world around him. Unlike the others, Istvan would not question his authority; he could, however, also wake up one morning and mistake Feronantus for a Mongol and take a knife to the old knight. Such was the unnerving simplicity of the Hungarian's mind.

How many more like him? Feronantus wondered. In the last forty years, how many had he trained to be just like Istvan? They came to Týrshammar, pink-faced and eager to devote themselves to a life serving the Virgin. They would be taught how to hold a shield, how to throw a spear, and how to fight with a sword. They would be taught to read and write so that they could understand the virtues of the order: honor, humility, selflessness, courage. They would be girded for battle and blooded on the field so that they understood the power and responsibility that came with the shield and sword. They would become men under his tutelage. He gave them purpose; in return, they swore to follow him—and others like him—for the rest of their lives.

To what end?

A breath of wind stirred the horsehair strands of the Spirit Banner, and an overwhelming longing to see Maria again swept over him. It was such an unexpected surge of emotion that his vision blurred with tears before he could stop them, and when he closed his eyes to keep them in, a few escaped. They rolled down his face and disappeared into his beard.

She would have comforted him. She would have wrapped her arms around his shoulders and pulled him close to her breast. He would have laid his head against her and been calmed by the steady pulse of her heart. She would have held him tight, and his breathing would match hers—slow and careful—and if he remained still long enough, he would hear the song that echoed in her heart. When she was happy, it would rise in her throat and slip out, a wordless tune that she was unaware she was singing, but the sound of it always made Feronantus feel as if he was doing the right thing. For all the confusion and chaos of those years in the English woods, the constant was Maria and her song.

He heard something that might have been a phrase of song, a whispered couplet, or merely the tinkling laughter of a young woman. He stood, opening his eyes and staring into the darkness beyond the meager flames of the fire.

Istvan lay as if dead: arms sprawled, eyes half-open, mouth gaping, a line of spittle creeping across his cheek.

The wind shifted, and the horsehair strands brushed against the shaft of the Spirit Banner.

Feronantus, his eyes not straying from the darkness around the camp, knelt and drew his sword from its sheath. The steel whispered against the mouth of the scabbard, and he heard a sighing echo from beyond the camp.

One of the two horses tossed its head and rumbled in its chest. Its hooves clattered against the ground as it shifted, but there was no nervousness in the sound. If there was something out there—watching them, *stalking* them—the horses couldn't smell it.

Feronantus grabbed the crooked stick he had been using to tend to the fire and shoved the tip into the coal until the wood caught fire. It was a pitiful torch, but the flickering light was as good as a tallow candle, which was better than nothing at all. Armed with sword and fire, Feronantus stepped away from the camp.

He walked deosil about the camp, the opposite direction of the normal night watch circuit, so that he would not be trying to look past the light of the torch held in his left hand. His night vision was poor, and the moon was but a thin fingernail low in the sky. He strained to hear any noises in the night as much as he tried to see anything moving beyond their camp, but as he finished his circuit, he had to admit he and Istvan were alone on the steppe.

The horses raised their heads and stared at him with stoic indifference. "It's nothing," he grumbled and he thrust the burning tip of the stick into the ground, extinguishing the flickering light. "Just the heartache of an old man," he sighed. He raised his head and stared at the sea of stars swimming across the vault of the sky.

Istvan coughed, and the sound was distorted as if there were something covering the Hungarian's mouth. Feronantus pulled his gaze away from the night sky and peered back at the camp.

What he saw made his heart leap in his chest. "Aaieah!" he shouted, darting toward the fire with his sword raised.

A shape was crouching over Istvan, poking at the Hungarian's face with bony hands. As Feronantus charged, the shape slithered sideways, moving like serpentine smoke, and then it leaped through the fire. Feronantus saw a flash of orange and black stripes, and thought he heard the rumbling growl of the tiger as the shape vanished.

The noise was coming from Istvan. Bent nearly double, the Hungarian was coughing from deep in his chest as if he were trying to dislodge something caught in his throat. Istvan hacked and spat; his throat clear, he started to swear—cursing the Mongols, his family, the sky, and even Feronantus in a voice haggard with exhaustion and pain.

Feronantus let him rant; it showed he was going to live and the noise was enough to drive off any predator still slinking about in the shadows. He picked up his scabbard and sheathed his sword, and he had just about decided all of the past few minutes were nothing more than nocturnal phantoms sent to invade their lonely minds when he spotted the marks in the dirt between Istvan and the fire.

There was a single set of naked footprints, as small as if made by a child or a tiny woman, and they did not match. One was a crooked foot, warped by age, and the other was less distinct but still a footprint nonetheless.

CHAPTER 13:

THE FIRES OF REVENGE

For the sake of his own inflated pride, Hermann of Dorpat had made Kristaps wait three days before deigning to agree to Cardinal Fieschi's request that leadership of the Teutonic Knights be turned over to Kristaps. During those three days, Kristaps learned a great deal about the prevailing attitude among the men. They were restless and the cold northern nights made their inactivity much harder to tolerate; they were ready for decisive leadership, and he knew he was the one who could give it to them. He was not one of those men who believed leadership was based in love or admiration. That quaint ideology was the sort of nonsense nurtured by princelings who were more accustomed to holding their mothers' tits than a sword. A conqueror took what he wanted and demanded fealty; those who failed to kneel were punished. It was as simple as that.

He knew what had to be done, and as soon as the messengers from the northern ports returned with a response from the letter he had sent, he gave the order. *The city is yours*, he told the men. *Take what you will, and take it with force. If a man raises his hand against you, cut it off. If a woman dares to resist you, take her children from her. And from each house, regardless of what you take, bring something of value to the main square where we will burn it. The fire we will set in Pskov will be seen in Novgorod.*

His men had embraced these orders, as he had known they would. They were here to conquer these northern pagans, after all. Hermann's approach had lacked the necessary ruthlessness. If they were going to lure Alexander back to Pskov, the threat had to be real.

His predecessors—Volquin and, to a lesser extent, Dietrich von Grüningen—had failed to create the proper environment of fear. Volquin had been obsessed with claiming territory in the name of the order, and he hadn't subjugated the pagan tribes. He had left enough of them alive that they had banded together—setting aside their old enmities to face a common enemy—and they had fought back. They had ambushed the Livonian Order at the river crossing at Schaulen, and the battle had been a disaster—the order had been broken and Volquin had been slain unceremoniously while struggling in the mud. The next *Heermeister*—Dietrich—had been so ineffective at Hünern that none of his men had bothered to wonder what had happened to the *Heermeister* when Onghwe Khan's Circus was scattered.

The Mongols, on the other hand, were perfectly ruthless. Kristaps had seen firsthand how they dealt with those they conquered, and he had found much in Batu Khan's approach to his liking.

The first bonfire was lit, and it smoldered at first, the flames struggling to find purchase in the damp wood. A thick plume of white smoke rose into the night sky as the second and third fires were lit. The night was clear and there was no moon in the sky. From a distance, the smoke would look like nothing more than a spreading fog.

Kristaps waited, warm in his heavy cloak and beaverskin gloves.

The scouts had also brought word that the Veche—the ruling council of Novgorod—had sent for Nevsky; the boyars had called their exiled prince home. Kristaps knew Nevsky would go to Novgorod—the prince needed the militia and any funds he could pry loose from the Veche—and while the prince was dallying in the city, the Teutonic army would move north.

A fierce grin spread across Kristaps's face. *I'm doing you a favor,* he thought. *As soon as word reaches Novgorod of what I have done here, you will have your excuse to leave all the petulant whining and in-fighting among the Veche behind.*

The first fire was a roaring pillar of flame now, tongues of red and orange licking the sky.

In the square, the white shapes of his knights were moving more erratically. Shouts and screams intermingled with the crackling roar of the fire, and as Kristaps watched, a trio of knights hurled a squirming shape into one of the fires. After that, movement became much more chaotic.

The people of Pskov need you, Kristaps thought, looking away from the panic in the square. He turned his gaze to the east, toward Novgorod. *Save them, Nevsky. Come to their rescue.*

✦ ✦ ✦

Hermann of Dorpat was waiting for him in Trinity Cathedral, drinking from a bottle of mead. Kristaps waved off the offer when Hermann tipped the mouth of the bottle at him. Wine was rare in the northern lands as grapes did not fare well in the hard ground and with the short summers, and the locals made do with a too-sweet concoction made from honey and dried berries. Judging by the tilt of the bottle when he raised it to his lips, Hermann had drunk most of the bottle already.

"Are they here?" Kristaps asked.

"Aye," Hermann said, lowering the bottle and wiping his lips. Light from the bonfires leaked in through the narrow windows of the church, elongating the shadows. Hermann's eyes kept twitching in his head as if he were seeing movement among the twisted effigies of the strange pagan saints.

"A fitting place to meet," Kristaps said as he looked about at the abandoned place of worship with its dust-covered floor and intermittent and strange shadows. Early on, people had taken refuge here, but after Hermann had put the priests and acolytes to the sword—one of the few acts he had done after taking Pskov that Kristaps approved of—few dared to openly worship. Only the truly wretched among the wretched sheltered here, though none were present on this evening.

"They're heretics," Hermann said. "This was the only place they would all gather." He drank from the bottle again. "There's no shame in being here, in accommodating the desires of men you want to make use of."

The Prince-Bishop wouldn't meet his gaze, and Kristaps wondered if the drunkenness was a sham. Hermann's face, while affable, was a mask, and had been since the Prince-Bishop had agreed to Kristaps's plan. It was possible that treason lurked behind those eyes, but it was not likely in the short term. Hermann was a man of station and duty. He would not risk everything on a game of pride, especially not when Kristaps still possessed the backing of powerful friends in Rome.

"There is no shame in doing what must be done to win the war," Kristaps said. "Show them to me. I would see faces and hear names."

Hermann indicated that Kristaps should step into the deeper shadows of the church, and as Kristaps strode down the empty nave, the Prince-Bishop whistled lightly. Hearing the Prince-Bishop's signal, several lanterns were uncovered and the altar of the church was bathed in light. A half-dozen of Hermann's personal guards stood near the front of the altar, and beyond them were a handful of mismatched men.

They were a mixture of sizes and shapes, a motley group that stood off from one another, as if each man were trying to keep all of Hermann's guards and the others in view. One had a large broken nose and numerous scars across his forehead; on his hip, he wore a curved sword similar to the ones that Kristaps had seen the Mongols carry, though this one had no noticeable guard. "That is Gorya," Hermann said. "He has served princes and warlords, but serves first those who have the most gold."

The second man had shaved his head, making it difficult to discern his true age. Living in the harsh wilderness aged a man quicker than a life within the walls of the cities, and Kristaps put him at somewhere between thirty and fifty—old by any martial standards. He had a pair of hatchets shoved through his belt, and his eyes were frosty and gray, like the ice on the river. "Onikii," Hermann said.

There were three more: Taras, who had a long mustache and carried a heavy axe; Vasya, a narrow-faced man cloaked in furs that Kristaps suspected he had caught, skinned, and sewn himself; and Makar, a slightly rotund man who appeared to carry no weapons unless they were well hidden beneath his plain robe.

"A priest?" Kristaps asked, nodding at the last. "Does he mean to convert the prince to Christianity?"

"He uses more subtle methods," Hermann said, and Makar inclined his head at the Prince-Bishop's words.

Poison, Kristaps realized. A coward's weapon, but what did he care how the prince was slain?

Men of Rus willing to fight their own kindred for coin. Men who know that who rules may change, and wisest is he who follows when the true masters appear. Volquin would not have failed if he had had men like this.

"Subtlety?" a voice rose from the niche beyond the altar. "I thought you wanted a man *killed*. Not an accident." The speaker wandered into the circle of lantern light, and Kristaps noted how the others shifted nervously at the sudden appearance of the newcomer.

"I am Iakov," the sixth man said, offering Kristaps a slight bow. Whereas the other men were weathered and battered, their faces marred by scars and age, Iakov looked like a young lad, not more than a year or two past his first beard. His face, finely featured as that of a woman of court, was framed by long brown hair that was carefully tended to, and his hands, likewise as delicate as a highborn maiden's, were small. His mouth was drawn into a perpetual smirk across his face, and he regarded each of the others as if he were examining hogs at a market. For all his apparent innocence, the lad's eyes betrayed him. They moved like a predator's, watching and waiting for the right moment to pounce.

"My sincere apologies for not being immediately present at this..." Iakov waved his hand dismissively at the others. "I was at prayer."

"You're too young," Kristaps said dismissively.

"For what?" the youth replied. "Too young to die? To kill?" He glanced at the one named Onikii and batted his eyelashes. "To love?"

In spite of himself, Kristaps was intrigued by the way the boy openly antagonized the other men, who were clearly accomplished killers.

"Where is this dandy from?" he asked Hermann, switching to German.

"Does it matter?" Iakov replied before the Prince-Bishop did. The lad spoke German easily with a noticeable accent. *Well traveled, then, or well educated*, Kristaps thought.

"You're not like the rest," he said to Iakov, still speaking in German. Iakov bowed at the compliment, and Kristaps noted that the lad kept his head up, his eye on the others.

"Have you killed anyone other than a rich relative or a drunk merchant?" Kristaps asked.

Iakov laughed. "Which was your first?" he asked in return. "The uncle or the merchant? I've done both."

"Skilled fighters," Kristaps snapped, ignoring Iakov's question. "Not pompous fools and leather-skinned old men. If those are all you have to your name, I am not impressed."

"Knights," Iakov replied. "Christians, Jews, Muslims. I have killed warriors in their prime, children at their mother's breasts, and shy young maidens. I have killed *boyars* on their horses and witches in their hovels. All before I was sixteen."

"Why should I believe you?" Kristaps answered.

"Because," Iakov answered, "you are afraid of me."

Beside him, Hermann of Dorpat emitted a small, quiet laugh.

"Don't mistake wariness for fear," Kristaps said.

"I never do."

Kristaps eyed the boy, considering just how much of what Iakov had said could be true and how much of it was pure bravado. He had said similar things in his youth—the brash braying of an untested warrior—though he had since learned that the measure of a man was his actions and not his words. While such bluster was not to his liking, that didn't mean such talk was empty posturing. *If half of what he says is true, he may be more than enough for what I need*, he thought.

"You men know each other," he said, switching back to the tongue they all knew. "Have you fought together before?"

They looked at one another with some muttering and nodding of heads. Only Makar abstained from admitting to knowing the others.

"And would you look to one of you as leader?" Kristaps asked, mainly to see their reaction. They shuffled about, trying not to draw attention to the boy, but Iakov stood still and all the posturing of the others accomplished was to clear a space around the boy—making it all too clear what they wouldn't say. *So be it*, Kristaps thought. *That cocksure arrogance is not without a basis, then.*

"They follow who is best at what they all do," Iakov sighed, lifting his shoulders in a girlish shrug.

"Did the Prince-Bishop tell you what it is that I require you to do?"

"He said that you wanted an important man killed." It was Onikii who spoke, his brutish, scarred face watching Kristaps in the same way a hungry dog watches a bigger beast it hasn't yet sized up. "There aren't many such men in this land."

But you don't know for certain, Kristaps thought, *and you want to hear me say it.*

"We will leave this city soon," Kristaps replied. "When we do, a savior will come. Someone whom these people will gladly welcome. That is the man I want slain."

He could have given Onikii and the others the satisfaction of naming their target, but he wanted to see their reaction. He wanted to know if they could muster the nerve to name the target themselves. If they could speak out against the man whom their fellow Ruthenians called a *hero.* It was one thing to ask a man to commit treason, even if you offered to pay him; but if he volunteered to do it, then the odds that he actually *would* were much better.

"Nevsky goes nowhere without five hundred retainers," Gorya said finally. "All of them are skilled. None of them will be weak."

"You will not lack for pay," Kristaps said, tacitly acknowledging the target. "The wealth of Pskov can be *redistributed* at my discretion."

"He who kills Nevsky will be hated in this land," Onikii said.

"All the more reason to use the money to go somewhere else." Kristaps nodded at Iakov. "The boy may have some suggestions."

There were other questions, though most of them were empty hypotheses or baseless objections. Kristaps had anticipated a certain amount of this pointless speculation. Hired knives lived by discretion; rarely were they known for being bold or being hungry for glory. But the fact that they asked all of these questions meant they were already thinking about and planning how to accomplish the task.

"Enough of this prattle," Iakov said at last, silencing the others. "I have never killed a prince, much less a son of Iaroslav, and for that reason alone, I will do this." He smiled at Kristaps, an eager glint in his eye. "They will help me, of course," he added, nodding toward the other killers.

"The people of Pskov will not let us escape to collect our pay if we do this," Onikii said. "These men want us to rid them of an enemy whom they are afraid of, and for what? None of us can do this thing and live."

The young man looked past Onikii's head to the shadowed effigies of the cathedral. "They say that he is wise and that he is brave," Iakov said, seeming to ignore Onikii's concerns. "They say that he has a ghost for an advisor and that *Valkyries* ride in his vanguard. He defeated Birger Jarl and ingratiated himself to a great Mongol Khan. I hear he is very beautiful." Iakov sighed longingly, and his gaze came back to Onikii. "I never took you for a complete coward," Iakov said mildly.

Hermann's guards stirred, sensing the sudden tension in the men standing on the altar. Hermann made as if to speak, but Kristaps laid a hand on his arm. "No," he said quietly. *I want to see what comes next.*

"You are a fool, Iakov," Onikii retorted. "Killing for coin is one thing, but throwing your life away for a foreign master who will abandon you is suicide."

"How can killing a prince and stamping our names on history forever be *suicide?*" Iakov asked.

Onikii was shifting his weight from foot to foot, his hands twitching toward the hatchets in his belt. Iakov, on the other hand, appeared utterly unaware of the bigger man's tension. The boyish young man with his effeminate carriage might as well have been standing in the back of the halls in some boyar's court, absently cleaning his nails, for all he seemed unnerved by the larger man before him.

"It can't be done," Onikii snarled. "You might as well charge the prince's host with your weapons drawn."

"You could," Iakov replied, "and that *would* be suicide."

Gorya laughed, and the sound was a signal for Onikii. He moved quickly, snatching one of his hatchets from his belt and lunging at the boy in a fluid motion that impressed Kristaps. Iakov hardly seemed to move: a pivot of his body was all that was needed to throw the measure of his opponent off enough so that Onikii's hatchet missed his nose by less than an inch.

"Slow," Iakov said, stepping to the side. A long knife flashed in his hand, drawn from some hidden sheath that Kristaps had not noticed. Onikii's left hand darted out to grasp Iakov's outstretched knife hand, but the boy's slender arm darted back as quickly as it had come. Onikii slashed upward with his hatchet, trying to catch Iakov, who only laughed as the blade missed again. The knife blade flickered in the lantern light, and Onikii's blood splashed across the floor.

Onikii staggered back with a grunt of pain, and Kristaps watched as Iakov held back from pursuing the wounded man. *The others may do this for coin,* Kristaps thought, *but not Iakov.* There was a perverse light in the boy's eyes, an eager delight at what was going to happen next.

Onikii drew his other hatchet and came at Iakov again, his weapons a blur of motion. Iakov nimbly evaded the charge, spinning around Onikii like he was dancing at a royal wedding, and Onikii coughed and stumbled. His hatchets slowed and when he turned, his legs moving slowly, Kristaps saw a flood of blood running down the side of his neck.

Iakov waved at Onikii, encouraging him to attack again. Onikii raised his hatchets, though the motion seemed to be very difficult, as if the weapons were made of stone instead of steel and wood. He took a step, and noticed the blood coursing down the front of his tunic. He stared at it, confusion written across his face, and when he raised his head again, Iakov darted forward, the long knife driving straight into his right eye socket.

"There will be no more discussion," the young Ruthenian said as he jerked his blade free and Onikii collapsed, quivering like a maimed dog. Iakov looked as though he'd just carved up an apple for breakfast. "You will have your dead prince."

He might actually do it, Kristaps thought, realizing he knew what Iakov wanted more than anything in the world.

◆ ◆ ◆

"Onikii's argument is one not so readily dismissed," the Prince-Bishop said as he steadied himself against the frame of the church's threshold. "Even if the man himself is…"

Kristaps paused on the porch of the church. The Prince-Bishop's face glistened in the light from the bonfires in the square; behind him, the church was dark. The body of Onikii would be found by the squatters who dared sneak back into the church, a nameless victim of the occupation of Pskov.

"As long as the prince lives, this war cannot be won," Kristaps said. "I would meet him on the field and kill him in battle, but why should I? Why should I waste all of our men when his death can be accomplished by stealth and greed?"

"The people of Pskov will turn against them," Hermann said.

"Of course they will," Kristaps said, "which is why I expect them to do it quickly before another one of them loses his nerve. Besides, if one of their own people slays the prince—and mark my words, he is not without enemies among the Novgorodians—who will say it was at our behest? Let them squabble among themselves while we take one city after another."

"Prince Alexander has brothers," Hermann said, staring dully at the bottle in his hands.

"Brothers who will need to take time to gather the allies he already has, brothers who do not have the victories to their names that he possesses. Kill the man, and his replacement will not be able to rally what remains against us. Not in time," Kristaps said.

"And if you're wrong?" Hermann asked, his voice almost lost in the night.

"Then they'll hate us more than they already do," Kristaps said. "And they'll discover how little they truly know about hate."

"What devil is it that hounds you?" Hermann asked.

"I only seek to do what is required of me," Kristaps answered.

"That is all any man seeks to do," Hermann said. He pushed away from the wall and stood close to Kristaps. There was a glint in the Prince-Bishop's eye, and Kristaps couldn't decide if it was the mead granting Hermann additional bravery or if the Prince-Bishop actually thought there was something that could be used against him. "Who wronged you?" the Prince-Bishop asked.

Kristaps said nothing. The scars on his forearms itched, burning with the memories he longed to purge from his mind. The wounds on his arms had long healed since the day beneath the earth, when desperation in the crucible had made him let go of the heavy shield whilst pounding water dragged him forward, both hands seizing the outstretched sword with its burning hot pommel. When he'd been pulled from the water, mutilated by the marks of his shame, his master had refused to meet his gaze. His brothers—*nay, they would never be his brothers, the cowards!*—had abandoned him.

And then Volquin had failed him. And Dietrich too. None of them had been strong enough. The masters of his order, the Templars, the Hospitallers, the Shield-Brethren. They all stood in a long line behind him, a line that ran through his memory like the flight of an arrow. All the way back to the mountain fortress of Petraathen and that day in the cave beneath the temple of Athena.

"I was deceived by our enemies, once," Kristaps said finally. "Deceived, wronged, and mutilated. I have not forgotten."

Hermann nodded slowly as if he understood, though Kristaps was sure the Prince-Bishop had no idea of what was being discussed. "You care naught about Rus, then?"

"Not in the slightest," Kristaps said. "It is nothing more than a wretched wasteland. Too cold to be of use to anyone."

"Is it merely duty then that keeps you here?"

"Duty and honor," Kristaps replied. "What else does a man have?"

"Indeed," Hermann said. The Prince-Bishop stepped back, his head swiveling toward the darkened church, and Kristaps suspected the Prince-Bishop was thinking of Iakov, the strange youth they had encountered in the desolate church. "What else?"

CHAPTER 14:

———

THE RETURN OF THE PRINCE

This was not the first time that Nika had seen Novgorod, but nevertheless the sight of the city took her breath away. Kiev had been the most beautiful city in the north, but once it had been decimated by the Mongol horde, that title had fallen to Novgorod, and Novgorod strove to uphold that honor. The afternoon sun sparkled on the white snow surrounding the mottled walls of the city, making the stones appear blacker than they were. All along the battlements, she could see people waving. They knew the *Kynaz* was returning, and they were eager to see their prince. The hero of Neva, the noble prince who would deliver them in this, their darkest hour. She found such notions quaint—dangerous, even, for those who hoped to survive in the wasted lands of the north—but she found the ease with which men fell prey to the hubris of being called a hero even more disturbing.

But Alexander had never claimed that mantle, had he? she mused as the prince's lengthy entourage of mounted knights moved toward the open gates. Most of her sisters were not part of the main procession; they remained in the vanguard, watching the wagons and supplies, along with the bulk of the men-at-arms. Alexander wanted to make a strong impression when he entered the city, but he did not want to alarm the Veche.

She had had opportunity to observe the *Kynaz* since she and the Shield-Maidens had joined his army, and while he seemed little more than a boy, he made decisions that displayed a wisdom far advanced for his years. He was eminently practical, rarely swayed by glorious ideals that were of little use in the field, and he appeared genuinely to care about the people whom he was sworn to protect. It was not difficult to see why men flocked to his banner.

Illarion rode with the prince's party, humble in appearance beside Novgorod's young war-leader. The bruise on his forehead was still visible, even though he tried to hide it by letting his white hair hang down across his face. Nika had heard several versions of the bout with the Northman Ozur, and she had congratulated Illarion on humanizing himself to the men, but Illarion had dismissed her praise with a wave of his hand. *That is not why I fought,* he had said. His reasons didn't matter, for the result was that the men now spoke of him less as a ghost and more as a mere man. She was considering challenging some of the Northmen herself with the hope that such bouts might have a similar effect for her sisters.

They were close enough to the walls now that she could make out individual faces among the crowd atop the walls. Fathers held their children on their shoulders, and the tiny faces were alight with joy at the sight of the prince's knights. Looking at the numerous fur-lined cloaks and hats, Nika was reminded that Novgorod's wealth stemmed from the fur trade. Crops grew poorly this far north, but there was an abundance of wild animals in the forests. Fur flowed south and west; in return, silver, gold, silk, and steel flowed into the city. If the Teutonic Knights captured Novgorod, they would have access to a wealthy trade route, and it would be very difficult to dislodge them from the north.

The Veche had finally come to their senses, realizing that paying tribute to the Teutonic Knights would be much more onerous than any demands put to them by Alexander. *But that didn't mean they were going to welcome him back with open arms,* she thought as she caught sight of the line of mounted men who blocked the way into the city proper.

Alexander held up his arm, signaling for his retinue to halt, and with the practiced ease of a life-long rider, he slid from the saddle of his horse. His cloak floated behind him as he strode toward the line of men. The people atop the wall were cheering and shouting, and he raised his face toward them and waved. Playing to the crowd.

He was *Nevsky* to them. The hero of the battle at Neva. He was, Nika realized, even more of an outsider than she and her sisters. The stories that surrounded him would terrify his enemies and impress those he hoped to make his allies, but the time would always come when words and stories were not enough and the would-be friend or foe would demand proof of the prince's qualities in exchange for respect. She had seen the devotion he had earned from his men, but it was not a hard thing to earn the love of those who fought in your service. Nor was it difficult to earn the love of the common folk.

The Veche were neither friend nor foe, and it was critical to sway them. *In the end, when lords and princes fight, it is always the people who suffer,* she thought bitterly.

The Mongols had circled Kiev for weeks, destroying the outlying villages and driving the displaced people toward Kiev. By the time they surrounded the city, it was overflowing with refugees and horror stories about what the Mongols were going to do once they breached the walls. The boyars of Kiev had been unable to come to a consensus as to their response to Batu Khan's demands for their surrender. They were still squabbling among themselves when the Golden Gate fell and the horsemen of the steppes poured into the city.

The Shield-Maidens had weathered the death of Kiev by holing up in their fortress cathedral and the Lavra beneath. They had saved those they could, but in the end, what Nika remembered was the screaming outside the doors, the sounds of chaos and destruction mingled with the horrific stench of the city burning. She and the others had prayed for hours, beseeching Saint Ilya, the Virgin, and any other god or saint who might answer for forgiveness and for strength, whilst outside the walls of the citadel Kiev was reduced to rubble.

For many months after, Nika and her sisters had fought back against those Mongols who remained behind, and after them, those who stumbled upon the devastated city and thought there might still be treasure to be found within the ruins. Then the Livonians came, and at first they had thought the knights of the west had finally come to their aid, but the Livonians were of a different mind. It was only when the Shield-Brethren arrived that she thought her prayers had been answered, but then a quarter of the remaining Shield-Maidens had left Kiev with them and not returned, leaving her to wonder if those who stayed behind had been truly abandoned.

The question had remained unanswered until the night she saw Baba Yaga. Until she had been given an unmistakable sign.

The line of mounted men parted and a contingent passed through—men in richly furred cloaks and peaked caps. One wore the distinctive robes of the Eastern Church—*the Bishop of Novgorod?* she wondered. The men reached Alexander and arms were clasped and words were spoken. From where she sat, Nika couldn't read much in the expression of the boyars who had come to greet Alexander.

She fidgeted in her saddle. Nika was a trained warrior, and capable as they came, but inaction, especially in formal settings, was uncomfortable. She let her gaze sweep across Alexander's retinue and then up to the walls, examining faces and postures. She knew she was looking for a threat, a reason to spur her horse into action, and while she doubted she'd spot anything, it was the most movement she could do without drawing unnecessary attention to herself.

After the initial greetings were exchanged, Alexander dropped to one knee and the bishop laid a cloak about his shoulders. He made signs over the kneeling prince and, judging by the start-stop motion of his mouth, Alexander and the Veche were now exchanging promises. They would most likely be presented as oaths of fealty—most likely sworn in Latin—but Nika knew such oaths were only as good as the intent of the men who swore them. She could imagine what Alexander was thinking as he repeated the bishop's words: *Yea, I will protect this city and its leaders, though they hate that they have to seek my aid and are secretly plotting to not pay my men.*

And the boyars, in response: *We promise to be loyal to your dictates until it is inconvenient. We offer our sons to you, though we wish you would simply go off and defeat these invaders without them.*

The bishop raised his face toward the sky and blessed these oaths: *Lord God bless this awkward lie of an allegiance of convenience.*

As she watched the *Kynaz* and Veche swear oaths to each other, it occurred to her that for all the double words and broken promises in the world, the true test of power was the ability to walk through these circles with their corruptions, their latticework of crisscrossing motivations, and still come out on the other side with the good of your people accomplished. A man might fall or fail in uncounted ways, but if he came through with that at least to say for himself, he would have done well as far as she was concerned.

The boyars and Alexander embraced, their spoken oaths making them the best of friends, and Nika read more stiffness in the boyars than in Alexander. He really was quite skilled in his ability to hide his true emotions, she marveled. A cheer rose up from the people atop the wall, and it was matched by shouts of joy from Alexander's retinue. The boyars waved at the crowds as they walked back to the city, as if the people were actually cheering for them. Alexander stood still, looking up at the people on the walls. Nika wasn't sure what he was waiting for. *They're not going to stop as long as he stands there,* she thought.

Finally, he raised his right arm in salute to the people of Novgorod, and then he lowered it in a gesture for his knights to proceed into the city. The retinue started slowly, parting as it passed around him. The men at the gates withdrew and the army of the *Kynaz* entered Novgorod.

Nika saw Illarion hanging back, and she nudged her horse through the men until she was beside him. Together, they waited until all of the men had passed and only Alexander remained. He saluted the people on the wall once more and then he walked—unhurriedly, his new cloak billowing behind him—into Novgorod.

CHAPTER 15:

UNEXPECTED VISITORS

The return of the scouts created a stir in the camp, and everyone gathered around the fire pit as Yasper and Bruno helped Haakon down from Evren's horse. The front of Haakon's leather doublet was stained black with blood, and the broken shaft of an arrow protruded from high on his back. His movements were sluggish and his head lolled from side to side as Yasper and Bruno tried to settle him on the ground.

Raphael pushed his way through the others and knelt by Haakon. "Keep him upright," Raphael said as he inspected Haakon's eyes and mouth. He slapped Haakon lightly as the Northman's head fell back, and Haakon jerked up with the blow, his eyes focusing on Raphael, but he still didn't say anything.

"No blood in his throat," Raphael said as he tugged back Haakon's doublet and gingerly inspected the arrow shaft. He probed with his fingers, eliciting a hiss of pain from Haakon. "I don't dare push it through. We'll have to cut it out." He looked around, spotting the pair of Seljuks. "Mongols?" he asked.

The word didn't need translation, and Evren nodded. He rattled off several sentences in the Persian dialect he and Ahmet used, and Raphael glanced at Cnán, who was trying to keep up with the excited Seljuk. "Something about a scouting party," she said. She frowned as she continued to listen. "And another group, I think. I'm not quite sure."

"Haidar," Gawain said as he joined the group at the fire pit. Gawain was not as tall as Rædwulf, who had journeyed east with the Shield-Brethren company, but his broad shoulders and big hands reminded Cnán of the fallen bowman. Gawain's hair was short but shaggy, and his beard was not so wild and untamed that his teeth weren't readily apparent when he smiled.

He was not smiling now.

Raphael sat back on his haunches and squinted up at Gawain. "Is he the one who you have been waiting for?"

Gawain traded a glance with Bruno. "Aye," he said.

Raphael sighed and got to his feet. "Let me take care of this first, and then we'll talk."

✦ ✦ ✦

While Raphael removed the arrow from Haakon and dressed the wound, the rest of the company began to assemble their gear. After making sure Haakon was comfortable in one of the tents, Raphael returned to the fire pit where Gawain, Yasper, Cnán, Vera, and Lian were waiting.

"What happened?" he asked, looking at Cnán as if he expected her to summarize what the others had been discussing while he had been working.

"Haakon stumbled upon a Mongol scouting party," she said. "He tried to run, but not before ..."—she gestured at her shoulder, indicating the spot where Haakon had been struck by the arrow— "and he tried to warn the Seljuks. As the three of them were heading back, trying to lose the Mongols, they stumbled upon another group of riders. Luckily, the Mongols thought these new riders were friends of our scouts and so they broke off. That's when they lost one of the horses."

"Do they think the other riders are coming here?"

"Undoubtedly," Gawain said. "Especially if they recognized Ahmet or Evren."

"Who are they?" Raphael asked.

"Men from Arabia," Gawain said, "Led by a man named Haidar."

"What is your relationship with this man?"

Gawain glanced at the others. "He and I were offered gold by the same man, to guard his caravan."

"And?" Cnán prompted when Gawain didn't say anything more.

"And there was a disagreement," Gawain said. "Partially about money. Partially about other things."

"Do they intend to take the horses, or are they seeking sterner justice?" Raphael asked.

Gawain shrugged. "You'll have to ask Haidar."

"I don't see any reason why I should converse with the man," Raphael said. He knelt and picked up Yasper's fire-poking stick. "How many?" he asked and when Gawain told him the number, he scratched twelve short lines in the dirt, and then drew a solid line beneath them. "This isn't our fight."

Gawain chewed on the inside of his cheek for a moment, and Cnán could guess what he was thinking. He and his companions had saved them from the storm. Was there a debt there that could be called? Would the Shield-Brethren stand by that debt?

She glanced at Raphael and was pleased to not be able to read any indication one way or another in his face. All traces of indecisiveness were gone. All she saw was the set line of his mouth and his hard stare—the face of a man who knew he might have to do violence and the utter calm with which he would attend to that task.

"They'll be here soon," Yasper pointed out.

"Aye," Raphael said. "That they will be. You may have saved the lives of my companions and me when you rescued us from the snows. I won't contest that claim, but any debt you think is inherently owed without our acknowledgement is akin to servitude and the Shield-Brethren do not abide by such claims, nor do we abide by those terms being applied to those under our protection."

"There was a girl—" Gawain started. "A woman," he corrected after noting Lian's glare. "The daughter of the caravan master. She knew horses, and he had her along to assist with the herd he was bringing to Samarkand. Haidar—the man in charge of the mercenaries hired to protect the herd—desired her. I disagreed with him. One night, he and a number of men he thought he could trust decided they weren't getting paid enough. One of those men was Bruno, who didn't find Haidar's solution very palatable. He warned me and we tried to protect the caravan master and his daughter, but..." He shook his head. "In the confusion, the herd was scattered, and over the next few days, we found each other, along with a number of the horses."

"Why didn't you keep riding?" Yasper asked. "After you got away and found some of the horses."

Gawain looked at him morosely, but it was Lian who spelled it out for the Dutchman. "Because of the daughter," she said. "She might still be alive."

"Haidar outnumbers you," Raphael said. "And you thought to even those odds by joining our two companies together."

"Aye," Gawain said. "That thought had occurred to me."

"And this is how you ask for our assistance?" Cnán snorted. "When Haidar is galloping for our camp?"

Raphael waved her to silence. "If we aid you in this matter, we do so because we deem your side to be the aggrieved party. And if we do, we will require compensation."

"What do you want?" Gawain asked.

"Horses," Raphael said.

Gawain showed his teeth when he smiled. "Any horse without a rider at the end of the fight is yours," he said.

✦ ✦ ✦

Raphael, dressed in his full panoply and astride one of the smaller horses from the paddock, rode beside Gawain, who was riding one of the Arabian mares, and Percival, who was riding the company's long-suffering stallion. They were heading south from the rock, following a narrow gully that traced a curving route back to the western end of the rock. Raphael carried his reins loosely in his left hand; in his right, he held his mace. Percival carried sword and shield, and his longsword was strapped to his saddle. Raphael's shoulders ached slightly from the weight of the maille already, and his helm felt tight on his head–signs that he had not been wearing his kit regularly enough.

When he had been putting it on, he realized that he hadn't fixed the broken links in the back where the Mongol arrow had injured him. Such carelessness was the very reason knights died on the field of battle. Their maille was a nearly impervious shield against arrows and swords, except when it was ill cared for.

Thankfully, the only one who carried a bow was Gawain. He had been both surprised and saddened when the Welshman had brought out the long oilskin bundle and strung the longbow. A longbow would make quite a difference, as he had seen on several occasions in the past, and seeing the bow reminded him of Rædwulf.

The twelve riders were clearly visible on the plain now, and as the gully turned east, Gawain reined in his horse and dismounted. He dumped his arrow bag on the ground and scuffed clear a patch on the hard ground beside the gully.

The gully was not more than a pace across, easily crossed by a horse and not much of a jump for a man, but it was as close to a defensive barrier as they were going to find. Raphael leaned over and glanced down. The gully was deep enough that a man could crouch within it and not be seen. He let his gaze follow the gully's path back toward the rock. He tried to spot any movement along the rim and saw nothing.

Percival's horse was nosing along the rim of the gully, seeking tender shoots of new grass, and the Frank pulled his reins slightly, reminding the horse of where its attention should be.

Gawain started sticking arrows, point first, into the ground. "Don't let me keep you," he grunted as he slid the fifth arrow into the ground.

Percival nodded and tugged his horse so that it would trot along the edge of the gully, away from Gawain.

"Try to keep your distance from them," Gawain said to Raphael. "It will make my job easier."

Raphael felt the muscles in his lower back twitch. "I'll remember that," he said. He set his horse after Percival and both men led their mounts in a large widdershins circle, urging them to run faster as they came back at the gully again. Both horses cleared the gap in the ground, and Raphael's helmet bounced precariously on his head for a moment after he landed on the far side of the gully.

The dozen riders angled toward them, spreading out into a large arc across the open steppe. From the center, one rider urged his horse out in front of the rest. Raphael and Percival slowed their horses. If the lone rider was interested in a parlay, Raphael would hear what the man had to say.

The man was dressed in the sort of hodge-podge of armor that was not uncommon among mercenaries: a boiled leather breastplate over a short maille shirt, stiffened leather on his shoulders and arms, heavy gloves, and a metal helm with extra pieces on the back and sides to further protect his neck. His skin was darker than Raphael's and his beard was trimmed in the Muslim style.

Transferring his reins to his right hand, Raphael raised his left in greeting as the man came within speaking distance. "*Salam,* traveler," he called out in Arabic, offering the abbreviated Muslim greeting that was appropriate for the circumstances.

The rider slowed his horse to a stop and returned the greeting. "Christians?" he asked, pointing at the sigil on Percival's surcoat. His Arabic was inflected with an accent that Raphael had come to know as influenced by the Turkic tongue. "Christendom is very far from here. Are you lost?"

"Not entirely," Raphael replied. "You?"

The man leaned on his saddle horn, smiling at Raphael. "No," he said. "I know these lands. I'm looking for some horses."

Raphael glanced over his shoulder. In the distance, against the dark bulk of the rock, he could make out a few of the horses, moving about the paddock. "And you think those might be them?" he asked, turning back to the man.

"They might be."

"Those are not the horses you're looking for," Raphael said.

The man frowned as if Raphael had just told him the sky was not blue or that the sun did not rise in the east and set in the west. "I wasn't asking you," he said, some of the civility vanishing from his voice. "In fact, I should be asking that one there"—he jerked his chin over Raphael's shoulder, indicating Gawain—"if he knows anything about those horses."

"He's not the man you're looking for," Raphael said.

The rider laughed, and there was little humor in his tone. "Why do you keep telling me that things that I know are not true? I am not blind. I can see Gawain right over there with his big longbow and his big arrows. I know that whoreson Bruno is here somewhere as well. I know those horses belong to me, and I'm here to take them."

Raphael shook his head. "Are you calling me a liar?" he asked. He turned his head to Percival. "He's calling us liars," he said in Latin.

"I do not care for such language," Percival replied, his voice muffled by his helmet. He lowered his spear, which he had been pointing at the sky, until the tip was directed at the rider.

"What did he say?" the rider asked, the bluster starting to drain from his face.

"He said he did not like being called a liar," Raphael told him. "What is your name?"

"What?"

"Your name," Raphael repeated. "We would know the name of the man who is claiming that we are ill-born men who speak with the tongues of snakes."

"I never said that," the man protested.

"You have said very little beyond veiled accusations," Raphael pointed out.

The man opened his mouth and closed it several times, and the last time he left it closed, muscles flexed along his jaw. "My name is Haidar," he said finally.

"I am Raphael and this is Percival," Raphael said, indicating his companion. "We are knight initiates of the *Ordo Militum Vindicis Intactae*, and we have been informed that you have engaged in the willful execution of innocents in pursuit of financial gain. How do you answer this accusation?"

"With your blood!" Haidar spat. He kicked his heels against his horse's barrel, twisting the beast's head around with his reins. The horse snorted and started, and Haidar galloped back toward his line of men.

"What did he say?" Percival asked.

"I asked an impertinent question," Raphael replied. "And now he wants to kill us too."

"You are such a poor negotiator," Percival said. He slapped his reins, and as his horse leaped into a gallop, he let loose with the Shield-Brethren war cry.

"That wasn't a negotiation," Raphael pointed out before he followed the Frank into battle.

◆ ◆ ◆

Gawain watched the two Shield-Brethren ride toward the line of Arabs, silently counting each of the long galloping strides taken by the horses. He and Bruno had long scouted all the terrain around the rock, especially after the sudden arrival of the strangers, making note of the places where they could mount an effective defense. He knew the distance from the gully to a single bush that had been trimmed in such a way that it appeared to be nothing more than a single tuft of dark leaves atop a naked stalk. That bush was the outward edge of his effective range with the longbow. Further than that, whether his arrow struck its target or not was fate and luck.

Haidar crossed the invisible line denoted by the bush, but the remaining riders were tantalizingly beyond it. *They'll come*, he thought as he flexed his fingers and waited, fighting the urge to put an arrow into Haidar.

He heard someone hiss his name, and he glanced down without moving his head. The Binder, Cnán, peered up at him from the base of the gully. She flashed him the sign that the others were ready, and he gave her a tiny nod.

Once the Shield-Brethren had decided that it was in everyone's best interest to stand together against Haidar, their plan had come together incredibly quickly. He had mentioned the gully and his range marker. Yasper had quickly seized on the gully as more than a defensive barrier, Percival had volunteered to be the lure, and Raphael had insisted on attempting to resolve the conflict without bloodshed.

Good luck, Gawain had said to him.

Success will not depend upon luck, the knight had replied.

The largest difficulty lay in corralling the enemy riders. The steppe was devoid of any significant land masses or defects that would create natural barriers and channels, and they had no time to erect such defenses. The rock was a natural defense, but if the riders got that close, they would be in their camp. They would have to move all the horses. No, it was better to meet them further afield.

Yasper had retrieved one of the cakes he was baking in the fire with a pair of narrow tongs, and had promised that he could manage to create a diversion that would drive the horses in a narrow path. *We just have to give them a target to focus on,* he had explained, and everyone had looked at Gawain.

Haidar knows about my bow, Gawain had argued. *They won't ride at me. They'll try to stay out of my range and circle around.*

Trust me, Yasper had cackled. *They'll come at you.*

I'll help convince them, Percival had suggested.

Gawain hadn't been entirely convinced, but no plan was ever foolproof, and this one seemed as good as any that he and Bruno had concocted over the last space of time.

The knights were talking with Haidar now, and Gawain calmly reached for his first arrow, setting it lightly across the nock. He lifted his head, testing the breeze on his cheek, mentally adjusting for the slight wind moving from left to right. He exhaled slowly, letting his shoulders relax and his eyes become slightly unfocused. His right fingers were resting lightly on the string of his bow, cradling the end of his arrow as he stood and waited.

He didn't have to wait long. As soon as he saw the horses move and heard Percival's war cry, he thrust all of the air out of his lungs and drew back the heavy string of his bow in a smooth motion— chest, back, legs, and arms all working in concert to draw the string. He held his breath for a second, peering along the shaft of his arrow, and then he released the string.

◆ ◆ ◆

The spear Percival carried was too short to be a true lance, but he couched it like one as he charged after Haidar. The mercenary glanced back over his shoulder once and, spotting Percival, he jerked his horse to the right, looping out across the steppe. Percival ignored him, knowing he wasn't going far, and concentrated instead on the line of Arab mercenaries who were now riding toward him as well, swords upraised. He kept the blade of his spear pointed forward, over his horse, as the beast galloped to meet the other men. He felt the shock of its legs pounding against the ground up through his pelvis, and he leaned forward in his saddle. At the last second, he swung the tip of his spear out, angling it directly at the closest man on his right.

The spear struck something firm, and the butt of the shaft was shoved painfully into his side. A second later, a sword struck his upraised shield, notching the top edge not far from his face. Then his horse was through the line and, using his legs, he turned it back toward the fray. The tip of his spear was red with blood, and he spotted the man he had hit, sprawled in the dirt. His riderless horse trotted aimlessly away from the battle.

Raphael had reached the line, and Percival watched as the knight bashed a man on the side of the head with his mace, knocking the Arab out of the saddle. Nearby another man slumped in his saddle, vainly plucking at the long arrow protruding from his side, and with a quick flick of his wrist, Raphael ended the Arab's pain.

Another pair were charging toward Percival, and he braced himself in the saddle and hurled his spear. The tip struck the Arab's shield in the upper portion, went through, and appeared to pierce the man's chest beneath. Percival caught sight of the man's stunned expression before he leaned back, still affixed to his shield, and fell off the back of his horse. The other rider thundered past, his sword banging on Percival's shield, and kicking his horse into motion, Percival drew his longsword from its sheath and pursued the rider.

Other riders were attempting to avoid the two knights entirely, riding their horses in a wide arc to flank the camp, but their horses shied away from plumes of red and black smoke that had begun to rise from the ground. Yasper had hidden alchemical smoke pots in the gully, and the dank and noxious cloud drove the horses back toward the center.

Back toward Gawain.

◆ ◆ ◆

Gawain had lost count of his arrows. It had been more than a year since he had been in battle such as this, and then he had been in the company of several other archers and they were well away from the heart of the battle. On the steppe, with the wind blowing the acrid smoke from the left and the confusion among the riders, he was concentrating heavily on each target, trying not to lose track of a specific horse and rider as they galloped across the smoke-strewn plain.

They were winning. Of that much, he was certain. There were only five riders left, and two of them were the knights. There were a number of horses wandering about without riders, and he didn't bother to count them.

He was looking for Haidar. He had lost track of the caravan captain after his first arrow had missed, and he had been distracted by the riders whose horses had approached the eastern bank of smoke pots. He had spent an arrow on each rider, and was laying the third across the nock of his bow when Raphael had ridden the remaining rider down.

Gawain sensed movement on his right, and he turned, drawing his bow. He loosed his arrow and swore as it passed over Haidar's head. The rider was leaning forward, presenting as small a profile as possible.

Gawain reached for another arrow, and his fingers encountered nothing but empty space. He looked away from his target, scanning the ground nearby, and saw no more arrows stuck in the ground. His arrow bag was several paces away, lying near the edge of the gully.

The top of Cnán's head was visible in the gully, and he snapped his fingers at her. "Arrow," he hissed, checking the distance to Haidar. The horse was coming fast. "Get me an arrow." When he risked another glance at the gully, the young woman was staring at him, mouth agape. "Arrow!" he shouted.

Cnán figured out what he needed, and she scrambled out of the gully like a fox darting for a fat bird. She stumbled over his bag, nearly impaling herself on several arrows as she tried to get one free of the canvas sack.

Haidar was sitting up, a wicked grin on his face. His sword ready, he whipped his reins against his horse, urging the beast to gallop faster.

This will be close, Gawain thought. Cnán extricated an arrow and thrust it toward Gawain, even as Gawain took a sideways step toward her. He felt the shaft of the arrow smack into the palm of his open hand, and without taking his eyes off his target, he put the arrow across his bow and...

It was facing the wrong way. The sharp tip was laid across the string.

Haidar's horse jumped over the gully, and Cnán screamed, leaping out of the way. Haidar's sword glinted in the afternoon light, and Gawain ducked, raising his bow to protect his head. The sword blade whistled past his ear, and he felt a sharp pain at the base of his neck, and then wetness start to spill down inside his gambeson. His bow was nearly wrenched out of his hands and he heard Haidar grunt loudly, and then as the horse galloped away, he heard the sound of a body striking the ground.

He turned, his right hand twisting the arrow into the correct orientation, and he caught the merest glimpse of Haidar charging toward him, sword upraised. He stopped thinking, stopping paying attention to what his eyes were telling him; he drew the bowstring back and released the arrow.

Haidar's savage cry was cut short with an audible gulp. Something bounced off his foot, and Gawain looked down to see Haidar's sword lying on the ground beside him.

Haidar was several paces away, lying on his side and mewling like an injured dog. His hands were plucking at a small bloom of feathers in his belly; protruding from his back was the long and bloodied shaft of Gawain's arrow.

CHAPTER 16:

THE WITCH IN THE WOODS

Nika waited until the hour just before dawn, when the sentries were most lethargic, when the weight of the night was heavy upon their shoulders and their thoughts continually strayed toward warm fires and furs. While the prince, his *Druzhina*, and many of the boyar's sons in the prince's army remained in Novgorod after the procession and feast, the bulk of the army had set up camp a few miles from the city, sprawling across the fields and forests near the river. This made it much easier for her to sneak out of the camp; she did not have to worry about scaling a wall or evading the Novgorodian guard. She moved carefully through the woods, her feet making no sound as she danced across the snow, and once she was far enough from the camp to be sure no one could hear run, she ran faster.

The previous night, as she and her sisters were setting up their tents, she had spotted markings on several trees. They were not the idle scratches left by a bear sharpening its claws or a deer knocking its horns against the winter-hardened bark. They were too similar, from tree to tree, to be an accident and had anyone else noticed the marks, they might have thought them to be symbols left by hunters or trappers. They might have been sigils marking the presence of a predator that might disrupt traps or indicating routes that could be easily obscured by snowfall, which would have explained why they were carved higher on the tree trunks than any man or woman could reach, but Nika knew otherwise.

They were a summons.

She crested a hill and found a small animal path that led her down the other side. She followed it, her eyes sweeping back and forth as she ran. She wasn't worried about meeting any deer or wolves. The prince might have far-ranging scouts that she didn't want to startle. They would be inclined to put an arrow into her before bothering to identify her.

By and by, the faint sounds of running water reached her ears, the gentle bubbling of a melting stream somewhere ahead, and she slowed, lest she come upon it unawares. Winter's grip was loosening, but the weather was still crisp and a dunking in meltwater would be dangerous. She was too far from the fires of the prince's camp.

So intent was she on keeping her eyes out for the stream that she did not realize she had stumbled upon a camp site until she stood in its center. It was so cleverly obscured by bramble and bowed trees that she would not have noticed it at all if she hadn't literally walked right into it.

It is only here because I needed to find it, she thought, as she turned in a slow circle. The grass had been trampled down as if by a herd of horses, and a small ring of mottled stones indicated a fire pit, though there were no ashes within the ring. Three of the stones were human skulls, and she felt her stomach knot when she realized they were small enough that they had to be the skulls of children. One was pale and gray, so old that the stark whiteness of the bone had faded; the second was darkened with ash and the eye sockets were darker holes; the jaw of the third gaped at her, the teeth smeared with a sticky redness. *One for those long buried,* she thought, *one for those we lost recently, and one for those still to die.*

Something massive moved behind her, the grinding sound of stone against stone, and Nika froze. Her heart was pounding in her chest, the loud echo filling her ears, and a slippery shiver ran down her back. She turned slowly, struggling to swallow the urge to scream. It was one thing to see a ghost at a distance, where it could be dismissed as a trick of fog and shadow; it was another thing entirely to be in the presence of a ghost.

Behind her, seated on a wooden stool as if she had been there the entire time, was a huddled figure wrapped in a cloak so dank and foul that its original color could not be determined. Wrinkled hands that were more birdlike than human poked out from the sleeves, and in the crone's lap was a mortar and pestle. The terrifying sounds that Nika had heard were nothing more than the noise made as the pestle ground seeds into a fine paste. The grinding motion sounded like a giant chewing rocks very slowly and very deliberately.

"Dusk, night, and dawn," the crone cackled. "They watch now, but once they were heroes. Like you. Like the one who has lost both his heart and his ear. Like the one who yearns for communion with the spirit."

Nika's mouth was dry, and the icy chill down her back was still there. It felt like a river of sweat was racing down her spine. "Mother crone," she started.

"Sit, little daughter," the crone rasped, her voice suddenly much deeper and much more menacing.

Nika obeyed, folding her legs beneath her.

"You have not told him yet," the crone said. Her voice was softer now, almost matronly in its tenderness.

"I haven't," Nika said. "He struggles with his despair. I don't know if he is ready."

"Who ever is?" the crone asked. "What of your sisters?"

This, at least, was an easy question for Nika to answer. "We train often with the *Kynaz's* guard, the *Druzhina*. They are eager"—she hesitated to say it so bluntly, but then decided there was no reason not to do so—"they are eager for the experience."

The prince's private guard was well equipped and a number of them had been battle tested, but not to the same degree as the Shield-Maidens. If Illarion had not said as much to the prince, she knew the Northman—Ozur—had most likely done so. Training with the *Druzhina* was much less contentious these days than it had been when the Shield-Maidens had first joined the prince's army.

"The *Skjalddis* have protected this land for generations, and I would expect them to be ready with their swords and spears," Baba Yaga said. "But who protects this realm when your numbers are few?"

"Our numbers?" Nika asked. "Against this Teutonic army?" She felt her face grow hot. "Or do you speak of what happened at Kiev when the Mongol horde came? They outnumbered us more than a thousand to one. It was a miracle that we were able to fight them off at all. Was that not enough?" Her hands tightened into fists. "Should we have ridden out in full panoply and engaged them until they brought all of us down?"

The crone put back her head and laughed, a long cackle that sounded like the call of a hundred geese. Nika got her first glimpse at the pale face beneath the hood, and the bright eyes that stared out of a shrunken face. "Little daughter, the Mongols pillage and burn, but they are like the winter snow—gone before the following spring," Baba Yaga said after her amusement bubbled away. "Rus has endured such conquerors before and will again. But they are not the true danger that threatens Rus. They are not the ones who mean to bend Rus to their will now and forever."

Nika tightened her fists and then relaxed them, understanding what the crone was telling her. "The knights of the red cross and sword," she said. "The Livonians."

"The sword and cross," Baba Yaga said, nodding her head. "And behind those, the two curved staves."

"We beat them once," Nika said. "At Kiev."

"Aye," the crone agreed. "But with the assistance of the *Skjaldbræður*. But you did not kill the one who mattered most. The disgraced knight."

"Who?" Nika asked, wondering who the crone was talking about, but she realized she knew. "Kristaps," she said.

"Aye," the crone said. "The one leading the army against you, against Rus. He is the one who came a-thieving to the caves of the Lavra. He is the one who binds the three of you together."

"The three of us?" Nika asked, looking at the skulls again and trying to remember what the witch had just said about them. *Dusk, night, and dawn.* "Who is the third?"

"He will come," Baba Yaga said. "He resists the path he must take, but he will find his way before this is done."

"And Kristaps is leading the Teutonic army?" Nika asked, trying to get a straight answer out of the crone on some matter at least. "Is that why he binds us together?"

"He bears the marks," Baba Yaga said. She held up her right arm and the sleeve of her robe fell back, exposing her bony forearm. On the pale flesh, a shadow writhed—a moon filled with stars that, as Nika stared, changed into a sigil of a tree bound by a circle, and then Baba Yaga slid her sleeve down again and the image was gone. "Some brotherhoods leave their marks, both on those they exalt and those they shame. Some marks are more apparent than others, to those who know how to see. This false *Skjaldbræður* knows what you and your sisters are. He is the greed of Rome, made flesh, but he is the champion of something much older."

Half-told stories and old wives tales flashed through Nika's head. She was no scholar of the history of her order, though like any of her sisters, she knew of the legacy that bound the Shield-Maidens to both Týrshammar and Petraathen. There were older stories, fables murmured by mothers to their daughters as they huddled before the hearth, stories of sundered siblings and of broken branches.

Behind all these stories were hints of an ancient animosity, a rivalry that had caused the first rift. It was always there, the wound that lay at the heart of the world. The wound that would never heal.

"Is that why you have summoned me?" Nika asked. Her mouth was dry and she yearned to scoop a handful of snow off one of the nearby branches and put it in her mouth.

"I did no such thing," Baba Yaga said. She peered at the contents of her mortar. "You came. You found me."

Nika could have contested that claim, but then she realized it was true, from a certain point of view. She had seen the marks on the trees and interpreted them in a certain way. She had left the prince's camp. She had wandered into this glade where the crone was idly crushing seeds. It was a twisted version of what had happened, but she saw why the crone was speaking this way.

"I need allies," Nika said. Baba Yaga wouldn't tell her what to do. She had to make her own decisions. The Virgin—in this case, the crone—supported the daughters of the shield. Nika knew the *Skjaldbrœður* were more inclined to seek guidance from the Virgin, but the *Skjalddis* were much more independent. They had to be; they thrived only when each sister accepted the burden of being a woman who carried arms.

"The Spirit of Rus is stirring," Baba Yaga said, and her cowled head lifted to take in the whole of the snow-covered forest that surrounded them. "A branch that was thought lost has been found. Things that have not been seen since the ancient times are making themselves felt again."

Nika's gaze wandered back to the stone circle and its three skulls as she wondered whether she should rejoice or be truly terrified at the idea of ancient *things* returning. The old tales were full of wonders, yes, but also of horrors. The skulls gaped at her. Dusk, night, and dawn. The fate of heroes was to be carved up into bloody pieces to be used in the rituals of others. *We lift up the mightiest amongst us*, she thought, *and devour them when they fall.*

"He isn't ready either," Baba Yaga said. "Illarion Illarionovich might think himself done with this world, but it is not finished with him. Ties of blood bind him to these affairs as surely as those of tradition and old power bind you and me. He will realize this soon enough. You will see it for yourself. You will know."

Nika's gaze lingered for a second longer on the blood-smeared skull and then she returned her attention to the crone. "Aye, and then I will tell him."

Baba Yaga set her pestle down on her lap and carefully poured the contents of the mortar out into the palm of her wizened hand. The seeds had been crushed to a yellow powder, and the dust settled in the deep lines of the old woman's hand. "Tell him what?" Baba Yaga asked, and then she raised her hand to her mouth and blew the powder at Nika.

Nika stepped back, coughing, as a cloud of yellow smoke billowed up from Baba Yaga's hand. It filled the camp within moments, stinging her eyes and choking her. Nika staggered back, her feet tripping over rocks and roots. Branches caught at her, shoving her in different directions. The fog dissipated quickly, and when Nika's eyes stopped watering, she found herself standing on the bank of a narrow stream.

There was no sign of the camp, and when she thrashed through the woods, she found no sign that it had ever existed.

◆ ◆ ◆

Illarion was with the prince when a breathless runner announced that the banners of the Grand Duke, Alexander's brother Andrei, had been sighted. "At last," the prince muttered. The Veche were, in the prince's privately expressed opinion, perpetually slow to act, and while the call for the militia had been quick to go out after the *Kynaz*'s arrival at Novgorod, the remainder of the preparations for war had proceeded sluggishly. The *Kynaz*'s army numbered more than four thousand and their camp filled the valley beyond the city walls. The arrival of Andrei's forces would swell that number, putting even more of a strain on the city to support so many men. The Veche could not ignore the strain such an encamped force put on the meager winter stores of Novgorod.

Illarion followed Alexander out of the prince's command tent, squinting against the bright morning light. To the south, winding their way toward the *Kynaz*'s camp, was a field of fluttering banners. Eastern crosses joined with armed beasts on brightly colored fields, and gilded helms gleamed in the sun. "Six hundred *Druzhina*," Alexander said, shading his eyes. "All mounted." He offered Illarion a tight smile. There would be, Illarion knew, nearly that number again in men-at-arms, squires, and other attendants.

A trio of riders galloped before the approaching force, two *Druzhina* flanking a tall man on a large grey horse. The Grand Duke was older than the prince and more battle-experienced. Many of Yaroslav's sons had fought the Mongols when Batu Khan had assaulted Rus, but they had been defeated and scattered. When Novgorod had exiled Alexander, Yaroslav had sent Andrei as Nevsky's replacement, but the Grand Duke had not stayed long. He was an effective leader, as far as Illarion knew, but the stories he heard said that Andrei was not as brilliant a tactician as his younger brother.

The Grand Duke brought his horse to a stop not far from Alexander and dismounted with a flourish of his cloak. A crowd had followed him in and when he took a moment to wave at them, they cheered his arrival. He was a larger version of Alexander, broader in chest and face, with the same red-brown beard, although his was thicker. Even as he smiled at the crowd, there was a hint of a darker mood in his face. *They cheer him*, Illarion thought, *but this army is here because of Alexander*. He glanced at Alexander, but was unable to read anything in the younger brother's expression.

Andrei strode up to Alexander and the two sons of Yaroslav regarded each other with a practiced ease that belied the tension Illarion could sense between them. It was Alexander who smiled first, and strode forward to embrace his elder brother with open arms. Illarion blinked, and the tension he had imagined was gone like a snowflake melting away on warm skin, and both men were slapping each other on the backs and laughing like the oldest of friends.

"We would have been here sooner, but the ice has been melting," Andrei said. "Many of the rivers are flowing free again. Getting all of these men across without losing anyone took a lot of time." He slapped Alexander on the shoulder again. "How many do we have now?"

"More than five thousand if you brought as many men as it seems you did," Alexander replied, smiling broadly when Andrei acknowledged his estimate. "Come," he said, indicating the command tent behind Illarion. "Let us eat and drink and discuss what we are going to do with five thousand men."

Andrei nodded, and the two men strode toward the tent. Illarion marveled at the manner in which the prince had deflected the earlier tension. *What* we *are going to do with five thousand men.* The *Kynaz* already had his battle plans in mind, but with a single sentence he had brought his brother into his confidence, suggesting that nothing had been decided yet.

Illarion caught sight of Nika making her way through the crowd and he waited for the Shield-Maiden. "I was looking for you earlier," he said when she reached him.

"I was…hunting," Nika said.

Illarion waited a moment for her to offer more but she didn't, and he shrugged and indicated the *Kynaz*'s tent. Nika ducked her head, and Illarion caught sight of something like relief in her eyes as she walked past him. He fell in behind her, puzzled by her distance, but he could ask her later.

Alexander nodded as they entered the tent, and before the *Druzhina* closed the flaps behind them, he ordered that Ozur and the other Northman commander be located and sent hither. "We might as well do all the planning now," he explained to his brother. He introduced both Illarion and Nika, and Andrei was cordial and graceful in his greeting. Illarion suspected the charm was more for Nika than for him. He had seen Andrei's eyes widen slightly when Alexander had mentioned Volodymyr-Volynskyi.

"Will five thousand be enough?" Andrei said once the pleasantries were done and they had all fallen to examining the battle map laid out on the table.

"Riders have gone to all the surrounding tribes and the men are still coming, but it is a mere trickle now," Alexander said. "Archers and infantry, mostly. Our *Druzhina* will provide the cavalry, along with the *Skjalddis* from Kiev."

Again, the emphasis. *Our.* Even though Alexander's company of mounted knights outnumbered his brother's.

"And the ghost of Volodymyr," Andrei said, regarding Illarion uneasily. "You are not as dead as I had heard. What do they call you?"

"Plank," Nika offered, a smile curling the corners of her mouth.

"Do you fight from horseback with such a piece of wood?" Andrei asked. "Or will you be on foot with the other…?"

Peasants was the word unsaid, and Illarion struggled to keep his tongue civil. He had felt this sort of animosity from some of the boyars of the Veche during the feast thrown in Alexander's honor, but there had been enough mead flowing at the celebration that it had been easy to ignore most of the jibes. But the undercurrent was there: they did not like him. He was one of them and he had surrendered to the Mongols. It did not matter the reasons why he had done so; all that mattered was that he was a reminder of what the Mongols had done to Ruthenian nobility. Being trampled to death by horses was brutal and it symbolized everything foul and barbaric about the Mongols. Illarion reminded the boyars of their own frail mortality. *But there is more to it than that,* Illarion realized as he looked at the Grand Duke.

"Would you care to step outside this tent?" Illarion asked. He, at least, kept his anger out of his voice, though it was there in his words. "I'd be happy to demonstrate."

The Grand Duke stared at him, his face reddening, and Alexander was about to interject when another voice interrupted the staring contest. "Gods, no," Ozur said from the entrance of the tent. "I can attest to his ability to raise a welt with a piece of wood." He pointed at the fading mark on his right cheek.

Silence filled the tent, and nearly everyone was looking to the Grand Duke for a reaction, and it came slowly. His beard parted as he smiled, and his mouth kept stretching as he let loose with a loud bray of laughter. Ozur joined in immediately, as did his companion, who did not know the context of Ozur's comment but joined his fellow Northman in revelry as a matter of course.

"I hope these Northerners are as fierce to fight as they are ready to laugh," Andrei said when the laughter ebbed in the room.

"More so," Alexander said.

"Good," Andrei said, and his gaze came back to Illarion again. "Do you advise, ghost, or do you lead?"

Illarion let his smile fade. "I would lead men as readily as you would, sir," he said.

"Enough," Alexander said, cutting his brother off before he could reply. "We have the same enemy. Hermann of Dorpat, the Prince-Bishop of Riga."

Nika cleared her throat noisily. "There is another," she said.

All eyes turned toward her, and she grimaced awkwardly at their attention. "The Livonians have their own man, and he is in charge of the army in the field."

"Who is this man?" Alexander said, his eyes narrowing. He did not ask the more obvious question of how she knew this information.

"Kristaps of Fellin," she said.

Illarion gaped at her, and Alexander swiftly judged his reaction to be one of intimate knowledge. "Who is he?" the prince asked again, this time directing the question at Illarion.

"He is a knight of the Livonian order," Illarion said, still shocked by Nika's news. "He attempted to defile the sacred places of Kiev last year. He is the First Sword of Fellin. Once he also claimed the title of Volquin's Dragon."

Andrei glanced at Nika. "A very daunting name," he said. "You fought him at Kiev?"

"We did," Nika said.

"And why have you not told my brother this news before this meeting?" Andrei asked.

"Because I did not know of it until shortly before this meeting," Nika said.

"Your advisors have their own spies?" Andrei asked, glaring at Alexander. "Does the Veche know?"

"The Veche knows little and wants to know even less," Alexander said dryly, attempting to defuse some of the tension in the room. Though, judging from the glance he gave Illarion, he was less than pleased to be castigated about the apparent secrecy of his advisors by his brother. "In fact," he continued with a final shake of his head, "they do not yet know what I am about to tell you: the Teutonics have abandoned Pskov, but not before putting much of the city to the torch."

Everyone other than Illarion started talking at the same time, and the prince had to shout over the hubbub of voices to make himself heard. As the assembled council quieted down, the prince turned to Illarion. "Of all of my advisors, you seem the least surprised."

Illarion nodded, and he gestured at the map on the table before them. "He's moving north, isn't he? The fires in Pskov are just the start. He'll burn and pillage as he marches."

"If the Teutonic order means to rule Rus after this is done, this is no way to earn the loyalty of the people," Andrei spat.

"They care nothing for that," Alexander replied. "When we have been forced to exact tribute from the tribes north of Novgorod for the yearly fur trades, it has always been understood that our purpose was not to make them love us. A hand can be extended to offer love or to strike fear; a ruler must know when to use each if he means to hold his throne."

Andrei reddened slightly at his brother's words, but managed to hold his tongue.

"He wants to break their spirits," Illarion said. "We are a land of scattered tribes and city-states more than we are a unified people. You just said as much yourself: *when you exact tribute from the tribes of the north.* You are a man of Novgorod first and foremost. Kristaps was part of the order that campaigned in the north ten years ago. He was *Volquin's Dragon.* He's wreaking havoc among the tribes, and the survivors will run to Novgorod. The city can't support that many refugees, and the more there are, the more the Veche will resent them. They'll lose control of the city."

"It is the same tactic the Mongols used in Kiev," Nika pointed out.

"He thinks I will come save the people," Alexander mused. "The Veche will want me out of Novgorod—fewer mouths to feed—and he thinks my pride will be unable to resist these cries for help."

"What is Pskov but a wounded child, crying out for you to rescue it?" Illarion asked.

Alexander's face tightened at the thought. "I think it is as likely that bored warriors need plunder to remain loyal to their masters."

"That may be true as well," Illarion said. "But Kristaps wants you out in the field. He wants to crush you, and by doing so, crush the spirit of Novgorod."

Andrei bristled at this. "The sons of Yaroslav will avenge their dead."

"I'm sure they will," Illarion said. "But none of them is Alexander Nevsky."

"Careful with that tongue of yours, ghost," Andrei ground out.

"Would you go to Pskov in my stead?" Alexander asked, his voice hard.

His brother sputtered for a few moments, growing red in the face again, but then he let out the air he had been drawing in, and his face softened. "No," he said.

Alexander sighed, and frowned at the map for several moments. "I am glad you are here, brother," he said, lifting his gaze and offering Andrei a smile. "You and I will march together. I am sorry you will not have more time to rest here at Novgorod, but we should march immediately." He looked at Ozur and Nika. "Send a runner to Novgorod. Inform the Veche of my intent to march. Tell them why. I'm sure they'll hear from their own scouts soon anyway." He put out a hand and stopped Illarion. "Go," he said to the others. "I would speak with you a moment longer," he said as the others bowed their heads and made to leave the tent.

Nika lingered, staring intently at Illarion as if she wanted him to understand some subtlety that he had missed so far. He frowned at her, and she only shook her head slightly before she left.

"Tell me about this man, Kristaps," Alexander said when he and Illarion were alone in the tent.

"When I first returned to Rus, after the death of my family at Volodymyr-Volynskyi, I went to Kiev," Illarion explained. "We met a party of Livonians, who were led by a man named Kristaps. These knights wore the old sigil—the red cross and sword that the order called its own before the battle of Schaulen. They were in Kiev's ruins, seeking to defile the Lavra where Saint Ilya lies buried. We stopped them, and Kristaps was the only one who escaped. Apparently he did not run far."

"What were the Livonians doing in Kiev?" Alexander asked.

"That question has plagued me since that day, *Kynaz*," Illarion said. "What were they seeking Kiev? Were they hunting relics or were they chasing something else?" He looked involuntarily at the map. Kiev was leagues south, now, and still the ruin it had always been. *Secret missions*, he thought. *What if the Shield-Brethren were not the only ones?*

Alexander drummed his fingers idly upon the maps as he contemplated Illarion's words. "There are other things you haven't told me," he said eventually.

"Aye," Illarion admitted.

Alexander seemed to realize what his fingers were doing and he glanced down at them and then at the map beneath. "When I accepted you into my service, I did so knowing you had secrets. All men do."

"I...I do not mean to keep them," Illarion admitted. "I do not understand many things that some would consider secrets, but if I cannot trust the veracity of what I know, am I serving you well by blurting out every oddity that I encounter?"

"No," Alexander laughed. "But let us concoct a secret of our own," he continued, more soberly. "Nevsky must go to Pskov because that is what the people yearn to see. They want to see their hero rescuing them."

"You must consider that it is a trap," Illarion said.

"Of course it is," Alexander replied. "But it is also the only territory in Rus that the Teutonics still hold. If I were to take that away from them, where would they go when they ran?"

"Back to Dorpat," Illarion said.

"And that's what the Veche wants to see," Alexander said. "They want to see the invaders driven out of Rus."

"But if Kristaps isn't in Pskov, what do you gain by going there?" Illarion asked. "We have no idea how many are dead or what the city defenses are like. We will be overwhelmed by the needs of the people of Pskov."

"Of course," Alexander said.

Illarion shook his head. "Then why are you going?"

"Me? I never said I was going to go."

"You said *Nevsky will go to Pskov.*"

"I did."

"But you are Nevksy."

Alexander raised his hands. "Nevsky is a hero. That is who the people want."

Illarion nodded, suddenly understanding the secret the prince wanted to share with him. "A hero," he said simply.

Alexander pointed to the map, indicating Pskov and then he let his finger drift. "And if a hero were to rescue a city that has been traumatized and beaten by an arrogant enemy who thinks his foe cannot strike back at him…" His finger came to a stop on a city beyond the borders of Rus.

"Arrogance is the folly of many a man who strives to be more than he should be," Illarion said.

"Perhaps Nevsky might remind him of this hubris," Alexander said, his finger tapping the name on the foreign city.

Dorpat.

CHAPTER 17:

ON THE MARCH

"I have some concerns about your plan," Hermann of Dorpat said as he reined his horse beside Kristaps. The Prince-Bishop wore a heavy cloak, trimmed with white fur; beneath it, Kristaps could see the glint of maille. The familiar outline of a sword disturbed the trailing edge of the cloak.

"So you've said," the First Sword of Fellin replied, returning his gaze to the line of men marching out of Pskov. He wondered if the Prince-Bishop had ever drawn his sword in combat or if the maille had ever felt the bite of a blade.

"Pskov was our foothold in the north. Giving it up is tantamount to fleeing."

Kristaps let his gaze roam over the city under discussion. He and the Prince-Bishop were observing the movement of the Teutonic army from a hillock less than a mile from the southern gate. Dawn had come less than an hour before, and the tendrils of smoke still rising from the smoldering fires were pale threads against the lightening sky. "Are we fleeing?" he asked the Prince-Bishop. When Hermann shook his head angrily, Kristaps shrugged. "Then why do you come to me and suggest that we are?"

Hermann flushed, and his hands jerked at the reins of his horse. "I have heard that you intend to recall our men from Izborsk and Koporye as well."

Kristaps nodded. The Prince-Bishop's consternation suddenly made more sense. Hermann of Dorpat had stood by when he had given the orders to ravage Pskov, and the Prince-Bishop had opened his coffers to provide the necessary coin to entice the mercenaries even to meet with them at the church. He had not said anything when Kristaps had sent word to the quartermasters that the army would march as soon as possible. Only now, when the men were on the move, did the Prince-Bishop have *concerns* that he needed to voice.

Izborsk and Koporye.

Most of the distain Kristaps had shown for Hermann's efforts in the north was in regards to the Prince-Bishop's lack of initiative in the last few years. When the Teutonics had first invaded the Ruthenian lands, they had done so with measureable success, taking and holding both Izborsk and Koporye. Conquering those cities had been victories that reminded Kristaps of Volquin's strategic method of bringing down an enemy piecemeal. And the occupation of Pskov had been a fierce blow to Novgorod, but the Prince-Bishop had failed to take advantage of the impetus provided by these victories. He had wintered in Pskov, and once his men had stopped moving forward, it had been easy to stay put.

But Rus would not give itself to the Teutonic crusaders simply because Pskov and a few other garrisons had been taken, and Rome wanted *all* of Novgorod. It was akin to being asked to capture an entire herd of wild horses and bringing only three stallions back.

"What good are garrisons in those cities if we fail to best Nevsky in the field?" he asked the Prince-Bishop.

Hermann scowled at Kristaps, offering no answer to the question posed to him. He jabbed the heels of his boots sharply against his horse's barrel and left Kristaps to watch the Teutonic army march alone.

The crux of the difference between the two men lay in the unanswered question. Hermann of Dorpat was a cautious man. His brother, Albert, had founded the city of Riga and built a cathedral there, earning the eternal gratitude of Rome. Hermann, who had been given his brother's title when Albert had died, did not want to live within the shadow of his brother's accomplishments, but Kristaps did not see how it was possible for Hermann to eclipse Albert. He simply did not have the same fire.

And what of the young Novgorodian prince who had beaten a Swedish army at Neva, the upstart commander who had instantly become a hero of the people after that victory? Would a cautious man like Hermann of Dorpat have any chance against a man like that?

A cautious man would wait for his enemy to give him an opportunity to attack, but there would be no such opportunity. Not unless it was created.

Pskov was a wound, a bleeding injury that the people of Rus could not ignore. The boyars of Novgorod would be frightened and they would call upon Nevsky to protect them. Nevsky wouldn't ignore them—not when they reached out to him like that—and he would show them, as well as the rest of Rus, that he was their one true champion.

For an instant, staring at the sullen walls of Pskov, he was reminded of the walls of Petraathen, and he clenched his teeth at the intrusive memory. A stray gust of wind buffeted his horse, and the animal shook its head in protest, eager to be moving.

Aye, he thought, tapping his heels lightly against the sides of his horse. He did not care for this land. It reminded him too often of the mountains around Petraathen, of the wild people who were scattered throughout the Carpathians and their pagan myths. It reminded him of Schaulen, and while he was loath to admit such a fear, he longed for the day when the memory of Schaulen did not haunt him.

A second gust of wind buffeted Kristaps, and when he looked over his shoulder at Pskov, he almost fancied that the rising tendrils of smoke were twining about one another, forming the twisted branches of a tree. But when he blinked, the branches were gone, and there was nothing above Pskov but a grey haze of death and despair.

Muttering a curse at the wind and the land alike, Kristaps turned his back to Pskov and rode after the Prince-Bishop. At Schaulen, he had been forced to run. In Kiev, he had been forced to run. Years ago, at Petraathen, he had run. *I will run no more,* he warned the demons that lurked in the dark corners of his heart. *This time, it is you who will run from me.*

✦ ✦ ✦

Their route was north and east of Pskov, a circuitous route to Novgorod, but one that allowed time for Nevsky to marshal a response to what he had done in Pskov. They also needed to gather the garrisons from Izborsk and Koporye, and one of the final messages Kristaps had received in Pskov before departing had mentioned the arrival of the boats belonging to the sons of Valdemaar. Danish marauders—long-standing villains in the eyes of the Ruthenians, but such enmity meant only that they were the perfect allies. His request for their assistance had been met with equal parts suspicion and wonder, more so when he had made it clear he cared little for any plunder the Danes might acquire during their campaign. *Help me break Novgorod,* he had written. *I care naught for the rest.*

It was not his land, and when it was conquered, he would not be the one who would have to administer it. That was the dreadful responsibility of someone like Hermann, who, for clearly prideful reasons, wanted that yoke. The more the people were traumatized, beaten into a state of ready submission, the more readily they would cling to whatever order was given to them. He found such obsequiousness somewhat ironic. It was not as if their own boyars were any kinder as rulers. Kings and princes spent their entire reigns waging provincial wars over such slights as the theft of daughters or fish or furs. While in Pskov, he had learned that the Veche of Novgorod sent out an army every year against the heathen nomads who roamed the northern mountains, brutalizing them until they gave up their yearly tribute of furs. His Teutonic army was just another oppressor.

The few villages they passed were already abandoned, the people fleeing for Novgorod, and he did not allow the army to tarry. They had a decent supply train, and there was no plunder worth taking in these ramshackle villages. It wasn't that he felt pity for these desperate people; he simply had no interest in the distraction that would be caused by allowing the men time to pillage the empty homes. *Let them think we are merciful,* he had said with a laugh.

Mid-afternoon, his scouts spotted a column of smoke among the trees and Kristaps took a company of knights to investigate. Hermann insisted on accompanying them, and while Kristaps could think of several reasons why he should have stayed with the main column, he said nothing as the Prince-Bishop and a small contingent of his bodyguard joined his riders.

Nor did he say anything when they discovered the village overrun by a party of yellow-haired marauders, who were systematically looting and burning each building. The sudden presence of the mounted knights created a stir, but the Danish invaders did not appear overly concerned. A trio of blood-spattered men approached the Teutonic company.

Hermann positioned himself in the center of the front line of knights. "Who are you?" he demanded. "What are you doing?"

Kristaps thought the answer to the second question was fairly obvious.

"Who are you?" the middle of the three Danes replied, equally nonplussed about the second question.

"Hermann of Dorpat, the Prince-Bishop of Riga, and you are…you are…" Hermann sputtered angrily, trying to find words to express his confusion and outrage.

"They are Danes," Kristaps said, nudging his horse toward the front of the company. "And they were invited."

"Aye," the Dane replied with a wide grin. "That we were."

"What?" Hermann exploded.

"I invited them," Kristaps said. "Are the sons of Valdemaar among you?" he asked the Danes.

"Valdemaar is king no longer," the Dane said. "Our brother, Eric Ploughpenny, is now king in Denmark."

"My condolences to the sons of Valdemaar," Kristaps said, "and my congratulations to the Ploughpenny family."

One of the other two Danes spat on the ground and was rudely elbowed by the spokesman. "You are the one who called for us?" he said to Kristaps. "I would have your name."

"I am Kristaps, the First Sword of Fellin. Once I was Volquin's Dragon," Kristaps said.

The Dane nodded. "I have heard of you." He hooked a thumb at the spitter. "This is Thorvald, and that one is Illugi. I am Svend."

Kristaps leaned on the horn of his saddle. "How many of you are there, Svend?"

"One thousand fighting men," Svend replied proudly.

Kristaps glanced over at Hermann, who was staring angrily at him. "And have you met much resistance during your march?" he asked.

Svend laughed and gestured at the wreckage of the village behind him. "This? This is but an idle afternoon's work. Barely worth descending from a horse for."

"They're fleeing for Novgorod," Illugi offered.

Kristaps nodded. "The Veche has put out the call for the militia then, and the families have fled for the safety of the city walls. Novgorod is building its army, though it will be filled with farmers and fur-traders. They will not be equipped to fight men such as you and me."

"Who is?" Svend laughed. "Come," he said, waving Kristaps forward. "We have raided their winter stores. There is some mead still. I would have you meet my lord. He will, I am certain, be eager to discuss the storming of Novgorod."

CHAPTER 18:

WHAT IS LEFT BEHIND

"It is a shame to lose the arrow," Gawain noted, and Cnán choked on the words caught in her throat. The longbowman finished wrapping his bow without another glance at the still form of Haidar. He picked up his arrow bag and started to walk calmly back toward the camp, but Cnán finally managed to clear her throat and bring him up short with a quick yell.

"We just can't leave him," she said, pointing at Haidar.

"Why not?" Gawain asked. "He would have done the same for you or me. Worse, probably."

The excitement of the ambush was still thrumming through Cnán's body, and she spoke more bravely—more openly—than she would have normally. "You're better than that," she said. "You're not a killer."

Gawain glanced at the rock for a moment, considering his response, and then he walked back to her. "What do you know of me?" he asked. "You think that just because I rescued you from freezing to death that I'll take pity on any wounded creature that I stumble across? In case you don't remember, he nearly took my head off." He jerked the collar of his gambeson aside, showing her a bloody gash along the top of his shoulder. "If you hadn't moved, you would have been trampled. I saved your life. Again."

Cnán flushed, but she held her ground. "We're not monsters," she said. "Look at him. He's in pain."

As if to buttress her statement, Haidar groaned and tried to lift his head. The area around the flower stuck in his belly was dark with blood as was the ground beneath him.

Gawain signed and put his bow and arrow bag down. "Would you have me put him out of his misery?" he asked, his hand falling to the knife in his belt.

"No," Cnán snorted. "We should...we should..." She didn't know what they should do.

"Come here," Gawain said, roughly grabbing her arm and pulling her along with him as he strode toward Haidar. "My arrow has pierced him all the way through. Men do not recover from wounds like this. They can last several weeks, but eventually their bellies swell up with poisons and they die."

He stopped several paces away from Haidar, and while he let go of Cnán's arm, he kept his other hand on the hilt of his knife. "What would you have me do?" he asked.

Haidar clenched his teeth and managed to lift his head. There was blood on his lips, and his eyes were already dull. As he tried to sit up, the arrow protruding from his back wiggled obscenely.

Cnán shook her head, disgusted by the lesson Gawain seemed intent on giving her, but unable to look away from the dying man on the ground.

Gawain took another step forward and then squatted on his haunches so that his face was closer to Haidar. "What would you have me do?" he asked the wounded man.

"Die," Haidar gasped, and he lurched at Gawain, struggling to throw himself upon the longbowman. His right arm, which had been hidden behind his body, appeared suddenly, swinging toward Gawain's face. Cnán jumped at the sight of the long knife gripped in Haidar's fist, but she was the only one surprised by Haidar's desperate act.

Gawain blocked Haidar's attack and stood, retaining his grip on the other's arm, dragging Haidar halfway to his feet. Gawain stripped the knife from Haidar's slack fingers and released his hold on the other man's arm. Haidar fell to the ground and tumbled back, the weight of his body snapping the arrow off. He screamed, arching his back and clawing at the broken shaft of the arrow. Gawain kicked him once in the head and he fell silent.

"Satisfied?" Gawain asked, holding out Haidar's knife.

Cnán shook her head. "No," she whispered.

Gawain tossed the knife on the ground near Haidar and stalked off to collect his bow and arrow bag.

Haidar's chest still moved, a tiny shiver in his frame that suggested he was still alive. His left hand relaxed, and a bloody bubble swelled on his lips.

Cnán clenched her fists and turned away. Her eyes were burning with tears and she feared she would not be able to hold in the scream that was building in her throat. Her body still hummed with the tension of the battle, and to be so forcefully confronted with the death of another human being threatened to overwhelm her. She was no stranger to killing, not since she had joined the Shield-Brethren, but all of it had happened at arm's length. This was much too close, too much as though her own hand had held the knife that delivered the final blow.

Standing on the edge of the gully, his face and hands blackened with soot, was Yasper. He was staring with shock at Haidar's corpse. He had been in the gully, marshalling his smoke pots, and she hadn't been aware that he had crawled to the center where she and Gawain had been. Yet, here he was.

She ran toward him, no longer thinking, and when he raised his arms, she bulled into him, burying her face in his stained jacket. All she could smell was the acrid scent of his phoenix eggs, and all she could feel was his arms encircling her and holding her tight.

◆ ◆ ◆

Lian was standing beside the paddock when Percival and Raphael returned. She and Vera had remained at the camp when the pair had ridden out, and though she stood on a rock and tried to see what was happening on the steppe, she saw little more than the tiny shapes of riders darting like swallows through the drifting smoke from Yasper's alchemical smoke pots. It was much different than the way the Mongols fought. The company was scattered, and they all had roles to play in the battle, but it was not organized in the same cohesive strategy that Mongol *noyon* used. These men were used to fighting on their own.

She had been thinking about Gansukh as Percival dismounted from his horse. "Eight," he said cheerfully. His helmet was off, and his brown hair was matted with sweat. The front and right side of his surcoat were splashed with blood. "We've recovered eight horses."

"Marvelous," Lian said distantly. She put aside the thoughts she had been exploring and smiled at the tall Frank. "And you are unhurt? All of you?"

"Aye," Percival said as he draped the reins of his horse over the rope rail of the paddock and began undoing the sequence of knots that held the rope gate shut. He glanced over his shoulder toward the steppe where the fighting had occurred. "Four prisoners too, I believe," he said. "Haakon and Bruno are bringing them back."

"Four?" Lian questioned the number. "What are we going to do with four captives?"

"They surrendered," Raphael said from atop his horse. The knight stared down at Lian. "We showed them mercy."

"Yes, but—"

Raphael nudged his horse forward and, even though the animal was still a pace away from her, Lian stepped back, feeling the paddock rope stop her from retreating any farther.

"You are a guest," Raphael said. "You will not question my decisions."

"My apologies," Lian said smoothly, dipping her head down in well-practiced contrition. She suppressed the urge to drop to her knees, though her legs did bend slightly before she caught herself.

She heard Raphael grunt, followed by the sound of his boots striking the ground. "Stop that," the knight said gently, touching her lightly on the arm. She raised her head and noted that he actually seemed embarrassed by her reaction, and she offered him a fleeting smile, letting him know that all was forgiven.

"Help..." He cleared his throat and tried again. "Could you help Percival with the horses?" he asked, offering her the reins of his mount.

"I'd be happy to," she replied. She curtsied briefly and then accepted the leather straps from him.

Raphael gave her a funny look, and then glanced over at Percival, who had undone the section of rope and was leading the first horse into the paddock. "I'm going to talk with Gawain and Bruno," he said. "Join us when you can." With a final nod at Lian, he walked off, somewhat bow-legged and stiff. Whether it was from sore muscles that were unused to riding and combat or from further embarrassment, Lian couldn't tell for certain.

"He doesn't like being in command, does he?" she noted to Percival as she led Raphael's horse through the gap in the rope.

"Few do," Percival noted.

Lian thought of Master Yelu Chucai, Ögedei's senior advisor and her one-time master. As the *Khagan*'s drinking had worsened, more and more of the administration of the empire had fallen to Master Chucai, and the Kitayan advisor had flourished under the increased workload. *Some do*, she thought, wondering which of those two types Percival was.

Fleetingly, she wondered the same about Gansukh.

Percival set about removing the makeshift saddle from the horse. He spoke in a low voice to the animal as he worked, in a language she did not know. She doubted the horse did either, but the words he was speaking weren't as important as the soothing tone of his voice. She liked hearing his voice, and imagined he was quite adept at reciting poetry. The ladies of court at Karakorum would find him quite extraordinary, and not simply because of his exotic features. Percival knew he was a beautiful man, and from his carriage and bearing it was clear he was of noble birth. But unlike so many noble-born sons she had seen in China and the Mongol empire, Percival displayed little of the arrogance that typically came with such station and blood.

Lian blinked, realizing she had been staring, and when she turned her head slightly so that she wasn't looking at him directly, she was surprised to notice a strange glow of light coming off the Frank. When she looked at him directly, the sun was merely bright in his hair and on his sweat-streaked cheeks, but when she looked at him out of the corner of her eyes, a subtle difference in his countenance was revealed.

Unconsciously her hand strayed to the place where Gansukh's lacquer box was hidden, and when her hand pressed against the fabric lying between her flesh and the box, the glow about Percival intensified.

She must have made a noise because Percival looked up from his work, his brow creased with worry. "Are you alright?" he asked.

"I'm fine," she said. "It's…" She let go of her robe, which she had been clutching tightly, and pointed at his surcoat. "It's the blood."

Percival looked down at his surcoat and seemed to notice the blood stains for the first time. "How unfortunate," he said. "This was my best robe."

Lian smiled at him, leaning lightly against the side of Raphael's horse. "It's your only robe," she pointed out.

"All the more reason to return to civilization as soon as possible," he said. He slid the surcoat over his head and let it fall to the ground so that the blood stains were not as visible. His coat of maille was a cascade of dull metal that made him appear as if he were submerged in water up to his neck. "Does this offend your eyes less?" he asked.

"Very little of you offends my eyes at all," Lian answered.

Percival acknowledged her compliment with a bow and he offered her the wooden comb he had been using to brush down his horse. "Perhaps the lady would like to finish while I attend to Raphael's steed," he said.

"I would," she replied. When she took the comb from him, she utilized one of the old courtesan tricks and ensured that their fingers touched during the transfer. She wasn't clumsy in receiving the comb from him; she merely allowed several of her fingers to drift across his as she accepted the object.

The sort of men who gave gifts to courtesans were the sort whose desires were well evident. All they wanted was what was hidden from their eyes by layers of silk robes. A touch—bare skin against skin—reminded them of what they sought.

Percival's cheeks colored slightly as he walked past Lian and began fussing with the saddle straps. Lian walked to the far side of the other horse so that she could look over its back at Percival as she brushed the horse.

He kept his back to her as he worked.

So like Gansukh, she thought, a little surprised at the wistful melancholy that settled on her.

✦ ✦ ✦

The four prisoners had been stripped of their kits and bound, hands behind their backs, to stakes driven into the ground. They were spaced several paces apart. Raphael knew it wasn't a permanent solution as the stakes could be pulled out of the ground if any man were given enough time to apply the necessary leverage, but the arrangement would do in the meantime.

Bruno sat on a nearby rock, a water skin dangling in his hands, his attention only vaguely directed at the prisoners. There were a few streaks of dried blood along his left ear.

"They put up much fight?" Raphael asked as he joined Bruno. He had stripped off his maille and undershirt and changed into a wool gambeson. Using a ladle of water from their stores, he had washed the dirt and blood from his face and hands. It was the closest thing to a real bath he'd had in several months.

Bruno idly fingered the tip of his left ear. "Not much," he said as he offered Raphael the water skin.

Raphael took the offered skin. He was expecting water, but the liquid from the skin burned his lips and he coughed and sputtered, trying not to let it get any farther into his mouth. "What... what is this?" What little he swallowed burned all the way down, as if he had just ingested a hot coal.

"Yasper and I have been working on the recipe," Bruno said as he took the skin back and lifted it to his lips. He drank deeply, without any visible stress. "The one on the left there is Mamut," he said. "I think I did something to his arm."

Raphael shook his head as Bruno offered the skin again, and to forestall any more discussion about Bruno and Yasper's little project, he walked toward Mamut, appraising the sweating man with a practiced eye.

Mamut's right shoulder had an unusual lump beneath his tunic and he was visibly quaking from pain. *Dislocated*, Raphael thought, *and compounded by having his hands tied behind his back.* He crouched beside Mamut and asked a question to which he already knew the answer. Mamut, understanding Raphael's Arabic, nodded, his eyelids fluttering rapidly.

"I'm not going to kill you," Raphael said gently. "I want to help." He touched Mamut lightly on the shoulder, above the lump. "I need to move your arm back in place," he said. "It will hurt more than you are hurting now, but after that, the pain will pass. Do you understand?" When Mamut nodded, Raphael crab-walked around the man and leaned forward to fumble with his bonds. The knots were tight, and after picking at them for a few moments, he cut them with his knife. "Lie down," he instructed Mamut, pushing against the man's upper back.

Mamut did as he was instructed and Raphael waved Bruno over. "When he did sustain this injury?" he asked.

"Does it matter?" Bruno asked, heaving himself off his rock.

"It might," Raphael said.

"I asked him some questions"—Bruno took a swig from the skin—"and I didn't like his answers." He swayed slightly as he did, the spirits starting to take over the function of his legs and torso.

"Hold him," Raphael said, and when Bruno knelt down and laid a thick arm across Mamut's left shoulder, he gently gathered Mamut's right arm in his hands. Mamut started to squirm, and Raphael put his left knee against Mamut's torso and quickly straightened Mamut's arm and leaned back, pulling as hard as he could. A grating noise came from Mamut's shoulder, soon drowned out by Mamut's shrieks, and then the arm hopped in Raphael's grip. The lump disappeared, restoring Mamut's shoulder to its normal shape, and the injured man pressed his face against the ground, weeping openly.

Raphael coaxed him back to the stake and tied his hands again, in front this time, so as to alleviate the stress on his reset shoulder. He wound the extra cord around the stake, which was now between Mamut's legs. "It'll do for a little while," he said to Bruno, who was watching with a raised eyebrow.

He slipped the skin out of Bruno's grip and took another drink of the fiery water as he wandered back to the rock and sat down. It didn't burn as much the second time, and there was a floral hint beneath the acrid taste of ash.

It felt good to sit and drink, and he wouldn't have minded doing so for the rest of the afternoon, but there was much to do yet. He caught sight of Vera and Gawain approaching, and he took a final sip—a very small one—before tossing the skin back to Bruno.

"Eight horses," he said to Gawain. "It would have been nice to get all twelve."

Gawain glanced at the prisoners briefly, checking each face to see if he knew the man, and then nodded at Bruno, who threw him the skin. "One took an arrow. The wind blew it off target," he said with a shrug. "We can probably round up the rest in a day or two."

"We probably shouldn't wait that long," Raphael said. "Besides, once these men get loose, they'll need steeds."

Gawain's face darkened slightly and Raphael wasn't sure if it was from the spirits or what he had just said. "I am not the only one who has been hiding, am I?"

Vera gestured for Gawain to share the skin, and Raphael watched her drink the fire water without any visible distress. "Those Mongol riders that Ahmet and Evren spotted might be looking for us," Raphael said.

"Might be?"

"It's hard to say if it is *those* Mongols specifically," Raphael dissembled and Vera laughed.

"Am I missing something?" Bruno asked.

"I think we both are," Gawain added.

"We're going to continue north and west," Raphael said. "North of Saray-Jük. There's a Khazar village beyond the big river. We'll resupply there and continue west. We could use a longbowman." He glanced at Bruno. "Bruno is good with the horses."

"Bruno and I have some unfinished business to the south," Gawain said, but then he noticed that Bruno wouldn't meet his gaze. "What?" he snapped.

Bruno shook his head.

Raphael suddenly understood what questions Bruno had been asking earlier, and he quickly put himself between Gawain and the prisoner. "I suspect there is nothing you can do," he said gently.

Gawain glared at Bruno. "What happened?"

Bruno sighed and looked down at the skin in his hands. "She's dead, Gawain. They're all dead. After Haidar ran us off, he went back and—"

Gawain launched himself at Mamut, but Raphael caught him before he could put his hands on the prisoner. Vera came up behind the Welshman and bound his arms with hers. Gawain struggled against both of them for a moment, and then relented. Tears silently tracked down his cheeks. Raphael carefully released Gawain and let Vera pull him away from the prisoners. Gawain struggled briefly, and then subsided, letting Vera direct him toward the tents.

Bruno and Raphael watched Gawain stumble away, and Raphael wished he could do more to offset the Welshman's suffering.

"Who is chasing you?" Bruno asked, breaking the silence.

"Mongols," Vera said.

"How many?"

"All of them, probably," Vera replied casually as if she were commenting on the mild weather they were having.

◆ ◆ ◆

The evening meal was a somber affair, and little conversation was shared among the company. While the steppe was showing signs of spring growth, the nights were still bitterly cold, especially when there were no clouds to obscure the stars. The company was making preparations to decamp in the morning, and Cnán had almost nothing to pack. Helping Yasper with his alchemy experiment was an excuse to stay close to the fire, though the usually talkative Dutchman was oddly reticent this evening.

"So Gawain and Bruno will be joining us," she said as he finished packing the first of his pots and started tamping ash into a second.

"Aye," Yasper said. "And the Seljuks too, I suppose. Though I heard some heated words from their tent earlier. I suspect they're not happy to learn that those Mongol scouts they spotted are probably going to return with others."

When he finished the first layer of ash, he applied himself to the delicate next step: getting the oblong shape of his alchemical egg out of the fire without breaking it. She had been full of questions earlier when he had moved the first one, part of her efforts to engage him, and he had tolerated her inquisitiveness for a while, but eventually he had asked her to stop pestering him.

And then he had immediately apologized for being rude to her. She had smiled at him, and had actually thought about reaching over and touching his shoulder, but had toyed with her hair instead, telling him no apology was necessary.

What he really needed was a flat plate of iron, preferably with a handle of some kind. He had had an instrument like that in his kit once, but the horse carrying all of his alchemical instruments had been stolen in Kiev, and she knew it was best to not let him dwell overlong on the theft. He tended to get morose. He had found a piece of shale that was flat on one side and not very thick. As he dug ash out of the fire pit, he made a pit next to the buried cake; once it was deep enough to hold the flat rock, he packed the shale into the ashes, flat side up, and then he filled the empty space around the rock with more ash. He had to work quickly; if he left the stone in place too long, it would get too hot to touch, and then he'd have to dig it out and start over once it had cooled.

The stone in place, he carefully laid his fire-poking stick along the far side of the cake and pushed it through the ash pit until it was resting atop the stone. He quickly dug the ash away from the edges of the stone and, gritting his teeth, he plucked the stone out of the ash. He held it close to the edge of the pot, and Cnán provided the sole bit of assistance she could by gently poking the cake with a stick so that it slid off the stone and into the pot.

Yasper dropped the rock, and blew on his fingertips briefly before crossing his arms and shoving his hands into his armpits. "A little hot that time," he said.

"Are you hurt?" she asked.

"No, no," he shook his head. "I'll be fine."

They sat awkwardly for a moment, and looking at Yasper with his arms crossed over his chest like he was hugging himself, Cnán started thinking about what had happened earlier in the day.

"Yasper—" she started.

"Yes, well," he said, interrupting her, "I suppose I should see to the rest of my gear." He pulled his hands free and inspected them. "See? They're not burned."

"That's good," she said, letting go of the words she had been planning to say.

He stood, dusting off his knees. "Do you think you could finish covering this?" he asked, pointing at the half full pot. "Equal parts ash and sand."

"I could," Cnán said. There was a lump in her throat.

"Ah, good, thank you." He hesitated, at a loss for what to say, which was so unlike him that Cnán found herself starting to smile. "Well, I'm going to pack, then. You can just leave these here when you're done."

"I will," she said.

He nodded once more and scampered off, looking like a bushy field mouse as he darted across the camp.

Cnán watched him go, trying to swallow down the lump in her throat. *What a funny little man,* she thought, and it was only as she started to layer ash and dirt into the pot that she realized he had left her in charge of his alchemical experiment.

She swallowed once more, the lump vanishing, and the smile she had been carefully nurturing bloomed.

CHAPTER 19:

FINDING THE TRAIL

"**H**orse," said Alchiq.

Gansukh looked down at the dark brown body. It was indeed a horse.

A single arrow protruded from the carcass at the base of the neck, and black blood stained its neck and withers. The scavenger birds had taken its eyes already and were starting to work on the rest of the head. The belly of the horse bulged slightly.

"Dead two or three days," Gansukh assessed, and his attention returned to the large rock that they'd been riding toward since mid-morning. He'd heard about the rock from a Cuman trader in the village near the Aksu River. It was a camp site used by smugglers and other merchants who wished to avoid the attention garnered by traveling along the Silk Road. The *Skjaldbrœður* would need supplies and fresh horses, and he did not think they would risk showing their faces in any village where they would stand out as foreigners. The Cuman had been reluctant to tell Gansukh the location of the rock, but after making some faces and offering some coin, Gansukh had learned the Cuman wasn't entirely sure. *You can't miss it*, the trader had pleaded with him, *once you get close enough*.

Gansukh knew how expansive the steppe was, and while he knew such a statement would undoubtedly be true, it was not a very helpful one. It was like being told that a hawk could not hide in a cloudless sky.

And yet, they had managed to find the rock, and, judging from the length of the arrow jutting from the dead horse's neck, they had found the men from the west as well.

The carrion birds they had driven off the horse had joined others who were circling the rock, drifting on lazy thermals caused by the massive stone blocking the flow of the winds across the steppe. "More horses?" he asked Alchiq.

Alchiq shrugged.

He had been less talkative than normal after recovering from his wounds, as if any conversation should include some mention of gratitude for Gansukh's ministrations but such acknowledgement was stuck in the older man's throat. Until the blockage was removed, Alchiq's ability to speak would be curtailed. Gansukh could have said something himself, but he had realized that to do so would only infuriate Alchiq all the more.

Alchiq nudged his horse forward and let the beast amble toward the rock. Gansukh pulled his bow out of his quiver and ran a hand through the arrows so they would come out more readily if he needed them. He laid one across his bow and clucked at his horse to follow Alchiq. Both animals were well watered and fed, and it was several hours before sunset. He judged it would take them an hour to get to the rock at this pace. Anyone watching them would grow bored, and they would have time to see any activity before they had to act.

But he suspected no one was at the rock, and he suspected Alchiq was thinking the same. The carrion birds only came where there was no danger to them. If anyone was alive at the rock, the birds wouldn't be floating overhead: they'd all be pecking at the dead horse. But they weren't. *There is enough for all of them*, Gansukh thought. Would the corpses they were sure to find be human bodies or would there just be more horses?

Would he recognize any of the bodies?

He'd been thinking about Lian more often than not since they had left the Aksu River, pondering why she had joined the *Skjaldbræður*. He doubted she was a prisoner. There was no reason why they would still be treating her as such after crossing the pass during the winter. The only value she could possibly have for them was her Chinese heritage and they were riding away from China. No, more likely, she was part of their company now, and he had spent hours speculating on what she hoped to find in the West.

In the one instance when he had mentioned Lian to Alchiq, the old hunter had dismissed her outright. *It doesn't matter*, he had said. *She isn't Mongol and she rides with those who killed our Khagan. She will die too.*

Alchiq preferred simplicity in all things. Thinking too much led to inactivity, and inactivity led to death. It was very simple, after all.

But Gansukh knew that Alchiq's bluster hid an incredible cunning and determination. They knew the band of *Skjaldbræður* they pursued did not have the Spirit Banner; in fact, the leader of the company—the only one of the Westerners whom Alchiq considered his equal—was not present. But they would know where the old *Skjaldbræður* was; if they didn't, it was merely because they hadn't found him yet. He and Alchiq suspected they were looking for him too, and there would be no wholesale slaughter of the company if they caught up with the *Skjaldbræður*. Not until the banner was found. Without it, they couldn't return to Karakorum. Without it, they were lost.

Three nights earlier, Gansukh had asked Alchiq if he thought about returning to Karakorum. *Why?* Alchiq had answered. *Easier to slit my own throat now.*

Karakorum, for all of its glory, had been a prison to Gansukh. The walls of the *Khagan*'s compound had blocked his view of the steppe and the horizon, and the arcane rules of the court were impossible to fathom. Even with Lian's help, he had barely managed to bluster his way into the *Khagan*'s confidence. So why did he want to go back? Was he not a son of the steppe?

But he didn't want to merely go back. He wanted to turn back the passage of the seasons too. He wanted it to be fall again, and to be at the court of the *Khagan*, trying to convince him to stop drinking. He wanted to be in the garden where he might chance upon Lian and engage her in some silly excuse for a lesson. He wanted to believe that he could help the empire.

Instead, the *Khagan* was dead.

If Lian had not run, would he have stayed with her? Would they have gone back to Karakorum with the others and participated in the *kuraltai*. Maybe Chagatai Khan would understand that he, Gansukh, had not failed, but that the empire itself had failed the *Khagan*. Gansukh allowed the fantasy to blossom in his mind. He would be pardoned by Chagatai Khan, even congratulated, perhaps, for having accomplished as much as he had, and he would be awarded a place in Chagatai's retinue. While Ögedei's brother and the other Khans argued over who would succeed the late *Khagan*, he and Lian would have their own debate. They could compare their impressions of the contenders. Gansukh would, most likely, advocate for Chagatai Khan, but Lian would deftly predict the actual victor of the *kuraltai*. She was wise in the ways of court.

He wondered if she had managed to be useful to the *Skjaldbræður*.

Gansukh roused himself from his thoughts and noticed that Alchiq's horse was missing its rider. He pulled on his reins, scanning the terrain for any sign of the old hunter. Alchiq's horse was contentedly munching on a bush, and his own horse ambled to a stop and began to crop at the same bush.

He heard a grunt and glanced down, spying a long gully that lay across their path. It was nearly invisible at any distance, and as he watched, Alchiq clambered awkwardly up the slope, a clay pot clutched in his damaged hand. "Smoker," Alchiq said as he tossed the pot at Gansukh.

Gansukh caught the pot and turned it over in his hands. It was a simple pot, but the insides and the rim were blackened as if something acrid had been burned within. He sniffed it cautiously and the hair on the back of his neck stood up. "Chinese powder," he said. It smelled like the night the Chinese had attacked the *Khagan*'s caravan during the journey to Burqan-qaldun. The Chinese alchemists had had a device that hurled iron and fire, and the smoke that had come from it had the same bitter scent.

"The short one," Alchiq said. He had spotted something to Gansukh's left and, indicating that Gansukh should bring his horse, he loped along the edge of the gully. Gansukh leaned over and gathered up the reins of the other horse and followed.

When Alchiq leaped over the gully, Gansukh brought the horses to the same spot and dismounted, draping both sets of reins around the center trunk of a bush. He appraised the distance across the gully and took several steps back to get enough of a running start. He landed easily on the other side and jogged over to where Alchiq was standing beside another body.

This one was male, and he had died from an arrow to the belly. Alchiq held up the broken tip of the long arrow, and Gansukh took it from him, curious about the arrowhead used by the Westerners. He had seen a *Skjaldbrædur* bowman put an arrow through men in armor and even a man and a horse together. The arrow that had pierced the corpse at their feet had gone nearly all the way through the man's belly. He shivered slightly, remembering the fight at the great bear's cave.

"I don't know him," Alchiq said.

"Who?" Gansukh asked.

"This one." Alchiq nudged the corpse with his foot. "And we killed the *Skjaldbrædur* archer already so where did these arrows come from?"

✦ ✦ ✦

They split up, riding away from the rock in opposite directions and then circling around until they were approaching from the other side of the monolith. Gansukh's horse needed little encouragement to gallop; the steppe-bred horses enjoyed running across the open spaces and he hadn't let his run free for several days. He crouched low in his saddle, the wind whistling in his ears. His eyes scanned the area around the rock for any sign of movement—any sign that a living person was aware of his approach. As he got close enough to the rock to scan the empty ground, he urged his horse to his left, circling back around to the southern side of the rock.

He spotted signs of human habitation. Strips of cloth tied to wooden stakes fluttered in the afternoon breeze. A sheet of canvas was stretched between an upright rock taller than a man and a pair of wooden poles that might have once been spear shafts. A length of rope hung between other poles, outlining a patch of ground for a horse corral.

Alchiq was already in the camp, off his horse and stalking toward the lean-to with his sword in his hand. Gansukh slowed his horse and raised his bow, nocking an arrow. He spotted a circular ring of stones that was most likely the camp's fire pit. He circled around the lean-to, his stomach muscles tightening as he passed across the opening that faced south.

He let out the breath he had been holding. The lean-to was empty. He lowered his bow and stood in his stirrups to take one last look around the deserted camp. *Nothing.* He tugged on the reins, slowing his horse, and as the animal circled around to the back of the lean-to, he threw a leg over his saddle and slid off.

He could smell the dead bodies now, and he lowered his bow as he approached the lean-to. Alchiq was already there, and having seen what they were both smelling, had sheathed his sword. "Three," Alchiq said as Gansukh came around the side of the lean-to, and he stumped off toward the fire pit.

Gansukh looked anyway, his curiosity pushing him to look on the bodies. He had to know who they were, or who they weren't.

The three were all men, dark-haired and dark-skinned. It was hard to tell from the condition of the bodies, but Gansukh thought they had all died from multiple arrow wounds. He examined the arrangement of the bodies and then scanned the ground around the lean-to. "They didn't die there," he said to Alchiq as he caught up with the old hunter.

"Dragged," Alchiq said. He pointed at a stretch of open ground where several wooden stakes had been pounded into the ground. They were almost in line, an arrangement that wasn't conducive to their being tent stakes. As Gansukh was trying to puzzle out the significance of the stakes, he realized what Alchiq was directing his attention to was the confusion of hoof prints on the ground.

"Mongols," Gansukh said. "They would collect their arrows, but they wouldn't bother dragging the bodies under cover like that."

"Someone survived," Alchiq pointed out.

Gansukh's horse whinnied, and both men turned back toward the lean-to. A dark-skinned man dressed in a filthy tunic and trousers was attempting to restrain Gansukh's horse long enough to get into the saddle.

"Don't kill him," Alchiq said calmly as Gansukh raised his bow.

"I'm not," Gansukh replied, a touch of annoyance in his voice. Man and horse were performing an awkward dance, and he was waiting for a clean shot that wouldn't endanger his horse. The man had gotten hold of the reins and the horse was finally calming down.

"He's going to steal your horse," Alchiq said.

"He's not going to steal my horse," Gansukh replied.

Alchiq let out a grunt that said he thought otherwise.

The horse was standing still but the man was on the other side of the beast now. In another second, he would get a foot in one of the stirrups and swing himself up into the saddle.

Gansukh held his breath for a second, and then exhaled slowly as the man's hands appeared on the horn of the saddle. He let go of his bowstring, the arrow flying in a shallow arc, and the man appeared from the other side of the horse, settling into the saddle. Gansukh's arrow caught him in the shoulder, knocking him askew, and his sudden motion spooked Gansukh's horse. The animal bolted, and the man fell out of the saddle in an awkward confusion of arms and legs.

Alchiq made another sound that Gansukh interpreted as approval, and they walked toward the lean-to and the stunned man. Gansukh didn't have another arrow, and so he slung his bow across his back and drew his sword.

The man was on his knees, his face pressed against the ground, whimpering into the dirt. The arrow protruded from the junction of his arm and torso, not quite in his armpit and far enough forward that if he tried to raise his right arm, he would jostle the shaft. Alchiq tapped the wounded man lightly on the head with the flat of his sword, and the man jerked upright. He was Persian, like the dead men in the lean-to, and his face was thin and sallow beneath a scraggly and unkempt beard. His lips were cracked and dry and when he spoke, babbling in a tongue Gansukh did not understand, his voice was not much more than a ragged whisper.

Alchiq said one word and the man stopped. He sagged back on his heels, nearly falling over from exhaustion. The fabric of his tunic beneath his right arm was damp with blood.

"Do you understand what he's saying?" Gansukh asked.

"Somewhat," Alchiq said. He spoke again, and the man stirred, his eyelids fluttering. He replied haltingly, and Gansukh sensed that the man knew his death was coming. Alchiq's questions were the only respite he was going to get. He didn't have the will to refuse to answer; he barely had the strength to speak at all.

Gansukh sheathed his sword and went to calm his horse. He didn't have anything to contribute to the interrogation. The sun was getting close to the horizon. They would camp here for the night. He might as well feed the horses and see about finding some water.

There was a mystery about what had happened at the rock. They could try to puzzle it out after Alchiq had learned what he could from the wounded man.

◆ ◆ ◆

Gansukh was poking at the ashes in the fire pit, thinking about starting a fire, when Alchiq joined him. The sun had fled from the sky, and all that was left of the day was a fading line of orange light on the western horizon.

"They were here," Alchiq said as he finished wiping his sword clean. Gansukh had piled Alchiq's saddle and bags on one side of the pit, and Alchiq laid his sword across his saddle and started to rummage through his bags for some dried meat.

"How long ago?" Gansukh asked. He had had time to think about the presence of the Persians and the Western arrow in the dead horse beyond the gully where Alchiq had found sign of the alchemical powders.

"A few days," Alchiq said.

"But?" Gansukh asked, noting the pause in Alchiq's reply.

"There's a war party between us and them. Several *arban*, maybe even a *jaghun*." Alchiq chuckled. "The Persian could not count very well."

Between twenty and a hundred men, Gansukh thought, not terribly surprised the Persian had had difficulty measuring the number of men who had found him and his three companions. "They were survivors of an attack on the *Skjaldbræður*?" he asked.

Alchiq nodded. "Hay-door," he said. "They were following someone named Hay-door. A theft of horses, somewhere"—he gestured toward the open steppe to the south—"out there."

"Several dozen," Gansukh replied. While scavenging rope to picket their horses, he had discerned the size of the paddock.

Alchiq found what he was looking for in his bag and sat down, his mouth moving slowly and surely about a piece of tough meat. "Horses," he said after some concerted chewing.

"Yes," Gansukh said. "They have spares now. They'll be moving faster."

"The Mongol war party will have extra horses," Alchiq said. "And extra men," he added, smiling wolfishly at Gansukh.

CHAPTER 20:

FEARFUL SYMMETRY

Feronantus woke to find snow on the ground, a layer of fluffy whiteness as if the clouds had settled down to rest and were determined to sleep well past dawn. He wrapped a heavy fur around his shoulders as he got to his feet and staggered away from the camp to piss. His back ached, his knees were complaining, and the only relief he felt was the satisfaction of emptying his bladder.

The veil of night was slipping away; in the east, the horizon was more purple than black and a few of the bright stars winked at him, wanting to get his attention for a while longer before the sun leaped into the sky and scared all the stars away. The flaming dragon that drove away the night birds with the glittering eyes.

There was no snow on the Spirit Banner, or on the ground in a rough circle around it. He was no longer mystified by the unnatural way in which the banner ignored the weather of the steppe. Was it sacrilege to be bored by the ineffable? Was he a heretic for not worshiping the stick? True crusaders were sustained by their faith, their unshakeable belief in something far greater than themselves, and history was littered with the corpses of men who stood fast against unbelievers and doubters. How could he be one of those men if he did not burn with the same zeal? He was nothing more than an addled old man, fleeing across a land dev-astated by men who believed in the power of this stick.

He raised his hand and ran his fingers through one of the horsehair strands, the hair rough against his calloused and chapped hands. For the first few weeks after he had taken it, when-ever he touched the horsehair in the morning he would imagine hearing an immense herd of horses, galloping endlessly across the steppe. Over time, the echo of the foam-flecked horses had faded until he heard nothing when he touched the banner, nothing but the slow rhythm of his heart.

Every night since he had imagined the tiger looming over Istvan, inhaling the Hungarian's lazy breath, his dreams had been turbulent. He was not one of those who frantically tried to capture the essence (or even the particular details) of a given dream when he woke, but he was plagued by the persistent sense that he was forgetting something.

This was one of the more nagging aspects of the *Vor*—the awareness of knowing without knowing how or why such knowl-edge was gleaned. It had always been this way, even before he had known of his gift. Peregrinus had seen it in him, and the harsh lesson learned while he had been shitting was not one he had ever forgotten.

Feronantus let his thumb rest against the gnarled bump on the banner. The spot was healed over now, as if it had always been a knot of scarred wood, and not—as it had been when he had first acquired the banner—a fresh cut that was only beginning to scab.

Some wounds heal, he thought. Others did not. He looked at the scars on the back of his hand, the old cuts and nicks that had faded to tiny white lines on his flesh, as if he were a map so faded nothing could be read but the vague impression of ancient moun-tain ranges. *Would that be the fate of the world?* he wondered. After he and every Shield-Brethren were long dead. Would the world be wiped clean by snow or ice? Or fire, even? An endless plume of smoke and ash, belching from some volcano that finally erupted for a generation or more?

The Shield-Brethren would be gone. He knew that much. He had seen it come to pass, and he knew he had a part yet to play in that untimely disappearance. Just as he knew it would require a hard sacrifice, which is why he had left the others at Burqan-qaldun.

What father wouldn't sacrifice himself for his children?

✦ ✦ ✦

By mid-morning, clouds obscured the sky, a voluminous layer of white that sank closer and closer to the ground. The wind danced around the pair of horsemen for an hour before deciding that it would blow steadily from the north against their faces. Feronantus wrapped strips of cloth about his head in a vain attempt to keep ice from building in his beard, and Istvan huddled in his saddle, cloak pulled tightly about his lean frame. Seeing they were going to be undeterred in their route, the wind looped up in the clouds and returned with stinging rain and pellets of snow that flew at them like a swarm of icy bugs.

There was little respite from the storm, and even if they had wanted to wait it out, there was no shelter on the steppe. Istvan threw a length of rope to Feronantus and both men looped their respective ends loosely about their saddle horns in an effort to not lose one another in the blizzard. His horse continued to plod onward, its mane coated with snow and ice, its head hanging dejectedly.

They had been through worse, Feronantus reminded himself. The last blizzard they had suffered through had been in the mountains, where the terrain had been much more treacherous. The path had been narrow, and if they had strayed too far, they would have stumbled off the edge of a cliff. On the steppe, there was little danger of falling into a crevasse or being crushed by an avalanche of snow. They had to keep moving until they found shelter or the clouds ran out of snow to pelt them with.

The rope jerked taut between the horses, and Feronantus dimly stared at it for a while before nudging his horse to close the gap. Istvan's horse hadn't fallen; it had merely drifted from the course they had been taking. Their pace was so slow that it mattered little if they wandered more west than north. They were in the middle of the empty steppe.

Feronantus's horse stumbled, and he clutched at the horn of his saddle. The horse continued on as if nothing had happened, but Feronantus felt the change. The horse was picking its way down an incline. It wasn't a steep slope, but they had definitely crossed a ridge line.

The fury of the storm lessened, and his horse picked up its pace. He wrapped his shaking hands around the rope and pulled up the slack. The snow slowed to a swirling cloud of fat flakes as he and his horse descended beneath the level of the steppe.

The snow wasn't sticking on the ground, and as he pulled the ice-encrusted cloth away from his cheeks and eyes, he spotted dark streaks in the dirt. No plants grew either. The ground was bare, marred by the black stains.

The rope slackened even more, and he brought his horse to a halt beside Istvan's motionless steed. The Hungarian was shivering uncontrollably, his teeth clacking in his mouth; unable to form words, he pointed instead. Several paces ahead of them the ground became soft, dissolving into a pool of slow-bubbling darkness.

"What is it?" he croaked, but his voice was nothing more than a dry whisper and Istvan did not appear to have heard him. Shaking off the layer of rime that had formed on his cloak, Feronantus descended from his horse and stiffly edged closer to the pool.

The ground around the pool was stained black, and a pace or two in front of the horses, Feronantus crouched and slowly tugged one of his leather gloves off. The ground was cold but not frozen, and when he raised his fingers, they were slick with the oily darkness. He sniffed at his fingers, and rubbed them together, feeling the sticky texture of the muck. The smell reminded him of old keeps, stone towers built in an age when windows were a luxury and the stone walls and ceilings were dark with soot from torches and candles. It reminded him of something else as well, a memory of castle walls and an unrelenting sun, beating down on an empty desert.

He stood quickly and backed away from the pool. "Greek fire," he swore, memories of the long siege of Acre coming back to him. It had been his first campaign after taking the Shield-Brethren vows. They had arrived in the Holy Land in the spring, and had joined the crusading army that sought to take Acre from Saladin. The crusaders had been camped outside the city for months, and disease was rampant in the camp. It wasn't until Richard Lionheart had arrived several months later that the crusaders were able to rally themselves. Richard had had siege engines built, and after pummeling the walls for a week, he had given the order to attack. He remembered the smell of the sticky fire poured from the walls by the Muslims. It fell like black rain, and the Christian attackers did not understand the danger until Muslim archers sent a volley of flaming arrows down. In an instant, the entire rank was transformed into a wall of roaring flame, the men screaming as the greasy liquid ignited and melted their flesh.

Istvan slid off his horse and staggered to Feronantus's side. The Hungarian's beard was coated with ice and his eyes were bright with a fevered light. "World fire," he murmured.

"No," Feronantus said, grabbing Istvan's arm.

The Hungarian turned his icy face toward Feronantus. "Is that not what you see?" he asked. "Is that not what you learn during the night when you hang yourself on the wood?" He raised a shaking arm and pointed at the Spirit Banner slung across Feronantus's saddle. "Is that not what she wants?" Fresh ice glistened on his cheeks.

"She?" Feronantus did not understand what Istvan was talking about. The Hungarian had been coherent when they had broken camp but, as when Istvan had stumbled into Feronantus's camp during the mountain crossing, the cold weather could trigger a resurgence of the mind fever as if it were a shield against the winter chill.

"You saved me once," Istvan said. "That debt must be paid." He drew his sword and Feronantus stepped back, unsure of Istvan's intentions, but the Hungarian made no move toward him. Instead, Istvan knelt at the edge of the pool and thrust his sword blade into the sticky darkness. When he drew it free, the steel was black.

"Go," Istvan said. "I will give her what she wants."

"I don't understand what you are telling me," Feronantus said. "I don't know who you are talking about."

Istvan fumbled one-handed in the pouch on his belt and produced his flint stone. "Go," he shouted at Feronantus as he slammed the flint against his blade. A shower of sparks leaped from the contact, and the horses whinnied in fear.

But they weren't reacting to the sparks.

Feronantus heard a low rumbling growl, and he slowly turned his head and looked to his right.

The tiger was less than ten paces away.

"Here," Istvan shouted, banging his flint against his sword again. "I am the one you seek." Sparks flew again, and the tiger snarled in response, revealing long white teeth.

Light bloomed behind Feronantus, and he heard a whoosh of sound as Istvan's blade was engulfed with flame. The Hungarian raised his weapon and charged the tiger.

CHAPTER 21:

TO PRAY IN PSKOV

Sending cavalry alone would have allowed Nevsky to reach Pskov more quickly, but if Alexander wanted to do more than simply storm into the city, an army that included infantry was required. As a result, it took nearly a week to reach Pskov. The city was patiently waiting for them, the walls and towers rising from the morning mist that flowed off the Velikaya, eerily untouched, given the horrors the city had endured.

The bulk of the men in Nevsky's force were infantry, foot-soldiers who wore lamellar armor over old maille, protecting their torsos, and battered conical helms such as those worn by the Northmen sat upon their heads. Long axes or spears were held by most, though the occasional sword, old and worn, hung from the hips of the few veterans among the many volunteers. Their clothes were well-worn, and there was little to no uniformity of color. Those who could afford the luxury of fur—sheepskin mostly—wore cloaks and gloves of the same. The greatest asset of these men was their number, and the fact that they were defending their homelands. The knights within the city, should they opt to not surrender, would have better weapons and armor, but that would matter little against the fervor and number of the prince's men.

The *Druzhina* were a different matter altogether, and Illarion hoped their presence would be enough to forestall any desire for martyrdom on the part of the defenders. The *Druzhina* wore fine maille and helms with aventails that protected the backs of their necks. No two men were armed identically, for these were professional warriors whose whole lives were brutal affairs. Some were the sons of nobles, or nobles themselves, but many were mercenaries that had taken up service with their *Kynaz* for pay. Swords gleamed on belts decorated with metal, and lances were tipped with white spear-points that caught the light.

In his role as the *Kynaz*, Illarion was a sight to be seen. He wore a coat of shiny maille beneath steel pauldrons on his shoulders and a long surcoat that bore the prince's coat of arms. His cloak was lined with fur, his shield painted, and his helm chastened with sculpted gold. His sword—the least ostentatious piece of his costume—hung from his saddle.

On his right, Nika rode a large black horse. She was similarly attired in colorful garb over her maille, and she carried the *Kynaz*'s standard, the banner snapping in the wind.

Behind them were three dozen *Druzhina* guard.

When they reached the gates of Pskov, Illarion expected to be greeted with a formal challenge, but he spied no watcher on the battlements. Their party slowed to a gentle trot, and Illarion nodded at Nika, who stood in her stirrups, holding the standard high. "The *Kynaz* of Novgorod, Prince Alexander Iaroslavich, also known as *Nevsky*, commands that these gates be opened and that the city of Pskov receive him," she shouted.

No answer came, and for a long time the only sound on the plain was the wind playing with the standard. Then, Illarion heard a scrabbling noise like a mouse behind a wall, followed by the louder clunk of a wooden bar being raised. The gate creaked open slowly as each panel was pushed back by a single individual. "Welcome, illustrious prince," one of the two haggard figures said when he had finished with the gate. "We are so grateful for your presence."

"Where is the garrison?" Nika demanded, continuing in her role as spokesperson for the *Kynaz*.

"There is no garrison," the man replied. "They left nothing behind."

Illarion looked more closely at the speaker. His face was a mass of dark bruises, and his right eyelid drooped low over an eye that was milky in color. The other gatekeeper limped, and his left hand was a mass of dirty bandages. "Ride," he snapped to his escort. He swallowed heavily as he prepared himself for what they were to find within the city walls.

A lingering smell of burnt matter—both wood and flesh—greeted them as they rode into the city, and Illarion marshaled his courage as the horses trotted through the empty streets. They passed the burned-out husks of buildings, the blackened timbers dappled with fresh snow, and here and there he spotted the ragged shapes of hungry children digging in the detritus for something to eat. He saw very few figures that were as large as the pair who had opened the gates for them, and a prickling of dread began to work its way up his spine. *They left nothing behind.*

When they reached the main square, Illarion nearly lost the contents of his stomach when he saw the carnage. Beside him, Nika let out a choking sob.

The bodies lay in a long line, with a large pile arranged at one end. The recent snow covered most of the corpses, and the winter chill had arrested the normal bloating and rot that would take root in dead flesh. Illarion couldn't decide whether the corpses being frozen was better or worse than if the weather had been warmer.

"They form a sword," Nika said in a tiny voice.

Illarion forced himself to look more closely at the arrangement of the bodies, and saw what Nika had spotted. The long line of bodies was the blade. In the pile at the end, there were two mounds that jutted out from the central shape that was longer than it was wide. *The cross-guard of a sword*, he realized, *and the pommel stone.*

In his mind, he saw the Livonian sigil. The red sword and cross on the white field. His fists tightened within his gloves, the fingertips digging into his palm so tightly they might have drawn blood but for the leather. Memories of Volodymyr, of ruined Kiev, flashed through his mind, and now, added to those, was the sight of the dead of Pskov. Every man or woman who could have held a weapon and stood against the Teutonic army was here.

Nika took off her helm and wiped the tears off her cheeks, though more were flowing. "I underestimated his cruelty," she said.

"We all did," Illarion said. Horrifying as the sight was, it was a spark that kindled a long-dormant emotion in his chest. Kristaps had left a message for all the people of Rus: *You are not safe; your* Kynaz *cannot protect you.*

And as he looked around at the timid faces of the survivors of Pskov, he saw little joy in the haggard and bruised faces. They kept their distance, shying away from the *Druzhina*. They were still afraid. *They don't see saviors,* Illarion realized. *They see another group of armed men coming into their city, and all they know is that their families and friends are dead. What is there left to save?*

Too late. Always too late.

"He's playing a cruel game," Illarion murmured. "Word of this will spread beyond the walls, and to every corner of the countryside. He seeks to demoralize Alexander's army."

"No," Nika said. "Look at these men. They want revenge for this. When the time comes, they will fight hard for the prince."

"The *Druzhina* will fight, regardless," Illarion said. "As will you and I and your sisters. But it is not us whom Kristaps strikes against. He wants to make the militia afraid." He gestured at the field of dead. "This is what happens to brothers and sisters, mothers and fathers. Everyone who has volunteered is going to be worrying about the families they left in their villages. Worrying that this will happen to them."

"They will not break Rus," Nika said. "Not like this."

"We have to give them solace," Illarion said. "We must find priests who can give them hope, who can offer guidance to our men as they help these people find their dead and bury them." His eyes burned, and he wanted to take his helmet off and wipe the tears out of his eyes, but he didn't dare reveal his face. Not yet. If the survivors saw that he wasn't truly the *Kynaz*, what tiny hope his arrival had given them would be extinguished. "Let us find the church. Let them see the *Kynaz* pray for their dead."

The anger burned hot in his chest. Beneath his helmet, tears streamed down his cheeks, and they felt like rivulets of fire coursing down his face.

Rus would not be broken, he thought. *Not like this.*

◆ ◆ ◆

As Illarion, Nika, and a trio of the *Druzhina* rode toward the Trinity Cathedral, Illarion found solace in remembering a visit to the city as a boy. It had been in the spring, and the streets had been alive with the festive commotion of commerce. He had slipped away from his father's entourage once to wander among the markets. He had seen fisherman, their catch fresh from the river; fur traders who had returned from months in the forests with bales of silver and black pelts; pagan traders, who wore colorful robes that were covered in strange markings, tried to sell him metal trinkets and woven effigies that offered blessings to the old gods of the forests and mountains. There were other boyars, like his father, dressed in silken clothes that were much finer than any of the rough clothes of the north. They rode powerful horses, tall steeds with shining manes and ribbons woven into their tails.

The arches of the church came into view, and the stone façade was draped with snow. Illarion's memory of a lively Pskov was brushed away, much like snow dashed off a weathered headstone by a man who has come to the graves of his wife and children to grieve. *How long would it take to bury all the dead?* he wondered as he stared at the foreboding church. The ground was still hard from the winter freeze. Should they stack the dead in empty houses until the spring thaw softened the ground? It was a morbid thought and he pushed it out of his mind. It didn't go far; he knew it would be back, haunting him when he tried to sleep.

No priest came out to greet them, and the great doors of the church gaped open. One of the panels had been torn free from its top hinge and hung crookedly, like a misaligned tooth in a skull.

"One of you should stay with the horses," Illarion said to the three *Druzhina*. He unhooked his sword and scabbard from his saddle and slid down to the ground. Nika swapped the standard for her spear before joining him on the ground. The *Druzhina* exchanged glances, and, based on some unspoken decision passed between them, two of the three got down from their horses. "Belun," one said as he fell in behind Illarion. "That's Zuhzyn." The second one nodded in response to his name.

"Very well, Belun and Zuhzyn. Let us offer our prayers for this beleaguered city. May God grant us mercy." Illarion took the lead, Nika and the others falling in behind him.

There was something here that put him ill at ease. It was almost impossible for Illarion to lay his finger upon it, but it unsettled him, like a bad smell whose source he couldn't place. He paused at the broken doors, peering inside in a valiant effort to see something in the interior gloom of the church. He called out a greeting, and heard nothing but the distant caw of a raven. Bird of ill omen.

A shiver ran down his spine and he gripped his scabbard tightly. He was inclined to draw his sword, but he couldn't. The

Kynaz would not enter a church with a drawn weapon. He was here as a savior, not a conqueror.

"What is it?" Nika asked, sensing his apprehension.

Illarion looked at the houses that surrounded the church, and then he raised his gaze to the spires towering above him. The raven cawed again, and he spotted the black bird perched on the edge of the sculpted roof. "A sense of dread," he confessed.

Belun guffawed. "Now?" he asked. "All the dead bodies didn't bother you?"

"Belun is right, *Kynaz*," Nika said. "There is a great deal of despair and death here. We've all felt it since the moment we entered the city. It will stay with us for a long time."

Illarion removed his helmet and tucked it under his arm. He pawed at his face, smearing the partially dried tears on his cheeks. How could they understand that he had seen much worse atrocities? He had stood on the planks laid over the families of Volodymyr. After he had risen from the dead and killed the black bones who had been looting the dead, he had walked to the edge of the field of planks. There had been bodies under those planks, and each step had been horrific. What if one of the victims was, like him, not quite dead, and his weight crushed the final bit of life out of them?

"Forgive me," he said. "I am tired. You are correct, Belun. It is better to feel something than nothing, is it not?" He nodded toward the dark entrance of the church. "Let us enter and pray for God to show us mercy."

Nika went first, followed by Belun and Zuhzyn. Illarion thought about putting his helmet back on, but decided that to do so would be to give in to the fear bubbling in his stomach. He took a deep breath and stepped over the threshold.

His eyes adjusted to the gloom of the church. The light from the windows in the apse was sullen and gray, and it made the interior of the church a mass of deep shadows and bleak stone. There were iron candelabras scattered throughout and wall sconces that still held stubs of candles. "Let us bring some light to this wretched place," he said.

One of the two *Druzhina* moved toward the inner wall of the church and fumbled with a pouch on his belt. After several moments, a flint was struck, scattering sparks. After several more tries, one of the sparks caught in the loose tinder the *Druzhina* was holding, and when he raised the smoking bundle to his lips to blow on it, Illarion saw that the figure was Belun.

Belun held the smoking tinder to the wick of one of the candles, still blowing on the dry twigs to keep the spark alive. A tiny flame wavered, dancing languidly, and Belun drew in breath to blow one more time, but when he exhaled, he coughed. The sudden gust of air was too much for the tiny flame and it went out.

In the darkness, Belun coughed again, groaned, and there was a clatter as the candelabra he was holding fell over.

"Assassins," Nika cried.

They weren't alone in the church. Illarion heard a scrape of leather against stone and twisted away from an adversary that was approaching from his left. He felt the sharp point of a spear slide off the side of his helmet, still tucked under his arm. He had no choice but to let go of the helmet or risk the spear getting tangled with his arm and scabbard.

✦ ✦ ✦

Nika heard the blood in Belun's throat when he coughed the first time, and even before the *Druzhina* fell, she was already in motion. The assassins in the church had been there long enough for their night sight to bloom, and they would be dressed in dark cloaks. Her garb would pick up what light there was, and judging by the stealthy manner in which Belun had been killed, other assassins would be in place to do the same to the rest of their party.

As she moved, she saw a glint of steel on her left, and she slapped the haft of her spear into her left hand as she made a shield of the wood pole. Her spear clacked against the haft of her attacker's, and the force of her motion pushed the point of his spear past her. The contact between their spears was brief, and as soon as the weight of his weapon vanished, she dropped the tip of her spear down.

A blurry shape moved in front of her, and she knew he was attempting to rotate around her makeshift shield and strike her in the head with the butt end of his spear. Nika snapped the tip of her spear up, intercepting the incoming strike, and she heard wood strike steel, which told her where the assassin's weapon was. There was enough room for her to respond with a jab from the butt of her spear as well.

Her blow stuck something soft and her attacker grunted, and his weapon clattered against the stone floor. Her eyes were finally adjusting to the light, and she could see the shape of her attacker well enough to aim the point of her spear at the man's neck. Metal flashed, and her spear was knocked aside. Her attacker had not chased after his dropped spear, but had pulled another weapon free—a Danish axe. It came scything at her, and she blocked high. The blade of the axe gouged a chip of wood out of the thick haft of her spear. She whirled her spear around, forcing him to keep his distance, and tried to keep her position such that the light outlined him more than her.

She could spare no attention to whether or not Illarion was still alive.

◆ ◆ ◆

"Who dares draw blood in this house of God?" Illarion shouted as he drew his sword. He doubted his question would do much to dissuade the men who sought to kill them, but the sound of his voice would alert his companions that he still lived.

He could not say the same for the others. Belun was on his knees, gagging on his own blood. Off to his left, Illarion caught sight of Nika and heard the clatter of wood against steel. He didn't see or hear any sign of Zuhzyn, and he had to assume the worst.

His attacker came at him again, a dark blur thrusting a spear at his midsection. He knocked the spear aside with both his sword and scabbard, and, realizing how foolish it was to carry the latter, he threw it at his attacker. He followed through with a thrust of his sword, and he felt his point slide off a leather cuirass. But that told him where his opponent was, and he twisted the blade of his sword as he continued to push. He flicked it up and felt some resistance as the tip of his blade passed through flesh, and when the man screamed, Illarion stabbed again. This time, his sword pierced the man's armor and the cries of pain stopped.

A tiny gleam of light bloomed on his right, and as he turned his head to look at it, he caught sight of movement out of the corner of his eye. A slender shape, more feminine than Nika but with steel in either hand, darting at him. *Knife and sword*, he realized, as he blocked the sword attack and countered with a strike of his own, attempting to keep the figure far enough away from him that the knife would be useless. The knife tangled with his sword, steel grating along steel, and he was forced to pivot away from the figure to avoid catching a sword thrust in the thigh.

The slender man—for Illarion realized it was, indeed, a man he faced—slipped in and out of the deeper shadows as if his flesh were like the wind. Illarion had never seen a man move so quickly; he caught a glimpse of a crescent-moon smile and cold, eager eyes before the sword and knife were back, cutting under his guard. Illarion jumped back, driving blows aside only to find his counterstrokes hewing through empty space as his enemy danced away from his attacks. After a few exchanges, where Illarion found his efforts becoming more and more frantic, he realized he was not going to be able to land a blow as long as the man was moving freely. It was akin to trying to strike a bird out of the air. Much better to strike at the bird on the ground, he thought, and during their next exchange of blows, he did not follow through with the counterstrike as was expected of him. Instead, as his opponent danced aside, spinning to the left, Illarion surged forward, lashing out with his foot. He connected with the man's hip, momentarily disturbing the other's preternatural dance, and he was close enough that he could use the rest of his body. He thrust with his shoulder and connected with the man's chest, and smiled at the sound of hastily expelled air coming out of his opponent's mouth.

He would only have a second or two before the man recovered. But he never got the chance.

Something hard and metallic rang off his right shoulder, and Illarion staggered.

There was another assassin, and only the steel pauldron on Illarion's shoulder had saved him from a sword blow that would have severed his arm.

✦ ✦ ✦

The axe hooked her spear, and Nika knew what was coming next. As the bigger man tried to pull the spear from her hands, she didn't resist. She slammed into him, the axe caught flat between them along with the haft of her spear. Her attacker grunted and exhaled loudly, sounding almost as if he were laughing at her for coming so close to him. He let go of the axe and sought to get his hands on her body.

She sidestepped his clumsy grip, putting her left leg in line with his and snapping a short kick with her other foot against his other knee. He screamed as the leg moved in an unnatural direction, and she drove the butt of her spear under his chin, knocking his head back and rattling his teeth. He gulped and gagged—she might have caused him to bite part of his tongue off—and as she stepped back from his slack embrace, she swirled the spear around and slashed the point across his throat, opening it from ear to collarbone.

Turning, she caught sight of Belun sitting with his back to the wall. Nestled in his lap, held upright by his hand, was a guttering candle. The light from the flame was yellow, but his chest was covered with streaks of crimson. His head was down as if he were dozing, but she knew he would not wake. Lighting the candle had been a final protective act on the part of the *Druzhina*, and a fierce hand gripped her heart at the sight of such selflessness. *He died protecting his prince*, she thought, *protecting Rus.*

The thought stirred her from the unexpected reverie, and she cast about for Illarion, the disguised prince. By the weak light of the candle, she spotted him giving ground to a willowy fighter with an arming sword and a long knife. Illarion charged into the man and seemed about to gain the advantage when a massive, fur-clad assassin emerged out of the shadows behind him and tried to cut off his arm with a single downward slash of a sword. The fancy costume of the *Kynaz* had saved Illarion from dismemberment, but the force of the blow was going to leave bruises if it hadn't broken any bones in Illarion's shoulder. The slender assassin danced away from Illarion, laughing like a maddened child, and Illarion struggled to face the man with the sword, confusion plainly written on his features. Which one to face?

Nika changed course, opting to go for the dancing youth instead of the fur-clad sword-wielder. For all of his confusion, Illarion should be able to handle the swordsman. The youth was another matter entirely, and he tittered with glee as he made eye contact with her. He seemed eager to dance with her spear, but Nika approached him with caution. Her weapon was only effective if she could keep him at range; if he got too close, his weapons would negate the effectiveness of her spear. Much like the other man she had fought, there could come a time when it was best for her to throw the spear aside.

He had to close with her. It was inevitable if he was going to kill her, and she didn't have to wait long for him to try. She knew he would. He was too eager for blood to be patient. As he darted toward her, she feinted with her spear. He anticipated her feint and responded in kind, but she didn't follow through. She merely struck again, on the same path, and because he had tried to be cleverer than her by feinting as well, he was still in the path of the spear. He twisted aside, displaying startling agility, and the tip of her spear struck just below his hip on the outside of his right leg. The point rang off metal and tore through his clothing, but it didn't penetrate his leg.

She had forced him off balance, and the slashing attack of his long knife only skipped off her maille. "A woman," he laughed as he caught sight of her beneath the open face of her helmet. "A woman killed Taras. How amusing."

She let go of her spear, grabbed the inside of his knife arm to keep him close, and drove her helmeted forehead into his face. "I'm laughing too," she snarled as she felt his nose crumple and blood spurt.

✦ ✦ ✦

Illarion was having trouble moving his right arm. The pauldron had been dented—maybe even cut—by the sword, and the padded gambeson and maille he was wearing beneath the armor were the only reasons bones hadn't been broken. He wiggled his arm, and the dancing assassin slipped away from him, laughing at his attempt. He caught sight of Nika moving past him, and then paid no more attention to the lithe boy as the fur-wearing sword-wielder was coming at him again.

He dodged, slipped, and then turned the slip into a clumsy roll. He cracked his head on the stone floor, and a burst of red and yellow flowers, like stars exploding across a meadow, filled his vision. He got his feet under him, wiped his hand across his face in a vain effort to clear his vision, and then spotted the big assassin coming at him. He raised his sword in time to block a heavy hewing stroke, and the assassin's blade struck sparks from his as it slid off. Illarion's pommel was pushed back, smacking his forehead, by the man's attack, and as he felt the other's sword slide off his, he thrust his arms forward and hammered the end of his sword against the other man's kneecap. He got to his feet, swinging his sword wildly with both hands, and he caught the other man just above the elbow with the edge of his blade.

They stood still for a moment, staring at Illarion's blade. It had passed nearly all the way through the man's arm, caught between the knob of the elbow and the muscles of the upper arm. Blood was already flowing—running down the arm, raining onto the floor.

Illarion wrenched his sword free, and thrust the bloodied tip into the man's startled face, thereby solving the problem of what to do about the half-severed arm.

The taste of blood filled his mouth as he turned, and he spit it on the floor, saying a silent apology to God for the sacrilege in his house.

He heard voices, followed by the impact of metal against bone, and he spotted Nika and the assassin engaged in a bloody dance. The lithe youth was trying to extricate himself from Nika's grip, and as Illarion lumbered toward them, the slender man slipped free. He made a half-hearted attempt to cut Nika once more with his knife before he staggered away from Illarion's oncoming sword.

Illarion chased after him, and nearly took a blade in the face for his efforts. The assassin had darted a few paces away, moving like smoke. Turning, he had thrown his knife at Illarion, and it was only a flash of light off the blade that warned Illarion the flung weapon was coming. He managed to deflect it enough with his sword that it bounced off his left shoulder instead of piercing the maille at the hollow of his throat. And then the assassin was on him, his arming sword flickering like lightning on a summer day.

As he closed with the slender assassin, every detail of the man's face stood out in crystalline relief. He had the sort of chiseled features that set the hearts of village girls aflutter, marred now by a shattered nose that had splattered blood across the lower half of his face. But for the eyes, he might have been a random boyar's son, blessed with beauty and good nutrition, but his gaze was empty of anything but a gnawing void. *Like a vicious, spiteful child.*

Illarion barreled into him, sword in hand. The arming sword in the assassin's hand checked his blade, and then wound beneath it at his face. Illarion pivoted, letting the weapon slide past his cheek. Had he been wearing a helmet, the blade would have caught his helm and twisted his head to the side. Had he an ear, it would have been sliced open by the passing blade. As it was, he lost only some hair. He wrapped his left arm about his opponent's extended arm, trapping him close, and then he brought his pommel down—hard—on the assassin's beautiful face, destroying it further.

The assassin drove his knee up, missing Illarion's groin and hitting him in the stomach instead. Illarion pitched forward, bending around the assassin's arm so that he couldn't withdraw it—and his sword—and he felt the assassin grab the cross-guard of his own sword. They both struggled, each trying to control the other, and Illarion felt his grip on the assassin's arm starting to slip. The assassin was trying to turn his wrist to lay his blade's edge against Illarion's throat.

The assassin jumped suddenly, and Illarion heard the distinctive thud of a spear being thrust into flesh. The assassin struggled, putting all of his effort in freeing his right arm, and Illarion held tight.

Behind the assassin, Nika pressed all of her weight against her spear, shoving it slowly but assuredly through the assassin's body. He writhed and screamed, blood flying from his mouth, but his strength was fading. He glared at Illarion, his face a mask of blood and hatred, and Illarion stared back, waiting for the light to leave his eyes.

It took longer than expected, but Illarion found himself in no hurry. This was the first time he could watch one of his enemies die, and he found it to be a comforting sight.

CHAPTER 22:

THE EMPTY HORIZON

Cnán hadn't imagined there was anything drearier than riding across the steppe in the fall, but there was: that same trip during the desolate heart of winter. They were rested and provisioned, their horses were in excellent shape (and they had spares), and the weather was relatively mild for winter on the high plains. Their situation was much improved over the mountain crossing at the beginning of winter, but this comparison didn't alleviate the boredom of the endless days of riding.

And it had been only three days since they had left the rock.

They had come across the sign of a recent Mongol encampment on the afternoon of the second day, and Raphael had immediately turned the company north, forcing them to ride well past moonrise before he allowed to make camp. There had been no fire that night, and everyone had loudly complained about being stiff and sore from a night on the cold ground. But the sun had come out mid-morning and followed them all afternoon, and by the time it came down from its high arc and slipped behind the western horizon, Cnán was sorry to see it go. It was almost like one of their company were leaving them.

They set up a camp in a tight formation, and Yasper put her and Lian in charge of collecting rocks for the fire pit. He had a collection of dried patties made from a combination of horse shit and grass and twigs that stood in for firewood and he started the fire with a pinch of powders from his alchemical stash and a piece from one of his phoenix eggs. The fire started with a whoosh of blue and green flame, and on the first night both Bruno and Haakon had drawn their swords when the colored flames leapt up from the temporary fire pits. The others teased them for several hours, but Cnán could tell that the idle ribbing masked their own apprehension at Yasper's strange powders.

The alchemist hadn't been as talkative since they had left the rock, and she didn't go out of her way to seek his company. Instead, she fell back on old habits and spent most of her time trying to get behind Percival's stoic shield.

He had given his gray Arabian a name. *Morgana. Was it the name of an old lover?* she had asked. *A family member? A fairy princess from some story of his childhood?*

No, Percival had replied to all of her questions.

"He spends a lot of time with that horse," she noted to Lian as the two of them huddled by the fire pit. Yasper's alchemical logs burned with more heat than flame, which was good after the initial burst of wild fire, but the alchemist did not have a large supply. They burned one each night, and Cnán found herself and Lian sitting by the fire as long as possible each night before dashing for their tent in a valiant attempt to bring some of the last warmth inside the canvas shelter with them.

"He does," Lian noted, watching Percival's shadowy shape move among the nearby horses. "Have you seen how he rides her in battle? It is almost as if he and she were one."

Cnán remembered Tonnerre, the trained warhorse that Percival had started their journey with. Morgana was a dutiful steed, but she had none of the training that Percival's destrier had had. Comparing the two was like watching a baby chick try to walk and a grown hawk soaring in the sky.

Lian had one hand tucked inside her robe, and Cnán knew what the Chinese woman was clutching. She had seen the tiny lacquer box a few times when Lian thought she had been sleeping. She had no idea what was inside the box but knew it was the single most important thing in the world to Lian.

"What's his name?" she asked suddenly.

"What?" Lian asked, her attention coming away from Percival and the horses. Her hand withdrew and she idly smoothed the front of her robe.

"The man you are thinking about," Cnán said, knowing that she had guessed right.

"There is no man," Lian said defensively.

"Is it him?" Cnán nodded toward the horses.

"No," Lian scoffed.

"Gawain? Haakon?"

"It is no one in this company," Lian said, cutting Cnán off before she could list every member of their group.

"But there is someone," Cnán pressed.

"There was," Lian admitted.

"What happened?"

"I stole his heart," Lian said, a sad smile tugging at her lips. "And I put his tent and all of his worldly possessions to the torch."

"You did no such thing," Cnán snorted.

Lian giggled and her fingers flew up to her lips in a vain effort to suppress the sound. "I did," she said. "You saw the smoke."

"Where?" Cnán thought back to the day when she had infiltrated the *Khagan*'s camp at Burqan-qaldun, intent on rescuing Haakon. To her surprise, the young man had already been out of his cage, along with a red-haired giant of a man named Krasniy. And Lian, who had been in the process of escaping from the *Khagan*.

"That fire?" she asked. "In the *Khagan*'s camp. That was your doing?"

"It was," Lian admitted.

"Your…your *lover*'s tent?"

"What happened to whose tent?" a new voice asked, and both women looked up as Bruno joined them at the fire. He had his skin of spirits and several small cups.

"Ask her," Cnán said, jerking her head at Lian.

"It's a long story," Lian said before Bruno could do such a thing.

"Does it have a happy ending?" Bruno asked as he unstoppered the skin and poured a measure into each cup.

"Not really," Lian admitted, and Cnán choked back a snort of laughter.

"Ah, well, it's probably not worth dragging out of you then," Bruno said with a smile. He offered each of them a cup.

Lian accepted hers reluctantly and made no move to actually drink the contents. Cnán sniffed her cup carefully and her eyes watered at the strength of the spirits within. "What is this?" she sputtered, holding the cup as far away from her as possible.

"Don't drop it in the fire," Lian cautioned her, a knowing smile on her lips, and Cnán snatched her hand back.

"Yasper's recipe," Bruno said. "I just drink it." He raised his cup and threw the contents into his mouth. He grimaced as the liquid went down his throat, but sighed noisily after it settled. "You know you're alive after a sip of that," he added, touching a thumb to the corner of one eye to mop up the tear starting there.

Cnán took a tentative sip, anticipating the worst—and it was worse than anything she had braced herself for. Her mouth burst into flame, and even though she tried to stop the liquid from going down her throat, it wiggled down anyway, lighting everything on fire as it fell. It hit her stomach and the resulting explosion was not unlike the burst of blue and green flame when Yasper ignited his shit patties. She gasped, choked, wept, and felt sweat start across her forehead and neck. "That's foul," she croaked.

"Aye," Bruno said. "But it will keep you warm tonight."

Another figure emerged from the darkness beyond the weak flames, and Cnán hastily shoved her half-empty cup at him. Haakon took the offered cup as he sat down. "What is it?" he asked.

"It'll put hair on your chest," Bruno said, saluting with his cup.

"I have hair on my chest," Haakon said. He sniffed at the cup.

"Why does everyone smell their cups?" Bruno asked. "It is pure spirits. Do Yasper and I look like we're connoisseurs of flavor?"

Lian threw back the contents of her cup in one quick motion. Her lips tightened and a shudder ran through her frame, but she swallowed the spirits with no visible discomfort. Bruno stared at her, his mouth hanging open.

"I spent time at the *Khagan*'s court in Karakorum," she explained. "Drinking wine and stronger spirits was one of the *Khagan*'s favorite activities. The rest of the court tried to keep up."

Bruno poured another measure into Lian's cup. "Ah, I have heard tales about how much wine flowed into Karakorum. It was the death of him, wasn't it? I heard he died in a hunting accident—fell off his horse while intoxicated."

Cnán stared at the slumbering fire. "Well, it certainly happened while he was hunting," she said.

"And if an event isn't *planned*, it could certainly be called an *accident*," Lian said.

Haakon finished off Cnán's cup and handed it back to her without saying a word, though he did make eye contact and raise his eyebrows. Cnán held out the cup to Lian, who poured half of hers into it. "Yes," Cnán said, raising her cup. "To Ögedei Khan and his *hunting accident*."

Lian echoed her words and they both emptied their cups. Cnán flicked her cup at the fire, shedding the last drops, and a finger of blue flame leaped up from the coals as the spirit ignited. "Good riddance," she said.

Bruno was peering intently at her and Lian, trying to read something in their toast. Lian collected Cnán's cup and handed them both back to the Lombard, who took them absently. "The other day, Vera said that you were being hunted by the Mongols," he started.

Cnán giggled. "*All of them*," she said, quoting Vera.

"Aye," Bruno growled. "What did she mean by that?"

"I think she meant *all of them*," Haakon said. He leaned forward stiffly, his range of motion not quite normal due to the arrow wound in his back. He indicated that Bruno should pour him a measure of the spirits.

"Why?" Bruno asked, pouring for Haakon and handing the cup to Lian who passed it along.

"Because I killed him," Haakon said.

"Who?" Bruno asked.

"It wasn't an accident," Haakon said quietly as he accepted the cup from Cnán. "He asked me to tell him about the sea before he died. So I did"—he shrugged and drank—"and then he was gone."

Bruno hiccupped and then let out a loud bray of laughter. "You three are having a go at me," he said. "Just because I'm drunk doesn't mean my wits have left me entirely. I know a bullshit story when I hear one."

Haakon tugged the sheathed knife from his belt and tossed it toward Bruno. It landed between the Lombard and Lian. Cnán had seen the knife before, but she hadn't paid much attention to it, and now that it was on display, she realized the leatherwork wasn't done in the style of the West. The handle of the knife was smooth bone, a polished piece of antler from one of the steppe deer. "Oh, Goddess," she breathed.

"What is that?" Bruno said, staring at the sheathed blade.

"I know that knife," Lian said thickly. She clutched her robe and visibly shrank away from the knife. "It was a gift to Ögedei Khan from his father, Temujin—the man who became Genghis Khan."

"It wasn't an accident," Haakon repeated.

◆ ◆ ◆

Cnán barely managed to get into the tent before she passed out, and Lian arranged the other woman's limbs and body as comfortably as possible. Cnán didn't stay that way for long, and by the time Lian prepared herself for sleep, Cnán had already sprawled over half the tent. Making room for herself, Lian flopped on her back and stared at the ceiling.

The concoction made by Yasper and Bruno was stronger than anything she had had at court, her posturing notwithstanding, and even though she was lying as still as she could, the world still spun. Under her blankets, she clutched the box containing the sprig and hung on.

Was she hanging on to more than just the sprig? She was far from home, and traveling farther away every day. Was she clinging to some hope that she could return to China some day? And if she did, where would she go? Her family was gone and she wasn't even sure if the city where she had been born and raised still existed.

Or did she think that Gansukh was going to come and find her? He had given her the sprig for safekeeping, but was it important enough to chase her? He had nothing else; deciding to fire his tent had been a spontaneous decision. She had needed a distraction while she fled the *Khagan*'s camp, and Gansukh's tent was the only one she had known would be empty.

But if that was the sole criteria, why hadn't she burned Munokhoi's tent?

Because the insane ex–*Torguud* captain *would* have come after her, and if she had to choose who was chasing her, she would much rather it be Gansukh.

Would he, though?

The tent kept spinning, and she tried to steady herself against the ground, but it didn't help. With a groan, she threw off her blankets and crawled out of the tent. She made it only a few paces, still on her hands and knees, before her gorge overwhelmed her.

She gagged and then threw up, her throat burning as the acidic contents of her stomach came out.

Once her belly was empty and the quaking heaves had passed, she spat several times to clear the foul taste left in her mouth, and then crawled away from the stinking mess that had come out of her. She had almost made it back to her tent when she sensed the presence of another person nearby. "Who's there?" she whispered.

A portion of the night became more solid, revealing Yasper. The Dutchman swayed slightly as he approached Lian and sat down with a thump next to her. He was carrying a skin and he offered it to her. "It's just water," he said when she shook her head savagely at the idea of drinking more of the vile spirits. "You look like you could use some."

She accepted the skin and drank heavily. The water tasted dusty, but it was cold and clean. "Thank you," she said when the pain in her throat had faded.

"You were drinking some of the spirits that Bruno had, weren't you?" he asked. "That is foul stuff," he continued when she nodded. "I think it'd be effective at getting a blood stain out of almost anything. I wouldn't drink it."

"But…but Bruno was drinking it," she said.

"Bruno likes retsina," Yasper pointed out. "It's a drink of the Greeks," he explained. "It's particularly bad because they didn't want the invaders thinking that they knew how to make wine. The trouble was the invaders stayed a long time, and the Greeks got used to drinking it."

Lian laughed lightly, and Yasper seemed pleased that he had said something funny. She let him savor the moment and drank again from the skin.

"How's Cnán?" Yasper asked. "Did she…?"

"She's sleeping," Lian said. "If you listen carefully, you can hear her snoring."

Yasper ducked his head and looked away. "I...I don't need to hear her snoring," he said. "I just wanted to be sure she...you two...I wanted to be sure you two were faring well after a night of debauchery."

"Dee-botch-air-ee?" Lian shook her head. "I do not know that word."

"Heavy drinking," Yasper explained. "Or merely: what Bruno does every night."

Lian laughed again. "We frightened him," she said when the laughter left her. "That is why he drank heavily. Haakon told him what he had done."

"Ah," Yasper said quietly. "Well, I suppose it was bound to happen eventually." He sighed and stared off into the night.

"Do you think the empire is chasing us?" Lian asked. "Do you think everyone knows?"

"Why would they?" Yasper asked. "Do you think criers have been running from village to village proclaiming the news? *Huzzah! Our immortal ruler is dead. Stabbed in the woods by a Northerner boy. But it's okay. We didn't like him all that much anyway, did we? Rejoice!*"

"Another Khan will replace him," Lian said. "They'll fight amongst themselves for the honor of being named *Khagan* by the *kuraltai*. Who knows if the next one will be better or worse."

"No one ever does," Yasper said. "We're like swallows. We just flit about"—he waved his hand like he was imitating the flight of a bird—"and hope to find a safe place to roost every night."

Lian leaned her head against Yasper's shoulder. "I do not want to be a swallow," she said.

◆ ◆ ◆

In the days following their departure from the rock, they saw signs of riders. Some were the same size as their company; others were larger. All were to be avoided. All of the Mongol *ordu* were heading for Karakorum; the steppe, which had been empty months earlier, was going to be less so as the weather improved. Clans would be moving east, and all of them were to be considered unfriendly.

Haakon continued to scout with the Seljuks, which meant he had hours to himself in which he could wallow in his own thoughts. His confession to Bruno the other night weighed on him. He knew he shouldn't have said anything, but the weight of that secret was difficult to bear. It had become heavier after his injury, too, as if the Mongol arrow were a reminder that he had taken something very important from the empire. At the time, he hadn't given much thought to what he was doing—Ögedei had been trying to kill him, after all—but as they traveled west, the import of his actions had started to sink in.

It had been his hand that had killed the Great Khan. He had taken Ögedei's—no, it was Genghis's—knife as a trophy. What had he been thinking? Did he think he could wear it proudly like it was some sort of badge of honor? Lian had recoiled from the knife as if it had been a serpent. It was evidence of what he had done.

The irony was that he, Haakon, was the one who had killed Ögedei. The others had ridden thousands of miles to kill the *Khagan*, and several of their company had died along the way, but they had arrived too late. By no direct action of his own, he had gotten there first. *Kill him quickly*, Feronantus had told him. *We have very little time.* As if he were slaughtering a pig for a *Kinyen*.

As he scouted the steppe, Haakon realized he hated Feronantus. The master of Týrshammar had not come for him; he had not even cared that Haakon had survived the Mongols' arena games and escaped the *Khagan*'s camp. *Kill him quickly* was all he had said, and then he had left him to bear the burden of his actions alone.

He had fought in the arena in Hünern—and he had won!— so that Onghwe Khan would not know that the best warriors of the Shield-Brethren had not been present at the Circus of Swords. He had bled for the order—he had killed for his master—and his forearms were bare. He had not yet made the pilgrimage to Petraathen and taken the final test. He was not a knight initiate, and yet he had sacrificed so much for the order.

His horse trotted up a slight incline and at the top of the rise, he pulled back on the reins. Off to his left, he could see the company, a long string of horses moving slowly across the steppe. Ahead of him were the tiny specks of Evren and Ahmet. He turned slowly in his saddle, looking for any other movement on the steppe.

His hand fell upon the bone handle of Ögedei's knife. *Drop it here*, he thought. *No one will ever find it. No one will ever know.*

The frozen image of Bruno's expression swam in his mind—equal parts horror and awe that mirrored what Haakon felt when he allowed himself to reflect on what he had done.

You have seen more of the world than I.

Those had been Ögedei's final words. Occasionally, Haakon would dream of the sea, even though it had been almost a year since he had seen it. The white spray as the waves battered themselves against the stark stones of the cliff below Týrshammar. Rainbows caught in the spray of sea water. The smell of the water and wind—like no other smell he knew and the smell that he would always associate with home. He had stood on the rocks and felt the thunder of the pounding waves. He had heard the endless song of the ocean—the grinding roar and the fleeting hiss of the waves.

Haakon's heart ached for the sea. He yearned to go home again. He didn't want to die here, on the steppes, so far from the sea.

He didn't want the blood that was on his hands.

◆ ◆ ◆

They stopped along a narrow stream to water the horses. While Percival and Gawain worked to switch saddles among the spare horses, Yasper, Raphael, and Vera wandered along the stream bed. There were heavy clouds to the north and west of them—the sort of clouds that carried heavy weights of snow—and none of them were terribly eager to plunge into icy weather again.

"The boy told Bruno about the death of Ögedei," Yasper said when they were well out of earshot of the company.

"Aye, so I have heard," Raphael said. He glanced at Vera, who was walking a few paces ahead of them. "We couldn't keep them in the dark forever," he said.

"We could have," Yasper said. "We're far from Christendom. There are many who don't like us in these lands. We don't have to give them an explicit reason to hunt us."

"You think Bruno and Gawain will sell this information to interested Mongol parties?"

"They might, if it meant saving their lives. They're mercenaries. Their only master is the coin."

"Then we don't give them that opportunity," Vera said, tossing the words casually over her shoulder.

Yasper raised his eyebrows and indicated with his hands what he thought of that idea.

"We're not going to kill them," Raphael said, responding to both Vera's statement and Yasper's frantic hand gestures. "They have done nothing to injure us."

Vera glanced over her shoulder at Raphael. He held her gaze and she grunted wordlessly—saying much without saying anything at all.

"I don't want to spend the rest of my life running," Yasper said. "You can disappear into the ranks of your Shield-Brethren, but where am I supposed to go? What am I supposed to do?"

"A haircut and shave will make you unrecognizable," Raphael said.

"That's—" Yasper stopped and sighed. "What am I trying to say?" he asked.

"I don't know," Raphael said. "You're the one who brought this up."

"What are we doing?" Yasper blurted out. "Where are we going? We crossed most of the world to do an unthinkable thing, and now we're going home as if nothing has happened. But something has—something both terrifying and magnificent. We saved Christendom, but we're not going to be welcomed home as heroes."

"That wasn't why we set out on this mission," Raphael reminded him.

"I know. I know," Yasper sighed. "It just feels like…we're running. We're running and hiding as if we are little children who don't want to be caught for having stolen a loaf of bread or a shiny gold bauble."

"What would you have us do?" Raphael asked. "Raise a banner proclaiming that we have assassinated the Great Khan and demand tribute from all the peoples we have saved? Bearing in mind that I don't know that we've saved anyone, much less ourselves. When we get back to Christendom, I suspect we'll discover that all those who died at Mohi and Legnica will still be dead, and all those cities like Kiev will still be razed to the ground. And before you ask why we bothered doing what we did, let me remind you that we did it to save those who were imperiled by the Mongol horde. Our mission was to prevent any further decimation of Christendom."

"I know," Yasper sighed. He kicked at a large rock, and it flew into a nearby bush that shook with rage at being so targeted. "I hate this place," he said. "It's endless and empty and it sucks away my will to live like—"

"It's not that empty," Vera interrupted, directing their eyes to the north.

In the distance, the clouds had parted, revealing a tiny curlicue of smoke that twisted into the sky. Yasper and Raphael squinted, trying to estimate how far away the source of the smoke was.

"A camp fire?" Raphael wondered.

"No," Yasper said. "It would have to be an enormous fire to generate that much smoke. That has to be at least a half day's ride from here." He scratched his beard. "What could it be? There aren't enough trees out here to make a fire that big."

"It's Feronantus," said a voice behind them, and they turned to find Lian standing not three paces away, her eyes locked on the tiny strand of smoke. She was holding her right hand against her breasts, clutching something tightly in her fist.

CHAPTER 23:

PLANK

After verifying that Zuhzyn was dead as well, Illarion sent the remaining *Druzhina* to fetch the rest of the honor guard and to give the order for the army to occupy Pskov. Only then did he and Nika proceed to light the candles in the church. They were joined by more *Druzhina*, who wanted to know what had happened; Nika only shook her head and pointed to the bodies and then to the candles.

Illarion worked slowly; the church was large and there were many candles. His rage, which had been a pulsating red veil draped over his eyes, slowly faded. He no longer felt as if he were standing with his feet in a fire; now he seemed to be standing on the edge of a vast field that had been burned black. There was soot on his boots and his cloak. The sky was filled with a black haze, and there were no stars in the sky. Each candle was a pinpoint of light, a tiny spark that gave him hope. When he lit the last candle and saw that there were still shadows in the church, he called out for more. *Find every living soul in the city*, he told his men, *and bring them and a stub of wax or tallow to the church.*

He was tired of the darkness.

The church filled, both with bodies and with light. Word of what had occurred passed quickly among those gathered, and the bodies of the assassins disappeared. Belun and Zuhzyn were brought forward and laid out before the altar, their bodies composed in peaceful repose. A pair of candles was set on the stone floor beside their heads, giving the impression they were crowned with shining halos.

The angry muttering of the army was magnified in the church, and soon everyone was talking loudly in order to be heard by their neighbor. Illarion's head throbbed, and his mouth was dry; he wished he could send someone to fetch a flagon of wine or mead, but this was not the time for celebration. He could make out snatches of the arguments that were raging around him.

A priest of the church had been located, and he continued to profess utter innocence in the matter of the assassins in the church. Illarion was inclined to believe the man's protestations. If Kristaps had ordered his men to slay the city's populace indiscriminately, priests would not have been excluded. In fact, Illarion was certain that priests would have been singled out as men to be put to the sword during the pillaging of Pskov. That this man had survived at all suggested he had been in hiding for some time. This was probably the first time the priest had been in his church in weeks. Moreover, why would Kristaps have left this priest alive if the man had known of the plot to assassinate the *Kynaz*?

The *Druzhina* were angry; most of them were upset at him for visiting the church without a full escort, though Illarion knew such anger was misplaced. They had followed his order, and he had told them to care for the city while he had gone to pray. But they were afraid that he would blame them, though he did not know why he should. He had not been killed.

He stared at the candle in his hand, and when he placed it on the sconce, he felt himself on the verge of the black field again. The soot covered his trousers and the whole of his cloak was covered with it. He looked up and saw stars.

"That's the last one," Nika said. "They're all lit."

He nodded slowly and lowered his head. He turned to face the overflowing church. *Druzhina* and city folk were arguing noisily, and the only beings in the entire church who were quiet and calm were the two dead men lying on the floor beside the altar and a cloaked and hooded man who was nearly before them, his hands clasped in prayer. Illarion's discarded helmet sat on the floor before the figure's knees.

"People of Rus," Illarion called out, his voice hoarse. He allowed himself to wish for mead one last time before he worked up enough spit to ease the dryness in his throat. "People of Rus," he tried again. "Why are we arguing over whether this man knew if our enemy had plotted against us? We know our enemy wants us dead. We know our enemy seeks to break our spirits in any way that he can."

He did not have all of their attention yet, but he could see it happening. Arguments were falling away and the gathered people were turning their faces toward him. So many hungry eyes and sallow cheeks! He was not one for grandiose speeches; that was Alexander's duty. But he was here as the stand-in for the *Kynaz*. If the prince would have spoken to these people, so, too, would he.

"This man is not our enemy," Illarion said, indicating the cowing priest. "How many of you had children baptized by this man? How many of you received a blessing from him, thinking that it was a gift from God? He has shown himself to be afraid, and I dare any man or woman in this room to admit that they have never felt fear. How he dealt with that fear is between him and God. It is not our place to punish him for being afraid. It is our responsibility to look into our own hearts and ask how we failed him."

There was some grumbling from the *Druzhina* with that last sentence, and several men glared at him as if he were speaking directly to them. Illarion took care to not meet any of their gazes; instead, he let his gaze roam toward the high ceiling of the church where a few shadows stubbornly remained.

He thought of his last meeting in the prince's tent, shortly before he donned the armor of the *Kynaz* and rode for Pskov. He thought of Alexander's finger, tapping the map. *Dorpat.*

"Pskov has suffered enough," he said. "I will not punish a city that has seen its people defiled and burned. I will not harm a people who have given their lives and lost their homes for me. I will not allow fear to rule the lives of those under my protection. I refuse to be cowed. I refuse to lie down and let my enemy trample me into the cold ground of Rus!"

At some point in that recitation, he had lost track of pretending to be the *Kynaz.* The words rising up from the anger in his belly were his and his alone. He raised his hands so that they could see the dark stains on his sleeves and arms. "I have blood on my hands," he shouted. "We all have blood on our hands, and it has been the blood of our families. *No more,* I say. If there is blood to be spilled, let it be the blood of our enemies."

The *Druzhina* liked that idea, and they cheered and shouted in agreement. The common folk joined in as well, though they were less enthused than the armored warriors. Illarion felt Nika at his side. She stood stiffly at attention, her face betraying no emotion, but he could see a glitter in her eyes that said she shared the sentiment echoing in the church.

"Our enemy sought to enrage the people of Rus by defiling this village. He wanted us here while he roamed free—out there in the wilderness, burning and defiling other cities. He wanted us to always be behind him, tripping over the dead and staggering through the ruins of his passage. He thinks our fear will grow so great that we will fall to our knees and beg him to stop. Stop burning Rus. Stop slaying our children." Illarion took a deep breath before he continued. "Is that all we are? Beggars too frightened to take up arms and protect ourselves?"

The church shook with the resounding shout that came from the throats of those assembled.

"Careful," Nika whispered to him in the wake of the roaring refutation of the crowd. "You are supposed to be the prince. Do not promise them something he would not give."

He offered her a sad smile, knowing better than she what the prince wanted him to do, who the prince wanted him to be.

"I came to you today in the guise of your prince," he said more loudly. "I came to you wearing the mask and colors of the *Kynaz* because that is who our enemy expected Novgorod would send to liberate Pskov. But Pskov did not need liberation. Pskov needed to be *reminded* of who it is." He swept his hair, some of it matted with blood, back from his missing ear. "I am Illarion Illarionovich, one-time son of Volodymyr-Volynskyi. I fought the Mongols when they came, and I failed to save my city. My family and I were put to death beneath the planks. When the black bone Mongols came to take their trophies from the corpses, the touch of their knives brought me back. They took my ear, but I took their lives!"

He held up his hands to quell the shouting and stomping of many feet that followed, and when the crowd fell silent, he continued.

"I am Plank. Wood hewn from the forests of Rus. Wood used to shelter the people of Rus. Wood stained with the blood of Rus. I am Illarion Illarionovich; I am Plank; I am Rus. Just as each of you are Rus, and this land is ours. It has always been ours and will always be ours. The Mongols, who numbered in the tens of thousands more than these invaders from the south and north, could not destroy us. Why do we fear them? Why do we suffer their presence in our fields and forests?"

It was a rhetoric question, but Illarion let it hang for a few moments and the crowd broke out into a hundred different voices, all sharing the same enthusiasm, the same desire to be Rus.

"If they want to come to our lands and burn our villages and slay our children, then I say we show them the same courtesy," Illarion cried. "I say we don't bother chasing this reaver as he wanders across our lands. I say we go to his home. Let us trample his fine tapestries and drink his wine. Let us piss in his fireplace so that it sends up a foul smoke. Let us burn his house and salt his fields. Let us eradicate any sign that he ever existed!"

Pandemonium erupted in the church at his words, and the great weight that had been pressing down on his back and neck was lifted by their raucous glee and bloodlust. He stood, eyes closed, and listened to their voices, letting the noise batter him.

He was brought out of his reverie by a touch on his arm. The hooded man who had been kneeling beside the bodies was standing next to him, offering him the *Kynaz*'s helmet. The man leaned close, speaking into his left ear. "You will need this."

Illarion started, recognizing the voice, and he peered into the shadows of the hood.

Alexander Nevsky put a finger to his lips. "I was never here," the prince said.

Dumbfounded, Illarion took the offered helmet and the cloaked figure of the prince stepped back into the rank of the *Druzhina*. Illarion turned to Nika, intending to say something to her, but the Shield-Maiden was staring into the crowd. When Illarion looked, he caught sight of the hooded figure.

When the figure pulled its cloak tighter about its frame, he saw the hands were withered and bony, like those of an old woman.

"Plank! Plank! Plank!" the crowd chanted, finding a single word to convey all of their emotions.

He glanced at Nika to see if she had seen the same apparition as he had, but she was staring at him. Her eyes were wide, and he couldn't decide if the root of her expression was fear or wonder.

CHAPTER 24:

THE CUNNING WOLF

Any question as to whether the approaching riders were Mongolian was settled when the six riders split into three groups of two. Gansukh and Alchiq slowed their horses to a mere amble. Alchiq rested both hands on his saddle horn, leaning forward with an expectant gleam in his eye. Gansukh made sure his bow was easily accessible, should it come to that, but he, too, tried to appear as relaxed as possible.

The first pair rode straight at them, while each of the remaining pairs circled to the left and right. It was a standard tactic, one both Gansukh and Alchiq had been party to on numerous occasions during their campaigning years. The pair in the front would be the ones most likely to start shooting arrows if it looked like Gansukh and Alchiq were going to be hostile. The others were meant to distract them, and they would circle around, passing each other behind the pair. The approach meant that no matter which direction Alchiq and Gansukh turned, they would have someone at their front and back.

Of course, they outnumber us three to one, Gansukh thought as he watched the riders gallop toward them. *Which means they're being cautious, and why is that?*

It was an interesting question, and he thought to suggest it to Alchiq, but one glance at the older hunter told him that Alchiq had already had the same thought. The gleam in his eye was nearly feral.

"Ho, free riders under Blue Heaven," Alchiq called as soon as the leading pair were within earshot. "We greet you with sadness in our hearts and nothing but the wind and sun in our hands." He raised his hands to demonstrate the truth of his words, spreading his fingers so that they could clearly see his missing digit.

Gansukh did the same, but he didn't raise his hands as high as Alchiq's.

The leading pair slowed, and as the other pairs thundered past them, Gansukh got his first good look at the riders. They were dressed in fur-lined jackets over plain *deel*, with fur-lined hats and boots. They wore purple sashes, and one of the two held his bow across his lap. The other one had a long scar on his right cheek that made his eye and mouth droop. "Ho, riders," the droopy-mouthed one called. "You are far from anywhere worth visiting."

Alchiq traded a knowing glance with Gansukh. *He's the ugly one*, Gansukh thought, *and yet he speaks for the rest of them.*

"As are you," Alchiq replied, not willing to be put on the defensive quite so readily. "Or does your clan lay claim to this worthless land? We have not seen a decent pasture in, what, a week or more?"

Gansukh said nothing. It was Alchiq's play. He wasn't going to draw their attention to him. Not yet.

"If it was land that belonged to my clan, you would be crossing it without permission," the scarred Mongol said. "I could even accuse you of attempting to steal our horses."

"The ones you are riding?" Alchiq shrugged. "We'd be happy to take them. If you could take off your saddles too, that would be most helpful."

The other pairs passed behind Gansukh and Alchiq, one pair inside the other, and they galloped back toward their companions.

The ugly one threw back his head and laughed. "You are full of bluster, old man," he said when he was finished laughing. "Did the last warrior you were so impertinent to take that missing finger of yours?"

"No," Alchiq said. "A wolf bit it off."

"A wolf?" the Mongol chuckled. "And where is the proof of this? I don't see a wolf pelt hanging from your belt. Did you give him your finger and get nothing in return?"

Alchiq looked at Gansukh, and Gansukh offered him a shrug. There had been more than one wolf to deal with. He had been a little distracted.

"Aye," Alchiq said, raising his maimed hand and pressing his lips against his stump. "I gave my finger to Blue Wolf, and Blue Wolf watches over me now. If I need him, I have but to shout his name and he will come." He dropped his reins and slid off his horse. "Would you like me to demonstrate?" he asked as he walked toward the pair. His hands were still open and empty.

The other one reached for an arrow but hesitated. Alchiq had left his sword hanging off his saddle. Other than a short knife in his belt, the old hunter was unarmed. The bowman glanced at the ugly one, who was looking at Alchiq with a bemused expression. "And if I call your bluff, old man, and nothing happens, what then?"

"Nothing," Alchiq said. "Nothing at all."

Alchiq's answer confused the ugly Mongol, and Gansukh had to admit he was confused as well. He couldn't figure out what Alchiq's plan was, but he knew the old hunter was up to something. He wouldn't have waited to be surrounded if he didn't have something in mind.

Alchiq stopped a pace away from the ugly Mongol's horse and stood there, hands raised. "What will it be?" he asked. "Do I summon the Blue Wolf or not?"

The ugly one chewed on his lip for a moment, weighing his options. His eyes flicked to Gansukh once or twice, but since Gansukh hadn't moved, the ugly one saw no answer to his dilemma. Behind him, the two pairs of riders slowed, sensing there was no need to keep circling.

The ugly one turned his head to speak to his companion with the bow. "Put—" he started.

As soon as his eyes left Alchiq, the old hunter darted forward. He slapped the nose of the Mongol's pony, which stepped back and reared. The ugly Mongol tried to stay in the saddle, but Alchiq kept moving, grabbing him by the jacket and hauling him out of the saddle. The second Mongol fumbled with his arrow, but by the time he got it nocked and the string pulled back, Alchiq had control of the ugly Mongol. He crouched behind the man, his knife at his throat. The bowman paused, trying to decide if he had a clear shot.

Gansukh cleared his throat loudly, trying to get the bowman's attention. The nervous archer didn't want to look, but he saw enough out of the corner of his eyes to finally look at Gansukh.

Gansukh had his own bow out and ready too. His arrow was pointed straight at the bowman's chest. He had a very clear shot.

The other four Mongols had their bows up and drawn too, and Gansukh noted that if everyone released their arrows, he and the first bowman would probably be the first ones to die. He held his bow steady, but he could feel a bead of sweat start trickling down the left side of his face.

"Now," Alchiq said without a touch of malice or threat in his voice. "Let's go over your options again. You may give us your horses or you may take us to your captain." He tightened his grip on the ugly man's jacket, and the man gasped as the knife pressed harder against the soft flesh of his throat. "You boys are too stupid to be out here on your own. I want to talk to someone smarter. Someone who will listen to what I have to tell him."

"I—" The ugly Mongol swallowed nervously and tried to pull his throat away from Alchiq's knife. "We'll take you," he said when Alchiq relaxed his pressure. "He's close. He's very close."

"Good," Alchiq said. "That's the first smart thing you've said so far. You might yet live."

◆ ◆ ◆

The camp was like many other camps Gansukh had seen over the years. The horses were corralled together in one herd and the center of the camp was defined by three large fires but the rest was a sprawling disorganized mess. He tried to count tents and gave up after he reached forty, and there was no point in trying to ascertain the size of the force by counting horses. Each man would have several. If he tried to judge the number of riders by a head count of the horses, he would be woefully off in his estimate.

They circled the camp until they were on the side closest to the horses, and the ugly Mongol led them up to a pair of younger men who were in charge of the herd. The scouting party dismounted, and one of the young men looked expectantly at the ugly Mongol who shrugged as he glanced at Alchiq and Gansukh.

Gansukh slid off his horse and approached the young man. He didn't have much left in his pouch, but he offered the boy a few coins. "Water them, please," he asked, "and let them roam a bit. But not too far."

The boy nodded as he made the coins disappear. The Mongol scouts wandered off, heading for the southern portion of the camp. Alchiq clambered down from his horse and studiously made no attempt to talk with the boy. As he and Gansukh followed the scouts, he adjusted his sword in his belt and glared at Gansukh. "It's an insult for them to not offer to take care of our horses," he said. "Court life has made you soft, boy."

"Court life has taught me civility," Gansukh replied. "You're the one who put a knife to his throat. He's got his own insults to swallow. He'll take it out on you as he can." When Alchiq continued to grumble, Gansukh grabbed his arm and made him stop.

"He wants you to pull the knife again. Or worse, your sword. He'll have witnesses. It will be justified. You have no friends in this camp."

"And you'd just stand there?" Alchiq snarled.

"Yes," Gansukh said. "Because I don't want to die a fool's death."

"No one is going to die today," Alchiq said.

"Did the Blue Wolf whisper that to you?" Gansukh asked. "Old Nine Fingers."

Alchiq jerked his arm out of Gansukh's grip and stalked after the other Mongols. Gansukh rubbed his face for a moment and then followed, half-certain that Alchiq was completely wrong.

The camp was a war party. Gansukh saw no sign of children or women. The tents were small, and there was only one *ger* and it was clearly their destination. They picked up quite a few of the other occupants of the camp as they walked, and by the time, they reached the *ger*, Gansukh estimated there were more than thirty men following them.

The leader of the party was a tall Mongol with a thick black beard and quick brown eyes. Hawk feathers were woven into his long hair, and most of the fingers on his left hand bore rings. He was listening to the ugly Mongol's report with a tiny smile on his lips, and his eyes tracked Alchiq and Gansukh as they walked across the shallow field in front of the *ger*.

"I am Totukei," he said when the scout finished his report. "This is my *jaghun*." He pointed at Gansukh. "Is he your *arban*?"

Alchiq glanced around at the crowd, and Gansukh noticed his lips were moving as he did a quick head count. "Your *jaghun* is like my *arban*," Alchiq said eventually. "Smaller than it should be, but I am certain it more than makes up for that deficit in its bravery and strength of arms." He nodded to Totukei, clasping his hands together, fingers of his left hand over his right fist. "I am Alchiq, once of Clan Hupti, but my clan has been scattered. We are steppe people, now and forever."

"And your man?" Totukei asked.

"I am Gansukh," Gansukh said. "Before I was Chagatai Khan's man, I served with Batu Khan during his conquest of Rus."

"Batu and Chagatai," Totukei said. "You are far from home, Gansukh."

"Like my companion, my home is the open steppe."

"If you are home whenever you are beneath Eternal Blue Heaven, then you do not need a destination, do you? Are you just roaming these plains like wolves without a clan?"

"A wolf without a clan is dangerous," Alchiq said. "Who knows who it might try to bite."

"That is true," Totukei said. "My cousin says you struck his horse."

Cousin, Gansukh thought. *That explains a great deal.*

"Of the two, the horse was more likely to respect my fist," Alchiq said.

Gansukh felt like he should say or do something before the situation got even further out of hand, but short of knocking Alchiq down and sitting on his head, he wasn't sure what he could do. And, like Alchiq said, who knew who the wolf might try to bite.

But Totukei just laughed. "I know you are not here to fight me or my family, Alchiq Old Wolf. You want something from me. That is what all this posturing is about. Let us set all this bluster aside and talk honestly. What do you want from me?"

"How many men do you have?" Alchiq said without missing a beat.

"Seven *arban*. Maybe eight," Totukei replied, equally businesslike.

"How many in the group we seek?" Alchiq asked Gansukh.

"Seven," Gansukh replied, even though he knew Alchiq was well aware of the number of *Skjaldbrædur.*

"You don't have enough men," Alchiq said.

Many of the crowd joined Totukei in laughing at the old hunter, who waited patiently for their humor to drain away.

"When I last encountered those we seek, they numbered eleven," Alchiq said. "I had a *jaghun* at my command. I lost more than half of my men."

"That is impossible," Totukei snorted. "Warriors of such prowess don't exist. With all due respect, Alchiq Old Wolf, your storytelling skills do not match your bluster."

"That is very likely," Alchiq said, "But I never claimed to be a storyteller. I have chased these men from the edge of the empire to its very heart and back again. I know how they think, and I know their weaknesses. You need me."

"I *need* you?" Totukei sputtered. "Why would I need you?"

"Because you're tracking them," Alchiq said. "You have been since your men stumbled upon the Persians at the rock, and eventually you are going to find them. And then you are going to die." He offered Totukei the wolfish smile that Gansukh knew well. "Unless you have my help."

CHAPTER 25:

WHERE THERE IS SMOKE...

Behind him, Feronantus heard Istvan shouting at the tiger and the tiger's answering scream of anger. He managed to get his hands on the reins of his horse, but Istvan's mount pulled away from him, the whites of its eyes showing. He lunged for the reins, missed, and swore loudly at Istvan's horse as it bolted, charging up the slope to get away from the angry tiger and Istvan's flaming sword.

His horse wanted to flee too, jerking its head in an effort to pull the reins from his hands. He went hand over hand on the leather straps, dragging the horse's head down toward him.

The tiger shrieked again and this time there was more pain than anger in its cry.

Feronantus glanced over his shoulder as he struggled with his horse. The cloud cover above the depression seemed to have thickened in the last few minutes, filling the sinkhole with more shadows. In stark relief against the shadows and among the fat snowflakes were Istvan's flaming sword and the angry orange and black shape of the tiger, circling one another.

He had to make a choice. If he let go of his horse so that he could go to Istvan's aid, his mount would flee too. They might both survive the tiger attack, but they would be without steeds. If he left...well, he couldn't leave.

Why not? Part of him argued. *You left the others.*

No, that wasn't how it had been.

Others before them too, the voice continued. *How many have you left behind now?*

He clamped his jaw shut to keep the voice from getting out. It was the venial self-doubt that plagued any warrior as he entered battle. Feronantus had endured it before, and he had even learned to suppress its voice. The *Vor* had shown him how, though it was much easier when the shimmering path of his future was visible.

But there was no such path available to him in the depression. He was both below ground and trapped beneath the cloud cover, invisible to the divine graces that might gaze down on him and deign to provide assistance.

Muttering an oath, he left off trying to control his horse's head and reached for the Spirit Banner instead. It was attached to the horse's saddle by several leather loops, and as soon as he started to pull the long wooden pole free, the horse jerked away from him, fighting to get clear of the obstruction and flee. He grabbed at his saddle, trying to reach his sword too, and the horse hopped slightly, its hooves pounding against the ground.

"Stop fighting me," he growled. What he really wanted was the small crossbow hanging off the back of his saddle.

Another scream ripped through the air, and this time it didn't come from the tiger's throat. Both Feronantus and his horse paused in their tug-of-war, and Feronantus turned halfway to look for the source of the cry.

Istvan was down on one knee, his smoldering sword no longer held as dramatically. He wavered as if he were falling asleep and then jerked himself upright as the tiger came charging at him. The beast veered away at the last second, dodging Istvan's slow-moving sword. It swiped at Istvan again, and Istvan managed to bring his sword around enough that the tiger pulled its paw back from trying to swat him.

They were at an impasse, and the tiger continued to circle Istvan, who made no attempt to get up from his position. The feeble movements of his sword cast few shadows, and with each wild swing, the tiger grew bolder. The second time it darted at Istvan to strike him, Istvan didn't get the sword around in time.

Feronantus left off struggling with the Spirit Banner and concentrated on drawing his longsword. He managed to get the weapon out of its sheath, and he let go of his horse's bridle as he crashed across the dark and lumpy surface of the depression.

Istvan was on his back, straining to reach his sword which had fallen out of his hand. It lay on the ground just beyond his straining fingers, and as he got his fingertips on the pommel, the tiger pounced and landed on his legs. Istvan left off trying to get his sword and sat up. The tiger bit at his stomach and was rebuffed by the maille. Snarling, it bit at his face and he shoved his left arm into its open mouth.

Feronantus was halfway there.

Istvan screamed as the tiger bit down on his arm, and Feronantus saw his right arm rise up, his hunting knife clutched in his fist, and then Istvan drove his arm down, plunging the knife into the side of the tiger's neck. The tiger shook him like a child's doll, but Istvan held on. When the tiger paused, Istvan pulled his knife free and stabbed again. The second time the tiger shook him, his arm separated—forearm and hand remaining inside the tiger's mouth.

Just as Feronantus was about to reach the beleaguered Hungarian, the black ground beneath Istvan's discarded blade burst into flame. Feronantus slid to a halt, staring at the flicking flame as it danced across the stained ground.

The tiger roared, spitting out Istvan's arm, and its eyes were bright with reflected fire. Istvan tried to stab it a third time, but the tiger brushed his arm aside and closed its mouth, with its many sharp teeth, around the front of his head.

The fire leaped across the ground, suddenly creating a wall between Feronantus and Istvan. It kept snaking across the ground, leaping from dark patch to dark patch. With growing horror, Feronantus tracked where the flame was going, and realized it was heading right for the slow bubbling center of the seep. The black heart of the upwelling.

Feronantus ran. He heard the tiger growl deep in its throat and he heard the sizzling hiss of air burning, and then the ground shook beneath him, and he felt the fiery hand of an unleashed giant lift him up and fling him out of the depression and into the endless emptiness of the snowstorm.

◆ ◆ ◆

He tumbled, spinning like a leaf caught by a zephyr, and dimly wondered why he hadn't hit the ground yet. He flew away from the eruption of orange and red light, his eyes closed against the glare. He could still see the strange outlines of fiery phantoms, dancing across his field of vision. They were hollow creatures, nothing more than the outlines of ragged dolls drawn in luminous fire. They twitched and darted away from him as he tried to focus his gaze on them, and when the bright light behind them faded, they faded too, turning to ash.

A light breeze caressed his face, and when he tried to open his eyes, the breeze held his eyelids down and he struggled to open them. If he knew where his hands were, he could raise them and push up his eyelids, but he had to see his hands in order to find them. But his hands were connected to his arms, which were connected to his trunk, and his head was attached to the top of his trunk. He should be able to feel his hands, shouldn't he?

He felt the breeze on his face, but otherwise, he was numb.

There was no light anymore, and even the ashes had turned black. He could see nothing. He could hear nothing. Other than the wind, he could feel nothing. Was he even breathing? As panic laid claim to his mind, he felt none of the physical sensations that accompanied fear. The more he struggled (in his mind, for he had no idea what his body might be doing), the stronger the wind blew, until it was a stinging storm, slapping him on the cheeks. The tempest increased, and he could feel the skin on his face rippling and sliding. Finally, with a herculean effort, he wrenched apart his lips, and the wind hurled itself into the cavern of his mouth.

Like a blacksmith's bellows, he inflated, and as he filled out, awareness of his body returned—from his neck to his chest to his arms, waist, legs, hands, and feet. He swelled up, and his ears popped loudly. His eyes snapped open too, and he found himself lying on his back, staring up at a white sky, filled with fluffy clouds and drifting snowflakes.

He lay still, watching his breath float away. His back was cold, and as he explored the ground with his fingers, he found it slippery and wet. *Ice*, he thought as he slowly levered himself upright.

He was not on the steppe. He was lying on a field of ice—a lake, he surmised. To his left were vague shadows that suggested a treeline. To his right, partially behind him, a small shape in a ragged cloak crouched on the ice. The figure was holding a long pole, and a string attached to the end of the pole disappeared into a hole in the ice.

Feronantus peeled himself off the ice and staggered toward the crouched figure. When he touched it lightly on the shoulder, the figure shifted slightly and then fell over. Skeletal hands peeked out of the cloak, and when Feronantus pulled back the hood, he found a mummified face. Judging by the shape of the hands and face, the body was that of a woman, and without taking the robe off the corpse, he had no idea how she had died. Both cloak and body were frozen stiff, and it would take a proper fire and many hours to thaw the corpse enough to remove the cloak.

The pole was longer and thicker than he thought a fishing rod should be, and when he pulled it free of the skeleton's hands, he realized it was the Spirit Banner, burned black and bereft of its horsehair streamers. The hole in the ice was two spans of his hands in diameter, and the water beneath the ice was a pale blue.

He pulled on the string, and felt a weight at the end. The water was cold, even colder than the ice, and the string burned his hands as he pulled it out. He pulled and pulled, and was starting to wonder how long the string was when he noticed a shadow in the water. Coiling the slack of the string around his arm, he gave another strong pull on the cord.

A frozen hand and arm emerged from the lake. Feronantus braced one foot on the edge of the hole, holding the arm out of the water. It felt like there was an entire body at the end of the string, and when he tugged the string, the resistance increased.

The body wouldn't fit through the hole.

The hand and arm were bare, though covered with a fine sheen of ice. The fingers were half-bent as if the hand had been holding something that had been yanked free shortly before being frozen in place. Grunting with the exertion, Feronantus rotated the arm. There was a scar on the forearm, the circular brand of the Shield-Brethren.

The ice distorted the sigil slightly, smearing the finer details, but when Feronantus pushed up his right sleeve, he thought the old scar on his forearm was a fairly close match.

He let go of the string, and the outstretched arm disappeared into the lake. He picked at the knot on the staff first with his fingers and then his teeth, loosening the string from the pole. He pulled the string free of the pole and let it go, watching it snake across the ice as its burden descended farther and farther. His heart seized for a second as the end of the string wiggled across the rim of the hole, but he didn't dive for it. He held fast and let it go.

His hands were black from the layer of ash on the banner, and he suspected his lips and teeth were black too. Using the staff to test the ice, he started to walk toward the tree line.

This was nothing more than a dream, and the sooner he reached the boundary of its imagination, the sooner he would wake up. One foot in front of the other. Just keep walking.

Feronantus...

Once he reached the trees, he wouldn't stop. He would walk as far and as long as necessary. Dreams could not survive a methodical assault. The more order he forced upon this environment, the less it could sustain itself. It lived off fear and uncertainly. He knew where he was going. He was—

Feronantus.

—heading for the trees.

The staff poked against the ice, and he listened to the rhythmic shuffle of his feet against the slick surface. Poke. Step. Step. Poke. Step...

"Feronantus!"

✦ ✦ ✦

As the Shield-Brethren company rode toward the boiling column of smoke, they regarded it with curiosity. What could generate that much smoke on the steppe? How long would someone have to gather fuel for such a fire? Was it a signal? Was it, like Lian thought, a marker indicating where they might find Feronantus?

But when they got closer, Yasper realized what it was: an alchemical fire. Naphtha, he explained to the rest, was a concoction used by the Byzantines and Muslims, and it was made from a combination of oil and water. The source of the smoke was a naturally occurring seep of the oily liquid used in naphtha.

The column of smoke had lessened by the time they found the depression from which it was issuing, and the winter storm that had been squatting over the hole had moved on, leaving the skies clear but for the smudges of dark smoke still lingering.

Raphael, Percival, Gawain, and Yasper dismounted from their horses and walked the last hundred paces to the edge of the depression. The ground around the depression was boggy, as if a heavy rain had recently fallen, and there were dark stains on the ground that Yasper explained had been expelled from the seep. Raphael wasn't sure what they were going to see when they reached the rim of the depression, but as they approached, he strained to hear any noise coming from the fire. The air felt oily, and when he inhaled there was a metallic aftertaste left in his mouth.

A haze filled the depression, and many of the seep stains were on fire, albeit with thin wispy flames. They were like tiny worshippers, emulating the image of their god who roared and danced in the center of the depression. The burning seep was a pond of black oil, and the flames that danced atop it were taller than any of them.

"Well," Yasper said, breaking the stunned silence of the quartet, "it's not as bad as I thought it might be."

"It is the very presence of Hell upon this world," Percival said.

"Aye," Gawain said. "The only thing missing is—no, wait, what is that over there?"

The others peered in the direction he pointed, and Raphael felt his gorge rise in the back of his throat. "It appears to be..."

It wasn't a man, that much was certain, though it appeared to be struggling to wear a man's shape. It had too many appendages, and there was no telling what was the front and what was the rear. The entire shape was blackened like a log that had been charred in flames for hours, and it was half-twisted around itself. Raphael found himself thinking that the creature had been simultaneously trying to curl into a ball like a tiny child and to run away. The result was something that looked like a crisped snail, flesh burned into an ashen husk.

"Whatever it is, it is dead," Yasper said.

"How can you be sure?" Gawain asked.

"Go down there and poke it with your sword," Yasper said. "If you *really* want to know."

"Aren't you curious?"

"No," Yasper shook his head.

"I am," Percival said. He reached over and grabbed Yasper's tunic. "Come, little alchemist. Let us see what the Devil has left for us."

"What?" Yasper sputtered, struggling in Percival's grip as the Frank started down the slope. "What are you doing?"

"I'm bringing an expert opinion with me," Percival said.

"It's not safe," Yasper squawked. "You don't want to breathe this air. Trust me. I've done alchemical experiments. I know what I'm talking about."

"Breathe shallowly and walk quickly, then," Percival said, his grip not faltering.

Gawain looked at Raphael, expressing his question with a raised eyebrow. Raphael shook his head. "I trust their examination will be sufficient."

"Lian spoke of Feronantus when she saw the smoke. He is the one you are searching for, yes?"

"Yes, he is," Raphael said.

"Do you think that monster down there is him?"

"No," Raphael said. He had been glancing around the rim of the depression while he and Gawain had been talking, and he had spotted an irregular lump on the far side of the depression. "But I wonder whose horse that is." He pointed out the hump to Gawain.

"That would appear to be a much less frightening corpse to examine," Gawain said.

"I concur. Shall we walk around the rim of this stinking pit?"

Gawain snorted. "I'm not going down there."

✦ ✦ ✦

While the knights of the order went ahead to investigate the column of smoke coming out of the ground, the rest of the company milled about, uncertain what to do. It was too early in the day to make camp for the night, and while none of them said as much out loud, they all had a desire to be far from the burning hole by nightfall. That meant watering, feeding, and changing the horses—tasks that reminded Haakon that, regardless of the sword he wore, he wasn't much more than a glorified stable boy.

"I'm going to scout ahead," he told Evren, making the signs they had come up with to explain rudimentary commands: two fingers, pointed at his eyes; four fingers, mimicking the gait of a horse; one finger, pointing in the direction they were headed.

Evren acknowledged his signs with a quick tap of several fingers against his forehead and a nod. Haakon caught sight of Vera looking at him as he climbed onto his horse, but he didn't bother saying anything to her as he slapped his reins and let his horse run. *Evren can tell her,* he thought bitterly as his horse galloped in a wide arc around the smoke-filled depression.

He knew this hole was going to be a beacon, summoning every rider within a hundred miles or more. Their group had happened to get here first, but he knew if they stayed too long, they would have company. Judging by the hoofprints he and the Seljuks had seen over the last few days, the visitors would be Mongolian. Haakon needed to spot them before they stumbled upon the aimless Shield-Brethren company.

His eyes swept the open plain restlessly, moving quickly over the long swathes of short grasses and the clumps of wormwood and scrub trees. He had seen all of it a thousand times over and most of the landscape had become little more than a blur. What he was looking for were aberrations—moving shapes or flashes of color that were out of the ordinary.

There was a herd of steppe deer to the east, and he chased them until he was close enough to pick out individual animals. He counted them twice, letting his horse slow to a trot, and once he was satisfied with the number, he pulled his horse south. Three dozen deer were an interesting statistic, but they were no threat to the company.

He rode south for awhile, squinting against the glare of the afternoon sun. There was a dark line stretching across the southeast, and he watched it warily. While he was a single rider against the immense backdrop of the steppe, he was not entirely invisible. Sharp-eyed Mongol scouts could see him as soon as he spotted them.

He spotted a spur of rock to the west and angled his horse in that direction. The outcropping was a line of gnarled stone that protruded enough out of the ground to create a ripple in the landscape. The ground rose up around the ridge and dropped away slightly behind it; overall, the stones didn't tower more than the height of a pair of men, one standing on the shoulders of the other. A line of spruce, like the wispy beards sported by many Mongolians, trailed behind the ridge, and Haakon suspected he would find some sort of pool at the base of the ridge. During the spring and summer, it would contain a tepid layer of warm rainwater; during the winter months, it would be filled with icy slush.

The basin was where he expected to find it, and he left his horse to drink its fill and munch on the nearby grasses as he quickly climbed the rock face. The top of the tallest rock wasn't much more than a pace across and the stone was cracked into three sections. He jammed his toes deeper into the crevices along the side of the rock and leaned across the top, trying to find the least jagged places to rest his elbows. He didn't want to present himself as an oddity of the landscape by standing up, but his somewhat precarious relationship with the rock allowed him to scan the horizon from an elevated location.

The dark line to the southeast was thicker, and as he watched it, he spotted a few other dots moving to and from the squalid line. He was pretty sure it was a Mongol war party, and he glanced up at the sun to gauge how many hours of daylight were left. *They might make it by nightfall,* he decided.

He descended from the rock and retrieved his horse, the more pressing realization of what he had seen thrumming in his brain. *A half day.*

That's all the lead they had on the Mongols.

His horse was annoyed at being pulled away from the moist grasses and he had to slap it on the hindquarters a few times before it finally started to run.

He slipped back into the simple mindset of scouting as the horse galloped across the steppe toward the drifting column of smoke, watching for anything unusual on the plain. Watching for outriders from the Mongol party. Watching for—

Haakon blinked several times and stood up in his saddle to get a better look at the thin shape he had spotted to the west. Having satisfied his first impression that he had spotted a human figure walking across the plain, he sat down and nudged his horse to his left.

As he got closer, details resolved themselves. The figure was a solitary man, dressed in black. He walked slowly and carried no bags of any kind. The only thing he carried was a tall walking stick, and as Haakon got closer, he saw that the man was tapping the walking stick on the ground ahead of him as if he were testing for sinkholes or slippery sand. The man's clothing was filthy with soot and dirt, and he seemed familiar to Haakon.

"Feronantus?" Haakon called, recognizing the man's weathered face beneath the layers of dirt and ash.

Feronantus didn't seem to hear Haakon. He kept tapping the ground with his walking stick and staggering onward, doggedly moving west as if he intended to walk all the way back to Christendom. His eyes were open, but he wasn't seeing anything of the world in front of him.

✦ ✦ ✦

They gathered around the dead horse as if they were eulogizing a fallen comrade. Without touching the body, Yasper explained that the horse had died from inhaling fiery air, much like the pair he and Percival had examined in the depression, though the horse had lived a few minutes longer than the other two.

"It is Feronantus's horse," Percival said, nudging one of the hooves with his boot. The saddle was blackened with ash, and the horse's mouth was coated with soot.

"I don't think it was Feronantus down there," Yasper said. "It was a man and a tiger, though they had been—" He made a series of complicated gestures that signified nothing more than his own confusion and then put a hand over his face.

"The tiger tried to eat him," Gawain said.

"It would have eaten him, if the fire hadn't erupted," Yasper said. "Whatever happened, happened so fast that neither could flee in time. They didn't even have a chance to stop fighting."

"Is it Feronantus or not?" Raphael asked. Like Percival, he had recognized the saddle on the dead horse, but there was no sign of the Spirit Banner, an omission that troubled him.

"Ah, not," Yasper decided. "I think." When Raphael glared at him, he spread his hands. "The tiger was chewing the front half of his head off, and the fire burned away most of his clothing. I'm not very good at identifying people from burned-up corpses."

"Were there other members of your company who might have been traveling with him?" Gawain asked.

Raphael looked at Percival for suggestions, though he had his own suspicions. According to Yasper, Eléazar had remained behind to guard their escape, and of the remaining pair of the lost company, he found it hard to believe that Rædwulf would have tolerated Feronantus's flight without the rest of the company. That left Istvan, the mad Hungarian who had bedeviled them during their entire journey. "It's Istvan," he said, giving voice to his thoughts.

"Aye," Percival nodded. "I suspect that it was." He shrugged slightly. "It is a pity that one of our company has fallen, but he fell in combat, did he not? What more could any of us ask?"

"That he did," Raphael echoed.

"He was fighting a tiger—on foot, and without a weapon, apparently," Yasper pointed out.

"That sounds like a fair fight," Percival said.

"That sounds like Istvan," Raphael said.

No one else had anything more to say about their fallen companion, and so they stood quietly for a few minutes, each conducting his own private memorial. It was Gawain who broke the somber mood eventually.

"Look," the Welshman said, directing their attention to a lone horse approaching from the southwest. "There is young Haakon, and he has another with him."

Haakon appeared to have a bundle of blackened sackcloth with him in his saddle, but as the young Northerner approached, Raphael saw that it was the huddled form of an old man. Of equal importance was the long staff strapped to the back of Haakon's saddle.

"I found Feronantus," Haakon said as he brought his horse to a stop. "He was walking west."

The master of Týrshammar was slumped in the saddle with Haakon, his thin hands with their stark veins clutching the saddle horn. His face was even gaunter than Raphael remembered, and his beard and hair seemed even whiter under the layers of dirt and ash that covered him.

"He recognizes me," Haakon said, "but he hasn't said a word yet."

Feronantus stared at the dead horse, a single tear tracking through the grime on his face.

"There's something else," Haakon said. "There's a war party of Mongols coming. They're about a half day behind us. We're going to have to ride through the night if we hope to get away."

"The plume of smoke is a beacon," Gawain said. "It doesn't matter if they saw him or not."

"Aye," Raphael said. "They're coming here for the same reason we did, and when they do, they'll find our trail. Riding through the night may mean only that we're tired when they catch up to us."

◆ ◆ ◆

The veil of night covered the column of smoke, but in the resulting darkness, the source became abundantly clear. It was a flickering orange glow on the steppe, a beacon even more clear in the dark than the smoke against the blue sky.

Gansukh and Alchiq left their horses behind a stand of spruce and crept cautiously toward the glowing hole in the steppe. There was a fire burning in the ground, neither of them had any doubt of that fact, and during their slow creep toward the hole, Gansukh had ample time to wonder how such a fire was fed. It had burned for several days at this point and showed no sign of going out. How was it being stoked? What was its source of fuel?

The glow of the fire made it easy for them to spot the *Skjaldbrædur* camp on the western side of the hole. They gave the fiery hole a wide berth, and crawled on their bellies the rest of the way as close as they dared get. The figures were covered in flickering shadows, and only a few of them were very still. The rest were occupied in frenzied preparations of some kind.

Alchiq put his mouth close to Gansukh's ear. "They know we're coming," the old hunter whispered.

Gansukh had to agree. Three of the male figures were hauling and digging, but he couldn't see what they were accomplishing. The dirt was being hauled off and dumped, but they weren't building any sort of retaining wall or defensive barrier. Beyond the camp, he saw the dim shapes of horses, suggesting the company had enough mounts to carry everyone, and perhaps a few more. The fire pit of the camp was obscured by a few tents, but he spotted two or three people who were moving around the fire. A man and two women, one of whom appeared to have long dark hair.

His heart lurched into his throat, and his fingers dug into the ground. Lian. He had given up thinking about what he would do when he saw her again. She had been on his mind nonstop during the first few months, but it was only as he saw her again that he realized he had been thinking about her less and less over the last few weeks. He hadn't given up hope of seeing her again—no, that wasn't it: he had come to the realization that he probably wouldn't and his heart had been quietly burying his feelings.

Not deeply enough, he thought, staring at the slim figure as it moved back and forth behind a tent.

"The armored ones," Alchiq muttered. "No archers."

Gansukh swallowed heavily, forcing his heart back down into his chest where it echoed loudly. "What?" he whispered to Alchiq.

"No sign of archers," Alchiq repeated. "Not like last time. That's good. But…"

"But what?"

"Even if they are unhorsed, the armored ones are hard to kill."

Alchiq jerked his head and crawled off, and Gansukh followed. They made a tiring circuit of the camp until they had a better view of the horses. When Alchiq drew up short, Gansukh nearly crawled into him. The old hunter hissed at him for his clumsiness and gestured for him to crawl around. As Gansukh was doing so, he caught sight of what had arrested Alchiq's progress.

Standing along the western verge of the camp was an old man carrying a long pole. The pole was braced against the ground and the man was standing very still, his face pointed almost directly at them. Gansukh froze, hardly daring to breathe, his heart pounding harder in his chest. Had they been spotted? Alchiq was likewise immobile next to them, and they remained that way for such a time that their slow breathing became the breath of one being.

Alchiq grunted and shifted slightly, moving his body a hand's span forward. There was no change in the watcher, and Gansukh realized that whatever the man was looking at, it wasn't them.

"It's him," Alchiq hissed, his voice even quieter than before.

He wasn't a man Gansukh recognized, but since Alchiq clearly did, that meant this elderly figure was the man they had been chasing all these months. Did that mean the staff in his hand was the Spirit Banner?

Alchiq thought as much, judging by the vibrations coming off his body. The old hunter moved again, shifting himself forward, but Gansukh stopped him by grabbing his calf.

"Even if you get the banner, you'll be on foot," he whispered to Alchiq. "They have horses. You won't get far."

Alchiq hesitated, a growl rumbling through his body. He wanted to try anyway; Gansukh could feel the frustration coursing through Alchiq's body. To be so close to their goal but unable to reach it!

A pair of figures approached the group of horses, and Gansukh tugged on Alchiq's leg to redirect his attention. As they watched the pair moved among the horses and, with much discussion, appeared to be separating them into two distinct groups.

"They're splitting up," Gansukh whispered to Alchiq, who grudgingly crawled back until he was side by side with Gansukh. "They're picking out which horses to leave behind and which to take with them."

Alchiq nodded in agreement, the growl still rumbling in his throat.

"The armored ones are staying behind," Gansukh guessed.

"Aye," Alchiq agreed. He watched the division of the horses a little while longer; then, with a lingering glance at the stoic old man and the staff, he signaled that it was time for them to depart.

Scuttling like lizards, they reversed their facing and crawled away from the camp in a straight line. Once they were far enough that the glow from the fiery hole was nothing more than a glimmer beyond the grasses, Alchiq stood up and brushed the mud and gunk off his *deel*.

"They hope to confuse us," he said. "When Totukei attacks, he'll find resistance, but he won't know that some of them have gone."

Gansukh's heart was hammering in his chest again. Would Lian be one of those in the group that fled? "When Totukei overwhelms them, he'll think he's found them all," he said. "He has no reason to think otherwise, does he?"

"Unless we tell him," Alchiq said.

Gansukh wrestled with how to answer, trying to decide what his heart was telling him. "Why would we?" he asked finally. "Totukei doesn't like you. You showed up in his camp, made a fool of his cousin, and told him that he wasn't fit for command. He'll want to kill them all just to prove you're wrong about them."

Alchiq grinned. "He will. Let him attack the *Skjaldbrædur*. We'll just chase after the group that has fled."

"By ourselves?" Gansukh asked. He cleared his throat and chose his next words with care. "You are not as adept with a bow as you once were," he said.

Alchiq spat on the ground, unconsciously closing his injured hand to hide his missing finger. "We'll have Totukei give us an *arban*. That will be enough for the women and the old man." He glanced down at his fist and realized what he had done and angrily slashed his hand at Gansukh. "Let's find our horses," he said, striding off with utter confidence that he remembered where their horses were waiting.

Gansukh let him go, his attention going back to the distant *Skjaldbrædur* camp. The steppe was quiet. There were no night birds seeking food, and no wind moving through the grasses.

His heart was still beating noisily in his chest, but it was calming down. He held his breath for a moment, listening and staring intently. Was something out there, watching them? He didn't see or hear anything, but the skin on his arms prickled with the sense that he was being watched.

"Lian," the word slipped out of him, and the spell holding him in place was broken. He shook his head and turned to follow Alchiq. There was nothing out there.

✦ ✦ ✦

Raphael was sure the second Mongol had spotted them, even though he and Haakon had pressed themselves as flat as possible against the ground. Haakon had drawn his knife—that may have been the sound that had alerted the Mongol—and the Northerner was lying on the blade, ensuring no glint of moonlight gave them away.

They had been expecting scouts, and when Evren had spotted movement on the steppe, he and Haakon had immediately darted off into the darkness. They had blackened their faces, hands, and clothing with ash, rendering them practically inseparable from the night, and as the two Mongols had crept along the western edge of their camp, they had followed them.

Raphael had recognized Graymane by his white hair, and confirmation of the suspicion they had all held for so long had been both a relief and cause for alarm. After all this time, Alchiq was still chasing them. The man would never give up. Could they kill him before he was responsible for the deaths of more of their company?

Neither he nor Haakon moved for some time, and finally they heard the faint sound of hooves against the hard ground. Beside him, Haakon led out a loud whoosh of air and rolled onto his side. "They're gone," he whispered to Raphael.

Raphael nodded as he sat up. "I recognized Graymane," he said. "The one named Alchiq."

"The other one was Gansukh," Haakon said. "I know him. He and Alchiq visited me while I was in the cage at the *Khagan*'s camp. He is an intelligent man."

"Did you understand what they were saying?"

"Aye," Haakon said as he sheathed his knife. "They know you're planning on splitting the party. Someone named Totukei will be leading the attack tomorrow. They're going to hunt Feronantus and the women with an *arban*."

"Ten men," Raphael said. "Did they say anything about how many men will be coming?" He gestured for Haakon to follow him, and started back toward their camp.

"He didn't, but if he thinks he can get ten men without telling this Totukei what he is planning, then there are probably..." Haakon shrugged, not wanting to quantify the size of the force.

"More than ten," Raphael said with a tight smile. "And probably fewer than a hundred. We've fought a hundred before. A *jaghun*. It won't be easy. Harder, in fact, because I want you and Vera to ride with Feronantus."

"What?"

"Cnán and Lian don't have any armor. Ten skilled horse archers will bring them down without much trouble. Especially out here where there is no way to minimize their approach."

"I want to stay," Haakon complained.

Raphael shook his head. "Your wound slows you down. You won't be able to help us. I should send the Seljuks too, but I need them." He sighed and looked up at the star-strewn sky. "I hope the Virgin will watch over you, Haakon. Ride hard. I don't know if we can stop them."

CHAPTER 26:

CHASING ALEXANDER

Kristaps began the morning with drills against three of the Danes—Thorvald and two others whose names he did not remember. The men of the north had a ferocity that he admired, and there was enough variation in each of the three's techniques to adequately challenge him. For all the planning and marching and pillaging, there had been very little actual fighting, and he found himself longing for it when he woke in the morning. It was a sure sign that he was beginning to dull, and to do so in this frigid land, so far from Rome, where all the world was set against him would have been a failure equal to the mistakes of his predecessors. The Livonian Order would vanish into the folds of history as a farcical order of thick-fingered, ill-witted fools led by doltish commanders who did not understand the basic rule of martial conquest: keep your steel sharp and ready.

Kristaps would have preferred to train with steel, but the Danes were not as eager as he to test the edges of their blades, and they drilled that crisp morning with wooden trainers. Kristaps detested the wooden clatter of the blades as they struck one another. Each echoing *thock* was a reminder that their exercise was reinforcing habits that would work against them on the real field of battle. The wooden swords bounced off each other; there was no tug of a blade's edge biting into the steel of another blade. The training master at Petraathen had laughed at Kristaps when he had complained one morning about using the wooden swords. *You don't train with steel until you are skilled enough to respect it*, the old *oplo* had told him.

He respected it. It was the only thing beside God that he did hold in any esteem.

One of the Danes, a thick-necked man with red hair and beard, came at Kristaps with a strong two-handed attack. Kristaps blocked it smoothly, gritting his teeth as the blades make their *thock!* noise, and when the Dane's blade rebounded off his, he struck back with a vicious strike of his own. His strike collapsed the Dane's defense, and the man cried out as both blades came down on his shoulder. He stumbled and fell on his ass, and Kristaps poked him in the belly for good measure.

Thorvald held up his hands, pointing his sword at the sky, and took several steps back. His companion did likewise, and for a moment the training yard was silent—gone was the infernal racket of the wooden sticks!—and then the respite was punctured by groans coming from the man on the ground and the sound of a messenger calling out his name.

Kristaps tossed his practice sword at Thorvald. "We're done for the day," he said, and, gesturing for the messenger to walk with him, he stalked back to his tent.

"What news of Pskov?" he asked once he was inside his tent, the walls affording him a tiny modicum of privacy.

"No news, sir," the messenger started. "There are other reports, from along Lake Peipus."

"Where?" Kristaps demanded.

"Near Dorpat," came another voice. Hermann stood behind the messenger, blocking the man's retreat. "He's attacking us." Hermann pushed back the nervous messenger and went to the table, where he found the map he was looking for and spread it out. "He's less than three days from Dorpat."

"How can that be?" Kristaps snarled. This was all wrong. Alexander was supposed to be pursuing him. The prince was supposed to be rushing to the aid of Pskov, where Kristaps's assassins would finish this war without the loss of any men from the Livonian Order. Instead, he was behind them, marching on Hermann's city. "It's impossible," Kristaps said, glaring at the messenger. "Our last report was that his army was still at Novgorod. He could not have marched that far so quickly." He stared at the map, his eyes moving frantically across the parchment, measuring distances. "You're wrong!" he shouted at the messenger.

"There's no report from Pskov," the messenger repeated, visibly nervous about the response his words were going to elicit. "Other scouts have heard of an army marching along the western shore of Lake Peipus, burning villages as they go. They march under the banner of the House of Rurik."

"Get out!" Kristaps barked at the messenger, who was quick to dart out of the tent. Kristaps dashed the map off the table and stormed about the tent, his fists clenching and unclenching.

"You're a fool," Hermann hissed, his face blazing with anger. "You burned his city and slew his people, and he has responded in kind. And where are we? Wandering north, in the woods, much like the prince in exile. We can't stop him before he gets to Dorpat. He'll win the war without having to fight our army. What sort of fool—"

Kristaps snatched up his sheathed sword with a roar, pulled the blade free, and leveled it at the Prince-Bishop, the point quivering less than a hand's breath from Hermann's throat.

"The messenger is wrong," the First Sword of Fellin said with exaggerated care.

Hermann did not move, though his eyes blazed with an equal fury. "And what if he isn't? You'll have been outmaneuvered by a boy. You'll have accomplished nothing and lost everything. This will be worse than—"

Kristaps's sword touched the Prince-Bishop's cheek and he fell silent.

"The messenger is wrong," Kristaps repeated.

Hermann would have nodded, but he didn't dare move his head with Kristaps's blade pressed against his cheek. Instead, he merely stared at Kristaps, waiting to see what would happen next.

Kristaps struggled to keep his anger in check. Without moving his sword, he glanced at the table for the map, and only then remembered that he had swept it to the floor. It was lying next to the wall of his tent, half folded on itself, its back to him. *Just like the messenger*, he thought furiously, *telling me nothing*.

Lake Peipus was north of Pskov, a natural barrier between Rus and the bishopric of Dorpat, and it would take them nearly a week to march around the lake in order to return to Dorpat. They had not left the city of Dorpat defenseless and the main citadel could withstand a siege for at least a week. *What was Alexander doing?* He couldn't hope to take Dorpat before the Teutonic army caught up with him.

It was a daring move, and it fit with the stories he'd heard of the battle of Neva, where the prince had been victorious against Birgir, the Swedish jarl. The prince's swift assault had caught the jarl off guard, and the day had belonged to the prince. But Neva had been a single battle, one that had settled the conflict, and marching on Dorpat would not have the same result. All that Alexander could hope for was to stir the Prince-Bishop's anger. It was a bold move, but it was also one that seemed ill-planned, almost like…"Revenge," Kristaps said, lowering his sword.

"What?" Hermann asked.

"There are no messengers from Pskov because Pskov is not ours," Kristaps said. "Marching into Dorpat is an act of revenge against what he found in Pskov."

"The assassins?"

"They have failed," Kristaps said with a smile. "But they angered him, and he reacted without thinking." He put his sword back in its sheath and gathered up the map from the floor and spread it out on the table again. "This is the action of a man who is driven by vengeance. It is said he is a peerless leader of men, and I know the allies upon whom he has come to rely, but he's also young, and has never once lost a battle. He is smart, and capable, but he lacks experience. He enjoys the invulnerability granted to him by a sense of audacity that hasn't run up against failure. All we have to do is bloody him once and he will be ours."

"But we have to find him in order to bloody him, and all I hear is that he is not where we expect him to be," Hermann snapped. "This gambit of yours, hoping to draw Alexander north, is suddenly looking like the work of a fool. If the prince is allowed to take Dorpat, you will find yourself with very few friends here in the north."

Kristaps smiled grimly at the Prince-Bishop, showing his teeth. "I am in no need of friends," he said.

Hermann let loose a sharp bark of laughter. "No?" he said. "Only a fool or a madman is eager to make such a claim." He shook his head and wandered away from Kristaps, pausing near the flaps of the tent. "You are far from home, Kristaps of Fellin. My fortunes are tied to yours, and if you fail, I will fail with you. The stain of your foolishness will last a long time." He laughed again. "I dislike you, that much is certain, but it matters not, for you and I are allies, and you need not fear my loyalty. I have no desire to betray those in Rome who sent you and my faith is as strong as any man's, but I do wonder if you know whom you truly serve?"

"I serve God and am here to do His work," Kristaps snapped. "It is clear to me what Alexander is trying to accomplish, and you seek to muddy it with too many questions. However, in order to calm your mind and spirit, I will take a company of the Danes and ride ahead of our army. I will verify, personally, what our scouts claim to have seen in Dorpat."

"And if you see what they see?"

"Then I will attack the prince's army myself. I will stop him from taking Dorpat, and *I will not fail.*"

Hermann started to reply and then stopped, his face slackening as he grew thoughtful. "Your patron in Rome has great faith in you," he said after a considerable silence. "Either that or you are being groomed for an extraordinary fall from grace."

"The only one who is going to fall is Alexander," Kristaps said. "Bring the army around the northern edge of the lake. March quickly, and don't worry about the supply wagons. They can catch up. There is still time to take advantage of this mistake."

◆ ◆ ◆

Kristaps and the Danes rode west, pushing their horses across the snow-dappled landscape like the Devil himself nipped at their heels. When they reached the frozen shores of Lake Peipus, Svend urged him to turn south instead of north. While the army would march around the top of the lake, he told Kristaps, they could cross at the middle. On the maps, Lake Peipus resembled a misshapen hourglass: two vessels pinched together. During the winter, it was possible to cross the frozen lake at the pinch point.

Kristaps ordered the men to increase the distance between each rider as they followed him across the ice-covered lake, but as he galloped across the frozen water, he realized his concern was baseless. The ice was so thick that the entire Teutonic army could have marched across without mishap.

As the Danes crossed, he split off teams of three and told them to ride ahead, seeking sign of Alexander's army. "Do not engage them," he instructed the scouts. "The prince has cavalry who will pursue you, given the opportunity. Do not let them see you. Just find them. And if you find any scouts of theirs, kill them."

The scouting parties liked his last order, and they eagerly rode off to find the enemy. The rest of the company rode into Dorpat like shadows crawling across the land, given speed as if energized by the hunt, horses moving with the eagerness of warriors who could smell battle in the lands ahead. They rode over rock and crag, through dips in the land and under snow-laden trees, outriders sweeping out ahead of them.

But their quarry remained elusive.

At the end of the second day of riding, they camped on a rise that afforded a clear view of the surrounding forest and waited for the remaining scouts to return.

Inactivity did not suit Kristaps, now or in the days before. Waiting was a necessity of warfare, but it did not come easily to him, and he did not enjoy it. He paced about his tent for awhile, and eventually left to hike the short distance to the top of the hill. He did not expect to look out over the forest and see signs of the Ruthenian army, but the view was more expansive than staring at the walls of his tent.

Dorpat lay to the north—he raised his arm and pointed—and Pskov was in the other direction. *Somewhere in between,* he thought, gazing at the forest encompassed by his open arms, *is the prince and his army. Where are you hiding, Nevsky?*

"Men who stand too still in the wind and the cold have a tendency to turn to stone."

Kristaps dropped his arms and glanced over his shoulder. The Danish prince, Illugi, had joined him. Illugi was not the most handsome of the brothers, but he had a brutal sort of directness to his carriage, and when he looked out over the world at their feet, it seemed that he saw what was ripe for the taking.

"I wonder if that fate has befallen the prince's army," Kristaps said. "Perhaps that is why our scouts have not been able to find them. We are looking for flesh and blood men and they are all gone."

"We'll find them," Illugi said. He had a stick of dried meat in his hands, and he tore a chunk off and held it out to Kristaps. "They know we're coming. The prince is either a fool or a fox. If he is the latter, he wants you to chase him. To be chased, you have to be seen. Sooner or later, our outriders will find them."

"And if he is a fool?" Kristaps asked as he took the offered piece of meat.

Illugi raised his broad shoulders. "Then he is camped outside Dorpat, waiting for us to crush him against the walls of the city. But I do not think he is a fool."

"Nor do I," Kristaps said. He bit off a piece of the dried meat and began to chew it. "How many times have you fought the men of Rus, Illugi?" he asked around the mouthful of meat.

"Thrice," Illugi said. "But never as openly as this." He held up his hand, lifting one finger after another as he enumerated his previous encounters. "Once we came for women, once for plunder, once to avenge the honor of my father." He closed his raised hand into a fist. "When blood is spilled, nothing but more blood will suffice to answer for it," he explained.

Kristaps grunted in response. He liked the simplicity of the Danish world view. "What do you know of the men of Novgorod?" he asked.

"They do not train for war like we do," Illugi said, "but they are not unskilled in the martial ways. Their soldiers are peasants, mostly, but not like the raw recruits called up by the levies in Christendom. The men of Novgorod rule themselves like the heathen Romans of old, and all men of age are required to take up spear, shield, or bow in the service of their prince when he calls them to war. They are not as practiced as the *Druzhina* of the House of Rurik, but they are not weak." He smiled. "They will give you a good fight."

"Have you fought these *Druzhina* before?" Kristaps asked.

"I have not, but I have heard stories about Neva. They are professional soldiers, *Heermeister.* Like your knights, but not so…" He trailed off with a shrug as if the detail were not that important. "Some are the sons of *boyars,*" he continued, "but most are mercenaries who serve because they get paid. All are capable riders and able swordsmen. Like your knights, they will dominate against infantry unless they can be pulled from their horses and stabbed to death." He shrugged again. "Their armor is not as good as yours. The metal in the north isn't as strong as the iron and steel from Germany. There will be archers amongst them, able to shoot from horseback, but not at great ranges, and quick to maneuver. You must drive through their heart and shatter them before they can pick us off."

"And Alexander?" Kristaps asked. "What do you know of him?"

"Little," Illugi replied. "Neither my brother nor I have met or seen his face, but we've heard of his exploits. Who hasn't? But I think that few men are equal to the legends told of them. Every man will eventually meet his match, whether it is a battle, a place, a time, or another man. Inevitably, we will face a foe we cannot defeat."

Kristaps arched an eyebrow and looked sideways at Illugi as the latter stared out across the snowy landscape. It was an oddly deep thought for one who seemed to know no greater joy than destroying his enemies. "That seems a thought made to comfort the heart after failure."

Illugi gave a snort. "Dying is seldom comforting, *Heermeister.*"

"All the more reason it should happen to someone else."

Illugi smiled at Kristaps, but it was a hollow smile. The amusement did not reach Illugi's eyes.

✦ ✦ ✦

During the night, a group of scouts returned with news of having spotted the prince's army. Kristaps ordered the company to mobilize before first light and as the morning fog was beginning to lift, they had moved into position within the forest.

The scout had reported that the war-party was marching toward Dorpat, following an old trade path that ran between the forest and a narrow stream. The stream was not so deep that it couldn't be forded, but it provided a natural barrier. Coupled with the forest, the path was a narrow route that would make for a good ambush.

The Danish company waited in the trees. The sun was masked by gray clouds and fog still drifted along the surface of the icy stream. Kristaps sat impatiently in the saddle of his stallion, watching his own breath mingle with that of the beast.

Troubadours tended to make over battles into laborious affairs, but what entertained the masses was never good battlefield tactics. It was best to strike quickly, with overwhelming force, and so break your opponents utterly. As he breathed in the frigid air, Kristaps promised himself that this day would not end with a desperate crawl through the blood-soaked mud and undergrowth as his fallen brothers were run through by scavengers picking over the bones of the dead.

He looked sideways, caught a glimpse of the Danish princes among their own men. Svend and Illugi wore half-helms and worn mail less fine than his own, and their swords were of an older make. Spears were in their hands, and many of their men carried bearded axes. Kristaps's own men wore maille, some with solid steel plates upon their shoulders, fine swords forged of southern steel, and oaken shields painted with crosses. As Kristaps turned his eyes once more towards the open space beyond the edge of the wood, he flexed the fingers of his sword-hand beneath his mailled gloves.

It would all be over soon enough.

He heard them before he spotted them, the rhythmic sound of boots and hooves against the ground. His horse stirred, eager to run. Kristaps slid his hand down to the hilt of his sword, acutely aware of the rounded edges of the grip through the leather and fur that separated his fingers from its surface. His lessons from long ago flooded through his mind as he opened himself up to the flow of the world between himself and the sounds of his enemies, breathing in energy and turning it to fiercely burning hate. He felt his eyes widen as he quietly slid his weapon free from its sheath and raised it into the air, where it could be seen by his assembled forces. There would be no shouts, no commands to alert their enemies. They would charge in silence, taking their enemy unawares before they had the chance to understand what was happening to them. The quiet sound of clinking mail to his right told him that the Danes were taking his cue and raising their own weapons. Lance-tips rose from the earth to level off where they would take men through the hearts.

Through the trees and the snow, Kristaps caught the glint of half-helms and heavy cloaks. He saw them coming, marching with an order rare to see among peasant levies, though not so perfect as free mercenaries such as were to be found in Germany or Northern Italy. He snapped his sword tip forward as he dug his spurs into his horse's flank.

The order was given, and the First Sword of Fellin was leading the charge.

Trees whipped past him, undergrowth groaned beneath the pounding of hooves and snow and earth flared upwards in a wild spray as the war horse carried him forward. The sound seemed to swell as he moved, echoing in the thunder of hundreds of others, rippling outward before them in a wave their enemy was becoming aware of too late. They burst from the edge of the trees in a panoply of furious steel, driving up the ground before them as the ordered line of Novgorod's citizen soldiers desperately tried to turn to meet the coming wave. One of the Danish riders had outdistanced Kristaps by the body-length of his horse, and he caught a glimpse of the rider driving his grey-tipped spear through the face of the foremost man, a flash of blood seeming to whip past before

Kristaps himself was among them like a whirlwind. Faces swirled around him like a river of flesh and bone and stupefied surprise.

He killed his first man before the soldier had managed to raise his weapon. The second died beneath the hooves of his horse. He hewed a man's arm from his shoulder and opened the face of another, cleaving his head in half and catching only a flash of the explosion of flesh as he whipped past like an avenging angel.

He wheeled his horse about as the charge spent itself, and surveyed the scene of blood-drenched chaos. The gambit had worked, the initial charge ripping what order had existed of the Novgorodians into bloody shreds. On the entire stretch of space their forces had occupied, the snow was stained with blotches of red where bodies had fallen, and across the mass of moving humans, men fought with desperate, chaotic abandon. It appeared that he had lost only a handful in the initial assault, and now his knights and the Danes rode back and forth through the chaos, hacking heads and running men through as a handful of Ruthenian men on horseback desperately tried to rally them. *Druzhina.* Turning his horse towards one of them, Kristaps flicked his sword to free it of excess blood and charged.

The *Druzhina* spotted him at the last possible second and managed to block Kristaps's strike, but was nearly unhorsed in the process. Laughing, Kristaps wheeled his horse about and cut low with a backhanded flick of his blade. The *Druzhina* screamed as the blade sliced across his thigh. As Kristaps came at him again, he got his sword up and thrust it at Kristaps's face. Kristaps turned the point aside and jabbed his blade low again. The man was too slow with his shield, and Kristaps felt his blade grate against maille and then penetrate something softer. *The metal of the north isn't as strong...*His sword came away with a heavy sheen of blood.

To his credit, the young Ruthenian did not give up. He launched a desperate strike at Kristaps's horse, hoping to down the Livonian's steed. Snarling, Kristaps beat his blade aside with the back edge and pulled his mount closer to the other man's horse. Before the man could get his shield in between them, Kristaps drove his sword through the *Druzhina's* armpit, where the inferior maille would be weakest. The sword pierced the armor, cut through the padded gambeson beneath, and pushed up through the man's flesh until the point came out again near his neck. The *Druzhina* jerked back violently, his helmet falling off his head, and Kristaps saw the face of a man less than twenty years old, his beard still spotty on his cheeks and chin. The *Druzhina* dropped his shield and grasped Kristaps by the shoulder in a dying effort to pull the Livonian out of the saddle with him. He dropped his sword as well and steel glinted in his hand as he tried to stab Kristaps with a short-bladed knife.

Kristaps released his reins and hammered his fist down on the other man's wrist, trapping the arm against his thigh. The man wiggled, desperately trying to get the knife turned so that he could stab Kristaps, and Kristaps grabbed his wrist. He rotated his arm up, twisting the *Druzhina*'s arm violently, and the knife spilled out of the man's grasp. Still holding the man's arm, Kristaps jerked his sword free of the *Druzhina*'s armpit and, reversing the weapon, hammered the man in the face with the pommel. At the same time, he shoved with his left hand, and the bloodied and dying man fell out of his saddle.

There were no other combatants around him and, somewhat surprised, Kristaps assessed the battle. The path was littered with dead and the few remaining Ruthenians were attempting to flee, and as he watched the Danes ride down the scattered remnants of the Novgorodian force, Kristaps finally spotted the trampled banner of the prince lying in the mud beside the stream.

One banner.

This was nothing more than a raiding party. They had not found the main force.

◆ ◆ ◆

The sun set over a carpet of dead, clouds parting long enough to let the yellow-red glow of evening color the killing ground the hue of bloodstained gold. Kristaps sat atop a rock near the stream, watching as the Danes stripped the bodies of the dead of anything of value, and those who were not yet dead were hastened on their way with a swift thrust through the heart or a hastily cut throat. The singers could weave their beautiful melodies about glory and honor, but ultimately every battle came down to the brutal task of glorified knife-work.

Kristaps had taken no wounds, and he cared little for the taking of plunder—none of the men dead before him on this field had anything that he might have wanted. What spoils there were would make the Danes happy. What Kristaps sought had not been present.

They had decimated a raiding party. If his scouts had stayed long enough to investigate the numbers of the men they had spotted, they would have realized the prince's *army* was not large enough to constitute any real threat to Dorpat. He did not believe that the prince would have sent only one raiding party into Tartu, and as he watched the Danes pillage the dead, he realized the prince's clever ploy.

The prince wasn't in Dorpat. All that was needed were a few men, a handful of mounted *Druzhina*, and a banner flying the prince's colors. Nevsky could scatter a dozen such raiding parties across Dorpat and the reports that would get back to Hermann and Kristaps would be conflated into the alarming news that the entirety of the bishopric was under attack. It was bait, and he and Hermann had fallen for it. The Teutonic army was rushing back to defend Dorpat, which was not under any true threat.

"I've never seen a man look so dour after a victory," Svend said as he knelt by the stream to clean the gore from his sword.

"Commoners with axes are not much of a victory when you are hunting a prince," Kristaps replied.

"Ah, but they are his people. We have pricked him, and we shall see how he bleeds. That is something."

"Aye," Kristaps said. "We've bloodied him."

"And now he must answer," Svend said happily. "Blood calls out for blood. He will come."

Kristaps looked along the path in the direction from which the ambushed party had come. *Would the prince come?* he wondered, though he privately thought the prince would not. *He's a fox*, he thought, recalling Illugi's words. *Having been seen, he wants to be chased.*

Kristaps would oblige him.

CHAPTER 27:

...THERE IS FIRE

Yasper started awake and blearily looked up at Raphael. The sky behind Raphael was purple, and the stars were twinkling. The alchemist groaned and closed his eyes. It was almost dawn and what little sleep he had managed to snatch was not nearly enough. Raphael shook him gently again and Yasper brushed the bothersome hand off like he was shooing away a fly. "I'm awake," he groused.

"It's time," Raphael said, belaboring the obvious reason he had woken Yasper.

"I know. I know," Yasper said. He opened his eyes again and flapped his hands at Raphael. "I'm getting up. I don't need any help."

His back and shoulders still ached from all the digging he'd done during the night. The ambush he'd planned required careful consideration, and it had been insane even to try to put it together in the course of one night. And then Raphael and Haakon had come from their nocturnal excursion and, after a whispered conference with Gawain and Vera, had informed him they were going to abandon the depression sooner than planned. Once Yasper had finished sputtering and complaining about the change in plans, he had realized that it meant he had to be less concerned about blowback.

The only reason he had allowed himself any sleep at all was the comforting thought that his plan had been made easier.

Yasper sat up, pulled on his boots, and stood up. He was already stiff, and the idea of spending the day on a horse wasn't a pleasant one. *It could be worse,* he thought as he ran his tongue over his teeth. *I could be dead in the next few hours.*

Cheered by that thought, he rummaged in his saddlebags for a few strips of dried meat. After washing his mouth out with a swallow of night-chilled water from his dwindling water skin, he gathered up a swaddled bundle and wandered toward the hole in the ground to check on his alchemical masterpiece.

He had conscripted all of the company to help dig trenches, raise foundations, and build partitions. Crisscrossing the depression were a maze of pathways that had been carefully filled with seep-stained dirt. The pool at the bottom of the hole still burned, but the flames had lessened, dying down to a height of less than that of a man. They would burn for years, he suspected, an eternal flame in the middle of the desolate steppe.

But they could also be snuffed out.

Bruno ambled up beside him, yawning widely, and Yasper winced slightly at the amount of air the Lombard was inhaling. The air coming off the fires of the seep made his head ache and his vision blur. He had spent enough time in closeted alchemical laboratories to know that many experiments vented strange gasses that were poisonous. And yet Bruno was sucking up the dirty air of the seep as if were as rarified as sea air.

"Are you ready?" he asked the Lombard.

Bruno grunted, idly scratching along his jaw.

Yasper led the way, the bundle held carefully in his arms. Beneath the layer of heavy cloth was the metal tube of a Chinese hand cannon. They had found it in the woods while tracking Ögedei's retinue, along with a satchel filled with various alchemical powders. Yasper had used most of the powders during their escape from Burqan-qaldun, but with the rest, he had figured out how to make the burning cakes that he called phoenix eggs.

Shards of the cakes, when crumbled and scattered across hot ash, would smoke wildly, and he had used most of one during the raid at the rock. The remaining portion of the first cake was sealed inside the Chinese tube, along with every other combustible ingredient in his possession. Rope was tied around the tube and the other end was knotted in a narrow loop.

Down near the pool of fire were two poles, the trunks of two young spruce trees that Percival had felled during the night. The branches and bark had been stripped from the trunks and the tops of the poles were lashed together, forming an X.

Yasper was sweating by the time he and Bruno reached the bottom of the depression. They had gone over what needed to be done several times so that there would be no confusion once they started. Yasper wasn't sure how long they would have, and he really didn't want to be dawdling near the lake longer than necessary.

He put the bundle down near the X of the poles and uncovered the tube and the looped rope. Slipping the loop over the tips of the two poles, he grabbed the other end of one of the poles. Bruno grabbed the other and when they carefully raised the poles, the tube dangled down between the angled poles.

"Quickly," Yasper gasped, and Bruno grunted in agreement. They sidestepped toward the pool, and Yasper had a momentary panic that he had judged the size of the pool incorrectly, but they ended up on either side. Bruno shoved the base of his pole into the ground, and Yasper did the same, trying to dig the butt of the spruce trunk into the ground enough that it would remain upright. The poles were leaning against one another, a precarious triangular structure, and slowly, carefully, he let go of his pole. The structure wobbled for a second, the tube swinging over the flames, and Yasper gasped. But it settled, and Yasper waved for

Bruno to let go of his end as well. The Lombard did, and Yasper did a quick mental five-count—waiting for the poles to fall over.

The poles didn't move. The tube turned lazily on the rope.

"Go," Yasper hissed at Bruno, who needed no further instruction. Yasper was right behind him, and both of them charged up the slope of the depression, trying to clear the hole before the tube heated up enough that its contents transformed. *Ignio*, Yasper thought as he scrambled over the lip of the hole and threw himself flat on the ground. *Here it comes.*

Bruno lay next to him, and the Lombard had his eyes squeezed shut and was covering his ears. As they waited, Bruno started to grit his teeth, squeezing his eyes shut even tighter. His expression was comical enough that Yasper almost laughed, but for the growing panic surging in his chest. Why hadn't it gone—

The ground rippled beneath them, a single shudder that made the hair on Yasper's neck stand on end. He held his breath, peering up at the sky with one open eye. A black mushroom-shaped cloud was roiling into the sky, but there was no column trailing after it.

Using his elbows, he carefully worked his way to the edge of the hole. There were a few scattered strands of fire burning in the hole—thankfully none of them was in any of his crazy trenches. More importantly, the surface of the pond was still. The fire had been smothered.

He slapped Bruno on the leg. "Get the tents," he said. "Let's build the phoenix nest."

✦ ✦ ✦

Dawn came on slowly, lightening the eastern horizon into a pall of gray clouds. The sun remained hidden away, and there was only a rosy glow that indicated it had risen at all. They kept the glow behind them, riding steadily.

There were five of them: Vera, Cnán, Lian, Feronantus, and Haakon. They had four extra horses and most of the drinkable water. Raphael's instructions had been to ride west until they reached the mighty river they had crossed once before. After finding a way across, they were to turn north and west again until they found the remote Khazar village where the trader Benjamin lived.

They could wait for the others there, if the Khazars didn't find their presence troubling, or they could leave a message with Benjamin that they had made it that far. After the Khazar village, they would head for Kiev, a journey that would take a month or more, following a route that Vera knew.

The decision to split the company gnawed at Haakon as they rode. After all this time, it seemed tantamount to failure to leave some of their company behind—a decision that did not, in his mind, seem to be in keeping with the tenets of the *Ordo Militum Vindicis Intactae*. Though Raphael had kindly told him that doing exactly what they were doing—staying behind to protect the rest of the company—was not uncommon in the history of the order. They were not martyrs; they merely understood the burden of being an initiate in the order.

Lian, who was showing signs of becoming an accomplished rider, brought her horse alongside Haakon. Her black hair has bound up in a ponytail and she wore a fur-lined hat and a shapeless cloak. From a distance, she could be mistaken for a man.

She had Raphael's crossbow and a small satchel of bolts. She had insisted that she knew how to fire a bow, and Raphael had had her show him with Ahmet's bow. She was far from proficient, but she knew how to aim and hold the bow steady. It would be skill enough with a crossbow if the Mongol riders got close enough.

A better weapon than a knife, Gawain had muttered to Vera while Haakon had been standing nearby.

Aye, Vera had answered, *but there is no reason to not give her both.*

"Did you see them?" Lian asked. Her tone was casual and she didn't look at him, as if she were merely passing some of the endless hours.

"I did," Haakon replied.

"Did they…Did you know any of them?"

"Aye," Haakon said. "One of them was Gansukh."

She nodded lightly, seemingly unmoved by his news, but he saw how tightly her hands were holding her reins.

"They're coming after us," Haakon said. He nodded toward Feronantus. "They want the Banner."

"Of course," Lian said quietly.

Haakon nudged his horse closer to Lian's and leaned over, touching her on the elbow. "When he…just before he left, he said your name," he told her.

Lian turned her head and looked at him, and he was startled by the shining light in her eyes in contrast with the frozen mask of her face. "I wish you hadn't told me that," she whispered and then she pulled her horse away, leaving him to wonder what he had just done wrong.

◆ ◆ ◆

They put the hole with its intricate trenches and swollen canvas covering over the black pool behind them, so that, initially, the Mongol riders wouldn't be able to come at them from all directions. The extra horses were hobbled nearby, though based on what little Yasper had told him, Raphael expected them to bolt when Yasper birthed the phoenix. He and Percival were wearing the full kits, and the weak links in the back of his maille had been repaired. Bruno and Gawain were wearing an assortment of greaves and leathers they had taken from Haidar's Muslims, and Gawain had meticulously counted and checked each of his arrows.

He had three dozen. If the Mongol commander, Totukei, had only four *arbans* and Gawain hit every one of his targets, the fight might be extremely short. But Raphael didn't think the Virgin was going to bless them in such an extraordinary fashion. There would be more Mongols than that, and Gawain had been tasked with doing as much damage as he could to their ranks with his arrows.

Gawain and Yasper were on foot. He, Percival, and Bruno were mounted. The others had left hours before, and shortly before sunrise, Ahmet and Evren had ridden north in search of the steppe deer herd that Haakon had spotted the other day. The Seljuks were tasked with stampeding the herd toward the depression. It was a desperate idea, but the more confusion that could be sown on the battlefield, the less organized the Mongols would be. The key to shattering their efficient swarming techniques was to keep them off guard.

"They're coming," Bruno said, pointing with his ax toward an undulating black line to the south.

"Let's get ready," Raphael said, plucking his helmet off the horn of his saddle and settling it on his head. Beside him, Percival stretched in his stirrups, eager for the combat to start. Raphael fleetingly wished he hadn't sent Vera with the others, but he had needed to send a strong fighter. *As soon as we're done here, we'll join them,* he thought, banging on the top of his helmet to make sure it was seated well. *Perhaps we'll even be in time to intercept Graymane and his* arban.

✦ ✦ ✦

Since there was no way to hide on the steppe, Alchiq's *arban* rode hard for the *Skjaldbrœður* party. Gansukh counted five riders, and his heart skipped momentarily when he couldn't pick Lian out of the group. But then he spotted two who were smaller than the others, and his heart started pounding more normally again.

Alchiq whistled at the others and their group split, dividing into three squads—much like they had when Gansukh and Alchiq had first been discovered by Totukei's riders. Bows were readied, and they started shouting battle cries as they drove their horses into battle.

Suddenly the *Skjaldbrœður* group changed direction, wheeling to the right, and then nearly as quickly came to a complete stop. Riders leaped off their horses and as the small herd of extra animals caught up with the main group, the *Skjaldbrœður* disappeared into a confusion of legs and manes.

The trio of Mongol riders on Gansukh's right were closest and they hesitated, unwilling to fire arrows indiscriminately into the confusion of horses, and as Gansukh watched, two suddenly pitched from their saddles as the *Skjaldbrœður* picked them off with their shorter-ranged crossbows. The third man pulled his horse away, but it stumbled—Gansukh couldn't tell if it was from clumsiness or if it had been struck by a crossbow bolt—and the rider leaped out of the saddle before he could be pinned by the falling horse.

A figure popped up in the midst of the group, standing in a stirrup, and it hurled something in the general direction of the second group. This group reacted more quickly, and the figure jerked as it disappeared, two arrows striking it square in the chest.

The thrown object turned end over end, a spray of sparks trailing after it, and when it hit the ground, it burst into a sheet of flame.

"Shoot the horses," Alchiq screamed. He raised his bow, pulling the string back with his maimed hand, and loosed an arrow into the throat of one of the horses in the front rank. The horse reared, spooking the already frightened horses near it, and when its front legs hit the ground again, they folded and the horse went down.

A second figure appeared, arm pulled back to throw another incendiary, and Gansukh—knowing the *Skjaldbrædur* maille was nearly impervious to his arrows—aimed for the figure's head. The figure brought its arm forward, but its aim was thrown off when an arrow from one of the other Mongols ricocheted off the metal helm. The object arced up instead of being thrown flat. Without thinking, Gansukh shifted his aim and loosed his arrow at the spinning object.

His arrow struck its target, and the bomb exploded, showering the steppe in a fiery rain.

◆ ◆ ◆

Vera had thrown the first of the three alchemical fire bombs that Yasper had concocted for them, and she had taken two Mongol arrows for her effort. They didn't penetrate her maille, and while Cnán was worrying them out of Vera's shirt, Haakon grabbed the second fire bomb. They had already taken care of the trio on the left; the group on the right was diverted by the wall of fire, and when he put his foot in the stirrup of his horse and levered himself up to throw the bomb, he was aiming for the group coming right at them.

The arrow bounced off his helmet, and he tried to correct his aim, but he was already committed. He fell out of his stirrup, staggering to stay on his feet, and through the narrow gaps in his helmet, he tried to spot the ill-thrown bomb.

Fire erupted overhead, and rivulets of flame cascaded down like a freak spring squall. The horses, which were already spooked, panicked and stampeded away from all the fire. He was struck in the shoulder by a running horse, spun around, and had to dart out of the path of a second horse. A third galloped at him, and when he tried to get out of its way, it shifted direction, still heading right for him.

He realized this horse had a rider.

The Mongol swiped at him with a curved sword, and Haakon ducked under the blade, feeling the tip scrape across the back of his maille, and he tried to grab at the Mongol's leg as the horse flashed past. His fingers encountered heavy cloth, but he couldn't maintain his grip.

He stumbled, trying to orient himself in the smoky pandemonium that the battlefield had become. A pair of horses still milled nearby, and beyond them, he saw the body of another horse. A horse and rider were charging him, and as he frantically cast about for something that he might use as a spear, he caught sight of the third fire bomb, lying on its side, its tiny wick still burning.

He scooped it up, and he felt the clay pot shift and crumble in his hand but he threw it anyway.

The Mongol tried to turn his horse, but the animal was coming too fast, and the horse screamed as it ran into the spray of fire that was flying from Haakon's hand. It reared, throwing its rider, and bowled forward, its withers and head crawling with fire.

Haakon had a glimpse of white teeth and the smell of burning flesh overwhelmed him as he leaped aside, trying to dodge the pain-maddened horse. He realized his gauntlet was on fire and was trying to shake the flames off when someone slammed into him and knocked him sprawling.

◆ ◆ ◆

"The Virgin watches over us," Percival said, drawing Raphael's attention away from the charging line of Mongols. He turned his head and looked to the north. A hazy cloud indicated that Ahmet and Evren had found the deer herd and had managed to stampede it in the right direction.

Indeed, he thought, *the Virgin does reward us in our time of need.*

"Yasper," Raphael called. "Time to redirect the herd."

The alchemist jogged forward, breaking the line of Shield-Brethren horsemen. In each hand he held a clay pot, stopped with mud and stuffed with a bit of oil-soaked cloth. Clutched in his teeth was a stick, one end of which was still smoldering. The alchemist jogged a dozen paces in front of the group and then stopped, glancing at both of the approaching herds of four-legged animals. He put one of his pots down, took the stick out of his mouth, and applied the hot end to the oil-soaked cloth. It caught fire almost instantly and, after judging distances once more, Yasper threw the pot as hard as he could toward the distant line of charging Mongols.

The pot hit the ground, broke, and scattered a wash of fire across the steppe. It wasn't more than a few paces long and not very wide, but it was bright and hot, and the herd of stampeding steppe deer shifted direction immediately.

Yasper lit the second pot and threw it to his left, spooking the deer again. The running herd was redirected, and the two Seljuks peeled away from chasing the group, no longer needed.

The stampeding herd of deer was now heading directly at the approaching Mongols.

"*Alalazu!*" Raphael shouted, slapping his horse on the rump. His horse leaped forward and he sensed Percival and Bruno spurring their horses as well. They charged after the running herd and the Seljuks fell in with them.

For God and the Virgin, he thought, steeling himself for battle.

✦ ✦ ✦

The only one of their company who was not surprised by the fiery rain was the old man, Feronantus. To Lian, he had been a strange addition to their company. The others clearly held him in high regard, even though he had abandoned them back at Burqan-qaldun, but since they had found him wandering on the steppe, he had been unresponsive and nearly catatonic. Raphael had tried to reach him during the planning of their stand against the Mongols, and she inferred that Feronantus had been some manner of military genius, but for all of Raphael's efforts, the old man had been monosyllabic in response. Even when Vera had given the command to circle the horses and dismount, he had complied readily and without comment.

When the arrow struck Haakon's ill-thrown bomb and the rain had fallen on them, pandemonium had erupted in their cluster of horses and men. Feronantus had remained stock still, staring up at the falling rain, clutching the burned stick that had once been the *Khagan*'s Spirit Banner. None of the falling streaks of fire had touched him, and as the horses spooked and ran, they instinctively shied away from him.

And then the Mongols had been on them. Lian had aimed her borrowed crossbow and pulled the trigger, knowing that she wouldn't have time to reload it. The bolt missed its mark, and she had scrambled out of the path of the charging horse. The rider missed her with his sword and was turning his mount for another try when Feronantus knocked him from his horse with the staff.

The Mongol flew out of his saddle, turned his fall into a partially successful roll, and charged Feronantus with a drawn knife. Feronantus swept the outstretched arm aside and jabbed the butt of the staff so hard into the man's face that blood flew when his head snapped back.

"Get the horse," Feronantus shouted at her, and she responded without even thinking, such was the strength of his voice.

The horse shied away from her as she approached it, but it didn't run, and she managed to grab its dangling reins. Speaking in a calm voice, she tried to soothe it. She tried to hide the terror that was still battering around inside her chest like a trapped bird.

She spotted Vera and Cnán, the latter being supported by the former, blood running down the side of her head, and she pulled the horse toward the pair. More arrows jutted from Vera's maille, but the Shield-Maiden did not appear hurt. Cnán, however, couldn't stand without help, and when Lian reached them, she saw that Cnán's eyes were glassy and unfocused. Her hat was gone, and the side of her head was sticky with blood.

"Take the horse," she said to Vera. Vera tried to argue but Lian shook her head. "She can't ride by herself, and I can't ride for two. Take her and go. I'll get another one."

She was grateful that Vera was eternally pragmatic and saw the merit of what she was saying. She helped Vera get the wobbly Cnán up into the saddle, and she held the horse still while Vera got settled behind the wounded Binder. "The Virgin watch you," Vera said as Lian handed her the reins, and Lian nodded in return as Vera drummed her heels against the barrel of the horse and it ran eagerly from the burning battlefield.

There were scattered fires all around her, and the smell of burning horse meat. An animal screamed somewhere off to her left, but she couldn't see anything through the haze. Her eyes watered and she started to cough. A Mongol corpse lay sprawled near her, a curved sword on the ground near his open hand. She scooped the weapon up, juggling the sword until she got it seated well in her hand.

Hearing muffled grunts, she tracked toward the sound of men straining against one another. She spotted Haakon wrestling with a Mongol, and as she approached the pair, intending to use the sword on the Mongol, they rolled over. The Mongol was on top of Haakon, his hands around Haakon's throat, his knee pinning Haakon's right arm against the ground.

"Gansukh?"

Hearing her voice, the Mongol looked up, staring at her.

Haakon pulled his arm free, revealing a knife in his hand. Genghis's knife, Lian realized, and she watched with horror as the Northerner stabbed Gansukh in the side.

"No!"

◆ ◆ ◆

Between the haze from the clay pot fires and the number of riders, it was difficult for Yasper to follow the battle between the Shield-Brethren and the Mongol riders. He wished, not for the first time, that he had a tree or a battlement to climb so that he could get a better view. As it was, he hopped from foot to foot, nervously waiting for some overt sign of who was winning.

Beside him, Gawain carefully tracked outliers of the skirmish, watching for patterns in the movement of the Mongol riders that would allow him to anticipate where they would be. They were at the extreme range of his bow; at that distance, luck and the vicarious whimsy of the wind would contribute as much as his own skill at archery to whether his arrow struck its target or not. The Mongols were too smart to bunch up, making for an easier target. A neat line of eleven arrows, their points shoved into the ground, were arrayed next to him. Two similar lines of readied arrows were spaced behind them, a half dozen paces separating each.

A light wind was coming from the north, and Yasper was hoping that it might switch to the west. *Would God bless them with such assistance?* he wondered. He glanced over his shoulder at the voluminous shroud raised over the pool in the depression. Attached to the center of the cover was a bundle containing the rest of his alchemical supplies and the second phoenix egg.

The Shield-Brethren were depending on his alchemy, and he tried not to dwell on how much his experiment relied on speculative philosophy. The canvas of the tents was moderately waterproof and he hoped it was impermeable to invisible vapors as well. If he was right, then the toxic fumes coming off the black pool would be collecting inside the shroud. He hoped the Persian alchemist Jabir ibn Hayyan was right about the flammable properties of those fumes when Jabir had written *Kitab al-Zuhra*, his treatise on alchemy.

Gawain's bowstring sang, and Yasper turned around in time to see a Mongol rider tumble off his horse. The tide of the battle had shifted and was coming toward them now, forming a wedge. At the tip were two riders in white tabards.

Gawain loosed another arrow. "Bruno's down," he said as he plucked a third arrow from the line arranged before him. The second arrow struck a horse that went down hard, throwing its rider. Another horse collided with the downed horse, putting another Mongol on the ground.

A line of riders peeled off from the main wedge, swinging out to Yasper's right. The Mongols weren't in arrow range yet for their less powerful bows, but the second group was going to try to flank Gawain, forcing him to split his attention between the two groups.

Gawain put an arrow through the chest of the lead rider of the flankers. "They'll be in range in a few seconds," he said to Yasper. "I could use that cover now."

Yasper scrambled over to the long panel of bound branches that Cnán and Lian had assembled during the company's preparations. It was nothing more than a rectangle of branches lashed together to form a makeshift screen. It was flimsy and had several gaps in it that were wide enough for an arrow to slip through, but it was better than no protection at all. Grunting, Yasper hauled it upright and, using the two handles that stuck out from the back side, he hauled it around to Gawain's right so that it stood between him and the oncoming archers. Just as he braced it up, he heard a rattling sound like pebbles against a wooden shutter and the panel vibrated slightly against his shoulder.

Gawain fired his penultimate arrow, and then grabbed the last one from the ground. He flexed his body, pulling the heavy bowstring back, and he held the fletching next to his cheek for what Yasper thought was an interminable moment. A few Mongol arrows stuck in the ground not far from him, and Gawain exhaled—almost sadly, Yasper thought—and the fletching vanished from between his fingers.

Gawain lowered his bow and ducked behind the panel with Yasper. More arrows fell around them and some rattled against the screen. One flashed through a gap not far from Yasper's left hand, and he yelped as the fletching buzzed against his skin. "Let's move," Gawain shouted and, each holding one of the handles, they retreated in tiny steps, heading for the next line of Gawain's arrows.

✦ ✦ ✦

As soon as they were in range, the Mongols started shooting arrows at them. The next thirty seconds were the most dangerous of their attack. Their advantage over the Mongols lasted only as long as they could remain as mobile as the horse riders, and if the Mongols targeted their horses, they'd be on foot, and the battle would be very one-sided. Fortunately the stampeding deer were still causing confusion among the Mongol ranks, and the arrows that flew in their direction were not well targeted. A number struck Raphael in the chest and arms, but none of them stuck in his maille.

And then they had reached the Mongol ranks, and their handheld weapons came to bear. Raphael caught sight of Percival taking a Mongol's head off with a single stroke of his sword, and then he lost sight of the Frank. A Mongol screamed at him as their horses rushed past each other, and the man's curved sword slashed his tabard and slid off his maille. Raphael clouted him on the side of the head with his mace, and the man tumbled bonelessly from his saddle.

A second Mongol came at him from his right side, and he got his mace around enough to deflect the man's sword so that it rang off the side of his helmet. He leaned over and punched the man in the face with his metal-studded gauntlet, and then followed through with a backhanded sweep of his mace that ended the man's life.

On his left, Bruno lost his hand ax in the shoulder of a Mongol, and as the Lombard pulled his sword from its scabbard, he was struck in the shoulder by a Mongol arrow. The arrow went through the leather guard, and Bruno sagged for a moment. He rallied, spurring his horse toward the man who had put the arrow in him, and delivered his revenge with a savage stroke of his blade. The arrow slowed him, though, and he wasn't quick enough in the saddle to block another Mongol's sword. Raphael saw blood on the Mongol's blade as the two combatants separated.

He kneed his horse toward Bruno, attempting to come to the Lombard's aid, but the Mongol was quicker, wheeling his short pony in a tight arc. Bruno was still trying to control his horse when the Mongol rode up behind him and thrust his sword into the Lombard's back.

Raphael hit the Mongol twice with his mace, but it was too late. The Mongol, his shoulder shattered and his head smashed in, fell off his horse, but his sword remained in Bruno's back.

Bruno leaned against his horse, his face bright with sweat. "It's bad, isn't it?" he said. He punctuated his question with a cough that spattered blood on the mane of horse. He looked down at the pattern of crimson dots, frowned, and then toppled out of the saddle.

There was no time to offer any prayers for the dead. Raphael wheeled his horse, looking for Percival. The Frank was still on his horse, his white tabard splashed with blood in numerous places. "*Alalazu!*" Raphael shouted, raising his sword high. "*Alalazu!*" His throat hurt from shouting so hard. He jerked his reins, turning his horse back toward the Shield-Brethren camp, and dug his spurs into the beast's side. The horse leaped forward at a mad gallop, and Percival shoved his way through a trio of Mongols and fell in beside him.

✦ ✦ ✦

It wasn't until he rolled off the *Skjaldbrædur* and the knife was wrenched out of his side that Gansukh realized the pain in his chest was not from seeing Lian. He sat down heavily, his hand limply trying to find the hole in his armor, staring at the strangely clothed woman wearing the fur-lined cap. "Lian?" he tried, and it sounded like someone else was saying the word.

The knight scrambled away from him, gasping beneath his mask. Gansukh's attention was drawn by the man's motion, and he saw the bloody antler-handled knife. It looked like a Mongol knife, but the man was dressed like one of the knights from the West. He tried to focus. There was something awry here; he just couldn't figure it out. *And where was all the blood coming from?*

The knight switched his grip on his knife as he readied himself to come at Gansukh again. Gansukh held up his hand, showing the man his reddened hand, as if to say *I am wounded already.*

Lian—was it really her?—was carrying a Mongol sword and she slapped the knight on the helmet with the flat side of the blade. She was shouting something at him that he didn't understand, and the man reacted to being struck on the head. He pulled away from her, putting up his hands. She paused, sword still raised for another blow, and he pulled off his helmet.

"I...I know you," Gansukh said, and the blond-haired knight looked at him. "Haakon."

"Aye. Aye," the knight said in the Mongolian tongue. "It's Haakon. No, wait," he added as Lian took another step toward him.

"Leave him alone," she said.

"He's—"

"Leave him!"

He kept his hands up, nodding that he understood what she was saying.

"I'm...there's so much blood," Gansukh said. "You...you stabbed me." He stared accusingly at Haakon.

Lian rushed at Haakon, and he bent his knees reflexively, dropping into an attack stance, but she only thrust the hilt of her sword at him, gesturing for him to take it. "Find a horse," she snapped at him. "The others are running. Cnán's hurt."

"What about...what about you?"

"Go!" she screamed at him, and then she rushed to Gansukh's side. He tried to tell her about the hole in his side, the one that was leaking, but she grabbed him and crushed her mouth to his, silencing his words.

◆ ◆ ◆

Raphael's horse took an arrow just before he made it back to the hole. He felt its back end skew to the side and then it stumbled. Yanking his feet out of the stirrups, he was ready when it tripped, and he leaped out of the saddle as the horse hit the ground. Raphael's feet hit the ground first, and he tried to outrun his momentum, but he wasn't fast enough and his dismount turned into a flailing roll that cost him his helmet. He was up and running a second later, keeping his head down and his eyes locked to Gawain, who was standing beside the protective panel they had made. The longbowman was shooting arrows as quickly as he could pluck them from the ground, and Raphael reached him just as he grabbed and nocked the last one in his line.

"To your left!" Gawain shouted, and Raphael dodged accordingly. He heard Gawain's bow sing, and felt the ground shake behind him as a horse plowed headfirst into the dirt.

"Burn it," Gawain shouted, and Raphael watched as Yasper darted toward the edge of one of the many trenches they had dug. The alchemist was carrying a smoldering stick and he thrust it into the trench, which burst into a line of flame. The orange fire raced along the seep-soaked trench toward the covering at the bottom.

The ground was shaking beneath him, the tremors of approaching Mongol horses. Arrows were falling all around, and many were smacking into his maille like angry bees hurling themselves against him. An arrow creased the back of his neck, and he felt blood start to flow along the collar of his gambeson.

The fire in the trench danced happily as if it knew what was coming next. Yasper had thrown himself down on the ground, covering his head as best he could. Raphael meant to do the same, but an arrow caught him high in the upper back, near the armpit, and it twisted him around. It might have gone through his maille; he thought he could feel a tiny pinprick of an itch in that spot. As he turned, the bottom of the hill came into his field of view and he saw the red flame race down and disappear beneath the canvas cover.

He would never forget what happened next. It was burned forever onto the inside of his eyelids.

The dirty canvas rippled and black lines squiggled across it, reminding him of the protective shield on the siege tower as he and his young brothers had charged the Muslim watchtower in the center of the Nile during the siege of Damietta. Barely blooded, so young, and crouching beneath a shield that was covered with Greek fire. The canvas tent over the seep pool turned back in an another instant and then vanished as a pillar of flame erupted from beneath it. The fire, burning bright and hot as the sun itself, leaped skyward, transforming as it flew into a giant bird with wings of a thousand flaming feathers. It screamed as it was born, a righteous howl of hellish fury, and then it wailed again, a heart-rending scream of terror as it died as quickly as it had been born. The ground shook as the earth tried valiantly to thrust this burning phoenix away from it, and the hole belched a geyser of black stones in the wake of the phoenix's brief resurrection.

Raphael covered his eyes, but it was too late. He had seen the bird. He had seen the branching pattern of its iridescent wings. He had looked upon its face and it had looked back at him, knowing him. It had looked into his soul, and he screamed in horror when it told him what it found there.

CHAPTER 28:

LURING THE DRAGON

Illarion's sword stopped a hair's width from the bare trunk of the spruce, hovering there at the end of his extended arm. He drew it back, then snapped the blade out again, powering the blow with his hips. With every repeated strike, the faces of his enemies, past and present, swam before his eyes, mingled with the faces of the countless dead, and the more he swung his sword, the more the faces leered at him. The purpose of such practice was not to hack through a tree trunk, but rather to exercise the control necessary to put the sword in the same place, every single time, without fail. Strike hard; strike with control.

His breath fogged in the cold air as he threw himself into the exercise. The blade was older than the ones he'd wielded in the south, single-handed instead of the two-handed longswords that were becoming common in the rest of Europe. He'd been trained with one such as this, years ago at the behest of his father. When he had fought in Onghwe Khan's diabolical Circus of Swords at Volodymyr, he had defeated several of the Khan's champions. He knew it well, and so every stroke was as near to perfect as he could make it.

Such practice, however, did not make the faces go away.

"I've never seen a man swing a sword so hard and hit so little so many times," Nika said behind him as he was returning to a ready position. He glanced over his shoulder and noted she was actually smiling. She had, of late, been as somber as he had been on occasion, and he was gladdened to see the return of her acerbic humor.

"I am practicing my restraint," he said as he straightened and sheathed his sword. "Given our activities of late, restraint is in short supply."

Almost immediately after his speech in Trinity Church, the *Druzhina* had begun making preparations to raid into Dorpat. On the one hand, he had felt no compunction about turning them loose, but on the other, he knew the people of Dorpat were innocent of the conflict between the Teutonics and Novgorod. He had selected a dozen older soldiers to lead the raiding parties, and had carefully impressed upon them the distinction between discord and destruction. They were free to show the banners of Rus and to burn homes and fields as they saw fit, but they had to do so with as little bloodshed as possible.

The ruse would not last long, but his hope was that the sudden appearance of the prince's banner in Dorpat would cause the Prince-Bishop to question Kristaps's leadership, and according to the few fast-moving scouts he dared send out, it appeared as if the panic was having the desired effect.

Nika held up a folded piece of parchment. "A message from the prince," she said. "He couches his language very discreetly, but I think he is pleased with your ambition and your willingness to make your own decisions in the field."

"Is he?" Illarion said as he took the proffered message. He read it quickly, noting the prince's ability to imply much while saying little of substance. "The Teutonics are marching around the lake," he said. "It worked."

"It would appear so," Nika said. "However, we're still in Dorpat." She glanced around the tiny camp. "And the Teutonics are coming."

"We should not stay long, then," Illarion said. "The prince suggests we make little effort to disguise our departure, and that we should take the most direct route possible."

Nika nodded. "I have looked at the maps," she said. "That route is due east, straight across Lake Peipus, which I am told freezes over in the winter."

An unexpected shudder ran up Illarion's spine, and Nika regarded him coolly. "I dreamt of such a lake," he admitted. "Not two nights past."

"You and I have seen strange things," she said, the look in her green eyes becoming unsettling in its intensity. "We have seen the same phantom, which binds us in a way that is not readily dismissed. There can be more to dreams than just old memories that won't lie still. You know that, and to pretend otherwise is to shame both of us."

He turned away, fighting to keep the very memories she wanted him to share from filling his mind. They came, ignoring his efforts to forestall them. The twisted tree. The dead knight. The river of dark water. The branding. His left hand reflexively rubbed the place upon his right arm where he'd been marked in his dream.

"I saw the old crone again," Illarion said. His fingers dug into the flesh of his arm, trying to dig out a wound that wasn't there. "I saw the old crone. I saw visions of war and death; I walked among the bodies of both friends and enemies; and I felt her touch upon me." He took a deep breath to master himself. "It was a powerful dream, Nika, but that is all that it was."

"Then why," she whispered, "is your arm bleeding?"

He knew what he would see before he looked down. In his agitation, he'd done more than rub the skin raw on his arm. He had torn the flesh. It was not possible that he had ripped his skin in as precise a pattern as was now marked in blood upon his arm, but his eyes told him otherwise. The tiny daggers of pain now lancing up his shoulder told him otherwise. *It isn't real,* he argued with himself as he raised his left hand, staring at the bloodied tips of his fingers. *It is merely a waking dream.*

Nika laid a hand upon his shoulder, and when he looked at her, the frantic fear must have shown in his eyes, for she looked momentarily alarmed, and her grip upon his shoulder tightened. "Listen to me," she said, "you are not the first to dream of her. There have been others."

"Madmen," he answered, "or those soon to be mad." Perhaps he *was* mad already, in truth. The shadow of a man once a warrior, now the ghost beside a prince, waiting for a chance to die nobly, or just to die.

"Women of my order," she insisted. "It is rare, perhaps only once in a generation, but young *Skjalddis* sometimes dream of the old crone. They do not die, they do not go mad—at least, they do not do so often." A ghost of the familiar smile flickered across her face, but it did little to dismiss the haunted look in her eyes. "Baba Yaga has long watched the *Skjalddis* from the shadows," Nika continued. "When she visits one of us, we listen, for such a visitation is both an honor and a portent. If you have been dreaming of her, Illarion, it is because she is trying to tell you something that you need to hear."

He shook his head as he wiped his hand across his arm, smearing the pattern of blood into a meaningless shape. The wounds still wept blood, but the flow was sluggish and would soon stop.

"What did she say to you?" Nika asked patiently, and Illarion sighed. She wasn't going to leave him alone about the dream, and perhaps the burden of it would be lessened if he shared it with another.

So he told her: of the witch woman's talk of blood and vows; of living and dying again and again. As he spoke, he tried to keep the dreadful fear from his voice, but it crept in regardless. He told her of the mosaic of the knight with the rose in its chest, of his son calling him *Ilya*, of the black bird made from horsehair, and of the sword that had hurt him. When he was done speaking, his hands were shaking.

Nika said nothing when he finished, and his heart fluttered in his throat. Had he made a dreadful mistake in telling her?

"I think if you tell that story to anyone else, they will think you are mad," she said, and her words did little to calm his restless heart. "But I believe you." She leaned against him, her face close to his. Her eyes were bright and clear. "But then, I think I, too, am mad," she said. "These are not times for people of sound mind. When the world burns, those who stay safe in their houses die first."

"My house has already burned to the ground," Illarion admitted with a smile that did not come easily.

"Yet still you live," Nika said. "The world is not done with you. Or with me," she sighed as if accepting something she had been resisting for a long time. "You've been marked by her," she continued. "I will not pretend to know why, but I can tell you that for all the terror and dread she inspires, she has never misled those she has advised."

Illarion looked down at his forearm, and when he wiped the blood away this time, the wounds were nothing more than raised irritations on his skin.

"The mark is as real as you make it," Nika said. "It is a symbol of a conflict far older than the one in which we currently find ourselves."

"All wars are," Illarion said. "Even when it was just boyar fighting boyar over lands or titles, or when it was the Danes or Swedes raiding our lands over a stolen daughter or a murdered son. But that is not the case for this conflict, is it?"

Nika gave a sad smile, and Illarion realized that he'd never once seen her look so tired. "No. It's older than my order or your Shield-Brethren or their predecessors. It's older than the stones of Kiev and the lineage of the House of Rurik. I do not know its origin; all I know is that it lies at the heart of the oaths we've sworn. It lies at the heart of an old tree that is no more."

She embraced him lightly, almost awkwardly, but at the same time, he found being enclosed in her arms more comforting than he expected. There was nothing romantic in her gesture; it was more of the comfort brothers and sisters offer one another.

"Let us lead our enemies to the ice," she said, resting her hands on his shoulders and looking at him directly. "She will show herself to you there, and then you will know what she wants of you." She offered him a tiny smile, though none of the humor was reflected in her eyes. "We'll all know what is to be done."

CHAPTER 29:

HOMECOMING

Four days after crossing the river, they found Benjamin. The trader, along with four horses, the same number of oxen, two wagons, and a couple of drovers, was sitting beside a fire, idly plucking the single string of a zither as if he had neither a care in the world nor a place to be. His drovers had spotted the five of them when they had crested the hill, and it had taken another half hour for their horses to amble down into the valley and reach the camp.

"Ah, my friends," the Khazar trader said as Raphael stopped his horse and dismounted. "So fortunate to see you again." He stood, beaming, and crushed Raphael in a tight embrace that made Raphael's knees tremble. He clapped Raphael on both shoulders, as if to ensure that the knight would remain standing, and then moved on to Percival, Yasper, and Gawain in turn. He did not hug Evren, nor did Evren seem to mind.

Benjamin was a stocky man who, due to his predilection for wearing copious layers of rich silks and fine cotton, could be mistaken for being fat. When the company had first made his acquaintance, he had come across as a humorless trader who only had time and eye for making a profit, but once the trader had taken a liking to the company, they had discovered an entirely different side to Benjamin's personality.

"You did not say *unexpected*," Raphael noted when Benjamin finished greeting the tired company.

The trader smiled roguishly. "Why would I use such a word?" he said. "That would be so very rude of me, would it not? Guests such as yourselves are never unexpected, especially when I have been instructed very clearly to keep an eye out for your tardy arrival."

"You've seen them?"

"Aye," Benjamin nodded. "They are at my village. They have been there for almost a week." Some of the humor left his glowing face. "The Binder—Cnán —is not well. She needs a real physician. Alas, my skills are—*pffft!*—of very little consequence."

"Cnán?" Yasper exploded, shoving past Percival. "What happened to her?"

"A blow to the head," Yasper explained. "One of those ugly Mongol swords, I believe. It bled a lot, at first, according to Vera, and it wasn't that deep, but she…she is reluctant to come back to us."

"We need to keep riding," Yasper said, turning back toward his horse. "Raphael. You must come with me. We have to help her."

Raphael didn't move, having already made a prognosis about Cnán based on Benjamin's lack of immediate concern. "You said Vera. Is she healthy? And who else?"

"The woman is like a piece of iron," Benjamin said. "She cannot easily be broken. Feronantus suffered a great deal during the winter, and a week of rest has done much to restore his spirit, but he is old, Raphael. This journey has aged him, and he knows that it will be his last. He is tired."

"Aren't we all?" Gawain muttered.

Benjamin glanced at the longbowman, and seemed to realize that Gawain had not been part of the company on their journey north.

"Who else?" Raphael prompted, not wanting be drawn into a lengthy recitation of the members of their company who had fallen.

"There's a boy, Haakon. He, too, has been aged by this journey, but not in the same way. He is a man, certainly, but in some ways, he has suffered more than I, and I am old enough to be his father."

"And a Chinese woman? Lian?"

Benjamin shook his head. "Those are all who are waiting for you. I do not know of this woman you speak of. You will have to ask your friends when you see them."

"And we should go and see them now," Yasper reminded them.

"How far?" Raphael asked, more for Yasper's sake than his own.

"A day's ride," Benjamin said. "Not that far."

"But too far to go tonight."

"Judging by the state of your clothing and your horses, yes." Benjamin shook his head. "Come. I have brought food and wine. Let us fill your bellies and provide you with some comfort tonight. Tomorrow we will reunite with your friends." He glanced at Yasper. "They are not going anywhere," he said. "They will wait for you."

"Very well," Raphael said. "We will dine with you tonight and rest." His knees wobbled again, as if the very idea threatened to bring about collapse. He looked at the others and realized that he was not the only one who relished the idea of a decent meal. He smiled at Percival and Yasper.

They had been traveling nonstop for nearly three months. For the first time, he realized, they were no longer looking over their shoulders. They were looking ahead, eager to see those they loved.

Hours later, his belly full and his head swimming with wine, Raphael lay on his back and stared up at the night sky, letting himself drift with the tide of wine moving about in his head. It had been several weeks since the blazing birth and death of Yasper's phoenix and they had been riding hard the entire time. When he let his eyes drift closed, which took little effort, he easily imagined that the back and forth motion he felt was the rolling motion of an exhausted horse, pushed near the limit of its endurance.

The fiery eruption in the depression had terrified the Mongols. Raphael did not know if they had seen the same flaming shape that he had, but whatever they had seen had been enough to send them fleeing in terror. He and Percival had collected Yasper and Gawain—Evren had joined them an hour later, astride a stiff-legged Mongol pony—and they had managed to point their frightened horses west. The mounts had been eager to run, and the small company had not held them back. The fire in the hole was taller than it had been before, and Yasper's trenches were also filled with flame, tendrils of fire radiating out from the central pyre. Unchecked, the fires would spread across the steppe, albeit slowly due to the patches of bare ground and the still damp brush. If it snowed or rained in the next few days, most of the little fires would be extinguished.

Yasper thought the central fire, however, would burn for years. *A legacy of my visit*, the alchemist had said, and the idea disturbed Raphael enough that he had not mentioned it again.

They had found the scattered dead of the Mongol ambush of their friends, but no sign of either Alchiq or Gansukh, a minor detail that kept Raphael glancing over his shoulder for the following weeks.

Even now, drifting off to a wine-disturbed slumber, he fretted about posting a guard, about having someone keep watch for the ghosts of the east that he feared were still haunting them.

◆ ◆ ◆

They picked up the winding track of a narrow stream, and Raphael recognized the trail that ran beside it. The stream wound around a hill covered with spruce and fir and then meandered across a flat plain. The residents of Benjamin's village tended fields of wheat and rye that lay on either side of the stream, and there were several orchards and a vineyard of some hardy grape that could be convinced to thrive in this climate. Beyond the fields, several dozen huts and houses of various sizes were arranged around a dusty square. The rabbi's house was near Benjamin's estate, a manor house that seemed overly ostentatious in comparison with the houses around it, but to Raphael's world-weary eye, it was respectably restrained.

A handful of children, too young to work in the fields but old enough to roam freely, met them as they forded the stream. Benjamin called them all by name and sent them off to let the village know of his return and of the fact that he had brought guests. By the time the company reached the village square, everyone in the village knew of their arrival.

Including Vera, Haakon, and Feronantus.

Raphael embraced Feronantus stiffly and clasped Haakon's forearm in the traditional style of greeting among the Shield-Brethren before he remembered that the boy had not been through the initiation at Petraathen. Somewhat embarrassed, he stumbled into an embrace with Vera, who covered for his gaffe by squeezing him tightly. He held her close, inhaling the scent of her. Her hair was shorter than it had been several weeks ago, and he could easily touch the back of her neck. "I missed you," he said softly, his words falling into the hollow of her throat.

She nodded, resting her hand on his cheek.

"Where's Cnán?" Yasper asked, a note of panic in his voice.

"She's resting," Vera said, disengaging herself from Raphael. The Shield-Maiden offered the alchemist a thin smile, which did little to assuage Yasper's concern. "I can take you to her, if you like."

"I would," Yasper said, fidgeting.

"She could use your skills," Vera said, turning her gaze back to Raphael.

"I will be there shortly," Raphael said.

As Vera and Yasper left for Benjamin's manor, the trader said a few words to his team of drovers and the men flicked their switches at the teams of oxen hauling the wagons. Benjamin called on several of the older children to assist with the horses. Everyone moved very efficiently—it was a routine they all knew very well—and within moments, the square was empty of horses and oxen and wagons.

"Well," Benjamin said, throwing his arms wide and indicating the village, "here we are. Everyone is together again. You are not pursued by a maddened horde of Mongols, and I hear that Batu Khan and the other Khans have discovered a pressing reason to return to the East. That is good news for Christendom, and excellent news for those of us who make our living moving goods along the Silk Road. It is a joyous time, yes?"

"It is," Percival said when it became clear neither Feronantus nor Raphael were going to say anything. "I suppose you would like to have some manner of celebration."

"Of course," the trader said. "In fact, I should go attend to that immediately." He glanced at Gawain and Evren and waved them along. "Come, you two. Let us open a bottle of wine and find soft pillows to put under our asses. We have done enough work for the day. I will send a boy out with water for these four. I suspect they will be talking awhile yet."

After the trader had departed with Gawain and Evren, Feronantus squinted up at the warm sun. "Did you find Graymane?" he asked.

"No," Raphael said. "And neither did you."

"He attacked us, along with the other one. What was his name?" The last was directed at Haakon.

"Gansukh," Haakon said.

"Gansukh," Feronantus echoed. "Haakon stabbed that one."

"We found the place where it happened," Raphael said. "But we saw no sign of Gansukh. Nor Lian."

Haakon stared at the ground, a light flush coloring his cheek and forehead.

"Am I missing something?" Raphael asked, and when neither man answered him, he moved on. "Do you still have it?" he asked Feronantus.

"Aye," the old man said.

"Are you going to tell me why you took it?" Raphael demanded. "Why you abandoned us? Why you made us follow you to the heart of the Mongol empire and then left us there?" His voice rose in volume until he was shouting the last few words.

"I…I have seen—" Feronantus started.

Before he could stop himself, Raphael stepped forward and punched Feronantus hard in the mouth. Feronantus's head snapped to the side, and a spatter of blood marred his lips. He raised a hand to his mouth and found the blood with his fingers. He raised his gaze to Raphael and seemed about to say something, but whether he was going to finish his previous sentence or say something else entirely, Raphael didn't want to hear any of it.

"Go to hell," Raphael snarled, and before the fury in his heart could vanish and he had to face what he had just done, he stalked off, heading after Vera and Yasper.

◆ ◆ ◆

"What happened to your hand?" Vera asked a few minutes later as he carefully ran his fingers through Cnán's hair.

"It's nothing," Raphael said.

Cnán was lying on her back on a small bed, her head resting on a soft pillow. Daylight was streaming in through the unshuttered window, and Raphael thought it might have been the same room where he had held his vigil for Vera after she and her sisters had been attacked by the Mongols. Cnán was aware of her visitors—her eyes tracked them as they clustered around the bed—but she did not speak. Her hair had been cut back, and Raphael wondered if Vera had done the same in an effort to elicit a reaction from Cnán.

"Who did you hit?" Vera asked, opting for a more direct question.

"No one," Raphael lied. He immediately recanted. "Feronantus."

Yasper let out a hiccup of dry laughter.

"Do you feel better?" Vera asked, not displaying the same level of amusement.

"No," Raphael said.

"Do you think he feels better?"

"No."

"Are you going to do it again?"

"No, probably not. Look"—he left off probing Cnán's head and turned to Vera—"I'm trying to work."

"Good," Vera said. "You have some skill there, at least, in contrast with your lack of respect for authority."

Raphael swallowed his words and returned his attention to Cnán. Vera stood up from the chair in which she had been sitting and placed her hand on his shoulder. "I'll talk with him," she said softly.

He offered her a grunt in reply; her fingers tightened briefly and then she left. The room was quiet for a few moments, save for the faint sound of Cnán's breathing.

"I…I like Vera," Yasper offered in an effort to dismiss the tension still filling the sunlit chamber.

"Aye," Raphael said. "I do too."

◆ ◆ ◆

At the end of the vineyard lay a tiny arbor of fruit trees arranged in an arc. Several benches made from rough-hewn spruce logs provided seating, and the view was across the stream and the wheat fields beyond. The fruit trees, when they were in full bloom, would screen the benches from the village, but as the trees had only started to bud, Raphael easily spotted both Feronantus and Vera sitting on the benches. He wandered past the pair and stood in front of the benches so that their pastoral view was marred by his presence.

"There's nothing wrong with Cnán," he said. "The wound was not that deep, and it was cleaned well after it happened. Her hair will grow back, although, unlike Samson, I do not think that is the source of her lack of spirit." He crossed his arms, felt awkward being so imperious in his bearing, and dropped them, which felt no better. "Yasper won't leave her side, which may be the best medicine for her right now."

"Having someone keeping a vigil can make all the difference," Vera said.

"Yasper once spent five months tending to the heating of a single alchemical experiment," Raphael said. "I am certain he will remain at her side as long as necessary. Seeing such dedication in our company for another is admirable."

Feronantus shifted on his bench but did not respond to Raphael's comment. As the silence among the three of them lengthened, Raphael felt a scream building in him—a wailing cry that reminded him of the angry shriek of the firebird.

"When did you have your vision?" he asked Feronantus abruptly.

"I did not say…" Feronantus stopped and regarded his hands for a few moments. "Understanding came to me a few weeks ago," he continued. "Maybe more than a month."

"After you crossed the mountains?" Raphael asked, though he was thinking, *After you left us.*

"Aye."

"Percival had several visions while we were journeying east, and it was during one of them that Alchiq Graymane was able to surprise Finn. Did you ever give any credence to Percival's visions?"

"They were his visions," Feronantus replied. "And if he had come to me and asked that we honor them, we would have... discussed them."

"But you wouldn't have turned back?"

"I can't tell you what I might have done, Raphael. I do not look back on my past deeds. I only look forward."

Raphael shook his head in disgust. How many of his brothers had been afflicted with this same madness? This pernicious desire, like that of a frightened child who seeks the approval of its father and mother, to be given purpose, to be rewarded with a sign that the right path had been chosen.

"I need for you to understand what I've seen," Feronantus said.

"Why?" Raphael demanded. "It is *your* vision. If you won't accept Percival's, then why should I accept yours?"

Beside Feronantus, Vera stirred and shook her head slightly, trying to dissuade Raphael from his choice of words.

"I have not had a vision, Raphael," Feronantus said plainly. "Not in the sense that plagues you so constantly. I am not like the boy you knew at Damietta. What was his name? Eptor? I do not suffer like he does. Nor do I become transfixed by the divine spirit like Percival, who does not even understand what has happened to him. I am not some poorly educated devout soldier who desperately yearns to be rewarded with some sign that his years spent killing men has earned him a place in a mystical pantheon. I have been a member of the order longer than you have been alive, Raphael of Acre. I was there, fighting for God and King, in the very streets you toddled through as a child. Some of the stains on the stones of the citadel wall may be from my blood. When I speak of seeing what is to come, I know what I speak is true because I have spent my entire life studying the patterns of the *Vor*."

"The *Vor*?" Raphael sneered. "That is nothing more than *oplo* mysticism, cheap words to make the young men train harder. Men do not see what is to come, either in or out of combat. The *Vor* is a lie."

"Like God?" Feronantus asked.

"I will strike you again if you utter another blasphemy like that," Raphael said.

"How I can blaspheme against that which I have never given my heartfelt loyalty?" Feronantus asked. "If the Church truly knew who we are, they would brand us heretics. All of us, including you—your relationship with that most educated of emperors notwithstanding." Feronantus let out a dry laugh. "Your heart stopped believing in God years ago, Raphael. It is the rest of you that has not yet let go."

Raphael lunged at Feronantus with every intention of following through on his earlier threat, but Feronantus calmly pushed his fist aside with one hand and slapped Raphael hard across the cheek with the other. Raphael staggered, more shocked than hurt.

"I let you strike me once because you needed to expel that hurt you have been carrying for so long, but I am not an old fool who will suffer disrespect from those who should know better." Feronantus's eyes were bright and they bored into Raphael. "And if you do not take your hand off your knife, I will break his left arm," he continued, his voice hardening even further. His eyes did not leave Raphael. "Not his right, because I am not a cruel man, but I will not hesitate to hurt him because that is the most efficient way to disarm both of you."

Raphael finally realized Feronantus was not talking to him, and he turned his head slowly and looked over at Vera, who was still seated, but her right hand was hidden behind her back, where he knew she kept her sheathed knife. "Vera..."

"He's right," Vera said, bringing her hand out and setting it in her lap. "I would have stopped if he had hurt you." She leaned forward, her mouth tightening, and Raphael saw in her eyes the same indomitable drive that he had seen that morning when they had ridden against the *Khagan*. "But I will turn that weakness in my heart into something else, Feronantus," she said, her voice as cold and hard as his. "You have lost your advantage by recognizing it."

"I know, Vera of Kiev," Feronantus said with a sigh. "You do the *Skjalddis* proud. You need not fear my intentions. I give you my word that I will protect him from bodily harm. I will be his shield."

"And I will be his sword," she said softly. "Always." She stood, making eye contact with Raphael and then staring at Feronantus until the old master of Týrshammar looked up at her. "Decide," she said, making sure that both of them understood what she was demanding of them, and then she left the arbor, heading back for the village.

"Decide what?" Raphael asked when she was gone.

"I mean to go north, with all due haste." Feronantus levered himself off the bench and stood close to Raphael. "We know the Teutonics are marching on Rus, and Vera would have us aid her sisters if we can."

"It's more than that, isn't it?" Raphael asked.

Feronantus was silent for a long moment. "There is something that must be done," he said finally. "Things that have not been a part of the world for a very long time have been awakened. They must be set on the right path."

"And that path lies in the north?"

Feronantus shook his head. "The path lies everywhere and nowhere, Raphael. The next step is in the north. All of us will be asked to make great sacrifices."

"All of us? Who do you count in that group?"

"You." Feronantus laid his hand upon Raphael's shoulder. His grip was strong and his gaze did not waver. "I would have you and Vera see what I see, Raphael."

"What of the others? Haakon? Yasper? Cnán?"

Feronantus smiled at him. "They're safe, Raphael. You brought them back. I lost too many of our brothers, but you didn't. You saved them."

◆ ◆ ◆

Gawain found the young Northerner wandering around in the stable. The trio of local boys who had been tasked with caring for their horses moved efficiently around the dawdling Northerner. Haakon was not the first to stand in the way while the boys mucked the stalls and fed the horses. "It's a good place to hide," Gawain said, and Haakon only glanced at him sheepishly.

"They're leaving in the morning," Gawain continued, jerking a thumb at the activity going on around them.

"Aye," Haakon said with a sigh. "I've heard."

"Are you going with them?"

"Why wouldn't I?" Haakon was perplexed by the question.

"I don't know," Gawain said. "Why are you hiding in here?"

"I'm not hiding."

"No?" Gawain shrugged. "My mistake, then." He gestured at the row of saddles arranged along the far wall. "I'll just get what I came for and leave you to your...introspection."

Haakon grunted, and Gawain wandered to the saddles where he busied himself. The straps were all tightly fastened and cinched to the right length. The leather had been cleaned and polished, and his saddlebags were in the common room he was sharing with Percival and Evren. There wasn't anything he needed to attend to, nor was a concern for his saddle the reason he had come to the stable.

"What...where will you go?" Haakon asked.

Gawain hid his smile and turned around. "South. Ahmet had a cousin who owns a few boats in Antalya. Evren and I were thinking of telling the cousin about what happened to Ahmet. After that..."

"You would become a sellsword?"

Gawain shrugged. "Nothing much else for men like us. I'm not one to swear vows of poverty and chastity, and the rest get caught up in wars that mean nothing to me. It doesn't sound like much of a life." He wandered back to Haakon and pointed out the open doors of the stable at the fields in the distance. "You could marry one of the local girls—I'm sure Benjamin could arrange such a union—and become a farmer. Work the land until your hands are covered with calluses and your back is curved by the weight of the plow."

"My father was a fisherman," Haakon said. He raised his hands and showed them to Gawain. "Different set of calluses."

"You don't have your father's hands," Gawain said.

"Aye, I do not," Haakon said. "His were never stained with as much blood as mine."

Gawain shook his head. "We all have blood on our hands, Haakon. We knew it was going to happen as soon as we picked up our first swords. It was a choice we made. You can't wash it off, boy. That's what makes us men. It makes us who we are."

"Do you know who the first man I ever killed was?" Haakon asked.

Gawain shook his head. "I didn't know the name of the first man I ever killed. I'm not sure I even saw his face."

"I did," Haakon said. "I watched mine die. His name was Ögedei Khan, son of Genghis Khan. He was the *Khagan* of the Mongol empire."

"Well, he's a bit more memorable of a foe than some Danish marauder wearing a helmet," Gawain said.

"You knew?"

"Aye, Bruno told me about your confession around the fire."

Haakon was silent for a moment. He toyed with the handle of the knife shoved in his belt, and Gawain thought it was probably the blade the boy had taken from the *Khagan*. "Get rid of it," he said gently.

"What?"

"The knife. It's a trophy, and as long as you have it, you're not going to be able to forget his face."

"I'm never going to forget his face," Haakon said.

"You will," Gawain said. "It will happen. It just takes time." He clapped Haakon on the shoulder. "Or a lot of wine. Come with me, young master. I will show you the rest of the world. Let us find a way for you to forget."

Haakon thought about Gawain's process, his fingers drumming on the hilt of the knife. Then, with a curt nod, he pulled the sheathed blade out of his belt and walked with stiff legs to the saddles. Standing before the one that belonged to Feronantus, Haakon pulled the blade from its sheath, dropping the leather cover on the ground, and Gawain wondered what the boy was going to do. Haakon hesitated for a moment, wrestling with some thoughts, and then he took several steps to his left and drove the point of the blade into the leather seat of a different saddle—the one belonging to Raphael. "I'm with you," he said to Gawain as he walked away from the stuck blade.

1242

VELJA NOC

CHAPTER 30:

THE LADY OF THE LAKE

Newly fallen snow coated the frozen surface of the lake, sparkling in the moonlight. The western shore was nothing more than a pale suggestion beyond the moon-lit lake, and if the Teutonics had watchers along the shore, Illarion could not see them. In turn, he hoped he and Nika could not be seen as they made their way along the ice-crusted eastern shoreline. Illarion appreciated that the moonlight reflected from the snow made torches unnecessary, but he still felt exposed.

Nika led the way, and he followed in her shallow footsteps as her boots compressed the shining snow. There was no sound except for the gentle slap of water against the ice beneath the surface of the lake and his loud breathing. The Shield-Maiden moved like a ghost. Overhead there were no clouds, making for a cold night, and the sky was awash with brilliant stars. But for the moon, it was a night identical to the one in Kiev months ago, when the ghostly fog had flowed into the city.

Alexander's camp lay behind them, far enough away from the shore that it was marked only by an orange glow through the frost-rimmed trees. The men were restless, and there had been a number of strenuous arguments in the *Kynaz*'s tent. Andrei did not argue with his brother in front of the soldiers, but Illarion knew that

Andrei was pressing Alexander to take the fight to the Teutonics. So far, the prince's conviction about Lake Peipus remained firm, but if the Teutonics did not attack soon, Illarion worried that the prince's position would crumble.

"You've sent good men to their deaths, brother," Andrei had said during their last argument, "and abandoned them when we retreated."

"There are no victories without sacrifices," Alexander had replied.

"Strange," Andrei had said, after a long pause, "to hear you say that, who alone amongst the Princes of Rurik's house would not raise his sword against Batu Khan, who brokered peace with our last conquerors. Now you're all verve and fire and talk of sacrifice." The lilt of the prince's voice had suggested an excess of wine.

"Tell me brother," Alexander had asked, his voice tired and sad, "would you have had me throw all that remained of Rus the way of Father and Grandfather? Would a Khan's slaughter in the streets of Novgorod have pleased you?"

"That is not what I speak of, Alexander," Andrei said. "I speak only of honor."

"Families have burned for honor, Andrei," Alexander said. "Tribes, villages, cities, have all given their lives up to the consuming fires of personal vendettas and sullied pride. A ruler's first priority is his people, or he is unworthy of his throne."

"Yet here you are," Andrei answered, "fighting to keep from one foe what you would not from another."

"The difference between you and me," Alexander finally said, "is that I understand that only the battles we can win are worth fighting."

Nika slowed, turning her head from side to side as if she were searching for some sign. Illarion saw nothing but snow-covered rocks and trees.

"There," Nika said, pointing to a cluster of spruce that leaned out from the rest of the forest. She walked over to the middle tree and reached up to brush away the intermittent layer of snow on the trunk. Illarion saw the mark then, and marveled that Nika had seen it at all. It was nothing more than a series of gashes in the bark—some long, some short—stripping away the dark outer layer to reveal the pale trunk beneath. "There will be another mark soon," she said. "Not much farther now."

Illarion glanced back the way they had come. He could still see the glow of the fires from Alexander's camp. "Is it not a risk to come this close to the prince's camp?" he wondered.

"She is very skilled at remaining unseen," Nika said with a wry smile. "And even if others stumbled across her, what would they do? I fear more for them than for her, should that happen."

"When I have met her in my dreams, she…" Illarion trailed off, unwilling to give voice to that which he feared.

"This way," Nika said. She continued on, and before he followed her, Illarion reached up and laid two of his fingers across the gashes in the tree. They were as wide as his fingers and he could almost imagine the hand that had swiped across the bark, gouging out the pair of marks. Suppressing a shudder, he hurried after the Shield-Maiden.

She spotted another mark and this time he saw it as well, pale scratches high enough on the trunk that they weren't obscured by snow, and she turned away from the lake, disappearing into the woods. He followed, clumsily thrashing through the snow-covered undergrowth.

Nika moved gracefully through the forest, and no matter how hard he tried to follow her course, Illarion foundered more often than not—stepping in hidden drifts, catching his cloak on spindly branches, tripping over hidden logs. He was sweating profusely by the time she stopped.

"How do you know these signs are from her?" he asked, partly as an excuse to catch his breath.

"Although they look like signs that fur traders and hunters might use, they have none of the marks that would indicate they were cut by a knife or an ax." She held up three fingers. "And they are too few to be made by a bear."

Illarion shivered. "How many times have you met with her?" he asked, trying to keep his annoyance from his voice. He knew that Nika hadn't told him everything, nor had he ever thought she would, but to think that the enigmatic witch was following and watching them was deeply unnerving. He could dismiss the dreams—though it had been harder of late to do so—but to be here, in the woods, about to confront that which had been haunting him was something else entirely.

Nika paused, turning her head slightly but not looking directly at him. "She is to be obeyed, Illarion. I do not call into question things greater than myself, especially when they call on me to fulfill my own vows."

Illarion said nothing, thinking of the vow Baba Yaga had extracted from him. *It is my turn now*, he thought.

Nika nodded past the line of trees in front of them. The moonlight played tricks with her face, casting it in an array of unsettling shadows. "What lies beyond these trees is for you to know," she said. "I am merely your guide, and I can go no further."

Illarion noticed a gap between two trees that he would have sworn had not been there moments before. He tried to find some parting words to say to Nika, but realized everything he could think of sounded as if he were not expecting to return. His relationship with the Shield-Maiden had been a strange one from the beginning, born of mutual pain and boredom—a sensation of having lost their place in the world. Their hearts had both turned to stone long ago, and no deep affection lay between them, but here and now it seemed that there was trust and understanding.

"I have not always been as kind as I should have," he said to her.

"Nor I," she answered.

In the silence that lingered between them, Illarion realized the value of her friendship. It was his turn to initiate the embrace, though she was as awkward as she had been the last time. Still, he caught a glimpse of something in her gaze that made him glad he had hugged her.

He didn't think the gap between the trees would be wide enough for him, but when he turned sideways and sidled through, he fit easily. The trees were packed more tightly together than he expected, and the gap turned into a narrow passage. It turned to the left, and he lost sight of Nika. He stopped, breathing heavily, and then set aside his fear and continued on. When the passage narrowed, he had to duck several times to get past thick branches that stretched across the gap.

The passage turned again, and he followed it, his sense of direction utterly confused. The passage took another of its impossible left turns—how many there had been now he couldn't remember—and he found himself standing in an open space in the woods. The ground was flat and clear, and there were no stumps or breaks in the ground that suggested trees had been cleared. The verge of the circle was marked by wooden stakes driven into the ground, and at the center of the clearing there was a ring of stones. A fire of cedar logs burned in the ring.

Illarion stepped into the clearing, turning about as his feet crunched upon the hard-packed snow. He thought he saw a shadow beyond the trees, hulking and unmoving, like a cottage elevated from the ground, though he could not see by what. When he approached the fire, he spotted three skulls carefully arranged on the stones as if they were watching the flames dance. One was gray, one was black, and one was smeared with blood that glistened in the firelight. He felt his guts tighten and his hand reflexively brushed the hilt of his sword.

"There is no need for steel here, Ilya."

At once, she was there, though he could not have said from whence she came. She was stooped and ancient beyond imagining, swathed in layers of furs. A cowl hid most of her face.

"Sit," she said.

Even though there was no chair or bench, he obeyed. The ground was cold beneath him, even through his fur-lined cloak. A distant part of his mind found it strange that he, a child of Rus who was no stranger to the endless winters, could be so chilled. Other parts of his mind were frozen with fear, unwilling to accept anything of what he was seeing and hearing. He knew a man's senses could be tricked, and he could assuage some of the fear with a reasoned reminder of this fact, but he could not dismiss everything.

"Do you know why you are here?" the crone asked. She reached out to draw warmth from the slumbering fire, and her hands were so gnarled that they looked to Illarion like the dried bones of a corpse.

"I have dreamed of you several times," he said at last. His throat was dry, though from thirst or terror he could not say. "In them, your words have been maddeningly opaque to me. I admit that I understand little of what you have said."

She let out a cackle of dry laughter, and when she turned her cowled head toward him, he saw her wrinkled chin and gaping mouth. "Is that why you have come?" she asked. "Do you seek explanation of your dreams?"

"No," he said, swallowing heavily. "I fear that a plain-spoken explanation will be even more terrifying than what I imagine."

She nodded slowly. "It is said that you are a ghost—a man with one foot still in the grave. You have seen what this fear brings out in other men. And you have seen the power of being a ghost too, have you not?"

"I have," Illarion said.

"Which do you prefer?"

"I asked for neither."

She nodded as if he had responded correctly a second time. "Which serves Rus better?" she asked.

"What does Rus need?" he asked in return.

She leaned forward. "Is this a game you would play with me, Illarion Illarionovich? Answering my questions with a question of your own?"

"Rus needs a savior," he said, answering his own question, but as soon as he had said it, he realized it wasn't the correct answer. "Rus has one already," he said. "Prince Alexander Iaroslavich."

She nodded. "He can save the people of Rus, should he desire, and they are the bones and the meat of the body that is Rus, but they are not the blood of Rus."

"You mean like royal blood?" Illarion asked. "He is far more regal than I." Illarion knew his heritage, as every boy raised in noble birth was required to. The first years of his life had been spent memorizing the names of his descendants, until he knew them as well as he did the young and old of his living family.

"Aye," she agreed. "The blood of Svyatoslav of Kiev runs deep in Rus, but it is more than that. Svyatoslav was the first. He gave shelter to my sisters and me. He swore a vow to us and we to him. We are bound, his blood and mine, bound to Rus for all eternity."

Her words confused him, and he let his mind wander over the family trees he had memorized as a boy. *Blood mattered*, he thought, *but not that of the royal line. Who else?*

We are bound, his blood and mine.

Nika had told him already. Baba Yaga had been a Shield-Maiden once, and it was with Svyatoslav that the Shield-Maidens had first found sanctuary in Rus. Svyatoslav had had many concubines, from which had sprung many bloodlines ennobled by their origins, but barred from his throne by birth. One—or more—of them must have been *Skjalddis*. He struggled to recall the dim beginnings of the family lines he had memorized as a child, and then the name came to him. "Malusha," he whispered. *Malusha, daughter of Grimhildr.*

"Aye, she is the one," Baba Yaga said. "You can cut back a tree so that grows no new branches, but unless you pull down the trunk, its roots will still spread, hidden from sight. Eventually, when the land is fertile again, new growth may occur. New leaves may sprout."

The fire crackled between them, and in the firelight, the skulls seemed to be grinning at Illarion.

"There is little magic left in the world," Baba Yaga said. "But a little is enough. You have not sworn the old vows; you have not given an oath to protect the old ways, but you have the blood. Your flesh bears the mark."

"Is that why you call me Ilya?" Illarion asked.

A small smirk passed across the gnarled, wrinkled mouth. "What that not a name you had as a child?"

"No," Illarion said. "It wasn't."

"Is it a name that suits you?"

Illarion stared at the ash-blackened skull. Its eye sockets were black holes that seemed to suck up the firelight. He knew her question was not as innocent as it seemed, nor as nonsensical. Dreams were often filled with strange dichotomies—sweet promises mixed with threats of horrific pain and suffering—and more often than not, the power of the dream realm made it easy to overlook the darkness lurking beneath the surface. There was no veil over his eyes now. He saw the skulls for what they were. He saw the emptiness within the eyes of the black one. He saw the blood-smeared teeth of the other one.

If he were offered a chance to take revenge upon those who had killed his family, would he take it? If a sword were put in his hand, would he not use it to protect those he cared about?

Would he protect Rus from those who threatened her?

"I am no saint," he said.

"No?" She cocked her head at him. "Who are you then?"

"My name does not matter," he said. He stretched out his right arm, pushing back his sleeve. The bare skin of his forearm was unmarked, but he could feel the skin itching. "Only my actions matter."

"Aye," the old crone answered. "That much has always been true."

She hobbled over to him and bent to draw his sword out of its scabbard. He tried not to flinch as she raised his weapon, but once she had freed it from the scabbard, she moved away from him, back to the fire.

There was no fanfare or ceremony to what followed. It was a simple, utilitarian ritual of the sort long left behind by much of the world, where priests sang dirges and let swing incense-burning censors. The sort of rite that would always be true.

She reached into the fire, which refused to burn her, and brought forth a handful of ash which she smeared on the hilt of his sword. Holding the blade carefully, she pushed the weapon into the coals so that the pommel was in the hottest part of the fire. When she lifted it free a few moments later, the handle smoked and the pommel stone glowed orange and red. She turned and peered at him from under her cowl. He did not look away, nor did he withdraw his hand.

She pressed the hilt of the sword against his palm. It wasn't as hot as he expected and he curled his fingers around the ash-covered hilt. She raised the tip of the blade so that the red-hot pommel stone pressed into his bare forearm.

His flesh burned beneath the improvised brand, and Illarion had thought that he knew enough of pain to hold his tongue against crying out.

He was wrong.

CHAPTER 31:

THE GHOST OF RUS

He woke with a burning sensation in his forearm from what he thought had been a dream. When he remembered what the crone had done to him, the sensation spread, racing up his arm and filling his chest. It moved up into his head, sweat starting from his brow and along his neck, and then it moved down, sweat bleeding from his thighs and calves. He jerked backward, opening his eyes.

The fire had been built up to a large bonfire, and he had been lying prostrate beside it. It had been the heat of the fire which had been distressing him, and as he gasped and blinked, struggling to discern how much time had passed, he took in the concerned faces peering at him. Nika and…

"Raphael?" he croaked. "Feronantus?" He blinked several times, not entirely believing what he was seeing, but the faces did not vanish. "Vera," he said, recognizing the fourth face. "What… what happened? Where am I?"

"You're lying in the woods near Lake Peipus," Raphael said. "As to why or how, we can't help you with that mystery. We found you here."

Illarion struggled to sit up, and saw a few other faces hovering in the background: Ozur and several of the Shield-Maidens. He looked over at the fire and saw that the stones were the same, but the narrow pit had been filled with fresh logs. There was no sign of the skulls. He tilted his head back, following the curling column of pale smoke, and gazed up at the night sky. "How long?" he murmured.

"A few hours," Nika supplied. "Your friends arrived while you were sleeping. They came from Pskov, intending to see the prince, but they met some of my sisters and learned you were part of the prince's entourage. Ziara finally told them that we had gone into the woods."

Illarion nodded slowly. His right forearm had been wrapped with a piece of silk, and it clung to his skin in several places where blood had soaked through. "Who wrapped this?" he asked.

"I did," Raphael said. "It's very clean and there isn't much blood."

"Did you see what it was?"

"Aye," Raphael said. He glanced up at Feronantus. "We are familiar with such a mark, though it has been many years since I have seen one that precise. Most flinch, just a little bit."

"I would imagine the circumstances under which he received it were quite different," Feronantus said quietly. "And yet, it would seem we are of the same spirit now."

"Aye," Raphael nodded. "I would imagine so."

Illarion felt something rising in his throat and he quickly turned it into a braying laugh. "My friends," he said, not wanting to dwell on the mark on his arm. "What are you doing here? It has been so many months since I have seen you. You were—" He broke off, not sure how to speak of the Shield-Brethren's mission.

"We were successful," Feronantus said, his gaze wandering toward the frozen lake. "But our work is not yet done."

"What work is that?"

Feronantus looked at Illarion again. "There is to be a battle on the morrow," he said, and his gaze dropped to Illarion's arm. "*We* all have parts to play in it."

"Aye," Illarion sighed, plucking at the silk wrap. "That we do."

✦ ✦ ✦

They spotted torchlight across the lake as they made their way back to the prince's camp—sure sign that Hermann of Dorpat's army had reached the far side of the lake. Ozur went ahead of the group to alert the prince, though Nika suspected the *Kynaz* already knew. The pale glow from the opposite side of the lake was hard to miss against the black and white landscape.

They were met by a group of Shield-Maidens not far from the camp, a handful of warriors who were ready for battle, and Nika found her heart swelling with pride at the sight of her sisters. In the days since Pskov, the *Skjalddis* had proven themselves time and again in the scattered skirmishes in Dorpat, and although the company of *Skjalddis* was nowhere near the size of the force that had once protected Kiev, they still numbered enough to warrant special placement on the battlefield. The men in the prince's army looked upon them with reverence now, as well as a bit of fear. Nika had heard more than one quietly refer to her as *Valkyrie* when they thought she was out of earshot. She thought such deference might not last past this coming battle, but for the interim, she was glad to know that the men of Novgorod would have her back as well as stand ready beside her.

The *Skjalddis* fell in on either side of the small company, and the sight of the well-armored Shield-Maidens cleared a path through the confusion of the camp as they were led directly to the prince's tent.

The prince and his brother were having the same argument they had been having for the last few days when they were announced and ushered into the narrow tent. There was barely enough room for all of them, but knowing that she was the least important person in the room, she squeezed into a corner and did her best to become unobtrusive.

Alexander sought her out regardless. "It is somewhat awkward to awaken and discover that my favorite decoy and his shadow have fled my camp," he said, staring sternly at Nika. "More so when strangers arrive, seeking a part in the battle tomorrow, and then I learn they are old companions of yours."

"My apologies, *Kynaz*," Illarion said. "Nika and I were—"

"It would be unwise to lie to me," Alexander interrupted.

Illarion held his tongue a moment, his fingers idly plucking at the silk wrapping around his arm. He glanced at Nika, and she lifted her shoulders slightly as if to give him permission to say anything that he thought necessary.

"Nika and I were consulting with the old witch of Rus," Illarion said.

Andrei swore loudly, earning a hard glare from his brother. "And who, exactly, was this witch?" Alexander asked, the tone of his voice suggesting that while he would tolerate this outrageous story born from the mind of an imaginative child, his tolerance had limits.

"Baba Yaga," Illarion said, eliciting another exclamation of disbelief from Andrei.

Alexander chewed on the inside of his cheek for a moment. "Baba Yaga?" he asked, eyebrows raised. When Illarion nodded, Alexander glanced at his brother, who glowered at him. "Continue," Alexander said.

"She was a *Skjalddis* once," Illarion said. "A defender of women and children. Somehow, when she became who she is now, she took on the role of protector of all of Rus."

Illarion unwound the silk bandage from his arm and showed everyone the inflamed mark on his skin. "She chose me to be her champion," he said.

"It is the mark of the *Ordo Militum Vindicis Intactae*," Feronantus said. He put up his own sleeve, displaying a similar mark upon his forearm. "We all bear it."

Raphael showed his forearm as well.

Alexander looked at the three scars, inspecting each one carefully. "And how do you come by this mark?" he asked.

"When we are ready, we are tested, and those who survive the test are sealed into service," Feronantus said, his eyes lingering on Illarion. "The flesh never forgets what the mind and spirit have vowed to do."

Illarion lowered his arm, hiding the mark from view. Feronantus's last statement was meant for him, and the reminder sent a shiver up his back. The old master of Týrshammar seemed to know more about his visit with Baba Yaga than he did.

"*Vindicis Intactae,*" Alexander said. "Defenders of the Virgin. Is that who you swear to protect?"

"Among others," Raphael said.

Andrei shook his head. "This is heathen nonsense, *Kynaz.* They have no place in your army. They will only serve to frighten the militia."

Alexander looked at his older brother with a raised eyebrow. "Frighten them?" he wondered. "On the contrary, I suspect they'll give them courage. I have heard stories of the Shield-Brethren. I hear that between you and your martial sisters there are no warriors braver or stronger. If I understand what these men are telling me, it would seem that the advantage in the coming battle is ours."

Andrei flushed and turned away from his brother to pour himself a flagon of wine. *Utterly unnecessary at this time of day,* Nika thought, but Andrei needed something to occupy his hands.

"We have one boon to ask of you," Feronantus said.

"I will grant it if I may," Alexander said.

"The one known as Volquin's Dragon," Feronantus said. "Kristaps and his men are ours."

"All of them?"

"Aye," Feronantus said, and Nika noticed the odd glance that Raphael gave him.

Alexander glanced at Illarion, as if to verify there was nothing else that would require his permission, and then he looked at his brother again. Andrei refused to look up from his flagon. "Very well," the prince said. "If all you require of me is that I believe in childhood phantoms and that I provide you with an opportunity to stand between me and our mutual enemies, then I see no conflict. I doubt the three of you—and all of the *Skjalddis* outside who are already thirsting for battle—are enough to stand against the Livonians and their mad leader, but I will not prevent you from seeking them out on the battlefield."

"That is all we ask," Feronantus said, inclining his head.

Nika caught Vera's eye and raised an eyebrow. The elder Shield-Maiden smiled grimly, and Nika knew she had her marching orders. *The Livonians it is,* she thought. *At least they will be easy to pick out against the ice.*

✦ ✦ ✦

After the meeting, Alexander asked Illarion to accompany him as the prince went to inspect the lake. They walked through chaos as the *Druzhina* prepared for battle while the men of the militia struck the camp. The noisy cacophony made Illarion's head ache and he was glad to get away from all the confusion and shouting. Close to the lake, it was peaceful enough that he could hear the gentle sound of water moving back and forth beneath the ice.

Alexander walked down to the lake's edge and beckoned Illarion over. "Do you see the ridges where the wind has melted the ice and then frozen it again?" He pointed to the uneven surface of the lake.

Illarion recalled his journey across the lake several nights ago. He had been concerned about his horse falling through the ice, and he had instructed the men to lead the animals slowly and carefully. Looking at the edged ice now, he realized *slowly and carefully* was the best speed a horse and rider could hope for. "They won't be able to charge us," he said.

"Not until they get to this shore," Alexander said. "Should I wait for them here or meet them on the ice?"

"Do you think it will hold?"

Alexander looked out across the glistening surface. "I am not the one who has been consorting with the supernatural," he said. "I would defer to you on this matter, Illarion Illarionovich."

"My Prince..." Illarion began awkwardly.

"Had I known that Hermann had left assassins lying in wait in Pskov, I would have gone myself." Alexander laughed at Illarion's expression. "No, perhaps not. At the very least, I would have sent more men. But I speak with the benefit of hindsight. Would I have been killed in the church? Would I have been as capable as you in dispatching the assassins?"

"Of course you would have," Illarion said.

"I would hope so," Alexander said absently, his attention on the far side of the lake. The glow of watch fires was brighter than before, suggesting that the army of Hermann of Dorpat was readying itself as well. "My brother believes I am not as clever as I think," Alexander continued, "and he is still unhappy about some of my previous decisions, but he will follow me. The *Druzhina* will follow me, as will the men of Novgorod, and I believe that we have selected the best possible field of battle..."

"But..." Illarion prompted Alexander when the prince trailed off.

"But I am pragmatic man," Alexander said with a faint smile. "I know that how the people remember the battle matters almost as much as the outcome of the battle itself."

"And what would you have them remember of this battle?" Illarion asked.

Alexander smiled at him then, a broad grin that showed many of his teeth. "I would have them know that Rus rose up against those who would attack her. I would have any who contemplate invading our lands think twice about the folly of such actions. I would have them fear to awaken that which slumbers in these forests."

Illarion's forearm itched and he fought the urge to rake his nails across his freshly branded skin. "I would be honored to assist you with that goal, my *Kynaz*," he said. "My blood is the blood of Rus, and it is yours to command."

Alexander grasped his forearm, pressing his palm against the silk-covered injury on Illarion's arm. He grabbed Illarion's wrist with his other hand, holding him still as he squeezed Illarion's arm. When he released his grip, the silk bandage was marked with blood, and there was blood on the prince's palm as well.

"The blood of Rus," Alexander said. He stepped out onto the frozen lake and crouched. He held his hand over one of the icy ridges and drew his palm sharply across the frozen edge, leaving behind a line of bright blood on the ice. "This is our blood," he said. "This is our land. I, Prince Alexander Iaroslavich of the House of Rurik, swear to defend Rus against all who wish to do her harm, and I do not stand alone in this defense."

Illarion held his breath, half-expecting something to happen in the wake of the prince's pronouncement, but the lake was silent. His forearm stopped itching.

"They will have to come straight across the lake," the prince said, standing up and returning to the shore as if nothing had happened. He wiped his palm clean on his tunic. "This is the only place where the ice is thick enough and the lake narrow enough to make such a crossing possible. Our *Druzhina* and horse-archers will hold back with the infantry in the center. I want you with my cavalry. The *Skjalddis*, if they are willing, will be our shield-wall." He tapped his foot on the ground. "Here. This is the place where it will end. Right here."

CHAPTER 32:

 ◣━

THE BATTLE ON THE ICE

Kristaps reined in his horse at the edge of the frozen lake, and the animal snorted with impatience. He had ridden a palfrey for the past few days to save his warhorse for battle, and now his destrier was eager for the charge. Behind Kristaps, the bulk of the army assembled—Hermann's Teutonics, his Livonians, the Danes, and the ragtag militia gathered from Dorpat. His scouts had tracked the fleeing Novgorodian marauders to the lake, and he knew that they had crossed the ice at the same place that he had a week prior.

He knew this would be the place where Nevsky would meet him in battle.

Hermann had argued that they should have crossed during the night. The moon had been out and the sky had been clear, making it easy to see well enough to guide the army across the lake, but Kristaps had dismissed the idea. This was Ruthenian land, and they knew it better than he and his men. The army had been marching hard for more than a week; they were tired and worn down. A night's rest—even though he knew most of the men would sleep uneasily knowing they would probably march into battle in the morning—would be more beneficial than an attempted sneak attack. Just as it was bright enough from the moonlight for the Teutonics to pick their way across the lake, so too could the Novgorodians see them coming.

Kristaps stared at the empty expanse of the ice, considering the plan of attack, as other riders came up beside him—the Prince-Bishop and the Danish sons of Eric Ploughpenny.

"They have better ground," Hermann said sourly. "We will have to march out to meet them."

Kristaps grunted. The Prince-Bishop's commentary needed some response but he didn't care to offer anything more than mere acknowledgement of the Prince-Bishop's *astute* observation.

Svend was less polite. "Are your feet getting cold, Dorpat?" the Danish prince asked. "The ice is thick here, and we have ridden across it before. It will not swallow us."

"Their infantry will be Novgorod militia," Illugi pointed out. "Like those we faced in Dorpat." He leaned over and spat into the snow. "A charge of heavy horse will break them and send them running."

"Are you volunteering to lead that charge?" Hermann snapped. There was little love between the sons of Ploughpenny and the Prince-Bishop, and after weeks of marching back and forth across winter terrain with little opportunity for plunder, the Danes were getting restless. They were testing the mettle of the man they served, and Kristaps knew they were wondering if there was a different opportunity than the one offered them by the Prince-Bishop. For his own part, Kristaps did not care if the Danes turned on Dorpat as long as they did so *after* defeating Nevsky and the Novgorodian army.

"We will all charge together," Kristaps said. "Straight across the lake. We will smash their infantry and gain the high ground. Once there, the rest will be easy. God is on our side, and fortune favors the righteous."

He had not intended to make such a zealous claim, but his words put a decisive end to the bickering. Hermann echoed his sentiment, crossing himself, and the Danish princes had the presence to bow their heads and repeat the words as well. *Allow us to kill them all,* Kristaps prayed silently.

A shout echoed from behind him, and then another and another. At first Kristaps thought the army was taking up his prayer, but then he realized the noise was coming from the massed group of infantry, the peasants who had been conscripted to fight for the Prince-Bishop. They were shouting and pointing, and Kristaps turned his gaze back across the lake. On the far side, men were massing along the shore, which in itself was not cause for alarm, but then he spotted the banners: the colors of Novgorod and the House of Rurik, and, in the center, a pair of banners that sported the red rose.

The Shield-Brethren.

What happened next filled Kristaps with apoplectic rage as the first of the Estonian peasants, screaming, turned and fled despite the shouts of the mounted cavalry to remain fast. The panic started as a trickle and then rapidly became a flood until a majority of the peasant infantry had quit the field, running into the forest as if the Devil himself snapped at their heels.

"Hold the line," Kristaps shouted, and his voice was commanding enough that some men hesitated. Kristaps pulled his horse around and cantered back to the scattered rank of infantry. "The next man who presumes to run at the sight of the enemy will be cut down before he reaches the tree line," he snapped, glaring down at the frightened peasants.

His horse, sensing his incandescent fury, pawed the ground heavily, spooking the men who stood nearest the angry destrier. Kristaps drew his sword and raised it high. "We outnumber them," he shouted. "We have more knights than they do. We have Danish marauders who feel no fear. You are better armed and armored than the ragged fools who claim to represent the people of Novgorod. Why do you flee in fear from an assured victory? God watches over us. God is standing right beside you, and when you strike with your weapon, He will be guiding your arm."

He waved his sword and turned his horse toward the lake. "We shall cross the ice together and smash their center apart," he shouted. "We shall rip into their formations like tusks ripping into soft flesh. We shall taste their fear and the blood, and having done so, we shall carve out the heart of their commander. And then nothing with stop us as we march on to Novgorod!"

A cheer rose up from the men around him—tentative at first, but growing in volume until he was certain it made the ice tremble. He brought his sword down, point directed at the banners on the far shore. "The Boar's Snout," he cried. "Let us march to victory."

His army recovered, the infantry falling into formation behind him, the mounted knights lining up on either side. He kneed his horse and it trotted eagerly toward the lake. Behind him, the morning air rippled with the sound of marching feet, of rattling spears and armor, and of the hooves of cavalry against the ice.

✦ ✦ ✦

They stood arrayed, weapons at the ready, faces staring across the water at the flying banners of the enemy, and from where he sat in the saddle, Illarion could feel their fear. It was hard to forget, after all that he had seen, that most of the men here were not warriors by trade. He had heard them talking around the camp fires, or between the tents, or in the midst of their drills. It was an army made up of bakers' sons and drovers, fur traders and merchants' children, carpenters and shepherds called to arms by an oath of service to Novgorod's militia.

The *Druzhina* were split into two groups, one on the north flank of the gathered infantry and the other—consisting mainly of horse archers—standing ready at the southern edge of the army. Illarion was surrounded by the prince's personal guard, and behind him were Raphael and Feronantus. In front, standing behind a line of shields with spears resting butt-first against the ground, were the *Skjalddis*—the front line of their defense.

"The Boar's Snout," Alexander noted as the enemy began to march onto the ice. He didn't sound surprised, and Illarion suspected the prince would have done the same if the situation had been reversed. "It can be broken," the prince said, his voice heavy with awareness of what was coming, "but at a heavy price."

The Shield-Maidens, Illarion thought, *first to fight, first to fall.* He nodded grimly at the prince, knowing Nika and Vera and others would not have it any other way.

The Novgorodian army had cheered when the pair of banners provided by the Shield-Maidens had been unfurled, and their delight had increased when the enemy's infantry had started to flee. For a brief and tenuous moment, Illarion had hoped that the whole of the enemy's host would collapse, but his wish was not granted. He saw a man wearing the red sword and cross of the Livonian order riding back and forth, and he knew that was Kristaps, exhorting the men to stand fast.

The Boar's Snout was a costly maneuver, but Kristaps still had the numbers.

The ranks of knights and infantry across the ice slowly fell into a wedge formation, fanning out from a quartet of riders at the front. A shout echoed across the lake, too far away for the words to be discerned, but not so the tone: mocking, challenging, defiant.

The prince answered the challenge. He let his horse walk carefully down to the ice, where he could be seen by both the enemy and the ranks of his men, and he drew his sword and held it aloft. "You are not welcome in Rus," he shouted. His words were picked up by the men of Novgorod, by the *Druzhina,* and by the Shield-Maidens. Illarion added his voice to the roar that was sent across the ice. *Go home!*

The prince kept his sword upraised, the blade shining in the morning sunlight, until the roaring chant of his army finally died. "It is time, men and women of Novgorod," he shouted, his head turning back and forth to look upon his army. "It is time to stand your ground for home and hearth. It is time to stand for Rus, for friends, for family, for Holy God who watches over us. Our enemy thinks he can break us as readily as a log might be split by an ax, but he is mistaken. He thinks he might be strong enough to shatter our ranks, but we will show him the error of his ways." Alexander turned his horse so that his back was to the lake and the enemy. "He thinks he can walk across this frozen lake and take this embankment. He thinks we will suffer his foot upon our land, upon Rus. What do we say to this fool, sons and daughters of Rus? We will tell him that he cannot cross this ground. He cannot have Rus!"

A roar of five thousand voices echoed in response, rising up from the chest of every man and woman.

Across the lake, the wedge started to move faster, the leading edge of horses galloping across the frozen lake.

✦ ✦ ✦

Kristaps's horse found its footing on the ice and its hesitant canter evened out. He urged the beast on, its breath a cloud that swept past his helmeted head with every breath. His spear was in his hand, his sword loose in his scabbard. He'd done this hundred times before, ridden the fury of the torrent forward like a man drunk on sensation. Everything sparkled with perfect clarity, and he slowly urged his mount faster towards the opposite shore. Not yet, not yet a gallop. They would need that surge of strength for the final push to smash through the enemy lines. He saw the Danes beginning to outdistance them and fought the urge to increase his pace. *The fools make themselves targets*, he thought fleetingly, and as if summoned by his thought, he saw a rank of horse archers separate from the eastern shore. They flowed like a flock of birds, not unlike the Mongols in their approach, and it was a beautiful display of precision riding. Unfortunately the majesty was marred by the torrent of arrows they unleashed. He saw the first few Danes fall and their charge weakened. Illugi shouted an order that was lost amid the thunder of hooves and the screams of the men who had fallen on the ice, and the Danish riders changed direction. Kristaps swore loudly as he watched the horse archers split effortlessly around the Danish charge, feathering around the riders like pairs of wings, all the while loosing arrow after arrow.

Kristaps lashed his horse, spurring it to a full gallop. The sons of Ploughpenny had chosen their own fate, but if their foolish charge managed to distract Nevsky's horse archers long enough for Kristaps's Livonian knights to reach the far shore, then the Danish sacrifice had not been entirely stupid.

Memories burned through his mind, humiliating beyond imagining, of struggles over a year ago beneath *Pescherk Lavra* in Kiev, where a handful of experienced Shield-Brethren and *Skjalddis* had defeated a force nearly three times their size. He had been forced to flee on a stolen horse through the wilderness like a common bandit. He could see the *Skjalddis*, standing shield to shield in the front rank of Nevsky's infantry.

The wind was rising behind him, as if in benediction of his course, and he could feel the fury of his brothers at his back as they urged their horses onward like tormented men.

The Shield-Maidens would bear the brunt of his charge. Kristaps smiled beneath his helm. It was a sure sign that God was with the Livonians.

✦ ✦ ✦

One of the leading horses stumbled and then tried to stop, which only resulted in a collision with the horse and rider behind it.

A second horse felt the bite of the ice against its leg and turned, no longer charging directly at the *Skjalddis* shield-wall. Alexander gave the archers leave to loose arrows, and a flight of arrows arced toward the crumbling Livonian charge. Men screamed and tumbled from their horses, leaving the animals riderless and confused. The Livonian charge came on, but Illarion could tell that it had been slowed. The Boar's Snout was no longer as solid a wedge as it had been, and in response to a shout from Vera, the *Skjalddis* lowered their spears and readied themselves to meet the charge.

Illarion looked away as the horses collided with the spears and shields of the *Skjalddis* wall, but he could not block out the screams and the calamitous sound of metal and flesh and wood slamming against one another. His heart was pounding in his chest, vibrating his entire body, and his head and neck were slick with sweat.

The wall bent under the initial charge, but it did not break, and as Illarion groaned with frustration at not being able to assist his friends, the prince's infantry massed around the bulge and helped hold the line. Swords flashed and spears darted. By and by, the enemy was driven down the bank and back onto the ice.

Clumps of Livonian infantry reached the rear of the struggling knights and entered the melee, and the surviving stragglers of the Danish cavalry plunged into the mass of swarming bodies as well. Still Alexander held back, watching the battle unfold with a stoic expression on his face. The *Kynaz* sat etched like an effigy of a stone saint, eyes locked on the battle as it played out before his eyes, waiting for something that did not yet show itself. The horses around him snorted and pawed the earth, and the men murmured as others died in their stead on the edge of the lake. Still, he waited.

Then, as the Livonian men at arms finished their crossing and the bulk of the enemy pushed against the line of *Skjalddis* and

Novgorodian infantry, Alexander Nevsky drew his sword, signaling to the *Druzhina* of his brother on the other side of the beach. "For Novgorod!" he cried, and the roar that rose behind him was deafening.

Illarion drew his sword and dug in his heels, the horse surging beneath him as Alexander and Andrei's riders drove down the bank of the beach towards the water, coming at the enemy flanks from the left and right. Stones, snow, and frozen grass gave way to ice as they thundered at their foes, and whether by the grace of Holy God himself, or because of the narrow range of vision provided by the helms of the Livonian Crusaders, the enemy never saw them coming, and Illarion was suddenly in a sea of horsemen. He rode beside the *Kynaz*, cutting through the lines like a sweeping blade. Across the ice, Andrei rode towards them, butchering his way through horses and men.

The strategy of battle was a matter of careful finesse and planning, of understanding the ebb and flow of struggling men, and of timing commands to perfectly match when the enemy was weak and you were strong, but beneath the planning and the careful tactics was the truth that inches and ground were won in the crucible with straightforward knife-work, and now was the time for the *Druzhina* and the Shield-Brethren to prove their worth.

Men at arms swept around him as he rode across the shoreline. The infantry, galvanized by their prince's charge, now rushed forward even as the Livonians reeled from the attack to their flanks. Illarion turned his steed, cutting down footmen and shattering the ribs of another knight beneath his armor. He pulled a spear from a dead man and drove it into a Livonian's chest with the fury of a gallop behind him, dropping him to the earth, where he had a moment's glimpse of infantry bearing down on him, festooned with clubs, axes, and long wicked knives.

Out of the corner of his eye, he saw a flash of red and white, and when he turned his head, he saw the mad leader of the Livonian order.

Kristaps.

✦ ✦ ✦

Kristaps put his spear through a young man in a half-helm and patched maille, the spear-point taking him through the throat and drawing an explosion of blood from his mouth. His horse's hooves crunched flesh and bone as some men gave way in terror and others fell beneath the force of his charger. He released the spear and drew his Great Sword of War. Although normally wielded with both hands while on foot, it was possible to wield the weapon one-handed from horseback, and the great cleaving blows with which he laid about served him well. His sword rose and fell, sweeping through bodies and trailing lines of blood as he severed heads and smashed faces. It was this for which God had made him, and he reveled in it.

He caught sight of an armored foot soldier, more slender than most, driving a man off his horse with a single thrust of a spear. The technique was familiar, and judging by the size of the soldier, it was one of the Shield-Maidens. He jerked his horse's head in that direction, and the animal forced its way through the melee. But she was gone by the time he reached the riderless horse, lost among the chaotic mass of men and horses around him.

A Novgorodian footman was charging his mount, screaming and waving his pike as if he were trying to shoo birds out of his vegetable garden. Kristaps turned his horse and beat aside the man's clumsy thrust. He brought his sword down heavily on the man's leather helmet, splitting his skull, and his horse snorted and side-stepped away from the dying man.

Kristaps looked toward the shore and saw that the line still held. Their wedge had failed to shatter the shield-wall, and his knights were slowly being forced back onto the ice.

"Rally to me," Kristaps cried as he raised his blood-stained sword in the air like a standard. The knights began to move, flowing as one, though not with the strength of their initial charge. The line surged after them, and Kristaps found himself forced to give ground. The line left corpses of their own on the shore and they were losing some of their cohesion as they moved forward, but they were moving, forcing the Livonians and Teutonics back across the ice.

A *Skjalddis* came at him, thrusting her spear up at his horse. She moved much more adroitly than the last man—perhaps she was even the woman he had seen earlier. He twisted in his saddle, avoiding her thrust, but the tip of her spear raked through his surcoat, grinding across his maille. He seized the shaft with his left hand and chopped down with the sword in his right.

She let go of her spear, avoiding his cut, and while he was dealing with the weapon, she drew her arming sword and unslung her shield from her back. "I am Zaria!" she challenged him, making her voice heard over the din of the surrounding battle. "This is for Kiev!"

Kristaps pulled his horse away from her as she cut at his destrier's legs, and he rained a heavy blow down on her shield. He had the advantage of position and strength, but she took the hit on her shield without crumpling. Chips of wood scattered from the painted surface of the shield like dead rose petals tossed into the wind. Fighting a man on horseback from the position on the ground put any warrior at an extreme disadvantage, and Kristaps gave her grudging credit for the courage necessary to try, but the line between courage and foolishness was thin, and he did not have the time or the patience to indulge a fighter whose tenacity amused him.

As she lowered her shield to thrust up at him again, he lashed out with his foot. He caught the edge of her shield, driving the round surface back at her head. Instinctively she got her head out of the way, which only exposed it to his sword. He brought his blade down, and she got her sword up in time, but the smaller arming sword only managed to deflect some of the strike from the more powerful greatsword. He felt the impact of metal against metal travel up his arm, and though he had not split her helm, he knew he had stunned her. She took two steps to the side, her sword and shield drooping, and when he raised his sword for another blow, she was only dimly aware of what was coming. She was still able to get her shield up as his sword came down again, but it was a futile effort, for his blow shattered her shield. She screamed, presumably since he had broken her arm as well. Her wailing cry was cut short by his next strike, which split her helm and her skull beneath.

As he flicked his blade to rid it of blood, he assessed the battlefield once more. Nevsky's line had reached the edge of the ice, and his cavalry foundered on the ice. The massed infantry of his army had arrived and he raised his sword once more, shouting for the men to rally around him. They still had superior numbers and they could break the Novgorodian line that was still wavering. He swept his sword down, screaming for the men to take the shore.

✦ ✦ ✦

As the enemy surged toward the shore again, the prince finally gave the command for his riders to charge, and the shield-wall splintered. Nika had seen Kristaps slay Zaria and as soon as she heard the command to make way for the prince's charge, she stormed out onto the ice. Horses thundered past her, and she knew they would reach the enemy first, but she was going to be right behind them, her sisters and the Novgorodian infantry at her back.

She put her spear through the face of Danish marauder, twisted the point free, and then drove the butt into the stomach of the man next to him. She shifted her grip, and jabbed the spear to her left, catching a third man in the shoulder. He was wearing leather instead of maille, and the point slid through the boiled leather as if it were silk. The man howled in pain, and because his open mouth was such an inviting target, she jabbed her point there too.

She felt a tremor in the ice behind her and ducked. An axe blade sailed over her head and she thrust backward with the butt of her spear, hitting something that gave way. She spun, keeping her spear ready, and faced her opponent—another Dane, the son of someone important judging by the quality of his armor. He slashed with his axe again and she darted to her left, but he twisted his weapon and the blade of the axe sheared through the wood of her spear. He grinned, thinking she was disarmed, but she saw his next attack coming before he finished reveling in what he thought was going to happen. She grabbed the haft of her spear in both hands, stepped in, and slammed it against his axe, below the broad head. She felt the blade bounce off her helm, but the main power of his stroke had been blocked by the wood in her hand. He snarled at her, showing his teeth, and she shoved up and back as she stepped in again, putting him in range for her knee to slam into his groin.

A funny expression crossed the Dane's face, and his grip slackened on his axe. She yanked back, catching the curved head of the axe with her spear and pulling the weapon out of the Dane's hands. She jabbed him in the face with the end that he had cut, knocking his head back. His helmet spilled off his head, and she whirled the pole around to collapse the side of his now-bare head.

"Svend!"

Unlike Svend, who was now dead on the ice, the newcomer was still on his horse and his shout warned her of his approach. She ducked under a sweeping blow from his rune-etched sword and thrust her spear between the horse's legs as it galloped by. The pole was wrenched from her hands as the horse tripped over the shaft. It screamed and collapsed on the ice, and Nika felt a brief flicker of remorse for having injured the horse so badly. She had time to draw her sword as the rider jumped clear of the thrashing beast and slipped on the ice as he tried to orient to her.

"That was my brother, you fucking bitch," the Dane shouted.

"Come join him," she snarled. She couldn't help but think of Zaria, and of her other sisters who would undoubtedly fall today. How many had fallen since the Mongols had come west? How few were left?

If this is the end, she thought, *then let this battle be a monument to every one of my sisters who has ever died. Let my sword carve a legacy on this frozen lake that history will never forget.*

The Dane charged.

CHAPTER 33:

THE VIRGIN'S MARK

Kristaps caught sight of Nevsky's banner across the melee and forced his horse toward the flash of red and gold. It was hard to build up speed on the ice, but he managed to get his destrier to a gallop. *Remove the head and the rest will falter,* he thought. *Kill the man and the legend dies.* His horse collided with a *Druzhina* who thought to intercept him, and Kristaps smashed the pommel once, twice, against the other rider before the smaller horse stumbled and went down. His horse leaped, nearly unseating him as it slipped on the ice, but it avoided the other horse and kept running. He fumbled for the reins, trying to control his straining mount as another *Druzhina* came at him. He got control of the reins and got settled again in his saddle. He swept his sword up and his longer blade meant that his tip sliced into the *Druzhina*'s arm and shoulder before the other man's sword was within range.

There was no one else between him and Nevsky.

The prince turned his horse toward Kristaps, presenting a smaller target, and Kristaps brought his sword around in a heavy blow as his horse closed the gap. The prince caught Kristaps's strike on his finely etched shield and responded with a short jab with his arming sword. Kristaps pulled his blade back across his body, absorbing the blow on the strong edge of the blade, and thrust beneath the lower edge of the prince's shield, putting his sword in that place where the prince wouldn't see it coming until it was too late.

The prince's armor kept the blow from being lethal, but he bent around the stroke nonetheless, his mouth straining open with a loud gasp. He swept his shield to the side as their horses passed. Kristaps's horse snorted and nearly threw him, but he managed to keep it under control and bring it around again. Nevsky had recovered from the previous blow and blocked Kristaps's second strike, but this time the force of the blow nearly drove him from the saddle. He was a strong man, and well trained, but Kristaps was stronger, and a better killer by far. Kristaps kept his horse close, and launched a flurry of blows at the prince's shields, tearing deep rents in the painted heraldry and letting fly the wood beneath.

At Schaulen everything had come apart because Volquin had been blind to the combined strength of the tribes arrayed against them. They had been trapped in the marshy ground along the river, unable to move as quickly, and the Semigallians and Samogitians had rained flight after flight of javelins into their ranks. The Livonian cavalry had been butchered while they foundered in their heavy armor. Kristaps would never forget a moment of that excruciating ordeal—crawling through the mud and muck while his brothers were slaughtered around him by men who wore little more than leather jerkins and fur bracers. The memory drove his sword arm with a relentless and rampant fury. He would smother the memory of Schaulen with blood—the blood of every man, woman, and child in Rus if that was what it took.

The prince remained in his saddle, huddling beneath his scarred shield, but he had lost his sword. The prince's horse was wide-eyed and skittish, and Kristaps's destrier was snapping at its flanks with its large teeth.

Kristaps raised his sword. One more blow was all it would take.

The sound of thundering hooves was all that warned him, and the shriek of the panicked horse came too late to avoid what happened next. Kristaps turned to see a horse bearing down on his right flank, out of control as the beast slipped on the ice in the midst of its desperate gallop across the lake's surface. The rider, unable to stop, raised a gleaming sword and launched a desperate cut at any part of Kristaps he might reach.

He couldn't twist any further and couldn't get his sword around in time to block the strike and so he bent back, feeling his balance go as the blade passed over his head. The horses collided and Kristaps launched himself backwards, trying to jump clear of his mount to avoid being crushed. Through the eye-slits of his helm, the world spun in a whirl of white and gray, and then he struck the surface of the ice with a thud that would have left him gasping had he not known how to control his breath.

He had lost his sword, and he cast about for it, spotting it on the ice not far from his right hand. He also saw a man coming at him, and he strained for his sword, getting his hand on it. He twisted onto his back, raising his sword, and caught the downward stroke that would have split his skull in half he had not moved. The tip of the attacker's sword gouged the ice next to his head. Slipping, Kristaps lashed out with his feet and connected with the other man's shins. The man staggered back and Kristaps rolled onto his side and struggled to his feet before the man could attack him again.

Breathing hard, bruised beneath maille and gambeson, seething with indignant fury, the First Sword of Fellin quickly assessed the situation. The horses were gone, as was the prince. The melee had drifted away from them, leaving nothing but corpses of men and horses on the ice.

His opponent was a slender Ruthenian, carrying a longsword and wearing a maille shirt and half-helm like he was. He could only see the lower half of the man's face, which was covered with a heavy beard that had once been dark and black, but was now heavily streaked with white. "I know you," Kristaps said.

"Aye," the man said. "I'm the ghost of Rus."

✦ ✦ ✦

Illarion had been separated from the prince shortly after the initial charge, and when he spotted Kristaps hewing through the crowd of men in an effort to reach the prince, he shouted loudly, trying to warn the prince. He was too far away to reach Alexander in time, and though he lashed his horse heavily in an effort to get it to move more quickly, he could only watch in horror. Kristaps didn't slow down as he plowed through the pair of *Druzhina* protecting the prince. The Livonian scythed through men as if he were merely cutting grain. *God protect me*, Illarion thought, *that man can fight.*

The chaos of the melee forced him to weave a lengthy path to reach the prince, clinging to the saddle when his horse stumbled perilously. He turned aside blows when they came and wheeled to evade collisions where he had to. He pushed his horse to a reckless speed on the ice, trying so desperately to reach the duel between knight and prince before it was too late.

Everything could be undone with the next stroke of the Livonian's sword. He had to stop Kristaps. He had to get there in time. The frothing breath of his horse rose like a cloud of steam as man and beast surged forward recklessly to the wheeling duel unfolding so close, but so impossibly far to reach when everything could be undone in seconds.

Kristaps was raining heavy blows on the prince's shield, and Illarion could see how each blow pushed the prince a little closer to the edge of his saddle. He slapped his reins hard against his horse's neck, pushing the horse faster than it wanted to run on the slippery ice. The wound on his forearm blazed with pain and he slapped his horse, urging it to run faster. His horse staggered and slipped, and Illarion realized that he was going to collide with Kristaps. He no longer had any control of his horse.

He swung his sword once, a desperate swing, and it hit nothing. He had no choice but to leap free of his saddle before he went down with his horse. He landed heavily on the ice, slipping to one knee, and he felt the frozen lake surface flex and groan beneath him. Kristaps had fared less well, and Illarion dashed forward to finish the Livonian off before the other man could retrieve his sword.

Kristaps was incredibly fast, and Illarion's heavy downward stroke was blocked at the last second, diverting the tip of his blade into the ice. Illarion was over-extended, leaning too far forward, and when Kristaps retaliated with a kick to Illarion's shin, he nearly pitched forward.

Illarion staggered back, regaining his footing and his measure. He didn't rush in a second time, and the Livonian knight managed to get to his feet.

He hadn't realized how tall Kristaps was, or how long his arms were. Suddenly he realized his longsword wasn't going to be long enough against the better reach of the greatsword.

Kristaps was staring at him, his head cocked to one side. He pointed slowly at Illarion. "I know you," the Livonian said, a mocking tone in his voice.

Illarion snarled his answer, struggling to hide his apprehension about the Livonian's advantage.

"Ghost, eh?" Kristaps answered. He laughed. "You're a disgrace," he spat. "You abandoned everything you held dear, including God. Your story may be a frightful tale for little children and old women, but I know you to be flesh and blood. And when I have sent you to Hell, you can sit with all the other men I have killed. There are many, and they were all better men than you." He pointed at the red-stained scarf around Illarion's forearm. "Did they mark you?" he asked. "Was it supposed to give you strength in this battle to overcome your enemies?"

Kristaps clawed at the sleeve of his maille shirt, pulling it up on his right arm. "I have one too," he snapped. "It means nothing."

Illarion stared at the smeared scar on the Livonian's forearm. The mark of the Shield-Brethren! Kristaps had been tested, but hadn't passed.

And suddenly it was all clear to Illarion, and he couldn't help but laugh.

"Stop that," Kristaps snarled, taking a step toward Illarion, his blade held ready.

"I feel sorry for you," Illarion said, and Kristaps reacted as if he had been stung by a bee. Before the Livonian could recover from his shock, Illarion leaped forward, his blade thrusting before him.

◆ ◆ ◆

The blow came with a cold fury, forcing Kristaps to pivot back and parry with an upward stroke. He tried to leverage his position into a thrust at Illarion's face, but the Ruthenian evaded it with a compass step, shuffling his feet across the slick ice, and his sword flicked at Kristaps's hands. *God in heaven, he's fast.*

The First Sword of Fellin rotated the hilt of his sword down, narrowly saving his fingers from being broken, and again tried to put the end of his sword through Illarion's jaw. Once more Illarion checked the thrust and responded with a cut at Kristaps's midsection. Volquin's Dragon struck it aside with the back edge of his greatsword and cut in response with the true edge at the Ruthenian's arms. Illarion parried, now two inches out of range due to his shorter weapon, and they separated, regarding one another as they circled like a pair of snarling wolves.

"I remember this exchange," Kristaps sneered. "One of the favorites taught by the Old Man of the Rock. Is Feronantus still alive? Still sending out boys out to fight his wars for him?"

Illarion was breathing heavily but his shoulders were straight and his footwork was careful and solid. Only his eyes betrayed his anxiety, and when he mentioned the old man's name, he saw them flicker toward the shore. "Your fight is with me," Illarion said, his voice cold and steady.

Kristaps smiled. "But he's here, isn't he?" He felt a strange feeling in the pit of his stomach—part elation and part something more primal. It wasn't fear; if anything, the debt owed to him was the source of a long-simmering hatred. No, the distant unease he felt was dread. If the old man truly was here, then not everything was as it seemed. Much like it had been at Kiev.

The ice creaked beneath them, and his stomach tightened reflexively.

There is no time for this irrational fear, he chided himself. Feronantus was old; he was in the prime of his life. He had the superior numbers. There was no way he could lose this battle. Even wasting his time with this Ruthenian—this man who claimed to be the *ghost of Rus*—would not deter him from his victory.

Kristaps moved first, and Illarion was forced to check Kristaps's sword by moving his weapon from low to middle. Kristaps pivoted to the right, letting the parry propel his weapon in the opposite direction which created a natural barrier to Illarion's expected counterattack. But the Ruthenian didn't follow through as expected, and Kristaps didn't pause to wonder why. He turned his hands and brought his edge up in a vicious cut toward Illarion's head.

But the Ruthenian wasn't where he was supposed to be, and for a second, Kristaps's mind was clouded with a noisy voice crying out that the man was indeed a ghost, for only a phantom could have moved that adroitly.

◆ ◆ ◆

Kristaps reversed his sword, sweeping it up with a stroke that would surely separate head from shoulders should it connect, and Illarion dropped to a half-crouch, keeping his sword covering his head in case Kristaps changed his mind. Footing on the ice was treacherous enough that such a move was foolhardy, for his center was woefully out of alignment, but getting low meant getting under Kristaps's guard. Illarion's sword was shorter; he couldn't keep fighting at Kristaps's measure. He'd never get close enough. This was the only way. As the greatsword sailed over his head, he leaped forward. Too close to thrust or cut, he drove the hard edge of his crossguard into the space beneath the bottom of the Livonian's helm. Kristaps wore a coif, a covering of maille over his head and neck, but the links were not as heavy as elsewhere.

Kristaps's head snapped back and his helm flew off his head, clattering across the ice. Illarion got a brief glimpse of the Livonian's sweat-covered face and wide eyes before the Livonian recovered from the painful jab in the neck. Kristaps grabbed for him, and Illarion darted out of the way, shoving a hand against Kristaps's elbow. Kristaps kept moving forward, though, and he snapped his arm back, catching Illarion on the side of the head with his elbow.

The blow skewed his helmet and made his ears ring, and he retreated another step, anticipating that Kristaps would try to hit him again, most likely with the heavy pommel of his greatsword. He hewed upward with his sword, hoping to connect, and felt the edge of his blade clash against Kristaps's maille.

Kristaps didn't come any closer, but he was still close enough for his greatsword, and Illarion brought his sword back into a defensive position in time to parry Kristaps's sweeping stroke. Kristaps shoved his sword off Illarion's and reversed directions, striking at the other side of his head. Illarion was forced to retreat, his parry crumpling under the heavy weight of Kristaps's sword.

He was struggling to catch his breath, and he kept slipping as he tried to center his weight. In the back of his mind, he thought he felt the ice flexing, but he pushed the thought aside. It didn't matter.

Kristaps came at him again, and Illarion remained on the defensive, blocking each strike but failing to find an opening where he could close. He heard a pounding noise and thought it was the sound of his blood in his ears, but he caught sight of movement on his left. A horseman was approaching, and he couldn't figure out if the man was one of Kristaps's or the prince's. He and Kristaps both separated as the rider bore down on them, and Illarion saw a flash of dark fur and the curved shape of a bow. Almost like…

The ice snapped beneath him and the ground shifted suddenly. A long groan followed as well as the sound of moving water, and Illarion's attention snapped to the surface of the lake.

When the shield-wall had forced the Livonians out onto the lake, the battle had spread out across the ice. As a result, he and Kristaps were no longer in the center of the melee, but they were far enough from shore to be surrounded by ice. While the lake was shallowest where it was narrowest, it was still deeper than a man's height. Should the ice break, he would freeze to death before he could climb out of the water.

Kristaps stood not far away, a murderous fury in his eyes. He shook his bloody sword at Illarion. "What will you do, ghost?" the Livonian shouted. "If you run, I might cut you down before you can reach the shore. If you stay and fight, the ice may break before you kill me and we will both die. What choice will you make?"

Illarion gripped his sword tightly in his right hand and waved Kristaps over with his left. "I will kill you, monster," he taunted.

Kristaps laughed as he charged.

◆ ◆ ◆

The Ruthenian dodged his thrust and moved to his right, keeping out of reach of his blade. The man fought well, and he had found his footing on the ice, but Kristaps had studied with the same *oplo*. He knew the techniques as well as Illarion, and when the Ruthenian tried to close and body-check him, he was already moving out of the way. Illarion kept coming, and it was all too easy to bring his hands up and slam the pommel of his sword into the side of the man's helm.

Illarion staggered, and Kristaps pivoted, intending to get behind the clumsy Ruthenian and finish him with a single stroke across the neck, but his leg refused to move like it should. Pain lanced up his side, breaking his concentration, and he nearly fell as his leg threatened to give out on him. Stumbling like a drunkard, Kristaps stared down at the bright flow of blood coursing down his thigh.

Illarion's sword had struck him on the hip as they had passed, somehow slipping beneath the maille skirt and over the steel that guarded his legs. There was no time to assess how deep the wound was. He could still stand and move, but the bleeding was severe.

For the first time in many years, he felt something twist in his guts that he had nearly forgotten.

He hobbled after the Ruthenian, raining blows down on him as quickly as he could. He would not succumb to the fear. He would not let it steal his strength. Illarion was tired. The strike against his helm had dazed him. There was still time to finish this fight. The thing in his belly drove him onward. To lose here and now, to die in this wretched place on the cusp of what was to be his greatest triumph, was unthinkable. He would kill this man, and then he would find the prince and kill him as well. He would still triumph.

But his first blow was checked, as was his second and his third. The Ruthenian did not have the strength to counterattack, but he was still managing to block Kristaps's strikes. He could feel blood running down his leg, the hot liquid filling his boot. With each stroke of his sword, he was closer to death. All Illarion had to do was keep blocking his attacks and eventually he would falter as his blood ran out. He had to end this fight.

He feinted, drawing Illarion's parry, and spun his sword into a savage thrust with all of his remaining strength. He felt the tip of his sword catch on the Ruthenian's maille, and then he felt the grinding motion of the rings parting beneath the force of his strike. He kept up the pressure on his sword and was rewarded with a spasm of pain twisting Illarion's mouth. He set his teeth on edge as he pulled his sword back, knowing the blade might catch on the ruined maille. He felt it come free and Illarion gasped, wrenching himself around Kristaps's blade, trapping it between his chest and arm.

Kristaps's attention faltered as he struggled to free his sword, and his vision blurred for a second. It cleared just in time for him to see Illarion bulling forward, his helm lowered. He tried to pull back, but Illarion's helm smashed into his jaw with such force that his left leg gave out.

He landed heavily on the ice, spitting blood and bits of broken teeth, and Illarion landed on top of him. Kristaps twisted on the slippery ice, trying to throw the Ruthenian off him, and he lost track of his sword. The Ruthenian reached for his face and Kristaps snapped at the extended fingers. The motion of his jaw sent shards of pain blasting through his face and he howled like a wounded bear. With a mighty heave, he shoved Illarion off his chest and rolled clear.

He came up on one knee, casting about for his sword, and Illarion slammed into him. The Ruthenian had cast aside his sword too, and instead he bore a narrow dagger in his hand. He ripped upward, and the blade dragged across the maille covering Kristaps's belly. He caught Illarion in a half-hug, struggling to grapple with the Ruthenian, and Illarion took advantage of the clinch to bury the dagger in Kristaps's left shoulder.

Kristaps spit a mouthful of blood into the Ruthenian's face, and as the other man flinched, he wrapped his hand around the hilt of the dagger and yanked it free. He slashed wildly with it, and the Ruthenian strained back to avoid the cut. He missed the pale swatch of skin that was Illarion's throat, but he felt the blade catch and tear through the maille directly below.

✦ ✦ ✦

There was blood in Illarion's eyes and blood soaking his gambeson beneath his maille. He stared stupidly at the blade in Kristaps's hand, dumbly trying to figure out how the Livonian had gotten it from him, and it was only as Kristaps tried to stab him again that he snapped out of the stupor that had enveloped him. He blocked the Livonian's thrust with his arms extended, hands crossed, and tried to clear to his left. Kristaps struggled against him, and the tip of the blade scraped across the front of his helm.

The ice shuddered beneath them, and Illarion lost his footing. He was still hanging on to Kristaps's arm, but his balance was awry and the larger man shoved him heavily, sending him sprawling onto the tilting ice.

How can that be possible? part of him wondered.

He banged his head against a protrusion in the ice, a large knob that couldn't have been there a few minutes ago, and his vision swam. He blinked and found himself standing behind his wife on the balcony of their home. He blinked again and saw his son, playing with other children in Volodymyr's broad square. He blinked once more and he was in the sitting room of his father's estate. Warm light flooded through the high windows, illuminating motes of gathering dust over books that were piled haphazardly around the roots of a tall tree that was growing out of the wall. *How can that be possible?*

Kristaps was standing over him, but his attention wasn't on Illarion's sprawled body. The Livonian was looking wildly around, a moaning noise coming out of his ruined mouth. Illarion struggled to sit up and pulled off his helm to see what was happening.

A scattered stream of blood-stained survivors were running and slipping and sliding across the ice. The invaders were retreating. Their charge had been broken and their ranks decimated. The prince had won.

As Illarion watched, men began disappearing, vanishing from view as the ice around them collapsed and crumbled. Very few surfaced briefly, struggling to climb out of the freezing water, but no one stopped to help any of them.

Kristaps eclipsed Illarion's view briefly, and he realized the Livonian was fleeing too, leaving a bright trail of blood in his wake. Illarion spotted his sword lying on the ice and he staggered to his feet, lurching sideways as the ice moved beneath him again. He grabbed his sword and started after the stumbling Livonian.

It wasn't over. Not until he was certain Kristaps wouldn't return. Not until the dead in Pskov had been avenged. Not until his own debts were paid.

His first stroke didn't penetrate the Livonian's armor, but the force of the blow knocked him to his knees. As Illarion came around Kristaps so that he could look the Livonian in the eye as he killed him, Kristaps lunged forward. Illarion danced back, but Kristaps managed to get a hand on his leg and pull him off balance. He fell onto his back.

Spewing blood and roaring incoherently, Kristaps launched himself forward, diving for Illarion. Illarion's dagger was held tightly in his right fist, and his blue eyes were incandescent with fury.

His expression changed when Illarion's sword pierced his chest. His momentum carried him forward, and with a horrible tearing noise, the blade emerged from his back. He grabbed at Illarion with his left hand, his fingers closing feebly.

Illarion felt a burning pain in his lower chest when he tried to inhale. When he looked down, he saw the hilt of his dagger protruding from his torso.

The ice tilted around him, and a hole opened beyond Kristaps's feet; the white ice vanished into a dark hole of icy water. Kristaps began to slide toward the water. The light fading from his eyes, the Livonian dug his fingers into the links of Illarion's maille.

Illarion wrapped his hands around Kristaps's, holding them tight to his belly. "Let us go together," he said. "As the brothers we never were." He jerked his body toward the hole in the ice. Kristaps tried to scream, his shattered jaw flopping horribly, and Illarion was spared hearing the awful noise as they slid across the ice and fell through the hole. Freezing water rushed over them.

He felt as if every inch of his flesh was being pierced by knives. The fog cleared from his mind, and in the wavering shadows of the water, he thought he saw the smiling faces of his wife and son.

He opened his mouth and didn't struggle as the cold water of Lake Peipus rushed in. Illarion let go of Kristaps—letting the bloody monster sink away—and stretched out his hand towards his family.

Let us go together…

CHAPTER 34:

THE OLD MAN'S LEGACY

When the prince gave the command for the cavalry to charge, Feronantus held out his hand to Raphael and shook his head. Raphael glared at the old master of the Rock but held his reins tight. Around him, the prince's cavalry charged, a thunder of horses and men, and in its wake came the men-at-arms, shouting and waving their weapons as they surged forward to help the *Skjalddis* hold the line. As the flood of men slowed to a trickle, Feronantus pulled his horse to the left, away from the tumultuous battle at the edge of the lake.

"Where are we going?" Raphael shouted. Vera clucked at her horse and followed Feronantus, leaving Raphael as the only horseman on the bank. With a loud curse, Raphael yanked on his reins and turned his horse after the pair.

Since they had left Benjamin's estate a month ago, Feronantus had spoken less than two dozen sentences to Raphael. He had conversed with Vera numerous times, but she had, maddeningly, refused to speak of what they had discussed. While it was clear that Feronantus was displeased with him, it had taken a while to realize Feronantus's displeasure had little do with anything that Raphael had done, but that it stemmed from Raphael's own disgust. And this only increased Raphael's dismay. How could Feronantus blame him for what had happened? More than once during their headlong ride north toward Rus and Novgorod, Raphael had considered refusing to travel another mile without some explanation from Feronantus, but he never could do it. He could never be that dismissive to his vows.

Even now, his head still filled with outrage, he followed Feronantus, *away* from the heart of the battle.

Feronantus led his horse down to the frozen lake and dismounted at the edge of the ice. He pulled the blackened Spirit Banner from its sling and, walking with the measured pace of a man used to icy terrain, he strode out onto the ice. Raphael and Vera left their horses as well, and before he stepped out onto the ice, Raphael looked over his shoulder once to check on the battle.

The line was holding and even seemed to be pushing the Livonians back toward the lake.

"We're exposed," Vera said to him as he joined her on the ice. She was carrying her crossbow in addition to her shield and sword. Her breath steamed from her mouth, and she stripped her helm off and threw it on the bank near her horse. Raphael did the same, realizing that out on the open ice, he wanted to be able to see anything that might be coming at him.

Bending his knees, he jogged ahead, catching up with Feronantus. "Where are we going?" he asked.

"Just a little ways," Feronantus said, pointing with his chin. He glanced at Raphael. "I owe you an explanation," he said. "I am sorry to have kept you waiting so long. I will tell you everything in a few minutes."

To his right, the battle reached the ice and the sound of swords hitting wood and steel increased as the Livonian infantry joined the battle. Raphael saw one of the two Shield-Brethren banners dip and then right itself. The banner belonging to the prince fluttered near the closer edge of the fray, and he thought he could pick out the *Kynaz* on his horse.

He also spotted the white tabard and the red cross of a Livonian. "There," he said, pointing. "Is that him?"

"Aye," Feronantus said. "That is Kristaps, the First Sword of Fellin. Also known as Volquin's Dragon. A terrible failure on my part."

"Failure? How are you responsible?" Vera asked, catching up with them.

Feronantus offered her a sad smile. "I trained him at Týrshammar. He was an incredible student, and I had high hopes for him, but…"

He stopped, seemingly at random, and placed the butt of the Spirit Banner against the ice and leaned heavily against it.

"He failed his initiation," Raphael finished for Feronantus. "You sent him to Petraathen, and he didn't pass the final test. Did he miss the sword?"

Feronantus shook his head. "No, he didn't miss." He touched the inside of his forearm lightly. "He grabbed the handle tight with both hands and held on."

"He dropped the shield," Raphael said, and Feronantus nodded sadly.

"Ah," Vera said, not bothering to hide her distain.

"The tree rots from the inside first, and the poison has already set in," Feronantus said. "Kristaps was the first fruit that was spoiled before it could even be plucked from the tree. There will be others, and we cannot weather change or adapt to the times as once we did. What we protect, what we teach, the purpose for our existence, must be *protected*. A branch must always survive, and the legacy must be carried on."

Feronantus tapped the Spirit Banner against the ice as if he were testing its thickness. "We talked of the *Vor*, you and I," he said to Raphael. "You do not share my conviction, and you have a strong dislike for those of us who stress the importance of faith in how we allow ourselves to be guided."

"Aye, that I do," Raphael said.

"Whatever happens next, I want you to remember one thing, Raphael of Acre," Feronantus said, staring intently at Raphael. "Your strength—your steadfast refusal to believe that we are anything more than men who are as faithful as we are fallible—is what will save the order. Never let go of that. Never falter."

Raphael stared at Feronantus, unable to decide what to say.

"Swear it," Feronantus thundered, slamming the Spirit Banner against the ice. "Swear an oath that you will never—"

"No," Raphael said quietly.

"Raphael—" Vera said, touching Raphael lightly on the arm.

"No," Raphael repeated. "I will swear no vow to you, Feronantus. I do not need such an oath to support me."

Feronantus released the Spirit Banner and clasped Raphael roughly in a tight embrace. Raphael struggled to breathe, and he awkwardly returned the embrace. "The Virgin loves you," Feronantus whispered in his ear. "More than you will ever acknowledge."

Over the old man's shoulder, Raphael stared at the upright Spirit Banner. No one was holding it in place and yet it did not fall.

Feronantus released him and embraced Vera next. Still staring at the upright staff, Raphael gingerly reached for it. As his fingers brushed the pole, it moved, and he grabbed at it quickly before it fell over. There was no hole in the ice where it could have been stuck, and he turned to Feronantus with a question on his lips.

The question died in his throat. "Look out!" he shouted, leaping forward to shove Feronantus aside.

A horse and rider were coming toward them. Raphael didn't know where they had come from, but he recognized the horse as a short-legged Mongol steed. He recognized the rider too from his white hair. *Graymane...*

The arrow from Alchiq's bow caught him square in the chest and stuck in his maille. He stumbled backward, bumping into

Feronantus. He heard Vera's crossbow string twang, and watched the bolt sail through the air where Alchiq would have been had he remained upright in his saddle, but the agile Mongol had slid to one side. As Alchiq popped back up, he raised his bow and loosed another arrow. Raphael had an instant to regret not keeping his helmet before the arrow spun past his face so close that the fletching burned across his cheek. He heard a guttural cough behind him, and as Vera shrieked and hurled her empty crossbow at the approaching horse, Raphael turned his head.

Alchiq's arrow jutted out from the base of Feronantus's neck. It was off to the left side and most likely not fatal. With a curse, Feronantus reached up and snapped the shaft of the arrow off several inches from his neck.

Raphael felt another arrow stick in his maille, high enough on his back that he knew Alchiq was aiming for his head, and he stopped worrying about Feronantus. The old man could take care of himself. He darted to his right, spinning wildly on the ice as he fumbled for his mace in its sling at his waist. Alchiq's horse was nearly upon them, and he didn't even bother gripping the mace solidly. He simply pulled it out of its sling and threw it at the horse's head. The heavy missile struck the horse's withers and the beast stumbled once.

It was enough.

The horse lost its footing on the ice and went down, throwing off Alchiq's aim. The Mongol tumbled out of the saddle, and both Vera and Raphael charged at the sprawling man, drawing their swords as they ran across the ice.

Alchiq came up to one knee with his bow, an arrow still nocked. Raphael tried to skid to a stop and change direction, but all he managed to do was slide across the ice, straight at Alchiq. With a wicked grin, the Mongol loosed the arrow and Raphael felt a heavy punch in the stomach. He was knocked off balance and as he fell onto his side, he saw Vera descend upon the crouched Mongol, her sword flashing.

He swept his bow up, intercepting her downward stroke. The bow split in his hands, fouling her strike, and he rolled forward, letting go of the mess his bow had become. Vera's sword tangled in the horn, wood, and sinew, and as she tried to clear her weapon, Alchiq was on his feet, slashing at her with his curved sword.

She twisted and would have parried his sword had her feet not slid out from beneath her. Her swing went wide, and Raphael heard the grating sound of metal against metal as Alchiq's sword slid across her mailled hip.

He struggled to get up, pulling at the arrow sticking out of his maille. A stab of pain lanced up from his belly, and he stared down at the arrow. It had penetrated his maille. Gritting his teeth, he grabbed the shaft with both hands and snapped it off, much like Feronantus had done with the arrow in his neck. The pain increased for a moment as he broke the shaft, but it subsided quickly, which told him the wound was not deep.

Vera was still off balance and Alchiq shoved her, knocking her off her feet. He didn't bother chasing her down, and after sparing a quick glance at Raphael, he spun on the ice and went for Feronantus.

Wielding the Spirit Banner like a quarterstaff, Feronantus caught Alchiq under the chin with the end, lifting the Mongol clear off the ice and sending him flying. Raphael heard the sharp click of Alchiq's teeth slamming together, and there was blood on the Mongol's mouth when he landed on the ice.

Raphael scrambled toward him, and Alchiq squirmed away like a spider as Raphael slammed his sword down, throwing up a spray of icy shards. Alchiq spun on his ass, lunging with his sword at Raphael's ankles, and Raphael knocked his sword away. He sliced down again, and this time he connected with Alchiq's thigh.

Alchiq howled, and bright blood spurted across the ice. The Mongol sat up, swinging his sword at Raphael's nearby arm. Raphael tried to pull his sword back, but it stuck—either in the ice or Alchiq's leg, he couldn't be sure—and so he let go of his weapon entirely to avoid being hit.

Vera appeared at his side, and she kicked Alchiq's arm back as he tried to swing at her. She swept her sword up in a vicious stroke, catching him just below the elbow. Alchiq screamed again, and there was even more blood on the ice as well as a hand still clutching a curved sword. Vera lifted her foot and stomped down heavily, twice, and Alchiq stopped screaming.

◆ ◆ ◆

Feronantus rested against the Spirit Banner and when the screaming stopped, he roused himself from the stupor that had been stealing over him. In the distance, he could still hear the sound of the battle and, peering across the expanse of ice that separated him from the general melee, he gauged the state of the battle.

The Livonians were still on the ice, but they were beginning to push back toward the shore again. *It is time*, he thought, and wearily pushed himself upright.

He didn't know what words he was supposed to say or if he should compose his mind in any special manner, and so he merely thought of Maria. He recalled walking with her through the forest in England, before he had taken the course of life that would bring him to this frozen lake and this moment, and the memory comforted him.

He lifted the Banner up to his knees and slammed it down against the ice. Nothing happened, and so he did it again, struggling to clear his mind of any confusion, of any uncertainly that this was not the right choice. He had seen this lake. He knew there was power in the Spirit Banner. He had felt it time and again since he had first picked it up in the Mongolian forest. The stick had been cold to his touch since Istvan's death and the fiery explosion in the depression, but he knew there was still magic in the staff.

There had to be, otherwise his life had been spent striving for something that did not exist. It was faith, pure and simple, that the world was stranger than any of them suspected.

He had seen the tree. He knew that it had flourished once. Just as he knew the staff had been cut from the tree, carried over the generations by men who had benefited from the radiant power in it. They may not have understood its power, and he didn't claim to understand it either, but he believed in it.

The staff slammed into the ice again, and still nothing happened.

He leaned against it, his hands shaking. He felt tears starting at the corners of his eyes, and at the back of his mind a tiny worm of doubt started to wiggle. Had he been wrong? Had he imagined everything?

A drop of blood splashed on the ice beside the butt of the Spirit Banner. He stared at it, wondering where it had come from, and then he remembered being hit by the Mongol arrow. He touched at the piece of broken wood sticking out of his neck and examined the blood on his fingers. Frowning, he put aside the distraction of the wound and gripped the Spirit Banner again.

The wood moved in his hand.

Of course, he thought. Blood requires blood.

He let go of the Spirit Banner, which remained upright on the ice, and using one hand as a brace, he gripped the slippery shard of wood in his neck.

"Feronantus!"

He paused. Raphael and Vera were standing nearby, and Raphael was holding out his hands, shaking his head. "Leave it," Raphael said. "I'll get it later. You'll just bleed more."

"I know," Feronantus said. "It has to be done. The old must give way to the new."

"Stop," Raphael shouted as Feronantus pulled heavily, tearing the broken arrow out of his body. Vera grabbed Raphael, holding him back.

Raphael was right. Blood spattered onto the ice and blood ran down his maille, soaking his gambeson underneath. His vision darkened and he grabbed the Spirit Banner for support.

The ice rolled beneath his feet.

He raised his head and looked at Raphael. "I'm sorry," he said. "If the order is to survive, you must know what is at stake. It is not merely the people of the world, but the world itself. Blood and branch, Raphael, we must defend it all." He lifted the Spirit Banner—the last branch of the old tree—and slammed it once more against the ice.

Someone screamed. He wasn't sure who. It might have been him. The ice buckled beneath the staff, twisting and shivering. He clutched the staff with all his might, his hands slippery with blood, and he slammed it down one last time.

He saw, stretching out from the point where the tip of the staff touched the ice, a series of twisting roots. They shot away from him, cracking and shattering the ice in an explosion of white light. Closing his eyes, he still saw the roots, burned forever into his memory.

She was there, standing beside him, coaxing him to let go of the blood-slick staff, whispering to him that it was time to let go. Her wings were made from thousands of iridescent feathers. When he looked at her face, he wept, knowing he had done the right thing even though it was going to bring pain to those he loved.

EPILOGUE:

NEW GROWTH

The ice had shattered in a long wide arc, a triangular shape with its vertices at the edge of the shore where the *Skjalddis* shield-wall had held the Livonians, the point where Feronantus had struck the ice, and a final point in the midst of the northern bowl of the lake. The area was filled with floating bergs and frothy water, and there was no way of knowing for certain how many had been lost in the lake. At the very least, the bodies of all the dead had been claimed by the water.

Raphael wept when he learned that Illarion was one of the fallen. His tears dried up when he was told that Kristaps was gone as well.

The surviving *Skjalddis* helped Raphael and Vera gather wood for the pyre, and they built a long shelf upon which they laid Feronantus. They laid the Spirit Banner next to him, and neither Raphael nor Vera commented on how shriveled and emaciated the stick had become since the ice had shattered.

Alexander spoke first, giving a eulogy to all of those who had fought gallantly, giving their lives for Rus and Novgorod. He said nothing about the miracle that had swallowed the enemy, and judging by the stony expressions on the faces of those assembled at Feronantus's pyre, there was nothing that needed to be said. They all knew what had happened and who was responsible.

Vera spoke next, and she gave a moving eulogy for those sisters who had fallen in battle. *It was the way they all hoped to be remembered,* Raphael thought as he listened absently. He was still confused and angry at what had happened, and his mind struggled to find a rational explanation for what he had seen.

But the only explanation that made any sense was not rational.

He realized Vera had finished her speech. Everyone was looking at him, and as he gazed back at their faces, seeing their expressions of hope and fear and wonder, he couldn't fathom what he would say to them that would make them understand. What words would give them comfort? What words would ease the pain and fear in his heart?

"My name is Raphael," he started. "I was born in Acre, which is a place far away from here. In the Holy Land. I never knew my father, and my childhood was filled with the endless threat of yet another army deciding it had claim to Jerusalem. I was born in a land soaked in blood, and I grew up hoping that someday the fighting would be over." He laughed bitterly, his cheeks wet with tears. "Feronantus, who lies here, accused me of being faithless, of being unable to let myself believe in something greater than myself, but that's not true. I do believe in something. It is hope. A hope that every time we pick up a sword instead of a plow that it will be the last time. That our shields will grow dusty hanging over our hearths, and that our lives can be spent planting and harvesting crops instead of burying our friends and family."

He turned to Alexander's brother, who was holding the long-handled torch. He took it from Andrei and stepped up to the pyre where Feronantus lay, his hands laid over his chest.

"Those who fell today gave their lives for us. Let us honor their memories by loving each other. Let us live off this land, breathe this air, fish this lake when the summer comes, because that is the great gift given to us by God, the Virgin, and our dead companions. Let us live, my friends, and in living, keep alive our hope for a world made better by our presence in it."

He thrust the torch into the oil-soaked branches of the pyre, and flames sprang up with a noisy rush. The wet wood hissed and popped, but the flames would not be deterred. A thick column of white smoke boiled out of the wood, obscuring Feronantus, and the fire crackled loudly as it grew in size.

Vera touched his arm, lightly pulling him away from the burning pyre. "Come," she said gently. "Before the ice melts."

"Good bye, old friend," Raphael said. He tossed the torch onto the pyre, and he and Vera walked back to the shore with Alexander and the others.

From the safety of solid ground, they watched the pyre burn. The flames licked and cavorted about the wood, savoring the meal they had been given, but as they grew in size and heat, the ice melted. One end of the pyre tilted up, the flames hissing in anger as the cold water of the lake quenched them. The rest of the flames seemed to grow brighter and taller, and the column of smoke thickened. Then, with a sudden lurch, the pyre twisted and disappeared, leaving nothing but a wide gash in the ice. For a moment, Raphael thought he could see the orange of the flames through the ice of the lake, as if the fire fought back against the cold embrace of the water. The cloud of white smoke drifted into the darkening sky.

"It will be cold tonight," the prince said, gazing up at the clear sky. "Come. Let us celebrate. We are still alive, and that means we can huddle together and curse this endless winter." He smiled at the ragged cheer his words elicited from the assembled company, and as people started to wander off toward the camp, he paused beside Raphael and Vera. "They were extraordinary men, both of them," he said, referring to Feronantus and Illarion. "They will become more extraordinary in the telling of what happened here today. They left behind no families, and so the stories of who they were and what they did will be how they will be remembered."

Raphael nodded, and after a moment, the prince offered a knowing smile to Vera and left, leaving the pair alone on the shore of Lake Peipus.

She stood next to him, her hand finding his. He knew he should say something, that he should go after Alexander and join the survivors in their celebration of life. It was what he had exhorted them all to do, after all.

"You held me back," he said eventually. It wasn't an accusation nor was it entirely a question. "I could have stopped him."

"From doing what?" she asked quietly. "Pulling out the arrow or breaking the ice?"

"Both," Raphael said. "Neither." He sighed. "I don't know. But you knew, didn't you? You knew what he was going to do."

Vera lifted her shoulders slightly. "One of my sisters, Nika, has been visited—several times—by the witch of old Rus. Baba Yaga. She came to Illarion too."

"Baba Yaga?" Raphael shook his head. "She's a story meant to frighten children so that they behave. *Listen to your mother, dear child, or Baba Yaga will come in the night and steal you away.* Fairy tale nonsense."

"The stories are wrong," Vera said. "She doesn't steal children; she protects them. She protects all of Rus. She's one of us, but she's not part of the world we know. Not anymore."

"And you think that is what happened to Feronantus? He became part of the world beyond our mortal being?"

"Of course he did," she said gently, nodding toward the bare lake.

"I don't understand," Raphael said.

"The world moves in cycles, Raphael. More than the simple turn of the seasons. Far grander cycles that reach past our meager lives. What is new becomes old and is buried or burned or lost, and from that loss comes something new again. Do you remember Yasper's firebird? Whence did he summon that creature? How did he create such a thing?"

"It was a trick of the light," Raphael said. "You've seen what he can do with colored smoke and flash fires. It was nothing more than an illusion."

"And today? Was that an illusion?"

"I...I don't know," he answered truthfully. "Why are you smiling at me?" he asked, noting her expression.

She wiped at her cheeks and offered him a tiny laugh. "Hope is a tiny seed," she said. "It must be carefully nurtured, but it can grow into something splendid. In time." She linked his arm in his. "We have time."

✦ ✦ ✦

From the wood, Nika watched Raphael and Vera as they left the shore of the lake. She waited until they were out of sight before she left the shadows of the trees and made her way down to the icy shore. She hesitated to go farther; the memory of nearly falling into the shattering ice was still strong in her head.

She walked along the shore, her eyes scanning the trunks of the trees along the verge of the forest for Baba Yaga's marks. When she spotted the twin gashes, she left the shore and returned to the forest, wending her way along a narrow deer path.

The prince's army would celebrate through the night and tomorrow they would begin to break camp, the militia disbanding as the peasants returned to their villages. The remaining *Skjalddis*, of whom there were but a mere handful, would remain with Nevsky, presumably filling out the decimated ranks of his *Druzhina*. The prince had won a victory that would be celebrated for generations to come, and the people of Rus would flock to him in droves. A dynasty had been created, here at Peipus, raised upon a foundation of the corpses of her sisters and companions. Even so, Nika was not bitter. Battles always claimed lives, and Illarion had gone to this fight with death in his eyes and a readiness to face what came after.

Nika was ready too. Her absence would not be noted. She had not reported back after the battle ended, and would likely be counted among the dead. None of her sisters had seen the same signs that she had, and she had known all along what would be asked of her once the battle was over.

At last, she came to a small clearing. She expected to find a fire, watched over by three skulls, but instead she discovered a small hut that sat crookedly on a pile of thick sticks. Instead of a door, there was merely a heavy curtain, and pushing aside the wool drape, she clambered into the hut.

Inside, there was a table, a chair, a narrow bed, several chests, and a tiny hearth in which a bed of coals offered a lambent glow. There was no one else in the hut, and she put several heavy sticks from the bin beside the hearth onto the fire, leaning over and blowing on the coals until a thin flame started to lick the kindling.

There was an old shawl thrown over the back of the chair, and as the fire slowly started to warm the tiny hut, Nika stripped off her filthy maille. She threw the shirt into the corner of the hut, followed by her sword and scabbard. She sat down in the chair and pulled off her boots. Reaching over her shoulder, she grabbed the shawl and pulled it over her. Stretching out her legs so that her bare feet were close to the fire, she settled down in the chair to wait.

I'll just take a short nap, she thought as her eyes drooped. *She'll be here when I wake up.*

When the hut lurched upward and began rocking back and forth, a smile drifted across her face but she didn't stir.

◆ ◆ ◆

Hermann was not terribly surprised to find a guest waiting for him at his estate in Dorpat. The campaign had ended in disaster, and he had struggled home with a fraction of the men he had departed with. Nevsky's victory at the lake assured that Novgorod and its provinces would be safe for many years from any efforts to dominate them. The whole affair had been a dreadful waste, and he said as much as he entered his great hall. "What was the point of all that?" he sighed as he stripped off his cloak and gloves. "We could have taken Novgorod; we could have expanded Rome's reach into the north. But we have squandered that opportunity now."

His guest rose from the heavy chair he had been sitting in by the fire, and he limped toward Hermann. He was a narrow-faced man, and his beard and hair were streaked with gray. He wore simple clothing with no sigils, and there was a weariness in his gaze that Hermann knew all too well.

"Is he dead?" his guest asked. "And all of those who would follow him?"

"Aye," Hermann sighed. A servant offered him a flagon of wine and he accepted it readily. It was good to be home again, out of the cold and away from the bitter campaign that had been a failure in so many ways. "The Ruthenians will be singing about this victory for years to come, but it is done. Kristaps is gone, and the last of those who remember Volquin's ambition with him. The Livonian ranks have been purged; those who remain—" He broke off with a bitter laugh and quelled it with a large gulp of his wine.

"What?" his guest prompted him.

"You were not there," Hermann said. "You did not see what happened."

His guest stood close. "Tell me," he said, his eyes glittering. "Tell me everything."

Hermann did, and as he told the fantastic story of the breaking ice, he felt a resolute calm come over him, as if this news were a final reckoning of the task he had been set to perform. He was merely a tiny piece in a much grander puzzle, and he found an odd contentment in knowing his place. Some philosopher had once said that the wise man learns to win what he wants by appearing to lose what his enemy believes he wants. Hermann had never been more than God's humble instrument, to be used how God's agents saw fit, but even he could not help but wonder at the strangeness of it all.

"Excellent," his guest said when he had finished. "And you are certain your men will tell this same story to anyone that asks?"

Hermann laughed. "I'm sure it will get even stranger before the summer. Nothing of what will be said will be true, but it will be all that anyone remembers."

"Exactly," his guest purred. "That is what my master hopes. It will give him all the excuse he needs to launch a purge against these heathen influences. It may seem like you lost a great battle today, but you will be compensated—exceptionally well—for your sacrifice. Rome is pleased."

"What of the Livonians that survived?"

"Oh, you do not need to concern yourself with them." The man limped to the long table and picked up a sealed letter he must have put there earlier. "I will be taking charge of those men."

Hermann accepted the letter and broke the seal. His eyes tracked to the name signed with a heavy flourish at the bottom, and then he read the letter carefully, which revealed to him the name of his guest.

"So, Dietrich von Grüningen, you're to be *Heermeister* again," he said when he finished reading the letter from Cardinal Fieschi.

"Aye," the man named Dietrich von Grüningen nodded. "I am. There is a final matter that must be settled with the Shield-Brethren."

✦ ✦ ✦

She was still getting used to the noise and stench of the market in Samarkand. The stalls were tightly packed in the alleys behind the stone buildings, and it was impossible to navigate the aisles without being jostled and bumped constantly. At first, she had hated the crowds and had refused to visit the chaotic marketplace, but after a few months of doing nothing but sitting inside their *ger* or watching their pair of goats slowly munch the short grasses nearby, she realized she would go stir-crazy if she didn't acclimate herself to the cacophony of city life.

Plus she couldn't stand the idea that, of the pair, she was the one who couldn't handle civilization.

She was leaning against a booth, examining a bolt of light blue silk when she heard someone call her name. At first, she thought she had imagined it. The voice was familiar, but out of context, and not one she had ever expected to hear again. When he called her name again, she looked up, a sudden jolt of fear running up her spine.

And there he was, dressed in a plain robe like one of a thousand itinerant merchants who traveled through the city while on the Silk Road. His beard had been trimmed and shaped in the Persian style, and there was a weariness in his eyes that his smile did not dispel.

"Raphael," she said, nervously tucking a stray strand of her long black hair behind her ear.

"God be with you, Lian," Raphael said, clasping his hands together as he came up to the booth. "It is a marvel to see you again."

"Yes," she said. "Quite marvelous, especially in a city this size, and so far from where I saw you last many months ago. But not a coincidence, I suspect."

Raphael glanced at the merchant standing behind the booth. "No, not a coincidence," he said with a smile. "But it has taken me some time to find you. I have been searching along the Silk Road for months. In fact, this is the fourth day I've been wandering around in this market."

"Is there a problem?" A new voice asked, speaking in Mongolian behind Lian.

Raphael's eyes flickered over her shoulder. "There is no problem here," he said smoothly in the same tongue. He raised his hands to show they were empty.

Lian turned slightly and put her hand on Gansukh's chest. "It's okay," she said, holding him at bay. She could feel the tension in his chest. "Let him speak his piece."

"Is this him?" Raphael asked, eying Gansukh carefully.

"Yes," she said simply.

Gansukh made a noise in his throat, and she knew he had realized who Raphael was. "*Skjaldbræður,*" he growled.

"Not here," Raphael said. "Just a…friend."

"No friend of mine," Gansukh snarled.

"Maybe that is not the right word," Raphael said hastily, "but I am not your enemy. Not anymore."

"What do you want?" Lian asked, more harshly than she intended, but Gansukh's apprehension was starting to bleed over to her.

"My master, Feronantus—you remember him, don't you, Lian?—believed in something…I do not know the outcome of what he sought, or if such a dream could even be realized, but—"

Gansukh shifted behind her, and she knew that his hand was on the hilt of his knife.

Raphael knew it too, and he held up his hands once more. "Please, I mean you no harm. Truly."

"Continue," Lian said, suppressing a shiver that wanted to run up her back.

"He took something from you," Raphael nodded. "Something more precious than…I think he believed it did not belong to your people, and I do not wish to argue the validity of that belief. The theft was his and his alone, but I have come to a vague understanding of his reasons. He took something ancient and tried to create something new with it, but I think he failed. He broke—" Raphael waved his hands as if he didn't quite know the Mongolian words to express what he wanted to say. "Imagine a vast lake covered with ice. Animals cannot drink from the water because of the ice, nor can we catch fish in the lake. But once the ice breaks, then life can return to the lake. Do you understand?"

"It is the cycle of the seasons," Gansukh said gruffly. "It happens every winter."

"Yes, exactly. Now imagine that the entire world has been eclipsed by that winter—a strangely fallow period when nothing truly grows because it is waiting for the ice to be broken."

"You want the sprig," Lian said.

Raphael closed his hands, and his expression held both hope and curiosity. "The sprig?"

Gansukh made as if to speak, but Lian touched him lightly on the chest to quell his words. "It came from the Spirit Banner. That was how I knew where Feronantus was. That was why we were drawn to him. And when I stayed behind with Gansukh, I felt more longing and despair than I thought possible for a group of people who were both my friends and enemies of the man I loved."

"Yes," Raphael said. "I guess that is what I am seeking." He seemed relieved.

"You did not know that I had it," she said.

"I hoped," he said. "Cnán said you had a treasure you kept with you at all times, and yes, I suspected your awareness of Feronantus was tied to it."

"Cnán?" Lian's heart fluttered. "She lives?"

"Aye," Raphael said. "Much to Yasper's continued delight. I saw them both shortly before I began my quest along the Silk Road."

Lian smiled. "I am glad to hear they are together." She leaned against Gansukh.

Raphael's smile faltered slightly. "I need the sprig, Lian," he said. "I need to finish what Feronantus started."

"I know," she nodded. "I've known since…" She glanced down at her rounded belly, and carefully reached into her robe for the hidden pouch sewn into the lining. The lacquer box was there, where it always had been, except for the brief time when Gansukh had carried it after the battle on the steppe. She drew it out and slowly offered it to Raphael, who took it from her with great reverence.

He wanted to open it, but he swallowed the urge and tucked it away inside his robe. "Thank you," he said, and when his hand came out again, he held a sheathed knife.

Lian sucked in a quick breath as Gansukh shoved her to the side.

Raphael held up the leather-covered knife to show that he meant no threat with it, and she saw that the knife's handle was a piece of deer antler. "This isn't mine," Raphael said. "It was taken by accident. The boy meant…Well, it's not true that he meant no harm, but he regrets this act of thievery." Raphael extended the sheathed knife toward Lian and Gansukh.

"It isn't mine either," Gansukh said after a long moment. He draped his arm around Lian, his hand resting on her swollen belly.

Raphael looked at where Gansukh's hand rested, and he turned toward the hovering merchant who had been wondering what manner of conversation was going on beside his booth. Raphael pointed at the silk that Lian had been admiring and wiggled the knife. The merchant made a face and held up his hands, rattling off a lengthy diatribe about the ridiculous state of affairs when he was expected to trade fine Persian silk for a handmade steppe rider's knife. But he still took the blade from Raphael and pulled it partway out of the sheath to examine the blade. His patter changed when he saw the blade, and his eyebrows inched upward.

"For the child," Raphael said. "It is a poor gift."

Lian reached out and fondled the silk. "It is a fine gift," she said quietly, her eyes filling with tears. "It reminds me of the open sky of the steppe."

"Yes," Raphael said. "Eternal Blue Heaven."

Gansukh's hand tightened on her belly.

Here Ends
Katabasis
A Medieval Era novel of
the Foreworld Saga

ACKNOWLEDGMENTS

JOSEPH BRASSEY
To the Subutai team, who made this possible; to my beloved wife and son; to the lovely people at 47North; and to my brothers and sisters of Lonin League, Seven Swords Guild, and The HEMA Alliance—this one's for you.

COOPER MOO
Thanks to Mark Teppo, who wrestled prose from multiple authors into submission while keeping the fight enjoyable. Thanks to Sir-Not-Appearing-In-This-Book, without whose leadership we wouldn't be here. Thank you to Angus Trim and Joseph Brassey— it was an honor and a pleasure to work with you gentlemen again.

MARK TEPPO
My thanks to my fellow co-authors, who bravely went into uncharted territory and put together a great story. I'd also like to acknowledge Neal Stephenson, Greg Bear, Nicole Galland, and Erik Bear, who helped lay the foundations of the story that we've taken a step farther.

ANGUS TRIM
Thanks to Neal Stephenson for the encouragement and the opportunity.

ABOUT THE AUTHORS

Joseph Brassey lives in the Pacific Northwest with his wife, son, and two cats. In his spare time, he trains in, and teaches, Western martial arts to members of the armed forces. He has lived on both sides of the continental United States and has worked everywhere from a local newspaper to the frame-shop of a crafts store to the smoke-belching interior of a house-siding factory with questionable safety policies. Joseph was a co-author of *The Mongoliad*.

Cooper Moo is a Seattle-based writer of non-fiction humor and alternate history. In addition to being one of the seven authors of *The Mongoliad*, Cooper's work has appeared in *The Seattle Weekly* and on *Slate* and *BoingBoing*. His autobiographical piece "Growing Up Black and White" was awarded Social Issues Reporting article of the year by the Society of Professional Journalists.

Mark Teppo has been the showrunner for the Foreworld Saga, and his contributions include co-authoring *The Mongoliad* as well as a number of the Foreworld SideQuests. He is the author of *Lightbreaker, Heartland, Earth Thirst,* and *The Potemkin Mosaic.*

Angus Trim is a skilled sword-maker and machinist who lives in the Pacific Northwest. He is adept in Western martial arts as well as tai chi sword form. His previous contribution to the Foreworld Saga is *The Lion in Chains.*

The Foreworld Saga continues
in these other great titles from 47North!

Novels

The Mongoliad: Book 1
The Mongoliad: Book 2
The Mongoliad: Book 3

Katabasis

Foreworld SideQuests

Sinner
Dreamer
The Lion in Chains
The Shield-Maiden
The Beast of Calatrava
Seer
The Book of Seven Hands
The Assassination of Orange
Hearts of Iron
Tyr's Hammer
Marshal vs the Assassins

Symposium (three-issue graphic serial)
The Dead God (three-issue graphic serial)

Find out more about the Foreworld Saga at foreworld.com.

Information about all of these titles and other forthcoming
titles can also be found at http://foreworld.com/store.